CW01513294

THREE SIDES OUT, ONE WAY HOME (*MALAYA 1956-58*)

The story of three Englishmen during the Malayan Emergency:
One was meant to be there, one thought he ought to be there,
and one of them really should have known better!

Dominique Allen

THREE SIDES OUT, ONE WAY HOME *(MALAYA 1956-58)*
Copyright © 2023 Dominique Allen

Book and cover design by Davina Hopping

Printed by Book Printing UK www.bookprintinguk.com

Remus House, Coltsfoot Drive, Peterborough, PE2 9BF

Printed in Great Britain

ISBN 978-1-7392004-2-8

"For John. Be of good courage, my love.
You walk with the best of stout-hearted fellows."

[The Promise Kept]

THREE SIDES OUT, ONE WAY HOME (MALAYA 1956-58)

"No one volunteers, for anything, ever ... but sometimes ... you're asked!"

Three Sides Out, One Way Home (Malaya 1956-58)

Also available by the same author
in The Salvaged Summer Trilogy:
Bk 1: *All for Overalls (Summer 1940)*
Bk 2: *If the Sock Fits! (Autumn/Winter 1940)*
Bk 3: *Raids, Rallies & Reserves (1941)*

Also, soon to be available by the same author
In the Gertie's Path series:
Not So Safely Forgotten (Spring 1942)
The Biscuit Tin Summer (Summer 1942)
Restless Torches (Autumn/Winter 1942)
The Tunisian Turnaround (Spring 1943)

For further details contact the scrawny author at:
dommyallen63@hotmail.co.uk

CONTENTS

CHAPTER 1
Docks and Dashes 9

CHAPTER 2
Trains, Tea and Luggage 23

CHAPTER 3
Airfields and Alibis 39

CHAPTER 4
Tracks and Tins 89

CHAPTER 5
Radios and Rackets! 123

CHAPTER 6
Covers, Clocks and Corners! 151

CHAPTER 7
Intelligence!? 197

CHAPTER 8
Bother and Bus Stops 215

CHAPTER 9
Ferries and Foraging 239

CHAPTER 10
Not So Soft Landings! 279

CHAPTER 11
Rehab and Rallies 315

CHAPTER 12
Markers ... and Making Sense of it All 343

CHAPTER 1

DOCKS AND DASHES

JOHN

He hadn't expected there to be a library on board a troopship, but then again, the voyage was going to take a long six weeks. John was also aware that most of the men below decks hadn't got their sea-legs yet … but he had.

At least by giving John library duty the officers could be reasonably confident that, should they wish to borrow a book, they wouldn't be offended by the stench. The arrangements suited all parties.

John would have his breakfast then sign in and stay at his post in the library for the rest of the day, reading. His duties were to dust the shelves, polish the brass around the porthole and keep the on-loan ledger ready for the officer to check once a day. He'd gained his sea-legs about six months prior to starting his basic training. It had been on a trawler trying to impress the father of a girl he fancied. He didn't get the girl, but he'd got his 'legs'.

Most of the visitors to John's library had been officers although the padre had looked in a couple of times. John hadn't been surprised to see the fellow about the place. A troopship this size and on their heading? There was bound to be the need for someone like that.

What John hadn't expected was for the dog-collar to belong to such a pleasantly approachable chap, he'd even asked John's opinion on a few of the books.

"You volunteered for the library?" the cleric had enquired.

John smiled. "There weren't many of us to choose from. I guess I polished up most presentable." It was John's turn. "You volunteered for this? Pretty rough bunch of Lads and it's going to be no garden-party where we're heading either."

The most appropriate response the cleric could have given John would have been 'just following orders', but he couldn't quite bring himself to say that. The hesitation hadn't gone unnoticed.

John waited.

Technically, originally, the cleric's 'orders' had come from his mother. However, after a little more thought he offered John the most candid response he could muster. "I don't think I volunteered and they didn't exactly order me, rather, they asked if I would like this and it was better than the other options on the table!"

"Sounds a good enough reason to me!" John agreed.

TAPS

Taps hadn't volunteered either. He'd been shanghaied and it was all down to that ruddy watchman's hut getting in the way!

"It's not mine ossifer!" he admitted to the policeman. But, even as inebriated as he was, he wasn't going to attempt to deny he'd been the one riding the motorbike. "Wasn't my fault though. That there shed snuck-up on me!"

The policeman wasn't too sure on that last part of the story and waited for Taps to offer a little more detail. It had been a long night already, the weather wasn't good, the watchman's hut was empty and the black-out meant there were no lanterns. The policeman could give him that much leeway.

However, the matter of the crowbar might take a little more explaining.

"Yes ossifer. No, that's mine alright!"

The crowbar had fallen out from Tap's jacket as he'd crawled to the kerb, hauling himself to a standing stagger, by the grace of the corner lamp-post.

"Didn't mean to do that!" Taps acknowledged the remains of the hut, crumpled into kindling from the 'nudge'. The motorbike was down on its side, remarkably unscathed considering, it's back wheel still spinning.

Taps could see he wasn't going to be able to wriggle out of this one. He wasn't that drunk! He might be able to explain away the gravel-rash, where he'd planted his palm in the skid, but the gnawed flesh down the length of his left thigh, bleeding and bruised, rather shredded any alibi Taps could conjure up.

The policemen had yet to say a word. His feet were throbbing from a long patrol, he'd retrieved the dropped crowbar and kicked the larger pieces of hut to one side off the road. He just needed the lamp-post-clutching Taps to explain his version of the night's events.

The blood was dribbling down Taps' leg, starting to soak across his torn trouser, the pain from his gashed hand was just about managing to balance the throbbing dumbness he felt in his head.

"Didn't see the corner, Sarg. Didn't see the gravel. Didn't see the hut! Sorry Sarg."

"You didn't see much, did you?" the policeman asked him, shifting his weight back slightly to stand clear from the range of Taps' potent breath.

"I did see there was no one there, Sarg. I saw that!" Taps attempted to straighten, none too convincingly. "No damage done. Except the hut, a bit, and I can fix that."

"I doubt that!" The policeman was looking at the state of Taps' leg. "As for the no damage? You need someone to look at that."

There was definitely no watchman in the vicinity, no lanterns to indicate where the hut had stood in the road and the gravel was loose. That part of the story he was clear on. The remainder? The motorbike and the crowbar, and Taps? Not so much. He waited.

"Sorry ossifer, not at my best. Motorbike delivery, Sarg. Last minute rush. Meant to be getting it over to the docks for shipment." The constable appreciated the promotion and that sounded almost plausible, except for the slurring and wobble. "Bit of a dash-job, Sarg. Doing my best, here," Taps offered pitifully.

They couldn't have been more than two hundred yards from the docks. This was the constable's regular patrol and he knew all too well how the warehouses tended to blend into one another this time of night, with sounds echoing and ricocheting between brick walls and steel hulls. Especially when they were loading the troopships. With lights glancing across from the haulage cranes and warehouses, distorted by open doors and high windows, it was disorientating enough for a sober man!

The policeman was already swearing at the missing watchman, whilst still holding on to the as-yet unexplained crowbar! "Dash-job to the docks, was it?" he queried.

Taps could understand the officer's suspicions. He wasn't convinced himself about what had happened, and he was the one doing the talking! He was still clinging on to the lamp-post for support and trying to get his bearings.

"Papers?" the policeman asked.

Taps sprung into action at that. "Got those! They're 'ere somewhere, Sarg." Taking both hands from the lampost, he plunged them into his jacket pockets and promptly crumpled to his knees on the pavement with a groan.

"Alright! Alright! You're drunk. I believe you."

The policeman helped Taps to his feet.

The hut had been on its last-legs anyway, hardly more than a couple of crates knocked together. Under normal circumstances the whereabouts of the missing watchman would have been of more interest than one slightly worse-for-wear delivery-rider, except for one detail, the crowbar that had fallen out of Taps' jacket!

"You were lucky this slipped out before you fell on it, could have been a nasty accident. And why *were* you carrying a crowbar?"

"Ah, well it's like this, ossifer ..." Taps took a breath, this was going to take a moment. "It was the crate's fault!"

The policeman wisely waited for the rest.

"The delivery was for one motorbike, but the crate had two more packed in with it. Thought I'd save time, not wait for me mate. He was late anyway. Thought I'd just bring the one over, direct-like. If I'd waited for me mate with the truck we could've loaded the whole crate, then unloaded the motorbike out at the docks. But he was late, and I had my crowbar handy. Just got to deliver one motorbike to the ship, Sarg. Didn't want to miss it, saved a bit of time."

Taps took another breath, before a finishing flourish. "I've got me papers and delivery-chit, see! Got the motorbike, and the ship's only over there somewhere, Sarg. Ain't it?"

Idiotic enough to be believable. The policeman took another look at the paperwork. That at least was in order. The motorbike and delivery-driver a little less so!

Taps was on his feet, with his unbloodied hand grappling up the length of the lamp-post again, whilst attempting to appear to be only casually leaning against it. The impression wasn't convincing anyone!

His head was starting to spin. "Please, Sarg. Just point me in the right direction and give me a shove, gotta get this delivered proper-like, don't I?"

There was a flicker of emotion from the policeman, a grimace. He pinched the corner of the piece of paperwork, peering again at the blood-smudged scrawl. 'One motorbike, one shipment'. "They're loading the troopship on the dock second left, straight down." He handed the paperwork back to Taps, but was keeping the crowbar.

"Please, Sarg, can I just have my bike back?"

"You're walking it, right?"

"I'll give it a go, Sarg." Taps' head was still feeling out of focus, unable to decide whether it was sufficiently drunk or just plain knocked lop-sided. His gravel-grated palm felt as bad as it looked, and his mangled thigh was throbbing like heck.

"Can you manage that? The walking and the motorbike?"

The policeman was having second thoughts.

"I'll just lean into it, Sarg. That should do the trick," Taps offered, "It was second left, wasn't it?"

"Second left," the policemen confirmed, watching as Taps approached the task of returning the motorbike to upright. To his jaundiced eye it looked more like a lucky lunge than a coordinated manoeuvre. Now both man and machine were standing, all the policeman had to do was get them moving safely off his beat.

Taps had a good grip on the near-side handle but spoiled the effect by aiming to grab the far side handle and over-shot. Everything began leaning away from Taps. He braced his legs to steady the weight back in his favour, but the pain from his injured thigh shredded his wits and the pleading groan was too much for the policeman to stay impassive, but Taps waved him back.

"S'okay, Sarg. I got this. I got this … whoooops!"

Taps' second attempt to push the heavy machine was thwarted by a slippery smear of blood from his grated palm.

"Oh, for crying out loud!" The policeman caught the motorbike. "I'll push. You just walk straight. That time you saved not waiting for your mate, wisely spent, was it?"

"Oh yes, Sarg," Taps assured him amiably. "You know how cold it gets round these parts and a couple of doubles does wonders for the chill."

The policeman would have reckoned it had been at least twice that but didn't bother arguing. "No harm done if we get this aboard the troopship. As for the watchman, if he'd been where he ought, then I'm guessing you wouldn't have done what you did?"

Taps had lost the plot, but it sounded like it was heading in his favour. "Cor, Sarg. Me, getting police-escort!"

The pair of them made quite a sight. Taps bruised and bloodied and barely managing to stagger forward; whilst the policeman, a good ten inches taller and twice the size across the shoulders, handling the motorbike with ease and occasionally Taps too.

Between them they got as far as the warehouse office that had been kitted out with a 'First-Aid Station' notice on the door.

"I'm leaving you here."

The policeman thumbed to the red cross, then nodded over to where two military police were standing on guard in front of the Port Master's office a couple of doors down.

"I'll give them your paperwork. Might come better from me."

"Couldn't have done it without ya, Sarg. Yer a wonder!"

With those parting words, the policeman felt Taps had said quite enough. Leaning the motorbike against the wall, he reached over Taps' shoulder, hammered on the first-aid door, then opened it and shoved Taps in.

The room smelt of paperwork, not bandage wrappers. Taps registered that much as he stumbled in. It was dark too.

"Hello!?" Taps took another step into the room. His voice sounded louder than he'd expected, and his head throbbed harder in the silence. If he could just find a chair that would help, first-aid offices usually had a nurse, but there was no sign of one yet.

"Ruddy dark in 'ere ain't it?" Taps struggled to reach for where he decided a chair ought to be, but the dockside lights were causing the room to sway, glancing through the office windows and rearranging the pieces of furniture. It was starting to annoy him.

"Nurse!?" Taps yelled, raising his voice for the first time since finding the lamp-post and instantly wishing he hadn't. The sudden increase in volume made his knees buckle under the weight of his head. The light-switch flicked on, just as Taps slid down the wall to the floor, uttering a second more feeble, "Nurse?"

It definitely wasn't a nurse who answered!

"Oh, I do beg your pardon. I thought this was a waiting room. Are you alright?"

Taps' blurred vision managed to take in a hint of the identity of the man that now swam in front of his eyes. A dog-collar? That might explain the stupid questions too.

"If you meet anyone hollerin' for a nurse, Vicar, they don't tend to be looking so 'alright," Taps informed the other man harshly. "What are you doing here?"

The gentleman with the kind enquiries stooped down and offered his hand to help Taps to the nearby chair. "What seems to be the problem?"

ARCHIE

There was a small brown leather bag and an only slightly larger suitcase beside it on the floor. The gentleman whose luggage it was, stood quietly for a few minutes, waiting.

"Travelling light, hey Vicar!?" Taps noticed. And the sight of that dog-collar had been sobering. Taps had got just enough of his equilibrium back to start sounding cheeky again.

Archie ignored Taps' chatter and continued his tut-tutting as he attempted to lift the torn cloth of the trouser away from the injured leg. Taps winced and went silent.

"It's alright, I know what I'm doing."

Taps hadn't known any vicars being trained in medicine, but his head was clearing a little. The motorbike was destined for cargo on one of those troopships out there, maybe this vicar was too. Then that made him a Padre. Taps knew that much. All the Army vicars were called Padres, and he'd heard some of those dog-collar officers had medical training, too. Something to do with them not being able to get into the doctor's colleges? Something like that.

It sounded reasonable enough for Taps to be going on with. So, Padre it was, then. Taps didn't really care if the vicar was a Padre or a porter, so long as he knew what he was doing.

Archie was still trying to assess the extent of the wound. "How did this happen?"

"Sorry, bit late, Padre. Got caught up on a watchman's hut!"

Archie didn't correct Taps' misunderstanding. He'd more immediate priorities. If the Lad was going to be fit to board, then he'd need to be cleaned up and pronto!

Archie had expected someone to come and fetch him, but he seemed to have been forgotten. It was not an unfamiliar sensation. With Taps' arrival Archie had been prompted to act, no more waiting now!

Between his head and his leg, Taps had almost managed to forget about the state of his gravel-grated hand until Archie started attending to it, already unwinding the grubby crumpled square of handkerchief the policeman must have given him on the walk over. Taps couldn't remember when that had happened.

Archie was tut-tutting again, muttering 'no, that won't do at all' under his breath.

Taps hadn't heard that sort of soft-chiding reprimand since he'd been at school and once they'd started rapping his knuckles with the ruler he'd got out of there sharpish. This padre seemed to know what he was doing, and Taps was in no condition to think beyond that.

Archie had his back turned to Taps by then, pouring water from the jug by the wash-hand basin into the bowl he'd put ready on the clerking-office table, just like he'd seen them do in his college nurse's office.

He couldn't remember exactly what they'd used to clean his scraped knees then, but he could remember what it smelt like. Archie loosened the third stopper from the little bottles on the shelf in the cupboard above the basin and gave it a good sniff, that was the one. Cotton wool, ointment, towel, bandage. So far so good. Safety pin?

No safety pin. He was sure there ought to be some, there were always safety-pins in the nurse's office somewhere, usually a couple pinned up near her watch. Archie could make do. "This is going to hurt but I've got to clean it. If you put your hand in the bowl down to your wrist, it'll help your headache too."

Taps didn't bother asking how the Padre knew about that. He'd figured as far as the dog-collar belonging to the troopship, hopefully the same one his motorbike was destined for. He'd almost forgotten about the motorbike. Sarg had handed it in, so as far as Taps was concerned it was delivered. Sorted.

Definitely a Padre Taps decided. Couldn't be a doctor. In Taps' experience doctors didn't talk to people like that! The Padre didn't talk over his glasses or down his nose!

Archie was stern but gentle, and he'd known what to do with the bowl of water and Taps' wrist because his own mother had always dabbed cold water onto her wrists whenever she had a headache.

Archie tended to Taps' injured leg, drenching the cotton wool to dribble the clean water downwards, to loosen the dirt and clean the wound. Thorough, undoubtedly, but he was taking too long for Taps' liking.

Taps was feeling a bit steadier in his thinking and wanted to get out of there before those military policemen came asking about the state of the motorbike.

"It's OK, Padre. Honest it is."

As Taps got to his feet he stumbled and knocked the bowl off from the table. The bowl went flying and Taps went down. Archie instinctively grabbed for the towel to start mopping, then reviewed his priorities and started to pick Taps off the floor, again.

The next thing Taps was conscious of was walking, heading towards the troopship, with the Padre beside him. There was someone walking in front, carrying the Padre's bag and suitcase. Archie had Taps' arm across his shoulders, effectively lifting him almost off his feet.

"Can you manage back there, Padre?" the Army man carrying the luggage asked without looking behind him.

"We'll manage." Archie had tipped his chin down towards Taps' face, his voice hushed. "Nearly there. Don't worry, Lad, you've made it. I don't know how you got into such a state, but at least you didn't miss the boat."

The clatter of the gang-plank was within reach, the crane-lights shone over their heads and the shouts were ricocheting around them.

"Motorbike caught the gravel," Taps managed to mutter, as he staggered one foot in front of the other, disorientated by the noises. It was cold and bright and someone was asking him another stupid question.

"He was delivering some of your cargo, I think he got into a bit of a scrape, but I'll make sure he gets aboard OK."

That sounded like the Padre was vouching for him, bless him.

"Thanks Padre, knew I could rely on ya."

Archie wasn't a Padre, he wasn't quite a fully-fledged vicar. Not for the lack of encouragement from his family. They'd all been for getting him 'nicely settled' in the local parish. Archie had done his best to refuse, managing to persuade them to have second thoughts at the prospect. Having him so close might prove embarrassing. After all, everyone knew whose son he was and they'd just go on comparing him to his brothers, which never reflected favourably on Archie!

It had been his family's second thoughts that had brought Archie here. His mother had managed to 'persuade' someone he would be ideal for the post. What the actual 'posting' was, Archie still wasn't precisely clear on, except it required a sea-journey and he was to pack for a 'warm climate'.

Archie understood there was a vacant church property in the middle of a remote parish and he liked the sound of that. Apparently, no one else liked the sound of it sufficiently to be willing to fill the post! His mother had seemed equally delighted at the prospect, almost relieved, Archie recalled. She'd given him all the necessary instructions and letters and nothing he 'didn't need to bother about' as usual.

It was the right ship, Archie had checked. Somewhere between the first-aid office and the officer on the dockside, checking numbers and paperwork, calling them up to the officer onboard directing 'traffic' to their relevant holds and berths, Archie and Taps explained themselves.

The officer at the bottom yelled up to the officer up top. "Civvies! Clergy and driver. Hey Padre, you said he came with a vehicle somewhere, didn't you?"

Archie only had time to say he thought it might have been a motorbike. That seemed to satisfy the enquiry. The officer scratched out 'driver' and scribbled 'porter', just to clear up any misunderstandings, against the bunk allocation next to the Padre's.

"OK, Padre. You two had better get stowed away. Keep your heads down, we're in for a rough few weeks."

Taps could vaguely remember moving along a loud tunnel with a lot of even louder doors, and someone suggesting he might need a lie-down. He could still hear the slamming and banging, but at least it didn't seem to be inside his head anymore.

The next time he took a look around the room it seemed calmer and smaller. Cramped but clean, and the dog-collar with the gentle hands was talking to him again. Taps wasn't sure what he was saying 'yes' to, but it seemed like Padre was expecting him to say 'yes', so he did. Then he went back to sleep.

It was only once the ship was underway and in open waters that Archie decided the uproar outside their cabin had quietened sufficiently for him to venture out. He'd done the best he could for the injured porter, but he needed some fresh supplies and there was bound to be a first-aid room on board somewhere. A stroll to get his bearings might be wise, and for some reason the idea of a 'remote posting' being fascinating came to his thoughts again, it had certainly proven interesting so far and the journey over was looking like it could be quite eventful too!

Chapter 2

TRAINS, TEA AND LUGGAGE

John

With the sea journey behind them there was a two day layover in Singapore, with the men bunking down temporarily at the Changi Base prior to catching the train to Prai, the nearest railway station to Butterworth.

After the ocean breezes the air tasted strange in Singapore. Not unpleasant, but they didn't so much breathe it as get drenched by it. The tea was different too, so light, it seemed they didn't so much drink it as inhale it.

"This here's a ruddy topsy-turvy place!" John muttered, prompting an immediate response from one of the other men.

"Well, what do you expect, we're on the other side of the world!"

Somehow that made just enough sense to be believable. Another man added his own recommendations. "It's the water, mate. You need to watch out for the water!"

There were certainly plenty of warnings doing the rounds amongst the men as they were taken to where they'd be spending the next couple of days before the troop train was ready for them.

"Hang on a minute. I've got to watch the water, breathe the tea and have a shower in the air? Just don't give me any more advice, or I'll be walking on me hands before I get out of 'ere!" John was glad to get off the ship and for the advice, but this land took some getting used to.

Before any of them got to the troop train waiting for them, there were a couple of days of lectures to wade through; 'instruction' on the local situation in Malaya. The theory sounded good, but it wasn't particularly helpful. The men didn't need to know the politics of the situation, and they certainly weren't going to be able to make sense of the religious sensitivities. Most of them couldn't even say what religion they were, except when asked they knew to say 'C-of-E, Sir'. As for politics, that went as far as cigarettes and alcohol. Anyone asking more questions than that and they were considered a little too nosey for their own good.

One of the sergeants giving the lectures at the Changi Base seemed to be an old hand at them. The men could tell as soon as they got into his sessions. He shouted at them until they were all in and sat down, then he slammed the stick down on his desk. "This is the way it is. This is what we want you to know. This is what we want you to do."

The Sarg kept it simple and to the point, presumably because he'd decided they couldn't cope with anything more complicated. He was right. Most of the men were still trying to cope with the heat and humidity.

Most of the men learnt more from the young officer, a bright new shiny thing. He was smart enough to start by reminding the men, "You're here to do a job. You don't want to be here, I don't want to be here and none of the locals want us to be here, but most of them will tolerate us only because the alternative is worse!"

He was also the one that began explaining about the Communist Terrorists, the CT, informing John and the rest of the men that Malaya was in the middle of a guerrilla conflict between the Commonwealth forces and the pro-independence fighters of the Malayan National Liberation Army, mostly ethnic Chinese.

John could follow that much, though it became clear not even the bright-young-thing of an officer was able to explain where the locals stood on the matter. That was anyone's guess!

The officer had patiently explained this wasn't a war, it was an 'emergency'. There was a difference. Not that any of the men could tell what that difference might be!

Someone piped up with: "So is it our-lot trying to stop them-lot from shooting at the other-lot, Sir?"

Another was prompted to curiosity with: "So, are we meant to be starting it, stopping it, or just getting in the way of it, Sir?"

"Sounds like war!?" John muttered under his breath.

"Nah!" the loud mouth sitting beside him offered. "If they're fighting proper-like, in uniforms, both sides, then it's a war. If they're gorilla-ing and surging-in-civvies, then it's an 'emergency'!"

The young officer had been listening and considered that last description for a moment. It was as good a definition as he'd heard that month. "Yep!" he nodded sagely. "That just about sums it up!"

The support for the Communist Terrorists seemed to come mostly from ethnic Malay-Chinese population. They'd already been able to establish jungle bases and were conducting raids on the colonial police and military installations.

"That's where you lot are getting in on it," he'd informed his class, before adding that the tin mines and the rubber plantations were also frequent targets, in order to make Malaya too expensive for the British to maintain.

As far as John could tell by the time the lectures were finished, once they got up to Butterworth Base it was going to be a 'search and destroy' strategy towards the CT, and a 'hearts and minds' mission towards the locals. The only problem John could see with that was no one seemed able to tell the difference!

The lecture was fascinating but only managed to answer the questions the men hadn't known they were meant to be asking. It hadn't really helped with the essentials.

The 'essentials' got resolved soon enough over tea in the mess, a short walk and a world away from the lecture hut. The English-speaking locals allowed on base were only able to reach the men at the mess hut, and from then on the talk got really interesting. Even if there was no getting off base this side of the railway station, that didn't mean they couldn't talk about it.

The next scheduled lecture helped make it simple. The 'white areas' were ok anywhere, anytime, once you were allowed off base. The 'grey areas' were with escort-only. That notion got a few laughs. Sarg cleared his throat and gave them a moment to remember where they were. According to the map he was jabbing at, if they wanted to get from one large city to another, the main roads were all a bit dodgy!

Then there were the 'black areas'. Serious places. Most of the countryside, as far as John could tell from the maps they were being shown. The black areas seemed to cover almost anywhere in Malaya that had either dense jungle or high mountains. Where there wasn't jungle or mountains there were plantations and ports, cities and civilians, and these were the targets of the CT.

The second day wasn't nearly as complicated and very different. They'd all had to go on the rifle range to refresh their arms. It wasn't like they'd had much chance to forget basic training, it had only been a couple of months previous. But the instructor explained it was in case they needed to secure the camp area at Butterworth.

By the end of the first hour John was amongst a mix of thirty men, RAF and Army, that found themselves bused onto the 25-yard range. They had five rounds of ammunition each to get set in, then a further five to make an impression.

After they'd finished, Staff Sargeant collected the targets. Some of the men were told "thanks you can go", leaving about a third of the men remaining, including John. Staff Sargeant was joined by another chap, RAF by the sound of him, but that wasn't made clear. He asked them if they wanted another try, on the 50-yard range next door?

John was with nine other men who'd said yes and followed the new RAF chap. The rest were duly packed off back to the bus.

Each man got another five rounds to set in the distance with the new weapon. Then a further ten. John checked his breath and his thinking. He was enjoying this. He knew where he was and what he was doing, that was all he needed to know. Ten rounds shot. After the targets were collected and inspected there were only six of them left, John, another RAF man and four Army guys. They were told they'd done well enough to have a further interview once they got back to camp.

On the bus back the men talked. They were all able to take a guess at where events were heading, and John was ready to consider it. He was hoping the interview might clear up a few 'hazy' points, if nothing else. By the time the bus reached the camp gates two of the Army guys had already declared they weren't going to be volunteering for anything and would say so. They didn't get asked.

Later that evening John got a message to report to one of the roughly erected basha offices scattered around Changi Base. Once there, the same officer from the range was waiting for him. His first words to John were not the question John had been expecting. "How well do you think you did?"

"OK. Felt good." It was an impudent response, John knew he'd fired well. *How* well it had been in comparison to the others he neither knew nor cared, at least that had been what he'd been trying to convince himself since the bus back to the camp. John had already been casually informed there'd only been one score higher than his that day. Then came the question John had been expecting. Would he be interested in doing 'something different' rather than working as a fireman-driver up at Butterworth?

John still hadn't decided how he was going to respond. He'd only been in Malaya two days and hadn't even got to Butterworth yet. He wasn't sure what he was getting into … in either direction! John tried to say as much, politely, to the officer. He didn't want to say 'no thanks' immediately, he wasn't stupid. But he wasn't ready to say 'yes' either, not without a little more know-how.

The officer seemed to realise that and handed John a piece of paper. "Here's my phone number, call me if you change your mind."

John had already been warned not to say anything about what had just taken place. Well, that was easy since he wasn't quite sure himself! The whole 'interview' had taken five minutes and about as many words. John hadn't said 'no', that much he was sure about. But he wouldn't be sure about anything else until he reached Butterworth!

Next morning, they were rounded up into trucks and transported from Changi down to Singapore railway station. The troop train had about 300 Army and Air Force personnel on board. John wasn't so much interested in how many were going in the same direction as him, as he was in if any knew more about where they were heading. He was hoping it might make the going a little easier.

John was wrong. There was nothing easy about the troop train! The humidity was horrendous, worse than on board ship. No one was throwing up on the train, which surprised him, what with the tea, tobacco, body odour and fumes from the engine, as well as the stench from the tracks, too! He had to smile at some of the comments from the men who hadn't realised the trains didn't have plumbing in this part of the world.

The delicately aromatic tea got John imagining how his mum would have enjoyed it. He could see her picking up her pinky at one sniff of the brew. It was a silly thought, but he couldn't shake it. He was holding a mug of tea, sitting on the floor of a train, somewhere on the other side of the world and what was he thinking of? Not tracking through an unfriendly jungle, but his mum back home and enjoying a nice cuppa with her. "Ruddy topsy-turvy place!"

Someone had already piped up with "How far to Prai?"

No one was sure, although they'd all seen the maps. John could already see it wasn't going to be the distance, it was going to be the days!

With no air conditioning and in the middle of summer, it was as hot as hell. John had been able to get to a window and as the train went round the first bend, he'd been able to catch sight of something that gave him an idea of what they were heading into. The train was pushing two flat-bed trucks ahead of the engine. The first was loaded with sandbags. The second had a machine gun on it, with a bunch of Army guys kitted out for war.

The guard didn't come for another hour or so, but was happy to inform them the railway was often the target of CT. They'd blow the track to try to derail the train before firing at the carriages.

"Nice welcome!" someone a couple of benches ahead of John observed.

"Nice welcome!?" the guard asked him. "You didn't think they wanted us here, did you? Why do you think this is an emergency!?"

There didn't seem to be an answer to that, at least not fit to offer the guard. Plenty of possibilities were suggested as soon as he'd left the carriage, though.

It was cramped and hot, even with the windows open, and cripes did it stink! But the noise from the other men was becoming a reassuring constant, like the movement of the train itself, lulling John into thought. The smell of tobacco and trains triggered a pleasant recollection. His thoughts wandered back to when he'd been just about tall enough to see over the top of the bridge wall, over the railway that ran by his home. He must have been young enough for his mum to be walking with him back from school. She was where the tobacco smell came from. He'd beg her to let him stay long enough to see the 'next one'. He'd tell her he knew it was coming as he felt the bridge under his feet pick up the tremor from the tracks below. The air rushed forward bringing the smell of the engine in plenty of time to be sure, and the smoke stayed long after the train had disappeared from view. His mum would always 'tut' at him for making her wait, but she never dragged him away from the bridge until the train was out of sight. He must have been very young.

Shaking off the memory, John had the sense to decide the sooner he got comfortable the better. 'Two days to Prai' he reminded himself. The luggage rack over their heads was empty as they'd all been told to stow their kit in the carriage at the back of the train, so John climbed up to the canvas banded rack and stretched out, shutting his eyes, listening to the shuffling sound as more of the men did the same. Whatever they were heading into, the best thing he could do was get his head down and sleep … whilst he could.

PADRE

The 'Padre' label had started on the way over and Archie hadn't the heart to keep contradicting them. It seemed rude, after they'd been so accommodating. Since then, it seemed simpler to go with the flow of the proceedings, until he found himself being shoved along the railway platform, to join the officers.

He'd been quite amazed by the architecture of the railway station in Singapore. Something about it had got him thinking of those 'dreaming spires' he'd left behind. The station must have been built at least a hundred years ago and the train wasn't a recent addition either! There was something reassuring about the antiquity of the train, at least the engineers seemed to be taking good care of it, Padre tried to convince himself that boded well.

It was all so fascinating, in a nerve-numbing sort of way. He'd followed the directions being yelled at him, although they'd been surprisingly polite about it, considering how stupid he must have appeared. He was sure they'd told him the exact opposite on at least three separate occasions. In the end the best Padre could think to do was keep a tight hold of his bag and just wait for someone else to nudge him along.

The platform was a microcosm of commerce in itself and the Padre wouldn't have minded more time to observe the various situations on display; market-bargaining, legal-advice, postal-workers and an apparent laundry business! Unfortunately, as fascinating as it might have been to linger, by then he'd been shoved up onto the step and into the officer's carriage.

"Come on, Padre. Sit down before you get knocked down! Train's going to take a while and the tea's hot, or do you prefer coffee? I can get you coffee, but it's not very good."

"Tea, please. Thank you." Padre sat down thankfully and with an exhausted sigh, smiled, and accepted the cup offered to him by the bright young officer.

It had only taken one person to refer to him as 'Padre' on board the troopship and the label had stuck, although a couple of the Lads had actually thought he was some sort of 'doc' at first. It was an understandable mistake. His first errand had been to go in search of a clean bandages for his injured roommate. The unfortunate individual had improved after the second day and, since then, Padre had been able to wander a little, listening to the stories of quite a few of the young men travelling on board with him.

There might have been some confusion in certain quarters as to why the young vicar was amongst them, but for Archie there was no such doubt: this felt, by far, the most useful thing he'd done in a long while!

No one had actually asked him to explain himself, so he hadn't. He was still waiting for someone to check! He had his passport and the Letters of Introduction his mother had arranged for him. But by and large everyone seemed to simply expect him to be there, and there he was.

"More tea, Padre?"

They began discussing the countryside they were passing through. It was much greener than those library photographs had led him to expect, they really hadn't done it justice.

As they got talking, the young tea-proffering officer proved to be quite a well-travelled man. "They have villages. Did you know that? Smaller than ours but with more people," the young officer explained, helpfully. "They don't have streams though, only rivers. It's the water you see!"

Padre must have looked a little surprised by that explanation and the young officer had elaborated. "There's a lot of water only it tends to gush rather than flow. Large rivers, small rivers, deep ones and dry ones, they're *all* rivers."

"Those 'streams' you see, over there. That's not water, that's people. They've been sent out from their villages. We can't let them stay there, it's just not secure enough," the young officer earnestly explained the principle. "We'll burn their fields, destroy their livestock and tear down their homes, all for their benefit! Can't have all those little villages scattered around where we can't keep them safe, can we? So, we bring them in. Somewhere secure." The young officer pointed out, for the Padre to follow.

"Markets and merchants, fields and farmers, rice and rubber, workers, trade and commerce, transport, that's what we're trying to keep moving ... in our direction. Trying to protect these people from the Chinese. We need them on our side, that'll be the 'hearts and minds'. You'll be getting involved with that Padre. Don't know how, though? I wouldn't be best pleased with anyone who'd just kicked me out of my village. I wouldn't have much 'heart' left for anyone doing that to me, but that's your department Padre!"

With that revelation to keep the Padre's thoughts nicely occupied, the smart young officer grinned pleasantly and finally drifted into a companionable silence.

Taps

He was back with the luggage, last carriage. It was quite pleasant back there, not much room, not much conversation, but quite comfortable.

Taps was quite at home there. The smell of dusty old wood and crushed dried leather rather reminded him of the back room of a cobbler's shop. He'd done some running for the cobbler when the poker game was on. He'd been small enough to nip around the back alleys and no one turned a hair. The smell of glue and boot polish at the cobblers had taken some getting used to, but once he had, it wasn't so bad. He'd managed to forget about that old shop since then, until the old wood and leather had shuffled those memories to the surface.

It must have been a good few hours before anyone came to check on him. He'd been wondering how long it would take them. There were at least a couple of guards his end of the train.

Once he'd recovered sufficiently, Taps had quickly located a 'reliable' store room onboard ship. Wherever there was a store room there was always an opportunity of some description, and Taps had learnt early how to recognise an opportunity. He'd been listening to the chatter and keeping his head down ever since then.

The talk on the troop train had proven just as helpful, it was heading through unfriendly country and Taps knew what 'black areas' meant as well as any man on the train. Armed guards were only to be expected.

Taps was quick at recognising what was expected in a situation. If he hadn't been he'd never have lasted this long. The bloke that came into the luggage carriage now was not an armed guard, that much Taps gauged instantly. He wasn't English either and was talking fast, but it wasn't what he was saying so much as his appearance and mannerism that Taps felt able to interpret most accurately. He seemed to be some sort of porter. Taps was small and had always had a somewhat rough-and-ruddy appearance, so maybe he'd blend in better than most of the travellers on board.

The fast-talking man seemed to be coming into the carriage with the intention of moving the kit bags and suitcases around to allow for more space.

"More coming on board hey?" Taps asked him.

The fast-talking man nodded happily. A repeated gesture this time for Taps to join him in starting to move everything.

No problem. They both set to, chatting in two completely separate languages getting on the with job in hand, efficiently and amiably.

Every piece of luggage had labels. Taps knew how to check kit bags; grab the labelled handle first, other hand round the bottom end, lift and let the bag twist over in the air. That way the label stayed at the front as they steadily began to stack them tidily from floor to ceiling along one side of the carriage. This seemed to be a much-improved arrangement, according to the sounds coming from the local porter.

The suitcases, presumably because they belonged to the officers and civvies, required a little more considerate handling, but sat better in their respective stacks, flat against the carriage wall.

There were a few more obscurely shaped items of luggage to deal with and they came across the occasional case-bag, but these were easily nudged in where the gaps allowed.

"Nicely done, don't you think?" Taps asked the local bloke.

The sort-of-porter seemed satisfied, with a vigorous nodding of the head. "Yes, please, thank you. Tea very much?" That certainly satisfied Taps! He sat down on the floor of the cleared area and drank the tea from the jar being offered him.

Taps took a pack of cards from his pocket. That didn't need any explanation either, although the version of poker the locals played wasn't one Taps was familiar with. There were a few false starts and a couple of angry outbursts, nothing the tea and cigarettes couldn't resolve though, and it wasn't too much of a stretch for Taps to get the gist of the rules.

Keeping his head down had never been difficult for Taps. His stature and complexion leant itself to no one taking much notice of him. Taps had learnt so long as he looked like he wasn't worth noticing, he wasn't! Which had served him well so far.

He wasn't afraid of hard work; it was just that he didn't like getting 'stuck' anywhere for too long. He certainly hadn't got bored yet, nor had he got into trouble, well not since the crowbar and the motorbike incident!

He rather liked the heat, and the cold tea was remarkably palatable. Not like the harsh 'gun-fire' brew he'd had to get used to onboard ship. "Nice brew!" he offered, lifting the jar in salute to his poker mate. Taps had a watch, and the sort-of-porter noticed it.

"Time?" Taps asked and told him what his watch said. He'd checked it with the station clock so Taps knew it was correct.

That seemed to satisfy the sort-of-porter who sprung up from the floor, opening the carriage door, apparently to check where they were. The man yelled back over to Taps. "Ready-ready?"

Taps checked himself before replying, "Ready-ready!"

He had no idea what he was agreeing to but was ready to find out, and he didn't have long to wait. They were coming into the next station. Taps had been right there was more luggage due.

"Right-ho!"

Taps put the pack of cards back into his pocket.

The sort-of-porter checked his response, "Right-ho! Yes ready-ready!" he laughed and beckoned Taps to stand by.

By now Taps could hear yells from the armed guards in the mid-carriages, exchanging calls to those ahead of them. There was no mistaking when they came into the station.

The green fields ran out and the buildings started to climb over one another. The grass and thatch were rapidly being replaced by stone and plaster, corrugated sheeting on some of the roofs and what looked like pallets and sheets for some of the walls.

Gravel dust and hot food. Ah, now Taps was really interested! The tea had been good, but Taps was hungry. He'd noticed the shouting getting louder and less polite, too.

What Taps really wanted was a decent sandwich, something to get his teeth into. There had been lots of dainty bowlfuls of interesting foods whilst he'd been in the camp. He'd enjoyed their fresh variety and they compared favourably to the stale sameness of food on board ship, but the local dishes hadn't been particularly 'substantial'. Taps really needed a good old-fashioned sandwich, but also needed to keep his head down!

This country had a lot of street-food sellers and Taps was expecting something similar to the railway station at Singapore, though whether he had time to find one and get something to eat, without being seen, was anyone's guess!

"More-bags?" Taps asked.

"Ready-ready!" The go-for-it was duly given.

"Ready-ready!" Taps confirmed, standing ready to jump as soon as the train started to stop. He could hear the men on the platform before he could see them. He could smell the kit bags and followed the way the rest of the porters moved.

No one noticed him. Just the way Taps liked it. When eventually one of them did, it was only to yell at him to 'hurry up'. It wasn't an order, just a general yell in his direction. Taps hauled and scuttled back to the luggage carriage. His porter mate was ahead of him. They might be small but, by crikey, they could lift and shift as well as any man Taps could name from his warehouse days.

Most of the new passengers on the platform looked like officers so more suitcases than kitbags this time. Taps noticed that much. They all seemed to know what they were doing, which made him a bit nervous. Thankfully he'd found a 'stray' jacket whilst they'd been rearranging the carriage earlier, before starting the poker game. Nothing was said when he'd slipped it over his shoulders, and by the time they were halfway through the poker 'Porter', as Taps now seemed to be known, had learnt enough of the local expletives to feel ready for the station.

He followed the general movement. The officers kept putting their suitcases and bags down, and Taps kept picking them up and handing them on over to the next porter, who started packing them into the luggage carriage. His poker-playing mate gave every impression of being glad to have someone doing the running for him and was grinning like a Cheshire cat, nodding every time Taps put the cases down at his feet.

He was about two-thirds of the way through the process when

Taps wondered why no one had thought of using a barrow. He took a moment to scan the station beyond the immediate vicinity of the suitcases. It was a far more basic structure, plenty of business, but less colourful than Singapore. There were barrows but they were all heading up to the front of the train. A different 'loading', Taps reckoned, but kept that to himself and just continued to porter on with his head down.

There were still no sandwiches in sight, but Taps had managed to learn the next station was Prai. Another day away, but he could wait. He'd stay in the luggage carriage until the trucks pulled up, ready to unload everything going over to Butterworth Base. Men, kit and all. A Base meant a kitchen. That was the next stop for Taps. There was a sandwich there with his name on it!

While they waited for Prai station, Taps' poker partner had taught him about the local set-up. Tea and cigarettes would keep him until then. The jacket worked as a pillow for a while but there was plenty to think about and keep him awake.

Taps still wasn't quite clear how he'd got this far! He liked to keep things simple and staying on base made sense. He might not have volunteered, but at least between the luggage and the kitchen, he knew where he was and what he was doing. 'Porter, hey?' he'd been called worse. If the men and officers were already calling him 'Porter', then that kept everything simple. He could live with that, and that's what this was all about, wasn't it!?

CHAPTER 3

AIRFIELDS AND ALIBIS

(RAF Butterworth)

JOHN

If the movement of the train hadn't been enough to rattle their sense of equilibrium, then the discussions between the benches in the back of the trucks, as they drove away from the railway station, had certainly shredded any residual belief that they knew what they were heading into.

Butterworth Base was a sight for sore eyes. The trucks had seemed to find it easily enough, although where they were on the map was anyone's guess. They weren't supposed to have that map, but someone had managed to find a 'spare' on a desk back at Changi. It did the rounds smoothly enough, but even after studying it most of them were none the wiser.

There was a lot of green, that much they could see for themselves, although the 'green' seemed to stagger up the sides of some mountains and glide impenetrably down others. In between there were roads and rivers, according to the fine blue and brown lines on the map, but which way and where they led was anyone's guess!

"Are we here?" one of the men asked, peering through the canvas out the back of the truck.

"If you lean out any further, you'll definitely be there." Another man grabbed the shirt of the first, and flung him back in. "Wait." Wise words.

John's first thought, with both feet firmly on the ground, was to get something to eat. It seemed most of the men were thinking the same. That and finding somewhere to wash.

Some of the men seemed to be under the impression when the train had arrived at the station that they'd have a break before travelling again. No chance! They'd climbed down from the carriages, got the feeling back into their backs and legs across the length of the platform, then picked up their kit bags from the unloaded piles and got into the waiting trucks outside the station. From there it was sit down, shut up and watch out!

The banter had quietened, though the cursing had got progressively harsher.

The guards at the Butterworth gates had recognised the trucks and they'd gone through without slowing. The men were shown where their tents were. There were a half dozen huts, mostly wood with a bit of metal about them. Unsurprisingly, the officers had them. There were a couple of garages too, conversely mostly metal with a bit of wood.

The tents looked by far the most appealing as their canvas sides had been drawn up and tied, basic but reassuringly familiar.

"Good to know where you are," John grinned, muttering to himself as he dumped his kit bag down on the nearest bunk, already looking from there to where the showers might be. "Neatly done." He approved on the layout so far. Nothing wasted, very efficient, pretty much what he'd been expecting, only within a space that defied description. "This is an airbase!?"

"Not yet it ain't," an earlier arrival informed him. "That's why we're here. Working at it!"

OK. John could do that.

The air flow through the tents had more substance to it than the ground beneath their feet, more dust than earth. John had already learnt about the monsoons, partly from those lectures back in Changi, more extensively from what he'd heard on the train coming over. Surprisingly informative location, that luggage rack!

John still wasn't convinced he'd made the right choice, but in his experience, when someone was asking him to make a quick decision about a situation he didn't know enough about, then it usually meant it was only going to get worse! John had kept the telephone number in his pocket since the 'interview' safe enough … just in case.

He was hungry but recognised he needed a shower more. Anyway, the first Lads over to the mess tent would be the ones best able to give him an inkling of what he was heading into. In the meantime, the showers weren't going to be so busy.

It was a simple arrangement with water-tanks up top, rope down with wooden handle, stand under and pull. There was a sliver of a bar of soap left next to the bamboo for the towel to be slung over. John had noticed that detail. There was a lot of bamboo around the place.

More bamboo than wood, as far as John could tell. Very useful stuff this bamboo and the corrugated sheeting too, by the looks of it! He could see where the perimeter fence was from the showers, and it was close enough to make him nervous.

Stripping off John let the water loose on his pale travel-bruised body. It was well rested but felt crushed by the weight of the water. It took him a moment to adjust. Better. Squaring his shoulders to it, twisting his torso, soap and scrub, planting his feet sturdily and pissing out the drainage from the rough brew of tea they'd been given to gulp down between platform and truck. He was more thirsty than hungry.

Drying himself as he walked back to his bunk, he saw a steady flow of men forming, traipsing between bunks, showers and mess tent.

"Regular and standard." John grinned at his own thoughts, catching up with a few more men heading for the food. The talk was about what they'd found so far, about what they expected to find and about what they hoped they didn't!

Most of the men hadn't felt able to eat for the past forty-eight hours. With memories of the troopship crossing still keen, caution-learnt: don't eat anything solid until you've stopped moving.

Something about what he was hearing reminded John of one of the lectures. What was it they were meant to be doing? 'Denying the Communist Terrorists food and resources? Providing the indigenous tribes medical and food aid?' John found himself hoping that someone, somewhere, was going to explain how they were meant to tell the difference between the two groups. Locals and indigenous, merchants and workers, he wouldn't be at all surprised if they were inadvertently helping those they were meant to be hindering! "Wouldn't be the first time!" John muttered to himself. He hadn't expected that to come out so loud.

"YaWot?" one of the Lads in front of him in the queue turned.

"Sorry, wasn't thinking," John explained.

"You need to round here," the Lad warned him. "They're all at it. Got to keep your eyes open. Sneaky blighters some of 'em!"

John was pleased to meet someone who seemed to know a bit more about the situation. He had plenty of questions and it looked like the cook was struggling to cope with the sudden surge of men wanting to be fed.

"Bottle-neck?" John queried.

"Looks like it," the man in front agreed.

Pleasantries observed they got down to business.

"So, who are they targeting? If we're using this as an airfield, then I'm guessing we're not far from the problem?"

"Not far?" the other man laughed loud enough to make John feel stupid, but he could handle that if he got the information he needed. "Not far? Mate! We're slap-bang in the middle of it. This is *all* in the middle of it. That's why it's a ruddy-emergency. The whole damned country is fighting with itself!"

John had attended those Changi lectures three days earlier, but by the time he'd got to the front of the grub-line, there was definitely a sense of a better grasp of the situation dawning on him. The Communist Terrorists, the CT, were sabotaging installations, attacking rubber plantations and destroying transportation and infrastructure.

"Right. So, they're going for everything that they can get to!"

"That sounds about the way of it!" the other man agreed. More men were in on the chatter, as they sat at one of the tables with plenty of opinions flying about.

"So, we're protecting the transportation then?" John checked he'd got that much straight.

"Some of us are. We're only meant to be going out on patrols at the moment. Some of us are guarding the local villages and protecting the plantations. I think some of us are meant to be on the driving until they get this airfield fully operational."

"Sounds about right," John agreed. He was a fireman-driver and from what he'd learnt so far, the driving would be the greater part of his workload for the next few weeks. That suited him nicely.

"Oh! Don't worry, we've got more engineers and construction crews coming in for that. They're bringing the heavy-duty gear too," another man at the table informed him brightly.

"What about the locals, the indigenous?" John was curious, he'd seen a few about the camp already.

"Strange fellas some of them, but at least we're not going to get them confused with the CTs, are we?"

"No, you can't mistake them!" John grinned.

His table-companions agreed, "distinctive" was an accurate description.

"What're they doing here?" was the next query.

John could answer that one, glad to offer his share of the

knowledge criss-crossing the table as they ate and waited to be ordered to do something else. "They're the local Dayak trackers and apparently our 'guides' once we start getting that far. They've been hating and hunting the Chinese long before this 'emergency' got started. They'll help us find the CTs alright, so long as we let them cut their heads off once we've finished with 'em!"

"Sounds like a good deal to me! Solves the problem, don't it? No more emergency and we can all go home again!?" another man gleefully offered, before shovelling another forkful of food into his mouth.

One of the other diners, adding his two penn'orth, soon put a halt to that optimism. "Unfortunately, there are an awful lot of Chinese-Malays that are sympathetic to the CT cause hiding in plain-sight. Not so 'distinctive'. In addition, not enough of the local Dayak tribes-people have been persuaded to trust us much either!"

"That's where 'hearts and minds' comes into it then?" They could agree. Finishing their food, they were ready to start exploring the camp, just grabbing a final refill of tea before leaving the mess tent, the dust and talking making them thirsty.

The best advice the older men could give the new-comers was "stay out of the way."

"Out of the way of what?" would have been John's next question. He never got to ask that one, as they were called over to the in-coming delivery.

John was just beginning to get a sense of what he was looking at. The airfield was under-construction from more than one direction! The onslaught of deliveries, of both men and machines, was making it resemble a Supply Depot rather than a working airfield. John had seen two aeroplanes come in, so part of the airfield was definitely working, but the constant traffic wasn't coming from that direction.

The rough terrain and hurried turn-around of traffic meant a constant need for drivers. That got John thinking, what about those trucks that weren't driveable anymore? Someone was going to need to do some fixing. No one else seemed to be interested and he knew his way around an engine. It didn't matter where in the world he was, if John was given an engine to work on, he could get on with that and make himself useful. It helped him think, to watch and listen, and stay out of the way of everything else going on!

John returned to his tent, which was, at least, less cramped than the train carriages and the beds were an improvement on the luggage rack. They had a locker each. John had unpacked his kit and the handful books he'd been able to grab. Seeing those books on the locker was somehow reassuring, and smelling the engine grease on his hands made him feel easier too, although he couldn't shake the feeling that everything was in the wrong place.

John hadn't decided yet if he was safer here or on the train. But he *had* discovered, that with his head stuck in an engine, no one recognised the fact he hadn't been there more than a few hours. They'd start talking and he kept on listening.

The drivers weren't only bringing information of what they were transporting but also the routes they'd taken, the local conditions and the areas they had come through, mostly 'grey', but some definitely darker than that! Good to know. He wasn't going to need to ask many questions, he just needed to keep his eyes and ears open, and John knew how to do that.

By the next morning the lectures at Changi were starting to make more sense. There would be jungle-training here, not so much to do with how to shoot but more to do with the practicalities; they were going to need a few days of those.

The instructor had changed tack and got them all sat down under cover in one of the tents getting to grips with handling their regular kit in jungle conditions. Not so simple. Everything was compressed, everything was more intense. John got the overwhelming impression that if you needed more time to think, you were already too slow!

They took a break about mid-day. John went back over to the mess tent and gulped down a couple of pints of tea before sitting down by the truck he'd been working on earlier. One of the local

Dayak tribesmen he'd seen walking about earlier, came over and started chattering to him.

From what John had heard so far, many of the local tribesman were tracker-guides and maybe this one could give him a few more pointers to the local situation.

John hadn't a clue what the bloke was saying, at least not for the first few minutes, until he realised it was English with a strange accent, and very fast!

John made a simple gesture for the local to slow down his chattering, that shut the tribesman up for a moment. Long enough for John to offer him a cigarette. That seemed to be what the bloke was asking for all along and they got on well after that.

John's ear was starting to adjust to the contorted accent, there was a 'click' to it that seemed to interrupt the vowels. Once he'd allowed for those, he could follow most of the shorter sentences.

By the time they'd finished their second cigarettes John had a grasp on the essentials of 'cigarette', 'tea', 'truck', 'engine', 'boot' and 'water', although it got a bit murky after that. The tracker was trying to explain how many different words they had for 'water', it was fascinating, but got John off-track from the engine. Before he got a chance to take another look at it the tracker disappeared, and John heard the shout for everyone back to the lecture tent.

The officer giving the lecture this time was getting a bit bogged down with the 'history' of the situation. John would have been happier with a 'more recent history' lesson and less of the 'ruddy green maps with blue strips on', and he wasn't the only one.

"Who are they kidding? Rivers don't flow like that."

"They're not rivers, they're dykes! They need to flood their rice fields with them."

Most of the men were just waiting for someone to tell them what they were meant to be doing there. The air was hot, dense and sticky, the jungle was dusty, dense and dangerous. The water tasted like earth and the air felt as damp as water! Most of them found by the time they got back to their bunks they hadn't the energy to talk anymore.

Dragging on a cigarette, John remembered the local Dayak who'd found him by the truck earlier. He didn't really want to talk but if it only cost him a few more cigarettes, a bit more information would be useful.

He'd heard a couple of the men bragging how they'd already got the measure of the place. John doubted that! He'd heard it all before at other camps. The difference this time was nothing was entirely what it seemed!

The local Dayak wasn't by the broken-down truck, but by the time John had lit a cigarette the tribesman found him. John offered before he was asked, that went down well. He started off by asking the tribesman's opinion of the mess tent.

If John knew what the subject matter was before the local started explaining, then he had a better chance of figuring out what the heavily accented words meant. Steering the conversation around to the gate, the showers and the officers was an interesting concept. They got on to a few more of the camp buildings, as there were a couple that seemed to be set apart. Here the local tribesman demonstrated his tracker-guide skills eloquently, he'd got those figured out. They were for the 'Army' units that came through, not regularly, according to John's new friend.

"Not regular Army units?" John asked him. The tribesman didn't seem able to use an English word for *how* regular or not the Army units were, only that they were 'Army'. By the time John had got them both a mug of tea, the tribesman had decided they would be friends. That was a relief.

It was getting dark. If John didn't start soon, he'd not be able to find his way back. The tribesman cackled at his concerns. John looked down into his mug trying to think how to break up their meeting, then looking up, the tribesman had already gone. "Must find out how he does that!" John chuckled to himself as he stumbled his way back to his bunk.

John's last thoughts that night were that so long as he attended to the lessons-between-the-lectures, wherever they came from, then he could work with an unfriendly jungle. It didn't take a genius to realise if you watched your step and kept quiet you were going to make steadier and safer progress than if you started thrashing and slashing your way through it! His tracker friend was going to be invaluable, especially if he could teach John how to be unseen in the jungle.

As far as John could tell it was all about movement. The movement of men through the jungle, the movement of trucks along the roads and the movement of harvests to the ports. 'Logistics' they'd called it.

The next morning followed the same routine, with lectures that seemed to lead to more questions than they'd started with. And John had a question of his own to consider: he'd begun to wonder if his new tracker friend could help him 'track' down a few spares for that truck he'd been working on?

John had always been a driver, whether it was a tractor on his uncle's farm, a Land Rover down across some of the flat marshy beaches of the Wash, or a fire truck out of basic training. His uncle had set him the challenge: "If you want to drive it, you've got to be able to get it working first." That lesson had stuck with John ever since, and whenever he'd had the opportunity to drive something new, he resolved he'd learn how it worked first.

An incident with that Land Rover back at training camp had proven the point! They'd managed to get it stuck on top of a scrubby crag, an awkward combination of a steep climb with deep ruts. His mates were all for just getting out and shoving it over the other side, but John knew if he'd let them do that, it would never have got them back to base. It took John working the engine in his favour, 'gears and wheels, in the right order,' and they'd got the vehicle tipping, able to grip enough ground to slough over the ruts, limping back to base without gouging out half the hillside or dragging the chassis. Sarg had enough to make a guess at the incident, but insufficient evidence for a charge.

John didn't see his tracker friend again that day, but the man found John the day after that, the same day they both caught sight of the Australians. Large and loud about everything!

"Australians don't do subtle!" John tried to get his tracker friend to appreciate the difference between the Brits and Aussies. They'd been getting on well what with the 'spares' surfacing. By then there were three more trucks waiting for someone to get back on the road and the concept of 'cannibalising' the worst-rated vehicle seemed to have a fairly direct, if worrying, translation to John's friend!

The Australians had come on to Butterworth intending to build themselves a runway. That wasn't the problem, especially as the RAF had already cleared most of the jungle from the area. John was more interested to see what sort of muscle the Australians were bringing to the task.

John was a regular at the garage hut by then. Essentially, he *was* the garage! There were plenty of tools around, but no one else seemed interested in getting them to work. John and the Dayak became garage-mates. They'd already got that first truck working on the third try, and by then had two more waiting, with a further two set-aside for 'spares'. It seemed like a tidy arrangement.

No one asked what he was meant to be doing, although John was fireman-driver if anyone asked. His paperwork was in order, and no one had told him to do anything else. His kit was straight and the jungle-instruction from the tent benches had been heavily supplemented by the wisdom dispensed by his garage-mate.

"You guide me around the jungle, and I'll guide you around this engine."

That was the deal and it worked to both their satisfaction. As for the tea and cigarettes, that translated equally well. His garage-mate had a fascinating version of the latter and seemed happy to share, but one sniff and John politely declined. "Better not, still on duty!"

The Australians managed to bring all their heavy-duty equipment up by rail. John wondered how they'd fared those last twenty miles by road from Prai station to the camp? They didn't have any trouble muscling into the airbase, filling every bit of space marked for them, rapidly running out of that and promptly trying to nudge over for more! That took a couple of remarkably restrained hours in the officer's mess 're-negotiating allocations.' Basically, as far as John could tell from what was repeated in the mess tent later, 'it ain't gonna happen.'

According to his garage-mate, the Dayaks weren't too keen on the Australians either. John suddenly felt rather sorry for the big guys, however it made sense, the last thing you'd want to do in this environment was stand out!

The Australians had all the newest vehicles, and their diggers and dozers were massive. The civvies they'd brought over with them were all engineers and John had heard about them too. What they *hadn't* brought over with them were any mechanics!

Their Australian airfield machines were larger, faster to respond and with more moving parts. They could do more work in less time, but only when they were working. The more the machines were engineered, the sooner something was going to stop working. John had seen it before: the more the men bragged, the more he stayed close, waiting for the first inevitable breakdown.

He hadn't had to wait long.

By the third day the Australians had recognised John was not only 'fireman-driver', but apparently the camp mechanic too. As for John's garage-mate, the little fellow, he didn't say much whilst the Australians were listening, but had a cackle that could break a mirror at a hundred yards when they'd moved on.

Between the training and lectures, the mess and his bunk, the only other place to find John was leaning over one of the truck engines, waiting for his mate to return from another 'errand'.

The Australians had almost everything they needed. They'd brought over they own engineers, highly qualified apparently, from the big mining corporations over there. They'd come with their own tankers too. And medics, which was always useful to know.

But not a single mechanic to fix a dozey engine amongst them? Evidently, they weren't used to working in the middle of a jungle, nor in such cramped conditions, and they hadn't been attending to their maps either!

It only came to light later that they'd needed to use a couple of guides, relatives of John's garage-mate, to stop the convoy from straying out from Prai. They had jungles in Australia and mountains too, just not often together and seldom where they needed to take the trucks over. It seemed, as John and his garage-mate listened, the Australians tended to build their roads straight through.

They needed a driver, not just someone who knew the area they were working in, but someone who could get an engine re-started and John got 'volunteered'.

What was not to like!? Sitting on top of a state of the art 'front-loader' in the middle of a clearing in the Malayan jungle, in shorts and boots, hat tilted back, a packet of cigarettes in his pocket, rifle strapped in front of the steering wheel. Not to mention the fact those Australians got their eggs and steak flown in fresh, for breakfast!

There was also the small matter that not so long ago, part of the 'new' runway the Australians had adopted had been used by the Japanese. It looked like they'd simply dug a trench and filled it with local tree-trunks.

John's garage-mate had plenty to say on the subject. Some of the local tribes had considered the Japanese a fine delicacy. He was happy to go into greater detail. None of which John thought wise to repeat to the officer who asked what he was 'jabbering-on about'. John suggested they kept on topic after that. He wasn't too sure how much the other men could overhear and comprehend.

John's local language skills were still fairly basic, but he was fluent in body language and expressive hand gestures. When it came to sending messages over an area where raised voices were inadvisable, 'signing' became part of their working day.

It was on one such occasion, when John was on extra-duties with the Australians, when the first on base emergency occurred. John had heard one of their aeroplanes coming in and it didn't sound right, coming in lower than it ought. It was hesitating and that was never a good sign!

It was scheduled in, but not on John's runway. He checked again; it was definitely heading his way. "Damn!" Now he was focused. The bomber was coming back from an Op, coming in heavy and loaded. "Damn!!"

From where he was John could clearly see the problem, he suspected probably even better than the guys further back in the tower, with their binoculars. They'd be looking for it coming in on the expected flight path, and it wasn't there.

The bomb had got stuck on release. John could see the doors slightly open, but only slightly. He'd have to get help and driving a heavy lump of a dozer that was a heck of an ask!

"DUMP-TRUCK!" he yelled, signalling over to his garage-mate who was ambling up the runway with a couple of mugs of tea.

Pointing up and over with just enough gestures in between to get the message across, the mugs were flung aside and the little Dayak skipped into a run, back to where the dump-truck was sitting.

It wasn't far as they'd brought it halfway over in readiness for work. 'Daks' got it started with a stomp and a jerk, bringing it up to where John could climb aboard, leaving the heavy-duty dozer idle and off to one side of the runway. With John at the helm of the dump-truck they raced back to the huts. Daks held on for dear-life but was laughing the whole way.

Both men were keenly aware of the position of the aeroplane. It was still on approach but getting ominously low. They hadn't got time to explain anything. They'd got the plan straight between the pair of them and knew what to do.

Thrashing the dump-truck up to the nearest hut, almost ramming into it, John jumped down without waiting to come to a halt, leaving Daks to make sure it did.

John hadn't stopped yelling but as his boots hit the ground it became more direct, shouting orders to Sarg and the men and ignoring their expressions. Sarg was roused to yell back, but only for a fraction of a second before he realised what John was saying, as much from the way John was shouting, as to what he said. That got them all moving.

"MATTRESSES. In the dump-bucket. Now!"

Daks was skipping off in the opposite direction to the officer's huts with similar intentions. But he wasn't going to be understood no matter how loud he shouted so demonstrated directly what he needed, equally eloquently, but by rather less orthodox means!

Thumping the nearest officer and catching him by the wrist before he fell back, then trawling him over to the nearest bed, tugging off the mattress and thrusting it into his arms. The few words he offered rapidly descended into "JOHN-JOHN DUMP-TRUCK."

Already merrily hopping over the tipped bed, Daks reached the next and did likewise, turning to the stunned officer left in his wake, "go on!" And 'go on' they both did, with more joining them.

In the few seconds it took for John to get Sarg to dash up to the tower and get the alarm going. Those same seconds proved sufficient for Sarg to realise the disaster John was attempting to thwart and, when the man needed to dash, he did it rather well. Sarg sort of picked up speed rather than ran out of steam. If John had more time he would have enjoyed the spectacle.

With the alarm raised everybody suddenly seemed to be running in all directions, mostly getting in John's way, but he'd got enough mattresses and Daks was coming with more. They needed to get them over to where the aeroplane could safely land, gently, hopefully!

Daks had got the unfortunate officer by the wrist again. The officer in question was twice the height of diminutive Dayak, but about the same weight, a weed of a thing, all legs and elbows. Daks had his free hand up and waving over to John, yelling as he ran, encouraging John to go faster. "JOHN-JOHN DUMP-TRUCK. OK. Full-up!" With his other hand clamped round the young officer's wrist, still hauling him along at most ungainly rate!

Finally, the officer caught up with the circumstances and, picking up his speed, impulsively leaned down and scooped up Daks, and began running with the Dayak under his arm instead.

"Jeep!?" Daks was laughing again. John could hear his shrieking cackle from the other end of the runway.

The pilot had seen it all. It would have been difficult to miss! He'd followed what John was doing.

OK, if John was willing to give it a try so was he. The pilot was out of options anyway and was already attempting to bring the aeroplane down, as gently as possible, on the furthest field from the camp.

It wasn't so much the dump-truck John was driving so recklessly across to the far-field, laden with mattresses, that got the Sarg speechless. It was the young officer with the local Dayak tribesman tucked under his arm, running after John's dump-truck, with Daks shrieking like a banshee and the officer waving like a maniac.

There was also the fire-truck right behind them, with a half dozen more of the officer's mattresses hastily strapped over the truck's roof, a couple already having been shed in transit; whilst the remainder of the mattresses destinated as 'cushioning' were being held down by the passengers in a random jeep following!

There was absolutely no way Sarg was going to attempt to report this one. He'd leave that up to the tower, but he sincerely hoped he got a chance to see the response when it came back!

As the fire-truck overtook the young officer someone thoughtfully suggested, "Don't you think you ought to put him down now, Sir?" The young officer duly deposited Daks and climbed into the jeep, whilst Daks was more than happy to wave them all on, apparently enjoying the show immensely.

John was glad to see the young officer had caught up with him, if only for the sake of the formalities. "D'ya want to give the order, Sir?"

The young officer looked from John up to the pilot, waiting in the cockpit and ready.

"No, I don't think so. But I'll back you up."

"Right-ho, Sir." John gave the nod to the men, and they began steadily wedging the mattresses under the belly of the tentatively landed bomber. The pilot kept his nerve and waited for John to give him the nod. John held the dump-truck steady as the mattresses in the bucket gradually began rising up to meet the belly of the aeroplane.

One by one the men stepped back and were gradually sent further out of range. John and Daks stayed where they were with the young officer. John had no doubt by now they had many more eyes on them, and likely more help would be coming soon. In the meantime, they just needed to stop anything from happening 'suddenly'!

John could see the look on some of the faces of the men sent away from the situation, no point in being stupid. Bit late for that! With the young officer staying put and Daks having caught up, no one wanted to miss out on the details.

When John gave the signal, the pilot opened the doors and let the bomb fall. Only then did the young British officer think to enquire. "Did anyone call the Australians?"

"Who?" the pilot checked.

"The miners!" John twigged, explaining. "They'll know how to take care of this one for you."

"Oh!" The pilot had lost the connection by then. He was just grateful to be able to feel the ground. John sounded like he knew what he was talking about, and the young officer was hopping again.

"I think they know." He pointed in the direction of the tower.

"Yep, that looks like the Australians!" John agreed, grinning, with his own better-late-than-never sigh of relief.

The Australians had judged it prudent to bring their ambulance with them and it was screaming over at full pelt, with four men in full 'disposal' kit holding on to its sides.

"Where's the rest of them?" someone asked sarcastically.

"Probably still having breakfast."

They were all laughing by the time the ambulance arrived. There were those heavy-duty grim-faced Australians, all ready for tackling the emergency, and the RAF chaps were just lounging around in shorts and vests by the jeep, having a cigarette.

"Really!?" the Australian officer asked the young officer, who looked to the pilot, who looked to John, who looked to Daks.

"Oh! Yes please, thank you, cuppa tea!"

"Does he think we're the canteen?" one of the Australians wondered. It didn't need much explaining, but just for the sake of good-form, the two officers spent another minute talking about 'the situation'.

Whilst the officers talked, the men of the disposal team got to work. John and Daks stayed near; it was interesting. They did it very neatly and had a few tricks John hadn't seen before.

"Must remember that one for next time," John murmured across to the pilot. The pilot was nodding, but also fervently hoping there wouldn't be a 'next time'.

The Australian officer overhearing John's remark, turned to him. "And we could do with remembering *yours* for next time, too!"

Afterwards the Australians even helped get the mattresses returned to their respective beds and invited the men back to their mess for a 'late breakfast', since, as far as the Australians were concerned, if they were hungry it was always breakfast! They had a good approximation to a cuppa as well.

The two officers went off together to confer with the pilot on how to report the incident. 'Joint response' seemed to apply fairly well.

The Australians might not have been the best drivers, but they were great flyers. In addition, they were also inscrutable poker players! Which explained how John lost the bet that saw him given the dare with the tanker truck!

John had thought he'd a pretty good hand, but the other guy had a better one. The subsequent dare was for John to drive the tanker backwards through the local market. It was the day after market day, thankfully, but John had already noted the local builders weren't too careful with squaring-off their corners and some of the roofs looked a little precarious. A knock against any of those clay-mud bricks and the whole building would come down.

There was a point to the dare.

The Australians hadn't yet been able to get the tanker through the market. They'd got it as far as the airfield and no further. Apparently when the road had been widened and resurfaced it had only been from the railway station to the airfield. After that it seemed to peter out, from there through the market town and villages. It broadened out and improved again as it approached the plantation, but in between it was a bit of a rough track of a road with some tight corners.

The Australians seemed unfamiliar with the concept of driving a large vehicle between narrowly spaced buildings. When they got to something in the way they either blew it out of the way or built the road around it. That wasn't an option around these parts. That wouldn't have done much for 'hearts and minds'!

The tanker needed to get through the local market town and if John could do it then all the better. The Australians would know it could be done and if it couldn't they weren't going to get the blame.

John took it slow and got Daks to guide him through. Daks was more than happy to oblige. He'd got a couple of packets of cigarettes to smoke whilst they were doing it.

John didn't look at where his wheels were going, he looked up at the sides of the buildings he was driving between. He'd already figured the building's walls would start to lean out as they got higher and if he smudged a few of the bottom corners then that was no more than a kick of dirt. Going slow and steady.

The worst thing he could have done was hesitate. Just got to keep going, one corner at a time, the straight lengths were easy. There were no streets as such, just a few buildings in line with each other. John and Daks could work with that, when any of the locals came out protesting Daks got them chattering and soon got them helping to clear out any stray laundry baskets or market stalls that had been left behind.

Finally, they got through!

They left the tanker at the far-end of the village and walked back through, stopping for some local coffee on the way. The villagers were happy with the Australian tanker out the way and as for the market-stall keepers, it was business as usual, better than usual. The Australians would be walking through their patch to retrieve the tanker!

John even got an invitation to join the Australians after that. He didn't mind their grub and liked the driving. He'd learnt better than to play poker with them and was impressed by their resources, but he wasn't tempted.

John had got a taste for the jungle by then and he liked Daks, they got on well together. Days and nights didn't mean much, if they were on shift they worked and when they finished, they ate. It was simple. But all the time the jungle waited for him, John could feel it, wondering if he were ready for it.

As they worked in the garage together John and Daks discussed the 'geography' of their situation. As a result, John's jungle-craft was improving. Perhaps Daks didn't always get the task done in the conventionally recognised format, but he got the job done. He made the jungle straight forward for John. Simple enough for him to understand that the only purpose you needed to keep in mind when going into the jungle, was the purpose of being able to get out of it again!

John had stopped asking questions in the lecture tent by the end of the third week. By the end of the fourth week the lecturers were checking with him.

He hadn't forgotten that telephone number he'd tucked away either, but his Dayak garage-mate was an intriguing fellow and John was beginning to want to know a more about what was *really* happening. John was also a great believer in the 'no harm in asking' school-of-thought. They'd made him the offer and given him time to consider it, which meant they were willing to wait. But just maybe he might prove useful up this way first.

"Better the devil you know, and all that", John muttered to himself, forgetting the ears on Daks. It had been hilarious trying to explain the expression, until both men managed to appreciate the literal translation.

When John finally got the chance to make a telephone call, he checked in with the Changi officer, giving a brief summary of where he was, what he was doing and why. The voice at the other end of the line didn't say much and John got the distinct impression they were already aware of most of what he'd just told them. He didn't ask how, especially as the voice at the other end of the line didn't sound like they would appreciate being questioned. John followed his example and after giving his 'report' went silent. The voice responded succinctly. "Very good. Understood. We'll be in touch."

John found himself laughing on the way back to the truck, because if that had been meant to sound like some sort of a threat it had missed its mark entirely. John prided himself on being able to take the measure of a situation without being too obvious and, as far as he was concerned, with what had just transpired, they were still interested. He hadn't asked why, he didn't need to know, they'd 'be in touch' according to the voice at the other end of the line.

"Well, good luck with that," John chuckled into the dark jungle evening.

He could already see where Daks was waiting for him, as his eyes had adjusted to the variances in light and dark and the myriad of shadows in between. His nose had got used to the scents of the tents, the huts and the other buildings. He could already tell what most of the vehicles were even in the pitch black, as well as what was coming in over the airfield by the sound it made over the top of the jungle. How high, how low, from which direction it was approaching and whether it was flying heavy with cargo. None of this information he offered to Daks, knowing full well that his garage-mate knew far more than he was telling too.

Between them and the vehicles awaiting their attention in the garage, they learnt each other's history, language, mechanics and medicine; in addition to John beginning to appreciate the local cuisine and customs.

"Interesting times, hey?" John enquired of his garage-mate. Daks grinned and gestured to the flask at his hip, John declined the offer but let him continue. Daks seemed equally content with how things were turning out, not as he'd expected either, but interesting times indeed!

PORTER

Taps, or 'Porter' as he was now known, disembarked with the luggage off the train, then followed it over in the back of one of the trucks to the camp at Butterworth.

There seemed to be some sort of Supply Depot arrangement going on just inside the gate, that was useful to know. Porter could always work with that! He nipped out with the kit and got hold of one of the sack-barrows. Handy that, just what he needed to be blending in. The jacket he'd found on the train was getting a bit grubby and he hoped to find something a bit fresher. However, for now he just kept on unloading the supplies and following the chap in front, a local chap by the looks of him, who seemed to know what he was doing. Porter didn't, so followed him!

If there were fresh supplies coming in, then there was bound to be a kitchen somewhere nearby. Sure enough, he could soon smell it. He could see the showers from there too, always good to know. There were a couple of huts behind the kitchen. Porter guessed storage and prep. It seemed a fair guess. That was enough for him to know for now, it was late and getting dark. In addition to which he stunk!

It wouldn't be the first time he'd fallen asleep on the floor of a storage room. He still didn't even know where this place was, not exactly, except that it was hot, sticky and dusty and the air was full of smells he didn't quite recognise, but a whole lot better than being hungry in the back of a prime-target railway train!

He could have waited hunkered down by the sacks of potatoes. He could have slept there. He could hear the water from the showers. He might have dared go over there, except he could also hear the shouts from the gate and the patrols returning. No, not tonight. He wasn't going to chance it tonight, Porter decided as he tipped and cleared the last of the loads. Best hunker. Maybe he could find out where that other kitchen-chappy bunked down.

That 'kitchen-chappy' Porter had been following was the camp cook. He'd got himself a very comfortable arrangement in the prep room behind the kitchen, a rough bunk with spare blankets. Cook hadn't stopped Porter helping him bring the supplies over, but once they were delivered, he turned and took one look at Porter, sniffed him and slapped his face.

"Not good enough!" he'd yelled at him.

That surprised Porter but pleased him too. In his experience a slap in the face was as good as a handshake introduction. He was in. Now he just needed to make himself useful enough for the cook to let him stay!

The cook was already making himself some late supper. "Me too?" Porter tentatively queried. He still wasn't sure how much English this local kitchen-chappy knew.

The cook moved the pan off the heat and stepped back over to face Porter, looking him up and down and sniffing him again, raising his hand, but this time Porter caught it, before it made contact.

"Got it! I need to wash. Where? Where wash?"

"Where wash, there!" the cook indicated the bucket of cleanish looking water and the scrap of an old towel outside the door to the prep room.

This was getting better. Emboldened, Porter ventured a second query.

"Clothes, wash? Clobber?" The cook turned and frowned the translation of 'clobber?' Porter ducked the next gesture. "Me clothes, mate? Need fresh clothes?" Tugging at his shirt, then his trousers. "Clean clobber?"

Cook grinned and pointed to one of the kit bags that had come in with the supplies to his kitchen stores.

"Oh, that's handy!" Porter agreed. Taking the kit bag outside with him to the water bucket and towel. He did a swift job of getting freshened up whilst the cook made them supper. The bucket wasn't as good as a shower, but good enough. The kit was on the large-size, Porter was no taller than the cook, but smaller round the middle by a good few inches.

"How's that?" he checked. The cook duly sniffed him again.

"Bit of an inspection hey?" Porter chuckled. If it meant him getting supper, then he could tolerate that. "All present and correct, Cookie."

Cookie wasn't taking that for granted but seemed satisfied and sat back down at the small table, set with two bowls.

"Cookie," he greeted the man formally for the first time, the slap didn't count, that was just by way of getting-to-know each other. They sat down together and drank tea. "Porter," he introduced himself.

From the way Cookie was explaining it, Porter wasn't expected to do any cooking, only the fetching and prepping. He could work with that. Cookie had gestured to the floor of the store room as being sufficient for Porter to sleep in. The cook snored, but no more than Porter did himself.

The last thing Porter remembered before shutting his eyes was how much cooler the air was down on the floor. He could raise his hand and lose sight of it in the darkness but could feel the air become thicker and more humid at that distance.

When he next opened his eyes there was shouting and shrieking, the sound of running boots and someone yanking his arm out of its socket. "Oi!" he yelled up at Cookie.

Cookie yelled right back, and Porter scrambled to his feet. "What already?"

"Ready already!"

Cookie had no problem telling him where to go and what to do. It was only half-English, but Porter had managed to get the gist of the local tongue on the train coming over here, wherever 'over here' was. He hadn't got the lingo altogether straight yet, but there were enough words in common between them to get the job done, it was a cook house after all!

Cookie went through what he'd be needing with comprehensive gesturing and shouting, then left Porter to get on with it, whilst he brewed up another pot of his infamous coffee.

Cookie also had a habit of swigging back a couple of bottles of cola, whilst imbibing the local kat chewing-tobacco. Porter hadn't seen it done that way before, but he'd seen enough to recognise when a man was under the influence. Cookie wasn't drunk and he wasn't stupid, he just needed to be able to work.

Porter could see that it was in his interests to keep Cookie happy, so long as they could keep the men fed then Porter had a place to sleep and stay out of the way, safe.

If Cookie was going to get that breakfast fit for the men's plates, he was going to need an extra pair of hands, if only for the trays, pots, and ladling! Porter wasn't afraid of hard work and preferred to be kept busy. The busier he looked, the more he would blend in and the better his situation would become.

Cookie grinned and shoved him from one end of the table to the other. Porter soon got the hang of it, between the yelling and pointing, it wasn't difficult.

The men were soon coming into the mess tent, and they seemed friendly enough, although Porter tried to stay in the background as far as he could to begin with.

It surprised the men there was an Englishman on the serving side of the tables until Cookie started flailing his arms and crashing the scraped empty trays into the sink. Porter took the hint.

"You stay back here. I'll clear away out there, shall I?" he suggested. More gesticulating and yelling followed. Porter snatched up the spare tea-towel. He didn't fancy trying to retrieve the one draped over Cookie's sweaty shoulders.

"I'll take this and the trays? Plates? From there to you? You stay here, OK?" Cookie nodded and shoved him towards the men. "Ok, got it."

Porter knew what to do, he'd worked in bars in the East End, it wasn't rocket-science. It was mostly knowing when to join in the banter and when it was wiser to avoid it. Stay silent and duck out of the way.

He'd been younger in those East-End days and had learnt plenty since. With the tea-towel and the tray he worked his way around the tables, clearing up after the men had finished and wiping down the tables in time for the next batch. Methodical. That's what the men liked to see.

Unfortunately, Porter was a little too methodical at one point, forgetting himself and not waiting for a couple of the men to step away from the table before starting to clear away their plates.

"Hey! 'Ang on there, we ain't finished. What ya doin 'ere anyway?"

"We'll clear this lot ourselves, mate? Shouldn't ya be in the officer's mess?" one of them challenged him.

Porter hadn't expected that to come up so quickly. It was his own fault, but he responded well. This was one of those situations where keeping your head down wasn't an option, so standing up to his full height, which didn't go much above the other fellas shoulders, he replied, "Just goin where I'm sent, mate," probably offering the most honest explanation of his circumstances in months.

The men hadn't really been interested but agreed with Porter. "Ain't we all!"

Cookie had started swearing again, calling for him. Porter just smirked. That went down well. It seemed he was just where everyone expected him to be, somewhere between the supply room for the kitchen and the mess tent for the men. That would do him nicely, for now.

He could do with a little bit more kit, but that might take him a couple of more days. In the meantime, having access to the stores was going to be convenient, and keeping an eye on Cookie was also going to be a wise precaution. Cookie wasn't the most sociable of fellows, but he seemed reliable enough when it came to getting food ready for the men.

Porter would have liked to have a bunk of his own, but again he'd probably be able to get something sorted on that front in another day or so. He ventured to have a shower that evening, and the men, now recognising him, just let him get on with it. Soap and a whole towel, crikey! His luck was changing for the better already! Maybe he could 'pick up' a pair of socks? Porter would have pinched a pair of Cookie's, but he didn't wear any, made sense, Cookie didn't wear boots either!

The opportunity to get his own bunk came a couple of days later for Porter. The sack-barrow had become his ticket for getting around camp, so long as he stayed away from the airfield works, too many vehicles and too many checks that way. And checks always made Porter nervous.

There seemed to be something due for the cookhouse at least every other day. On the days between deliveries, so long as he had something in the barrow no one asked Porter why he was taking it that way.

On one of those barrow-forays Porter was checking out a couple of the men's tents. He didn't go with the specific intention of taking anything, at least not anything that would be missed, but there was always something useful left outside the tent, as if no one wanted it. Well, if no one else wanted it, Porter certainly wasn't going to see it go to waste!

There was plenty of space in the stores behind the prep room since Porter had started organising it and Cookie didn't need to go in there anymore.

Cookie was OK, especially as the day progressed and the cola and the tobacco began to kick in. He was well-mellow by supper time and only ever slapped Porter's face first thing in the morning. It was a pretty sharp learning curve but Porter was quick enough, it was becoming a bit of a ritual, almost reassuringly so.

Porter was halfway between the second of the tents he was scouting out. Not much to show for it. More soap and a couple of shirts. It might have been the men had left them out for the laundry boys to find, if they had then they were going to be disappointed. No harm done they'd just have an argument then get a fresh batch from supply, they could do that, Porter couldn't.

Boots, socks, shorts and a couple of shirts, almost the full 'kit'. Porter was feeling rather well pleased with himself. He'd been pushing the box of tins on his sack-barrow around for a couple of hours. He ought to be getting back before Cookie got started hollerin' again.

"Oi! You!" Plenty of calls and shouting going on around the camp, but this one had a particular ring to it, immediately getting Porter's attention. "Oi, yeah-you!" There it was, that call of home, the East End.

John was yelling to the porter with the barrow. "Bring it over here, will ya!?"

Porter could see what the problem was at a glance. John had one of the jeeps up on blocks as the trailer had twisted on the hook. He was trying to bend it back into shape so they could release it.

John and his garage-mate were both calling him over. No one else seemed interested in helping and Porter couldn't leave a fellow East-Ender stranded!

John couldn't let go of where he was, or they'd lose the tension they'd got so far. They just needed a bit more leverage. "Bring your barrow over will ya? Needing a counter-weight."

Porter hastily stuffed the recently 'lifted' shirts down in between the cans in the box and trundled over.

"Porter ain't it? Seen you in the mess tent. Cookie's Lad?"

"Yeah, looks like it, don't it!" Porter agreed, as vaguely as he dared. Enough for to John to recognise the accent.

"East End?"

"East End," Porter grinned. He would have shaken John's hand except John didn't have any free at that moment.

"Come on, climb over there and see if that works."

Porter followed the directions, clambering over to where he could apply his own body as an effective counter-weight, lifting the barrow up behind him with the box of tins still on it, to maximise the effect. That helped.

"How did you manage to get it caught like that?" Porter asked, as he climbed down, retrieving his barrow and box. They could all hear the jeep hook starting to loosen.

Waiting, none of them dared move, except Daks who seemed to delight in taunting the process by collapsing into a fit of the giggles. Fortunately, John held him steady long enough for the trailer to fall free, with a very satisfying clatter down to the ground.

Unfortunately, Porter mistimed his grab, catching the barrow but not the box. The tins began rolling across the garage floor and the two shirts crumpled out from where they'd been stashed, in full view of John and Daks. Porter didn't move. He held onto the barrow and waited for whatever came next.

John had seen the shirts, even if he hadn't before then, he did when Daks reached for them, cheerfully giving both a good sniffing.

"What is it with the locals and their noses?" Porter blurted.

"Ah, you want to have respect for their noses and their ears, and mind yours too," John gave Porter a look, then repositioned his stance so anyone beyond the garage couldn't see what they were talking about. "East-End, hey?" John repeated.

"Yeah, East End. Bit outta my depth!" Porter admitted ruefully.

"Looks like it! Bit low on kit too, are you?" John queried, taking the items from Daks and returning them to Porter.

"Low on proper-paperwork is what I am! Got a job in the kitchen, but that's about it."

There, that was it. The whole story, sort of. Porter waited.

Daks was chuckling as he picked up the tins, repacking them as Porter hastily attempted to stuff the shirts back into the box on the barrow.

John took another look at the man standing in front of him. He'd seen him about and now he'd heard his story. It had taken all of two sentences, but that was his story and as reasonable as any other story he'd been offered in this country so far.

"No bunk then?" John reckoned.

"No bunk," Porter confirmed.

"Need a bunk?" John asked, just to be clear on that point.

"Oh, yes please!" Porter responded, with such a plea in his voice that John burst into laughter, before waving them to follow him to the back of the garage where there were two bunks. One was meant to be for Daks, but John wasn't convinced he'd ever used it.

"We've got a spare. If you can get it back, without anyone challenging you, you can have it. Can you sort out the bedding?"

"Oh yeah, I can do that," Porter assured him. "Thanks!"

Gratefully taking possession of the bed frame, he began struggling to secure it to the sack-barrow with the box of tins still in the mix and only two straps to secure the whole configuration.

John put his hands up. "That's not going to work!" He called to Daks, who'd started jabbering-on about something else already. "We're gonna have to give him a hand, Daks."

As ever, Daks was happy to oblige.

Porter moved round and took the head of the bed, Daks took the tail-end and John took charge of the barrow.

"Come on, it looks less obvious if we're all doing it! They're used to me doing something stupid around here!" John told Porter.

Porter grinned thankfully but shook his head in disbelief. He wasn't sure what to make of this development. They were both laughing with Daks jabbering the whole way.

No one challenged them. No one even asked what they were doing with the bunk, halfway between the garage and the back of the kitchen.

"Told ya!" John propped the barrow up against the corner outside the prep room, as Porter finished moving in.

"If they think you're easy with what you're doing, then they'll be easy with you doing it!" John told him. "Daks taught me that."

PADRE

Padre had all his papers. They just seemed to be the wrong ones! He had his certificates and Letters of Introduction and hadn't actually intended to get on that train in particular, but when he tried asking which he was meant to be on, they kept nudging him along with the officers looking for their carriage!

After that he'd found that interesting young man who seemed so informative about the country, so helpful, and Padre had been gasping for a cup of tea, such a refreshing blend, and the conversation was charming. Well, after that it didn't seem polite to point out he wasn't meant to be on that train!

That had been Padre's mistake. When he'd eventually got to where he could check the address on the paperwork with a local map, he'd found that train conductor hadn't been wrong: this was indeed just about where he was meant to be.

The address he was looking for was in one of the local towns. "Out here?" he'd asked the next clerk he came to, to check again. The clerk didn't mind, it wasn't everyday he was asked where 'here' was by a Padre.

At Prai, Padre had been guided to accompany the other officers in the transport waiting to take them to Butterworth camp. Why Padre had waited until then to ask someone again, even he couldn't fathom.

"You're not lost!" the camp clerk assured him brightly.

"Well, I'm sure that's a very good thing, to know one is 'not lost'. But I've still no idea where I am!" Padre offered candidly.

The clerk checked the maps and showed him. "We're here, but that's there. But if I was you, I wouldn't go that far yet. Wait until some of our Lads can settle you in. Really oughtn't to be going that way by yourself!"

That left Padre in a quandary, what was he meant to do in the meantime?

"Oh, no problem, Padre. We've got a Chapel tent. You'll be very comfortable there, ready for Sunday Service then, won't you?"

"I will be?" Padre asked, astonished, relieved and doubtful in the same breath. "What day is it now?"

The clerk grinned. That happened a lot, especially with newcomers. He checked the calendar on the wall beside his desk. "We're here. That'll give you enough time before Sunday, won't it?"

With no indication to the contrary, the clerk assumed Padre was accepting the position and proceeded to direct him on to where the Chapel tent was.

Padre took his time in the walk, there was a lot to take in. He'd noticed the showers on his way over to deposit his suitcase and bag. He might benefit from taking advantage of the apparent lull in their occupancy, and picked up his towel, then rummaged for a moment to find his wash-bag. How long had it been since he'd had a shower? "Oh dear!"

It was further to the showers than he'd thought, navigating between the various arrangements of tents and men getting themselves similarly settled in. There seemed to be a lot of shouting but none of it directed at him.

He was almost at the showers when a familiar voice called his name. "Hey Padre, nice to see you've got your bearings. Join me for supper?" It was the charming young officer from the train.

"Is it that time already?" Padre checked his watch. He hadn't done that for days, it seemed a rather pointless exercise. "Supper?"

He'd already forgotten what date the clerk had told him it was, but at least he knew the day, so he was making progress. Padre was about to apologise for the state he was in.

"No, you're right! Not enough showers, but they'll get that sorted soon enough. I don't think they were expecting so many of us in one go. Though I don't think we're all meant to be staying here, some of us are getting shoved on pretty quick."

"Oh?" the Padre must have sounded alarmed because the officer immediately put his hand on his shoulder.

"No Padre, not you! We need you here. Sunday Services and all that! They haven't had that sort of thing properly attended to for months."

"Oh?" Padre relaxed a little, although he couldn't explain why. During his in-training college days, he'd occasionally undertaken the local parish vicar's duties. He'd done so diligently, as it had given him the opportunity to study the various elements of the services appropriate for different occasions, one of which must surely suit this one.

Padre had listened well during the train journey and felt fairly confident he could adapt his understanding to the expectations of the camp's congregation. He was here, after all. And they didn't have anyone else!

The men seemed genuinely pleased with his celebration of Sunday Services when it came to it. A couple of them actually waited behind and congratulated him, which made Padre wonder what his predecessor had been like. But as no one offered him that insight, he thought it wiser not to enquire.

It had only taken a couple of weeks to arrange to get him into town. It wasn't so much a 'grey' area, as more a matter of logistics, as the clerk informed him when he checked. "We're just not sure where this address is."

Padre couldn't help him there. He hadn't even known the direction he was meant to be going after the ship got into dock. "Yeah, we heard about that, Padre. We nearly lost you back there," the clerk chuckled. "Don't worry, Padre. Give us a couple more days and we'll have it sorted," the man sounded optimistic. "Can't have our Padre going off in the wrong direction now, can we?"

It had taken them a couple of weeks to locate the address, then a couple more days after that, before there was anyone who could accompany him.

"A car? Oh, I don't mind walking, actually I rather prefer it," Padre automatically protested, then apologised for his thoughtless blurt. Even he had realised no one walked anywhere on their own beyond the camp gates. He might not be wise to the ways of the jungle, but Padre wasn't an idiot!

John had been given one of the officer's cars to drive for the errand. It had been a while since he'd driven anything quite so fine. So far, he'd only had the one chance to get out of camp and that had been driving that tanker for the Australians. Whilst it had been an experience, he hadn't really had a chance to take a look around the town on that occasion, and John was hoping this trip would remedy that. Some of the other men had come back with some strange stories, but Daks had put him right on most of those.

John was all smartened up and waiting for Padre. No garage-duties today, he'd even polished his boots. Well, at least he'd kicked most of the dust off them! His instructions had sounded much simpler than he expected the task to actually be, if the stories were anything to go by.

John was just about to question how the church had actually got the address in the first place when the Padre came over to him.

"Are you waiting for me?"

"No. I wasn't waiting for you, Padre!"

"Oh! You're not expecting me then?"

"No, I'm expecting you, Padre. But I'm not waiting, I'm checking. This address of yours, where did your lot get it from?"

Padre wasn't quite sure how to answer that query, especially since they weren't so much 'his lot' as his mother's, but he wasn't going to try and explain *that* to John.

"Do we have any directions to get started with. I'm sure we can ask someone once we're in the town?" Padre ventured.

He didn't know any of the locals but guessed that John might, at least he'd seen John about the camp with the little Dayak guide!

John could sense Padre was looking for Daks and shook his head. "Something he needed to get sorted. He'll be back before we are, Padre," John explained, "you'll get used to that."

"Is there anyone else we can ask for help?" Padre wasn't doubting John's abilities to find the address and he'd heard plenty about John's driving skills from the Australians!

Padre was concerned that the camp clerk already thought he was something of an idiot for not knowing which day it was and the only other gentleman he felt able to approach for advice was the young officer he'd met on the train, but he was otherwise occupied.

"Come on, Padre, can't be that bad. We'll find it."

"Got room for one more?" Porter asked. He'd seen John with the car, and he was restless. He was getting on well with Cookie, finding the stores easy to handle, but he could do with a stretch of the legs if there was one in the offing?

"What you like at navigating?" John queried.

"I can usually find my way around," Porter offered.

Padre didn't have any objection, the more the merrier as far as he was concerned, but Porter checked with John, reminding him quietly, "I'll not get out the gate otherwise. They're not going to question you, not with the Padre here, are they?"

That was true and John needed to be able to keep his eyes on the road. He didn't expect to have any problems getting into town. However, it wasn't called an 'emergency' for nothing! Neither Porter nor Padre were armed. John was.

In the meantime, the problem wasn't going to be getting into town, so much as being able to find their way back out again. John had only been through that once in the tanker and he'd walked back, and that had been with his Daks as guide.

Padre was more than happy with Porter's inclusion in the party. Another pair of eyes would help, wouldn't they?

"I don't think they name their streets, do they?"

"I'm not even sure they actually have streets, Padre," John ventured, looking to Porter for confirmation.

"Doubt it. Most of the locals don't even wear boots," Porter muttered.

Getting through the gate had been simple enough and the road was clear all the way to the edge of town. John had been expecting a few vehicles coming in the other direction.

"Must be another of their market days, traffic's always different those days, sort of crushed up at the start and end of it!" Porter wondered helpfully, "What day is it, Padre?

"No idea, what day do they hold their market?"

John could only tell him what he'd heard. "Every other day seems to be some sort of market day."

Porter had heard something similar. "If they're having a problem getting through to town, then it's either a market day or they're having a party."

"Well, that sounds like fun!" Padre tried to sound optimistic.

"Depends what they're celebrating, Padre." Porter had learnt of a few 'options' from when he'd been able to catch Cookie in one of his more coherent moments. He was quite chatty then. Porter was hoping it was only a market day in the town up ahead of them.

It was, in fact, market day, and that threw up another problem in finding somewhere to park.

"Might have to walk from here, Padre? Porter, wait by the car." It wasn't a question.

Porter nodded, he didn't fancy walking-off anyway and there was plenty to see from here.

John had got the car as far as the edge of the marketplace. It was a sort of square, but with what felt like eight lanes of traffic going through it in all directions and every other house seemed to be another route in and out of it! It was quite hypnotic to observe the flow of business and, quite frankly, Porter was just glad to have got this far.

"I'll stay with the car, Padre." He nodded the confirmation to John, who tapped his side by way of a 'and keep your nose clean and your eyes peeled'. That being understood, John was ready to start the search for Padre's mission house.

Padre hadn't been clear on whether it was actually a mission house. He had a vague idea of what a mission house might look like in these parts, from the photographs he'd researched in his local library, but was quite certain his mother had other ideas.

Padre wasn't sure what John was looking for, but he seemed

to be the one knowing the directions to take, whilst Padre had the address written down on the letter. So, between them they had as much as there was to go on.

When they eventually arrived it wasn't what either of them were expecting! As for the mission house's occupants? They didn't appear to have been expecting anyone at all!

The neighbours seemed friendly enough, curious and quiet. They seemed to recognise Padre's rig though, so that was a good sign, although they were a bit wary of John which was also probably a wise precaution.

John and Padre sat together on the front doorstep, neither of them feeling ready to find what the inside of the building looked like. Judging by the state of the exterior there wasn't going to be much of a 'welcome'.

"Could be worse," Padre offered after a couple of minutes. "At least we found it!"

"Could be worse, Padre," John countered. "Might not be able to find our way back to the car."

Padre looked suddenly alarmed at the prospect, "Oh dear!"

"Don't worry, Padre," John reassured him. "Come on let's take a look inside. We don't want to leave Porter on his own for too long, he'll get worried about us."

A few members of the local wildlife had already made themselves at home, but a shove with a handy broom took care of them.

"Come on Padre, just needs a lick of paint and a bit of a tidy up, but everything's in order. I mean you've got four walls, a floor and a roof, most of the doors are standing. Though I wouldn't lean too heavy on that stair rail, if I was you."

Padre was wandering through the rooms. John was right, all the 'basics' were there, admittedly maybe under twenty years of dust and ancient, but still there, more or less. Not much else, but the basic would do nicely to begin with! Except in the kitchen. The kitchen appeared to be the most well-occupied of all the rooms.

"That's interesting."

What was even more interesting was that half the furniture they'd expected to see in the house appeared to have been relocated, through the kitchen, into a small courtyard.

Following the furniture, John and Padre took the courtyard route out to another street, that seemed to offer a far less circuitous route back to the market square.

"Interesting, indeed!" John agreed with Padre. "Are you safe for us to leave you here tonight? I can bring you back with us, if not. It's not a problem, they're half expecting me to, you know."

Padre hadn't known that, but now he was here he wasn't going to abandon his post. He'd accepted the mission, at least his mother had on his behalf, and the alternative was the local parish back home, and this had to be better than that!

"No, thank you, but do please ask your office if they can get a message arranged for me to let my church office know I've got here. They'd probably like to know that, don't you think?"

"I think they'll be amazed to know that!" John told him roundly, but duly agreed to pass on the message.

They both went back to the car and were pleased to see Porter still there. Padre had wanted to pick up his own luggage, to reassure himself he could find his own way 'back home'.

John checked he started off in the right direction. "Front doorstep is that way, kitchen yard is that way," he offered helpfully, arms in opposite directions as he grinned broadly.

Padre's own smile was only marginally less mischievous. "Good to know, thank you." And with that he picked up his leather bag and small suitcase and strolled off, soon disappearing into the market day crowds.

"I wish him luck," Porter muttered. "I've a feeling he'll get on alright, not too straightlaced, but quick enough to pick up on what's proper in a situation. That'll count for a lot around here."

John was nodding, but not ready to commit to an opinion.

"Come on, seen enough?"

Porter hadn't been wasting his time whilst waiting either. He'd seen enough to feel he might 'get on alright around here' too and had begun formulating plans. John was looking forward to hearing about them on the way back to camp, it would make for an entertaining journey!

The kitchen yard had definitely been easier to find, once Padre had deposited his luggage upstairs, minding the rickety stair rail on the way. He went in search of the linen cupboard, finding it on the third attempt, together with a good idea of what the problem had been for the previous occupant.

Padre tipped the remaining bottles of alcohol down the sink!

A pot of tea seemed in order, and he'd brought some tea in his suitcase for just such an occasion but, as this was a market day, a stroll would do him no harm. "A little bit of the local colour, introduce myself maybe?" Padre wondered to himself.

By the time he returned to his kitchen and got the kettle singing ready for that long-awaited pot of tea, not only was Padre pleased with the day's progress, but felt far more 'settled' than he'd expected to.

It definitely wasn't the sort of market day he was used to! Although the library pictures had gone some way to preparing him for the sights he ought to expect, the smells and sounds were something! "Rather exhilarating really," he observed to himself. He enjoyed the way everyone seemed to be happy talking at once and seemed capable of having an entire conversation in that form. "Remarkable!"

His appreciation had not gone unnoticed. At one point he almost applauded a pair of dealers working their way through the technicalities of a bargain. It was all over a crate of fizzy pop. "Really? Remarkable!" Apparently, the Americans had introduced the locals to the stuff, without realising it would become such a sought-after commodity.

The central town houses around the marketplace and those belonging to the more prosperous merchants and notables of the society were rather imposing, built of well-laid mud-clay bricks, with doorsteps and window frames. The lesser dwellings further out were more slapdash slab constructs of mud-mashed with a bamboo frame. Well-seasoned, they'd withstood the test of time and looked it.

The town had been established centuries before, by traders who had found it a convenient point for their paths to cross as well as avoiding the areas that, even then, were perhaps less than ideal for travelling through.

The central town houses looked conventional enough and the immediate streets behind the marketplace were quite presentable, considering the space and building materials available. A few of the plantation owners had town houses, built in their own compounds, a comfortable distance from the hubbub of town. In between were the sprawling homes of those with neither wealth nor position, built from a combination of tent-fabric and bamboo props.

Padre was astounded by what could be done with bamboo. Some of their gardens were planted in hammocks that hung from the modest verandas, farm-animals were pets, and pests were dinner!

Beyond the outskirts of the town there were the rice fields staggering up the side of the mountain. He could clearly see the road the tanker must have taken on its way up to the plantation. Somewhere out there the Dayaks had their villages. He'd seen a few of them, both at the camp and in the market place. There appeared to be quite a number of distinctive groups of peoples living in the town.

Padre wasn't convinced yet how well they got on with each other, but at least on market days they tolerated their differences. None of them had said anything offensive to him directly, so Padre was prepared to wait and find out for himself.

Farmers, merchants, traders, workers, clerks, and a few official-looking personages too, Padre had noticed. Perhaps he ought to pay his respects? He was quite certain at least two had seen him, but hadn't introduced themselves, maybe they were waiting, unsure of him.

Padre was considering how to make a good first-impression. His mother had drilled that into him. A cup of tea would help him think as he sat out with the mission house furniture, in the small back yard behind the kitchen, listening to the evening coming down.

The Dayaks, he decided, were very definitely interesting people. Their manners were so different from the other market traders and visitors. Watching them Padre could see the distinctions between the various tribal communities, depending on their home-village location or favoured trading method.

Coming back into the mission house kitchen Padre had cause to remember those locals, trading over that crate of fizzy pop. Indeed, he was pleasantly surprised the mission house had a fridge at all! What had been left inside? More fizzy pop. The stuff didn't agree with him, but Padre guessed the Dayaks might appreciate it. Maybe he could trade them for a few books?

He missed his reading books. He'd only managed to pack a few of his favourite. For some misguided reason he'd thought there would be 'plenty more books' already waiting for him at the mission house. He didn't know why but according to those library photos there had never seemed to be a shortage of 'donated' books about the place. Not here though, it seemed! Padre wondered what had happened to the fellow before him and his books!?

By the time the next market day came about, a couple of days later, Padre had already been contacted by the camp. They'd received his enquiry and the clerk was able to inform Padre there was a telephone already in town, somewhere; but he'd be sending one of their engineers to 'come by on his way over from the station'.

However, when it came, it was a military convoy that arrived from the station, with said-Engineer and on market day. "Oh dear, not wise," Padre muttered, as the officer in the lead car tried to shout his way through the crowd.

Padre hurried across the square and gestured for the officer to sit back down and switch the engine off.

"You can't go shouting at them! They'll only think you want to start negotiating a bargain. The best thing you can do is leave the cars where they are and walk through, slowly, Sir. It works better! You mind your manners and they'll mind theirs."

The officer sat back down, although he didn't look too happy about it. The Engineer on the other hand cheerfully clambered out, ready to take a walk with the Padre. The chap had just spent two days on a train with that bully of an officer and a quietly considered conversation would do him nicely.

"How about you leave me the motorbike and we can wheel that through, I can get back to camp under my own steam. Wouldn't want to hold you up, Sir? And Padre won't steer me wrong."

The sullen officer didn't wait to hear what Padre had to say on the matter. As far as he was concerned, he'd only taken the irksome diversion to deliver the Engineer. That being done, if the man wanted his ruddy motorbike, there was no reason for the officer to hang about, so he didn't.

"I'll help with that, you're taller than me so they'll see you coming." Padre suggested, taking the motorbike out of the Engineer's hands.

"But I need you to lead, Padre. I don't know where I'm going."

"No, but he does." Padre had seen one of his Dayak friends coming round the side of the stalls.

"Pop home, will you? We'll follow," Padre instructed the grizzled man with the stature of a boy and a grin to match.

"Pop home?" The Engineer asked with a raised brow, as he dutifully followed the local, whilst looking back at Padre, pushing the motorbike.

"Oh, they know which way 'pop home' is."

"Pop home?" the Engineer nudged again, as they got through the market. Their guide would walk a few paces then stop and do a bit more jabbering-on to one of the market day traders. It all seemed friendly enough and unhurried, as he walked with his backpack and toolbag, whilst the Padre followed, pushing the motorbike and seeming quite at ease with the whole arrangement.

"He knows the way very well and comes around three times a day since my arrival," Padre explained chirpily. "He seems to be the mission house housekeeper. I just call him 'Pops', hence the 'pop home'!"

That reminded Padre of something else he'd been meaning to mention. "I wonder? Have you heard how they like fizzy pop around these parts? My predecessor seems to have left in somewhat of a hurry and there was a lot left in the old fridge, with more in the broom cupboard. I thought, well that's useful!"

"It certainly was for you, Padre!" his walking companion agreed amiably.

"Indeed, yes. My Dayak friend here has a lot of uncles and cousins who like fizzy pop, apparently."

The Engineer could guess what might be coming next.

As the Padre began, "I was just wondering, when you're next coming by, we're on your way, aren't we?"

The Engineer agreed the town was indeed, between the train station and his current work site, and bringing a few bottles of pop over to the mission house would put him in Padre's good books.

He'd heard about Padre's recent Sunday Service at the camp. It had made a good impression, not too much of a sermon, hardly a 'lesson' at all, more a rambling story with some funny anecdotes and maybe a bit-of-a-moral at the end of it. The Lads had certainly enjoyed it and although the officers had considered it a little unconventional. A courteous and coherent Padre was a vast improvement on his predecessor!

Padre would continue to do the occasional services for the camp but, from now on, he would be based at the mission house in town. The camp was scheduled to be getting its own replacement chaplain, but when he was going to arrive was anyone's guess!

John had brought back a fairly optimistic report on the Padre's capabilities and certainly the Engineer had no qualms with giving a 'so far so good' assessment, although he was also beginning to get a hint of Padre's 'innovative' approach to his situation.

They'd got through the main throng of the market day traffic by then and were reaching the back streets that led to the kitchen yard entrance to the mission house, easy to find, with the furniture outside.

"You're looking like a café out here Padre? Much left inside?" he wondered.

"Oh, I have a nice little bed and a book-case upstairs. Sadly, not many books yet, but I'm hopeful of making a start on that soon enough. Not much in the other rooms, but I don't need much."

From what the Engineer could see, that was just as well. Padre had noticed his expression and attempted to reassure him.

"But the bathroom works adequately and the kitchen is in remarkably good working order … considering. But I'd rather like to be able to report in to my church office, to let them know I've arrived and I have no telephone."

"Ah, that explains the message for me." Unfortunately, the Engineer was about to give him some disappointing news.

"Sorry, Padre, but I'm not authorised to wire in a telephone for you. Not here. Only allowed to put them in official and military buildings. I'm surprised your church office didn't organise that for you?"

"Well, they didn't really contact me at all. It was my mother!" Padre sighed. He'd been hoping to avoid having to explain that part of his situation.

The Engineer was smiling as Pops found his own way into the kitchen, bringing himself out a bottle of pop and cups of cold tea for

Padre and his guest.

"Or would you prefer coffee, Pops does much better with coffee?" Padre enquired politely.

"They do know their coffee around here," the Engineer admired. He'd had some experience by then, when visiting a couple of the plantations.

Padre took the cup of cold tea back and offered it to Pops, with a kindly, "panas, please." Not demanding, not correcting, just a suggestion. Turning to his guest, Padre explained, "he's good with the kettle but gets it confused with the tea-pot sometimes."

With the hot tea served, the Dayak housekeeper sat on the back step and enjoyed his pop, bottle in one hand, long-stemmed smoking pipe in the other.

The Engineer was still wondering about the mission house telephone dilemma. "Didn't your office tell you this would be difficult?" He knew he was repeating the question, but it felt the best way to start deciding how he could help Padre.

"They didn't actually tell me anything! They wrote back to my mother, and she gave me the Letters of Introduction they sent her, but I haven't heard anything since then."

The Engineer nodded sagely. "Often happens like that out here." Wiser not to refer to the Padre's mother's hand in the matter.

"I can take a message and get it sent direct from camp, if you like?" he started. "But it might sound better from you, maybe through the telephone at the government office in town, it's around here somewhere! We should be able to find it between us."

Padre felt stupid. Why hadn't he thought about not having a telephone at the mission house? He'd never considered the possibility. His mother had always had a telephone at home, she had insisted on it. But she wasn't here, so she couldn't insist on anything! That last thought came unbidden, but rather wonderfully to Padre's thoughts. He was smiling to himself, as the Engineer continued.

"I thought you did all your direct calls by prayer, Padre?" he teased, as they drank their hot tea together. "Is this your calling?"

"Do you know I rather think it is!" Padre declared, surprising himself. It was bold and impetuous, but sincerely meant. "I rather enjoy being close to the market place and the kitchen yard. Meeting people who want to talk, rather than the far-more-formal front room. They don't find that comfortable and, to be honest, neither do I!"

"Then, Padre," the Engineer lifted his tea cup in a salute to his host, "sounds like you've got yourself a very agreeable arrangement. Just so long as we can keep that 'pop' in 'pop-home', hey?"

They spoke briefly of Padre's predecessor and, without going into details, it seemed he'd been rather too formal in his dealings with the locals. It had been proven rather unfortunate for his health.

"You know, I could take my motorbike back to the railway station and be back here before it's dark with another crate of pop for you, Padre?" the Engineer suddenly offered.

"I'll have just enough time to find that government office and get a call over to camp, to let them know I'm staying overnight at the mission house with you? They can pass that up to your office, how's that sound? That way we'll both have done our reporting-in and we'll know where the town telephone is, ready for next time, and you'll have extra pop in stock!?"

Padre was delighted with the plan, but wondered if it might be acceptable to add a little extra to that errand.

"How about you take Pops on the back of the motorbike? He can carry, while you steer, and he'll make sure you and your motorbike get back from the station safely?"

"Good idea, Padre," the Engineer grinned. He'd been right about this one. Common-sense and quick to pick up on local know-how.

The trip to the railway station wouldn't take so long this time, not now that the market was getting cleared away for the day. With less traffic and no convoy, he made much better progress. Pops was happy to jump on the back, taking charge of the toolbag that had been strapped there.

By the time they'd got back to the mission house kitchen, the return errand with the extra provisions had taken a slight detour by way of one of the Dayak villages. Pops had taken half a dozen of the bottles out of the top crate, in exchange for a crate of live chickens. They'd gained quite a few admiring glances from the locals back into town after that.

Pops seemed to consider this nothing extraordinary and having seen the state of some of the loads managed on the back of barrows and bicycles, the Engineer was impressed by Pops restraint in his trading!

"Oh, how marvellous! I was wondering what I'd do for supper." Padre knew a very good recipe with chicken. He did the preparation whilst the Engineer fixed the fridge, and Pops went off somewhere to let his friends know how they were getting on.

"Will you be coming this way regularly?" was the next obvious query from the Padre.

"I will now!" chuckled the Engineer. The mission house was, as Padre has described, 'basic but sufficient' as far as furniture was concerned. Not uncomfortable, the beds were clean and the blankets and sheets, although a little musty, had been kept well stored. They ate supper together and the local coffee was 'interesting'.

The call had eventually got through, from town to camp, so they'd be getting through to Padre's office soon enough. No one mentioned the crates of pop and chickens.

The night's supper had been pleasant enough, "a little bland, but I'll make sure I fetch some fresh herbs from the market before you come for supper next time," Padre considered the following morning.

"Next time, Padre? Even I don't know when that'll be. I go where I'm called!"

"Don't we all, my son! Don't worry. I'll have a chicken supper ready for you whenever you next come over."

"Deal!" the Engineer grinned. He liked the sound of that invitation. "And in that case, I'd best make sure I come with another crate of pop, too!"

Padre was shaking the Engineer's hand, as Pops, who seemed to have taken up residence in the kitchen yard, looked on with a grin lighting up his grizzled face, adding his own nod to the arrangement.

The Engineer was just about to take his leave when Padre added one more request, if he would be so kind, to pass it on to the relevant department at the camp.

"Do you think they might be able to find me a spare bicycle? It would be awfully useful."

"I think we can do that, Padre. Plenty of them about the place. Are you sure you don't want a motorbike?"

It hadn't gone unnoticed how the Padre had been admiring the Engineer's chosen mode of transport. It was obvious Padre knew his way around it.

Padre considered it but decided it too much to hope for. "A bicycle will do me nicely to begin with, I don't think I shall be trying to go too far for a while yet."

"Very wise, Padre. Not to go too far too soon around these parts," the Engineer approved, waving his goodbye.

"We're going to need some food for those chickens, aren't we?" Padre asked his grizzled friend, as they turned back into the mission house.

Pops seemed quite enthusiastic about that notion. Padre didn't always follow everything his housekeeper was telling him, but they seemed able to make sense of each other.

Padre was still wondering about that chicken supper last night, it had been very simple and nourishing, but it needed a little more flavour. He could remember his mother's cook did a very good chicken supper, a sort of stew, but finer than that. He would need to have a look at what the market had to offer. He could already hear it getting started. Pops had disappeared already and that usually meant he had business of his own to conduct. Padre could take his time and do a bit of wandering around.

Funnily enough when he used only his ears, closing his eyes, those first sounds of the local market getting started reminded him of those he'd known back home. The comparison was only possible in those initial fleeting moments, before the colour and smells swept over his senses, like nothing Padre had known before! He quickly decided which he preferred.

"Very aromatic, enthusiastic," he observed to himself happily, before adding, "and just a tad chaotic!"

Flamboyant! That was the word he was looking for, as he continued through the streets. He'd just glimpsed a book stall, "Oh, how perfectly wonderful!"

Pops came back before supper, asking if they were having another chicken evening? Padre thought that sounded a very sensible suggestion.

"Good practice," he agreed. He'd try and remember what his mother's cook had used in her recipe, then maybe add a dash or two of his own 'flamboyance' to the mix.

CHAPTER 4

TRACKS AND TINS

PORTER

The clerk at the camp's Supply Depot was starting to get careful. It might have something to do with that box of tinned beef Porter had swiped the week before. This time the clerk was counting the boxes off the back of the lorry, not just counting the lorries!

The tins of corned beef hadn't proven much of a problem. It was surprisingly easy to hide a cardboard box in a store room full of them and Cookie didn't go into the store room himself anymore. Why would he? He had Porter!

Porter had also got more confident in his tray-handling skills, between kitchen and mess tent. Most of the Lads recognised him now and, far from making things difficult, it seemed to have simplified so much!

He'd spent so much of his life trying not to be noticed for various reasons. But that had all got left behind at the docks, with half his wits, he sometimes thought! What on earth had possessed him to get himself brought into an airfield base? Where most of the men were armed and all were savvy to suspicious movements!? And yet Porter found he'd never felt so at ease and 'at home'! Not just in the camp,

but amongst the men and the locals, that came over from the local town.

He felt useful. No, more than that. Happy to be useful and, for Porter, that was quite a revolutionary concept! He still had a few dealings along the way but only when the opportunity was too obvious to miss, or necessity pressed him, and those didn't count!

Cookie wasn't an unreasonable chap. He'd stopped slapping Porter awake every morning and hadn't said a word about where the extra bunk had come from. He didn't even mind about Porter 'borrowing' those spare trousers from the kitchen kit bag, after all it wasn't as if he wore any! Cookie preferred one of the local sarongs and, so long as he kept his shirt and long apron on, no one complained.

Porter was clean, fed and able to hold his head up and walk around camp with no one batting an eyelid. It took a day or two for him to realise he wasn't looking over his shoulder anymore either, he was starting to look ahead!

Invariably if Porter wasn't in the kitchen, he was 'portering' something from somewhere to somewhere else in the camp, with his trusty sack-barrow, just as John had told him, 'better than paperwork anyday.'

Porter had even been asked to take a couple of messages to the office. He'd done his best to look presentable, giving himself strict orders: 'keep your head straight'. He'd taken the written note, knocked and entered the outer office. Don't say a word, don't try and salute, he reminded himself. He was civvy, his kitchen apron announced his status. The errand was to hand the message over the desk. If they looked up, all he had to do was say one word: 'message'. That was it and nothing else.

Evidently Porter had done this so well, he'd been summoned repeat the task. It seemed as well as moving-things, he was seen as camp-messenger. This could be a very useful devel for Porter!

It was a startling discovery to make; when he f

instructions he'd been given, completing the task in the way he'd been told, everyone seemed to have confidence in him. Why hadn't he done that before?

No papers was still a bit of problem for Porter. He was fed and clothed, but he wasn't actually earning any money, which was why he'd needed to 'divert' a few of the supplies from the lorries. No one was going to buy from him in camp. He needed to get it to market and that was his next problem.

There was plenty of traffic about the camp, but Porter needed a legitimate reason to get through the gate. He could have gone with the Australians, but he'd avoided them so far. Too loud for his taste. He could have probably thought up some reason to drive one of the officers into town, when they needed to attend to some business or other, or to the railway station, but they tended to be a little too 'polite' in their chatter, which meant they asked too many questions of his background, not a comfortable situation for Porter.

Porter had been looking for John to see if he had a spare jungle hat. That was the one bit of kit he hadn't been able to 'find' yet. Cookie's kitchen hat was alright between prep room and mess tables, but a jungle hat would help him feel a little easier around the camp.

The communications engineer was also in the garage. Porter had come over expecting to find John. They were both disappointed, no 'spare' hat and no John! The Engineer was also a civvy, like Porter, and greeted him as a fellow. "Hat? Oh, I've got a couple, unless you're looking for regulation type. Mine aren't quite regulation, but they do the job well enough. I'll do you a trade?" The Engineer introduced himself with that invitation.

He was talking Porter's language now. "A trade?"

"Yeah, you're a driver, aren't you? This is the garage. Don't you work with John and Daks? I'm sure I've seen you over here working with them?"

It was true Porter had been over to the garage a few times. He'd been in the right place at the right time with his sack-barrow. Since then, he'd collaborated on a few more unorthodox 'mechanical issues' that John had encountered and needed an extra pair of hands on. Daks did very well but tended to do more walking and laughing at the pair of them.

"If you can do an errand for me in town, I'll give you my second hat. How's that sound?"

"Sounds good, what's the errand?" Porter queried, not quite believing he'd been stupid enough to agree before asking the 'what?'

"I promised Padre a radio. Couldn't get him hooked up with a telephone, but fixed his fridge and told him I'd try to get a radio over to him. Can you manage that?"

Porter would have been happy to oblige, but if he took one of the cars through the gate he was bound to be stopped.

The Engineer could see the hesitation in the other man's face. "I've got his address. I know most of the vehicles don't do well getting around that part of town. How about using my motorbike? I won't be needing it for a few days."

"That would certainly make it easier," Porter agreed, with a relieved sigh. A motorbike, hat and goggles was definitely going to make it easier for him and an errand for the civilian Engineer to Padre in town, no one was going to question that.

"A 'spare' radio?" Porter queried. "That's a bit unusual?"

The Engineer grinned, rather pleased to explain how he'd managed it without putting a request through official channels. "You're right. It is. But one of the Australian officers brought it over with him and they've already got three over there. I told them about Padre and after that it wasn't so difficult."

It sounded like Porter was going to be able to get his tins to market after all and with no one turning a hair, if it all went according to the plan he was now formulating.

"We can't let Padre down now, can we?" he agreed with the Engineer. "Where's your bike?"

It turned out the Engineer had been called out in the opposite direction and he'd have to leave soon or miss his place in the convoy. "Always safer travelling that way," he cheerfully offered, before belatedly asking, "you going to be alright on your own?" as they walked back to where the motorbike was.

"I'll be fine, but just to keep this 'proper and above-board' could you write me a note? What with your motorbike and Padre's radio, a note might be called for, don't you think?"

"Quite right!" the Engineer was surprised he hadn't thought of that already. "Can't have you getting stopped for no-good-reason!"

Porter got himself sorted whilst the Engineer did the necessary paperwork. It was a bit of a rush-job. "This should be enough to give you a pass?" he offered the note across, along with the address for Padre and the radio packed in a cardboard box.

"Yeah, that should do it."

Porter could get as far as town, and he'd already heard the mission house was 'past the marketplace'. The Engineer's vague address of 'pop-home mission house' wasn't much more helpful.

"They probably won't be expecting you to get back before tomorrow. I'll make sure one of the Lads lets Cookie know," the Engineer offered helpfully, as he hurriedly began grabbing his own kit.

"You know what these padres are like, any chance for a bit of company and they'll be inviting you for supper before you know it." The Engineer spoke from experience. He also mentioned how the walls of the mission house might look a bit worse-for-wear, but the bedrooms were surprisingly comfortable. "Better than your regular bunk … for a couple of days."

"Deal?"

"Done!" they shook hands on it.

The Engineer picked up his toolbag and found his place on the convoy heading out. Porter picked up the two cardboard boxes and strapped them down to the back of the Engineer's motorbike, tucked the paperwork into his pocket and got started. With a market to get to and the prospect of a comfortable bed for the night, Porter was smiling as he got out onto the road heading into town.

There was already traffic going that way and more coming, between the railway station and the plantations. Some of the heavy lorries were taking cargo on to the port. Busy day. That worked in Porter's favour. No one would notice one small motorbike in amongst that lot.

It would thin out by the time he got into town, most of those heavy jobbies weren't going to get through the marketplace anyway. Most days were market days of some description, in town, according to the way Porter understood it.

'Awkward angles.' Porter was ready for those. The motorbike made it easier. He patted the pocket with the paperwork. The gate might not have stopped him but there were always going to be a few official-types hanging about the place on market days.

Porter knew the mission house wasn't directly on the marketplace, but everywhere in town sounded as if it were just off to one side or other, or behind the marketplace. Then he'd seen Padre himself, over by the book stall. Hard to miss amongst the rest.

"That's a good start." Porter started wheeling the motorbike purposefully through the crowds. He knew better than to try and call ahead, waiting till he was within arms-reach of Padre, before speaking.

"Hey there, Padre! Got your radio. Delivery from camp."

"Oh, thank you. I was wondering if they'd manage to find one for me. Bless you."

"Engineer couldn't make it this time. Called out, but he'll swing by next time he's heading for the station." Porter made the apologies.

"Thank you. It's nice to be remembered," Padre nodded and gestured for him to 'walk with me'. Porter wasn't going to object. No one was going to challenge Padre.

"Aye, Padre. But if 'they' forget about us, just for a while, maybe then we can get on with what we really need to do."

Padre wasn't quite sure if that was the proper way of looking at the situation but couldn't argue with it either!

"It is rather liberating, isn't it?" he admitted, as they made steady progress with bike, boxes and books, through the market day throng.

With that much cargo it wouldn't have been sensible to attempt going through the short side-alley route to the kitchen yard of the mission house.

"We'll take the long way round, it'll be easier."

Padre guided them, as Porter pushed and puffed behind him. Happy to take his time and look around, plenty for him to take in.

"Can you manage all that?" Padre turned around, hearing Porter's breath coming a little louder.

"I'm doing good, Padre. Better than expected, to be honest."

Padre had to admit, just between the two of them, so was he!

There were places to pause, to take a step back from the traffic, to stand and drink a cup of coffee. The server knew Padre. 'Pop-home', the man recognised, as he brought the tray. Padre accepted for them, thanking him in his own language.

Porter was impressed, asking, "Pop-home?"

"Oh, that's on account of the chickens. I'll explain when we get back. It'll be easier to talk then."

Porter heard Padre use the local words for 'thank you' and repeated them, pleasing the coffee-server, who grinned and bowed them on their way.

"Did I say that, right, Padre?"

"Almost, but very politely." Padre chuckled, quick to reassure the puffing Porter. "No harm done, we'll have you fluent in the less formal words, ready for next time."

"Thanks, Padre."

Pops was there to take the motorbike into his care for the duration of Porter's visit. "Don't worry he'll have it back for you, before you're ready to leave," Padre assured the other man as they both watched the grizzled little man cheerfully staggering off with the Engineer's motorbike.

"Books, radio and what's in there?" Padre enquired, as they unloaded it all onto the kitchen table.

"Oh! Those are for me to do a bit of trading whilst I'm here. I wasn't sure of the going rate around here, Padre. Any advice?" Porter hadn't hesitated, blurting out his intentions. He'd even asked for the Padre to help him! What was he thinking? He'd never been so reckless before. But this place was different, 'reckless' meant something else entirely. It was just as Padre had said earlier, in the market, 'rather liberating!'

Padre hadn't batted an eyelid. He considered Porter's query as he made them both a pot of tea and searched through his stores for where he'd put the biscuit tin. "Going rate? Ah now, that depends on what you've got to trade? And what you want to trade it for? Around here, a crate of fizzy pop goes for a crate of live chickens."

Porter made the connection. "Pop-home!"

Padre told him about that first evening and the significance of the chickens. It was after market, but before he got tired. That was always the most pleasant time to take a walk, not to go anywhere, nor see anyone, nor even to get anything in particular done. Just a stroll. To listen and watch the evening.

That first evening when he'd got the chicken soup started, he still couldn't work out how it had happened! The kitchen was a little too warm and he'd opened the doors, tried sitting in one of the chairs in the yard for a while, but he'd felt restless. He'd taken a walk along the narrow-alley, not far, but by the time he returned to the kitchen yard there was already a woman with four children around her knees and all she carried was a large bowl. An empty bowl. Padre could only guess they'd recognised him, or at least the chicken and the dog-collar!

Well, that's as good an introduction as any. All those letters his mother had 'arranged' for him and what had it really needed? A bowl of chicken soup! They'd sat and ate and he'd listened. He hadn't understood a lot of what the woman said, but that didn't seem to matter.

"So those are your local 'chicken soup church services' then, Padre?" Porter wondered.

Padre hadn't thought of it in those terms, but now it had been mentioned, he considered it. "I rather like the sound of that. I would like to be able to provide traditional services here at the mission house too. But I'm a great believer in gently does it and if that means chicken-soup-and-listening for the time being, until they need more, then those are the 'services' they'll find here."

Porter grinned. "Sounds like a plan, Padre."

Padre hadn't realised he had a plan, but it seemed he did! He could manage from his own funds for a while. His needs were modest enough and the more times he'd been able to make the chicken soup, the more came visiting to his supper-services. Sometimes they would talk, and Padre would always listen.

Porter had been listening too. He liked Padre and was genuinely glad to be able to bring the radio to him, but could see Padre was going to need more than that to support his supper-services. He had no way of knowing when that Engineer was due to swing by the railway station again, with a fresh batch of fizzy pop, but hoped it wouldn't be too long. "He'll have to come back to check on the radio, won't he? He's the communications engineer, after all," he reasoned optimistically.

They drank their tea, dunked their biscuits, and talked about radios and chicken soup for a couple of hours. The sounds of the market began to soften into the background of the evening. Unfortunately, something else was becoming more strident! Padre decided he had to say something about Porter's pungent odour. He needed a bath and, ideally, before the chicken soup was ready for serving.

"If you're intending to get any trading done today, you ought to get out there whilst there's still interest," Padre suggested. "And by the time you're back, the bath will be ready for you." It was subtle and in as direct a manner as Padre felt comfortable with.

It hit its mark, with Porter bursting into laughter, almost dropping the last quarter of the biscuit into his tea cup.

"OK, Padre. Fair-dos. I'll get myself cleaned up before supper-services. Hang on a minute, did you say bath? As in a bath tub in a bathroom, not tin in the back yard job?"

"Very particular about that sort of thing in a mission house they are," Padre assured him solemnly, enjoying the other man's astonishment.

Porter's enthusiasm for a 'proper' bath was very encouraging.

"Can I get you anything from market, Padre? How about I see what they've got? Maybe I can use it as first practise with how the deals get done around here?"

"Just mind your manners," Padre strongly advised, as he waved Porter out the yard and onto the lane that led back to the market stalls.

Porter liked Padre and the mission house would make a nice little base for him in town. No downside. Keeping 'respectable' with the locals and under-the-radar of the authorities, hot baths and pleasant conversation? Yes, that definitely sounded like an opportunity for Porter.

Padre might be a little irregular when it came to his 'services', but the locals seemed not unduly disturbed by his presence. As for Porter, he found himself with the box of tinned beef walking back into the market day melee. It wasn't quite as frantic as it had sounded a couple of hours earlier. He was looking at the tables and stalls. Some traders didn't have stalls, only a blanket on the ground or a tray on front of them and some were just walking around with random objects, haggling with anyone that walked in front of them.

That's what happened next.

Porter bumped into one of the locals with his own cardboard box.

"Snap!" he muttered with a smile. "Same?" he asked.

The local looked down at his own cardboard box and then to Porter's. Porter's offering looked significantly fresher. To the local that seemed as good as reason as any to make a deal.

Porter was suddenly put on the back-foot. He hadn't expected to be doing a deal like that. Instantly, he realised if this was his first trade in the market, he had best abide by its rules, or he would never make a second one!

If Porter didn't ask to look in the local's box, then the local couldn't ask to look in his. In the few seconds it took both men to register the details of the exchange, both reckoned it was a fair deal!

"Deal?" ... "Deal." ... "Done!"

They exchanged boxes and nodded a bow, before moving apart and being swept in opposite directions, before either man could take a look at the contents and comment.

"That went well."

Porter chuckled to himself, as he began walking deeper into the market. This time at right-angles to the way he had been heading. He was holding the box and still not thinking about looking into it. Somehow, instinctively, it felt rude to do so, not until he was somewhere out of the market, back at one of the side-alley cafés.

"A first-aid tin! Really?"

He'd opened the cardboard box and seen the insignia on the lid of the tin immediately. Something he hadn't considered until that moment: would the exchange be in local currency or English? According to what he read on the lid of the tin it was neither. An

Australian first-aid tin.

"I wonder where that fella got this from?"

As soon as Porter asked himself that question, he was guessing the other guy would be asking something similar about now.

"Well, Padre will be pleased with it!"

When did Porter start making deals to suit others? When did that happen?

There were a couple of locals drinking coffee in the same café and they smiled across at Porter. Maybe they'd seen him earlier walking back to the mission house with Padre. They started jabbering, but Porter wasn't keeping up. He smiled cautiously and nodded slightly, just enough to stay polite, but not enough to agree to anything he hoped!

They didn't seem to wish to intrude on his business further but when Porter had finished his coffee and stood up to leave, retrieving his cardboard box, one of them enquired "pop-home?"

"That's right." Porter grinned with relief and made his way back to the mission house and a hot bath.

The showers back at camp were always available, good for cleaning off the dust, but Porter enjoyed a good soak! He was also wondering if Padre had any clean clothes. That might be a good idea too.

"Fair exchange!" Porter decided by the time he'd got to the front door. "First-aid tin for a proper hot bath!?" Padre thought that sounded very reasonable and welcomed him back.

Porter stayed overnight with Padre at the mission house. The bath tub was indeed bliss. There was not only a change of clothes waiting for him when he was ready to emerge, before chicken soup services were due to commence, but also dry towels and clean sheets on the bed made up for him in the second bedroom.

According to Padre, Pops was very attentive to such matters and the motorbike was duly returned next morning. But as that also seemed to be a market day, Porter didn't feel inclined to rush to get back to camp.

The Engineer wasn't going to miss his motorbike for a few days, and by this time Porter not only had that pass out of camp, but also letters from Padre giving him a pass into town!

The two men had spoken of how they rather enjoyed having a foot in both camps. Porter liked being able to move around. "Cookie needs me, when it comes to stores, that's useful for me too, but I can't resist a good market day's trading."

Padre seemed to be finding his own path at the mission house, with his interpretation of 'gently does it' with the chicken soup suppers. He also enjoyed receiving the occasional invitation to go up to camp to provide more traditional Sunday Services. "I think some of the men just like to know some things never change, no matter where they are." They could both understand that.

Porter would have liked to have taken the motorbike out for a spin along some of the roads. It was fascinating countryside, he thought, admiring the hillsides and mountains as he looked beyond town. If it wasn't for the emergency, the CT, the language barrier and the fact that he wasn't legally meant to be in this country ... yeah, it would be a lovely day to take the motorbike for a spin on those roads!

He did get stopped by one of the police official-types, but not because he looked suspicious, and before he'd even had a chance to start to think about doing anything untoward. Porter had got stopped because he'd been recognised! Apparently, someone had told the official that Porter worked for the church and could make radios and mend watches!

Porter wasn't too sure where the 'make radios' might have come from, but knew *exactly* where the 'mend watch' reckoning had started ... and that hadn't been his fault either. It had been someone else's argument!

It had been on an errand for Padre, and Porter had been exploring one of the side streets when he'd almost got knocked sideways by two marketeers arguing with the café owner. Porter could tell that much from the gestures, no matter what language they were using!

The men doing the shouting seemed to be saying the café owner had got it wrong, he was telling them he hadn't. It looked like one of the men was saying the watch they'd sold him was right and the café owner seemed to think not. Porter hadn't been in that much of a hurry and, quite honestly, the argument intrigued him.

The owner was trying to push the two men out of his shop, and they didn't seem to want to go. The volume had gone up and the shoving was getting a little less friendly, but there was one particular gesture that Porter recognised, whatever language they were speaking. He recognised the tapping of the watch that way!

He'd walked over quietly, no quick movements. The marketeers seemed to recognise him as coming from camp and helping Padre. They called him over to their side, which immediately prompted the café owner to direct his yelling at Porter. Porter had stood his ground and tapped his own watch, just as he'd seen the café owner do. Instant translation.

The café owner showed him his watch. Porter turned his wrist over and the café owner did the same. Unstrapping the man's watch, Porter took the small pen-knife he always carried and flicked out the back. Seating himself down at the nearest table, in the middle of the café. The two shouty men sat down immediately and went silent. Well, that was an improvement for starters!

No one spoke, just attentive curiosity. It would have been intimidating if Porter had a mind to let it be. He didn't. He knew what he was doing.

Porter fixed the watch and calmly handed it back to the café owner, who looked at it in amazement, shook his wrist a few times, tapped the glass with his finger, then stared at it again, just to be sure, before taking a step back and generously welcoming them all into his café.

Porter would have been quite happy to continue on, to join

Padre at the mission house, but the café owner had other intentions. There was coffee and it was good coffee, better than Pop's tea! That was something else Porter had discovered, when you drank the café coffee around these parts, you knew you had!

That had been how the story had started, of a man working for Padre who knew how to repair watches with just a tap, a flick and a little bit of tinkering!

The café owner had come over with more coffee and some food. The two marketeers turned out to be local regulars and had insisted Porter share their meal. As the owner was providing it for all of them, Porter could see the funny side, and that seemed to help the conversation along.

Whilst the three of them ate, the owner had disappeared into the back room, next minute only to re-emerge bringing out an old mantlepiece clock, putting it onto the table in front of them. "Yes please?" the man promptly requested.

"Oh!" Porter's chuckles had faltered. "Won't do me any good tapping that one, now will it?" he said, demonstrating his dilemma to the owner, tapping the glass of the clock face, then putting his ear to it.

The owner had copied Porter's action, repeating his request. "Yes please?"

Porter took his small pen-knife out again, bringing the table lantern nearer to give him more light and moving the plates of food aside. His two dining companions did likewise. The owner took his cue and brought another lantern over from one of the other tables.

"That's better, thanks," Porter had nodded, but kept his gaze on the clock, turning it round and then over. It didn't look damaged and it wasn't that old. It had obviously been well polished.

As well as the blade on his pen-knife, Porter also had a small screw-driver. Carefully opening the back, Porter leaned in, studying the workings. The two marketeers and the café owner did likewise.

"Oi, back-off! Give a fella some light to work-by 'ere!"

He'd raised his voice which startled the patrons to take a step back, but they didn't look happy. Porter attempted a different approach, waving his hands wide, brushing the top of the table, to show them he just needed 'elbow-room'.

The plates and cups were duly cleared from the table and the spectators moved their chairs back, before resuming their seats. "Yes please?" the owner enquired.

That would suffice, Porter nodded and resumed his peering. Just as he suspected, it was clean inside. Nothing loose. "Just needs a spot of tinkering," Porter muttered to himself, his hands steady, his words low. No one spoke, although someone was puffing on a pipe that smelt rather pleasant.

It took Porter about four minutes more than he would have been comfortable with, that made five minutes in total. Enough for the coffee to get cold. The owner went off to refresh it and one of the locals was handing his friend another cigarette. Porter straightened up and relaxed his shoulders.

"There you go. Try that." Closing the clock up again, Porter tapped the front with the knuckle of his middle finger, then put his ear down to it, just to be sure with all due ceremony. He knew they appreciated that around here.

He pushed the mantlepiece clock back away from him, into the middle of the table, and moved the lanterns further from where they'd been singeing his eyebrows. "Any more of your excellent coffee there?" he asked, talking normally again and glancing over to the owner, who was poised in readiness ... and delighted.

Promptly putting down the pot of coffee and fresh cups, he lifted the clock up in both hands, looking it over in wonder, then listened, before watching the hands moving, as if he had never seen them doing that before.

That had been where the 'mend watches' notion had come from. Porter could guess that much. Although what *that* had to do with *this* local official had him nonplussed, for the moment... but he was willing to find out!

It turned out the official was a local policeman, who'd somehow managed to lock himself out of his office and believed someone of the church wouldn't be too loud about his predicament! The man graciously helped Porter walk his motorbike over to the door in question, whilst Porter started fumbling in his pockets, trying to see what he had that might be able to do the job.

The policeman seemed to have broken his key in the lock. "Ah! An extraction!" Porter examined it, identifying the problem.

The policeman could speak a little English which made the exchange between the two men slightly less haphazard. "Ah, there's a knack-to-that!" didn't quite translate the same as it did in the East End, but the policeman managed to comprehend all the same.

"Need to tap it out," Porter was explaining, as he began working the job. "It's not breaking-in, not if you're just tapping the old key out, now where's the spare?"

The concept of having a spare key also seemed to be lost in translation. Eventually, however, the policeman managed to make the full extent of his dilemma understood: he couldn't get the proper authority to order a new lock and key, unless he was able to get into his office.

"It's all about appearances, ain't it?" Porter beamed, as he suddenly wrenched the pick and got the door opened with a discrete flourish.

Five minutes later, he left the Engineer's motorbike with the policemen whilst he took the written request for spares, complete with the appropriate stamp, over to what passed for the town's municipal offices, just off the market square. Porter hadn't seen that one coming, either!

"Getting a spare key by regular-channels, who would have guessed!" He chuckled to himself as he followed the directions for getting there.

A senior flunky waved him in. The letter was given and received, and the keys located. Smoothly done and another lesson learned. As

Porter walked back across the square there was a change to his step … and to his head. It was something about this place, about himself. Porter was feeling a sense of pride in this new responsibility.

By the time Porter was heading back over to camp he didn't have much to show for that box of tinned beef he'd gone with, except for a pocket full of helpful letters, clean clothes and lot more self-respect!

Porter was just mulling over those facts and the events that had led to that realisation, when he was stopped. Not a road-block, but definitely a hold up. And not a particularly amicable one, either!

A couple of mining engineers seemed to have lost their bearings on route to where they were meant to be going. They appeared to be a South African and a Canadian. They were being stopped by a group of locals. Porter had nothing to do with any of it. So why had he stopped!?

Talk about a language barrier? Cripes, what a combination! It seemed the locals had got it into their heads the miner's vehicle was a logging-truck in the wrong place!

Porter yelled out "Stop" in their local language. The most senior stepped forward. Porter got off his motorbike and did likewise. The senior asked "From camp?" Porter nodded. "*To* camp," he confirmed, even more adamant in his gestures and including the miners, as being with him.

"Right?" he checked with the senior local, producing the letter from the town policemen. That seemed to do the trick.

He took forward position ahead of the mining lorry after that, and the locals waved him on, then swore at the driver for not having proper papers with him. Porter yelled at the lorry driver too, for being such an idiot. "Don't yell back, that only encourages 'em!"

He didn't look back, not until they got the gate of the camp. He had the Engineer's motorbike and the letters, but they weren't called for. The officer at the gate wanted to know what Porter thought he was doing bringing the mining lorry back with him?

Porter was just about to reply with something along the lines of, 'What? You'd rather I left them back there!?'until the officer recognised him as being Porter from somewhere between the kitchens and stores. Bit of a rough diamond, by all accounts, but seemed willing enough to be useful!

"Doing an errand for the Engineer, or was it Padre?" The officer didn't seem to need a response to that, so Porter didn't.

The miners did the talking from there on, and plenty of it! They were shown into the camp office to explain themselves whilst Porter took the motorbike safely back to the garage and waited for John and Daks to catch up.

Cookie would probably be wondering where he'd got to. Maybe he ought to drop-by and see if he needed a hand? Porter got as far as getting the motorbike sorted, but didn't get back to the kitchen, before he was called to the office. The miners weren't sure how he'd managed to get them out of the misunderstanding with the locals, but they were mighty glad he had.

"Just needed a bit of explaining and a bit of flapping paperwork. Really it was the motorbike that made the difference," Porter explained to them. He could see from their faces they hadn't caught on. "Around these parts, loggers never bring motorbikes with them!"

The officer politely coughed back a knowing chuckle. They'd escort the miners back to the road, going in the right direction this time. Turning to Porter, both mining engineers duly apologised for the inconvenience.

"You're welcome," Porter told them and meant it.

JOHN

Cripes! When it came to rations out on patrol, John was learning you'd be better going hungry, although Daks seemed happy to give them a try!

Daks had been getting the idea that John was only meant to be working in the garage. Unfortunately, so had John! Next patrol going out, Daks found John getting himself ready and decided he couldn't let 'John-John-dump-truck' go without him.

The other men on patrol were happy enough to have a second guide. "Personal scout?" one of them enquired.

John growled at them. "Don't knock it."

He'd been happy to stay in the garage but knew that wasn't why he'd been sent up there. 'Fireman-driver' might be what it said on the paperwork, but every man on camp had more than one job.

He hadn't woken in the best of moods, but that suited the orders and John too. Going on patrol in a good mood was not to be recommended. It made for stupid mistakes. Better to start off grumpy and get back in one piece. He indicated to Daks they'd take up 'tail-end', a silent gesture that hadn't been recognised by the others, but was respected. That would be useful too.

John could see a couple of the other men had experience. He didn't ask where or when but noticed. One of those men started walking, so they all started walking. They wouldn't be needing the guides yet but having one up front and one 'tail-end' was in their favour no matter what happened in the next couple of days.

On the map, it had only looked like a few miles. Through the jungle it looked like three days.

There wasn't much talking between them, regardless of mood, after they left camp. They had their kit and their orders. They didn't need to talk about much after that. The truck dropped them off as near as it could. They checked everything, then got started from there.

It was a slog of a patrol. Don't walk fast and don't walk tall. Stay down and stay slow. Move with the jungle, not against it. Mind your feet but look ahead and, whilst you're doing that, keep your ears on a 360.

They all knew who they were meant to be looking out for. None of them thought they'd find them, but if they were able to get out with some intelligence, that would be helpful to their superiors. They had a setting and expected to find it crossing a path in the next four or five hours, but that was about as much information as they had to go on, so far.

The tracking didn't start until they lost sight of the road. Daks was efficient. He didn't like the guide up front, so was well pleased with his position. That boded well too. John took a side-step and began walking beside Daks.

As they walked, Daks taught him what he knew. Every different leaf, whether it was on a branch over the heads, brushing against them, or beneath their feet; every leaf seemed to be able to tell them something, according to Daks, of what had come through here before they'd arrived.

Daks occasionally would pick at one but he didn't cut anything, unless he intended to keep it. A couple of times he swung his knife, releasing it from his belt and swinging it up in a wide arc, in silence and without warning.

John twitched at the first time, as he felt Dak's movement. The snake dropped from the branch to the floor. Daks grinned, bent down, picked it up and tucked it into his belt, behind his pipe. Turning to John, as he slipped his knife back into his belt. So smoothly the other man didn't even flinch.

Daks had timed it so the sound of the snake dropping, matched the stride of the men's boots. All they noticed was Daks adjusting his belt.

The second time he did it, Daks suddenly dropped down to his haunches. The sound of it startled the others and, although he was behind them, they instantly copied the signal.

John raised his hand, clenched fist. They listened. Daks had heard something. No one was going to move or make a sound until he'd decided what it was and where it was coming from.

Daks tapped John, John indicated two men to their left, about ten yards. They were moving which meant they didn't know the position of the patrol. If the patrol started moving the other two would be aware. They stayed silent and down, until Daks tapped John again.

John had heard it this time too. The 'targets' were still moving to their left, further away up ahead. Now the patrol could start tracking them.

Even before they'd started to resume a standing position, never mind take a step, Daks had taken the knife from his belt holding it in readiness, grinning with a menace that John had to admire.

John wasn't sure he was relishing this patrol, nor convinced of the 'intelligence' of it, either. The only thing he'd come to appreciate so far was that he had a lot to learn and having Daks by his side was his best bet for getting through this!

He could feel the sweat dribbling down his chest, the creases in his shirt already feeling uncomfortable. Glancing at the measure of the scant covering Daks had, it seemed a whole lot more practical. Dak's knife was something else John was admiring, a damn sight quieter than what they'd been issued with. Easier to move too, in these surroundings.

Nothing else was heard through the rest of that first day although when both guides compared notes, they seemed to agree the patrol was still tracking two men.

No one expected to sleep, rest was hoped for, but they'd make do with whatever they could get. They hoped to be able to eat something and they needed to drink.

Daks and the other guide disappeared for a while. The men had already started to brew up, when the lead guide stormed back in and kicked their fire, snarling at them, "Idiots!" Cold rations and wet tea, that would have to do.

John might not be as experienced as some of the other men in the patrol, but he seemed to be the only one actually bothering to listen to what the guides were telling them.

It wasn't just about listening, it was about watching the way the Dayaks did things. The ties they used when they needed to carry things, how they got water, how they kept themselves clean, although jungle 'clean' had a different meaning than 'camp-clean'. You didn't so much clean off the jungle, as clean yourself into the jungle. At least that was the way John understood it and followed Daks' example. Crouching down beside him to eat, he opened the rations they'd been given: tinned beef, biscuits, sugar, tea. John scooped the sloppy beef out of the tin with the biscuits, then put the tea into the beef-tin and poured water on top, before swirling the sugar into the mix. "That'll do nicely!" John muttered, downing it, looking over to Daks, who gave him a doubtful half-smile.

"That's it, haven't got anything else," John explained. Tins were safer to carry, but heavier than dried goods. None of it was very appetising, but they were all too hungry to care.

John could remember thinking how simple it was in camp at the garage: work, eat, sleep. Yep, same on patrol: walk, eat, watch, not so much sleep. The difference was, in the jungle everything around you was trying to stop you getting out of the jungle!

John hadn't been asleep, just resting his eyes. He'd leant up against a tree, crouching down with his hands on his rifle ready, hat low. At no time had his ears been asleep.

What was Daks doing, eating? Huddled-down cupping something between his hands and gnawing at it with gusto? Daks had taken the men's empty beef-tins and made a trap with them. John forgot himself for a moment. "How the heck did ya?" Daks silenced him but signalled him to come over. With the slightest movement of the fingers, whilst the hand never loosened its grip, cupped around his dinner.

Lowering his voice, John stepped over the intervening men. "OK, I give in, how the heck did ya do that?"

He still wasn't sure exactly what it was that Daks had caught. It was bigger than a rat and furrier, a wild piglet of some sort. It had a lot of belly about it.

Daks had managed to roast it somehow, without using any obvious fire. He showed John how it was done, digging down into the jungle floor, burying the fire, using the sides of the pit as a roasting dish. The wood bark cover kept not only the smoke contained, but also the scent.

"Clever," John murmured in admiration. Daks tore a piece of the remaining carcass and gave it to John. It smelt like meat and John wasn't feeling picky. "Got anything else to go with it?" he teased his mate.

Daks chuckled and reached deeper into the pit, retrieving the snake he'd tucked in his belt earlier, skinned and wrapped in broadleaves.

"Can I eat the leaves as well?" John asked, tentatively sniffing at them. Daks indicated they were edible, although personally he wouldn't have bothered.

They threw the bones beyond the perimeter, then tied the re-emptied tins with the twine the other guide had brought over for the task.

Daks and the front-man showed John and one more Lad, still awake, how to tie the tins. It seemed to be all about where you put the knots, each of the four tins slipped in between them. One tripped the sound, two more clamped the trap and the fourth tin held the arrangement, with the quarry inside, until it could be retrieved.

Unfortunately, they'd woken the rest of the patrol before they'd finished practising. John stayed on watch. Daks didn't think they should be sleeping anyway, and John took his cue from him. Lesson learned.

John's voice was hoarse and hushed, it didn't sound like his own anymore. "Which way tomorrow?"

Daks pointed the direction, then indicated distance.

"D'ya think we'll catch up with them?" John could see Daks was wondering whether he ought to be honest or kind. John wasn't sure what his garage-mate decided, but the answer was 'No.' Both men nodded and waited until they could sleep, as two more Lads took up next watch.

John had just about been able to feel his hands relaxing, he'd shut his eyes, his ears still open. When he opened his eyes again one of the patrol was standing over him with a tin cup of hot tea.

"Oh Corp, bless ya!" John murmured, feeling the bones in his back cracking up against the tree as he got to his feet, taking the cup gratefully and feeling the warmth in his hands.

"When did we start the fire?"

Corp thumbed over to the front-man guide.

"Make the most of it, that's the last til next time."

"Got it. Thanks!" John checked for Daks, who'd disappeared again. It seemed he'd decided to go ahead, before coming back, ready to repeat the answer he'd given John an hour or so earlier. It was still a 'No.'

"Out of range?" John queried as they packed up and got ready to start moving again. Daks nodded, looking as disappointed as John sounded.

John had heard why some of the Dayaks chose to join their patrols. It had nothing to do with the wages and they sure as heck didn't need the intelligence. They certainly weren't interested in persuading the CTs to realign their allegiances! From what John had learnt, as far as Daks was concerned, if he got near enough to those they were now tracking he'd be returning to his village with a trophy. The guy wouldn't be doing any talking after that and the best the information officers back at camp could do would be to gather their intelligence from the guy's pockets!

If the first day had been a slog, then the second day was ten times worse! It felt like a crawling stumble. If they had been grumpy the day before, today they were crackling with the fury of frustration. How could they have been so close only twenty-four hours earlier. They hadn't lost their target, so where had they gone?

They were through to sometime in the afternoon and most of the patrol had begun to be able to feel the way the day changed. They could smell the air was leaning towards night, away from the sun.

The heat got heavier, not so high. John felt as if they were walking through a bog of sweat and a haze of stale breath, but the tiredness no longer registered.

They'd stopped thinking about eating but missed their cigarettes. Most of the men hadn't spoken a word since yesterday, but they hadn't noticed that either. They could hear more now, above the sound of their own thoughts. They could feel the ground beneath their feet, all the way up to their finger-tips. The leaves moving, no longer seemed random, it was all connected.

That was the only way to get through a jungle, wait until it finds you and follow. The jungle holds the way, don't expect to make your own way through it.

They'd learnt from the night before. None of them were hungry, but they drank what remained of their tea and waited for Daks and front-man to return with whatever they decided was fit for supper. No one slept, they were too close to catching their quarry.

Tomorrow was the last day. They'd need to be where the lorry could pick them up. They all wanted to finish this patrol, but they all wanted to get to those two men they'd heard yesterday. A day ago? It felt like a month. They hadn't slept since.

Waiting for the light to change they watched the shifting shades that filtered through from the canopy above them. None of them checked the sun was up there anymore.

Front-man and Corp were up ahead when it was light enough to move again with two more men in between a few paces back. They'd got to the path they should have reached a day and half ago! Nothing there, nothing even to indicate the CTs had ever used it.

John and Daks were at the back, heads up, backs bent forward, feet lifting clear of the dusty path, slow, hands steady, eyes swivelling, ears tipped.

There was something! Something wrong! NOW!

John didn't see anything but heard Daks suddenly tense.

Daks' foot tilted, then braced on the path, ready to leap. John crouched down, even before the Dayak waved him to follow his lead, John was already down there beside him.

Daks gestured, two fingers pointing to his eyes, then doing a one-eighty at the wrist indicating where the CT were. John followed Daks' signs, only then realising the rest of the patrol hadn't stopped. "Damn," he muttered between clenched teeth.

John couldn't shout a warning. As he crouched his hands found the dust of the path by his boot. Pinching a pebble, he flicked it over to catch the shoulder of the man a few paces ahead of him. The man shrugged and scuffed his boot. Enough to warn the rest. That was all it took.

After nearly three days and two nights in the jungle, the flick of a bit of path-dust and a scuff of a boot. Warning given.

Ambush!

The front-man heard the movement behind. In the same movement it took for him to get down, he grabbed at Corp's shoulder, trying to bring him down with him. Too late to be quiet now.

John yelled up. "Corp! Ten o'clock, three yards! Grenade!" Front-man lunged, just as the rebel got up to lob. John and Daks were already in front of the two men hesitating in the middle distance. John snatched Corp's belt and yanked him backwards, away from where the grenade was flying. Daks leapt over both Corp and the grenade's flight path, with every intention of getting his trophy off the CT in the side-ditch, before front-man got the chance.

The two men who'd been hesitating now ran forward, clueless, directly into John and Corp coming back at them. John still had hold of Corp's belt. He lowered his shoulders and charged both the idiots rushing towards them, sending them flying backwards.

They had maybe two seconds grace, if that. They knew to the inch where the grenade had landed and waited for the explosion.

It came strangely muffled.

When the dust settled the remains of the CT's body was sprawled over the grenade crater.

Daks stood up from the side-ditch, furious.

Front-man stood up, beaming, holding his trophy high.

John looked to Corp. "Go on Corp, your turn. You ask him to give that bit back!" John looked over to front-man, offering his congratulations. "Good timing mate!" Then to Daks offering his commiserations. "Never mind Daks, next time dump-truck!?"

Daks smirked from Corp to John. "Nice catch!?"

Corp got to his feet and brushed himself off, adjusting his belt. Looking to the two men that had been knocked backwards, stunned and stumbling to their feet. "You two, make yourselves useful. Go through his pockets."

Neither Daks nor front-man waited for the lorry to pick them up. They wanted to get back home and tell their side of the story. At least that's what John told Corp. What Daks actually indicated was that they couldn't stand the smell of the patrol anymore. John agreed with Daks, they did stink!

The patrol needed to get to the showers. They needed to get something to eat, after that. They didn't need to talk to anyone else, they didn't need to see anyone else. Then, after that, they just needed to sleep.

It must have been a full day later when John woke next although he couldn't be sure, and cared less. He needed to go for a walk, to clear his head and then eat. He was hungry.

He'd just been walking around the back of the airfield and had been thinking about the market book stall in town, wondering when he could get over that way again, when he found himself hearing something that shouldn't be there.

There was a bit of a racket going on round behind one of the more remote sites. Nothing to see over that way. No reason for anyone to be there. John could definitely hear something off about it.

It reminded him of something he'd felt back on patrol.

When John went over to investigate, he found a couple of young locals merrily trying to take the top off an old but live mortar shell with a hacksaw blade!

"Idiots."

They didn't have a clue what they had, only that they might be able to sell it if they could just break it up into manageable pieces to fit into the basket of the bicycle they were sharing!

John didn't want them to get hurt and he couldn't leave them there, going at it like that! He managed to persuade the pair to let him take it away and blow it up safely.

Once they realised what might have happened, they were jabbering their thanks to him from one end of the airfield to the other, talking so much one of them nearly steered the bicycle into the officers' wash-rooms!

John walked back with them, reminding them as fiercely as he could in front of Sarg at the gate, without laughing at the expressions on their faces, "Shouldn't be messin' around back there". He checked with Sarg, "You OK letting them go?"

Sarg gave the young salvagers a look that left them in no doubt that if he'd been the one to catch them at it, they wouldn't have been let off so lightly. The pair got the message.

John let Sarg see them out, whilst he waited for the next truck heading into town. It still needed a few more Lads before it was full. In the meantime, the two misguided salvagers had cycled on ahead.

John saw them again in town, through the market. He was almost at the book stall and could already see which title he was heading for. He tried to avoid the young salvagers, but they were having none of that, bringing over what they'd evidently decided was payment due with them, one large fat live chicken!

What was John meant to do with a live chicken was anyone's guess. John remembered hearing someone had a tame snake on camp, somewhere, that ate live chickens, but didn't think he could get back with a live chicken under his arm, and the chicken didn't seem to approve much of his choice in books, either!

John had caught a glimpse of Padre near the book stall. He could probably catch him up before the truck was due. Padre had a back yard at the mission house. That's where a chicken belonged, John decided. Definitely not in the back of the camp, nor being wrestled with an armful of books.

PADRE

He'd just been meant to be making a telephone call over to his Head Office, although Padre was rather hoping they knew he was there. "Better safe than sorry." It certainly would have made the explanations easier.

The Engineer had said he'd call it in from camp, but Padre hadn't heard anything since and was starting to wonder. Maybe he'd forgotten, after all he was a busy man. Padre was doing his best, but it would be helpful to have a little bit of direction from Head Office as to what they expected of him.

The mission house 'supper-services'. comprising bowls of chicken soup and cushions, seemed to be working well, as far as Padre could tell. More locals were visiting and some even stayed and had started talking. He was always happy to listen to whatever they had to say and learn more of their expressions and phrases, gradually discovering their situations and the ways things were done.

"Making progress," he'd thought. They were recognising the dog-collar around town and seemed happy enough to say hello to him. He wasn't going to try and teach them anything, except maybe to trust him. "Gently does it," Padre reminded himself, happy with that.

He seemed to be on a rota, with the camp chaplaincy now in place. The regular chap seemed to do three Sundays and then one somewhere else, so Padre was his stand-in for that Sunday. The camp services were always Sunday mornings, so never interrupted the mission house suppers.

"So far so good," Padre told himself. He enjoyed the trips over to the camp catching up with some of the Lads.

The camp had a telephone of course, but Padre was only there on a Sunday and Sunday didn't seem the right time to be bothering the clerks. The Engineer had mentioned there was a telephone in town and Padre had decided it would be useful to know where, just in case of an emergency.

Padre had been able to follow some of the lectures he'd overheard whilst in camp about the current situation, although he still wasn't too clear on why it was being referred to as an 'Emergency'.

It didn't feel like an emergency at least, not so much in town. The market seemed to be thriving, colourful, noisy and mostly amicable. Indeed, rather better behaved than Padre had been led to expect on the train journey up.

Padre wondered if maybe he'd arrived during a lull in the 'Emergency'. Surely the nature of such situations was that they had a tendency to flare-up? Were they expecting something, or had it happened already? Had he missed it? Either way, Head Office really ought to be letting Padre know about it!

He had the address of the municipal building he was looking for. He'd been led to believe it was almost directly on the market place but when he'd got there, there seemed to be quite a few likely looking buildings.

Padre made two false starts, both of which had been politely received and he'd been patiently redirected. The second had gone so far as to write the address down for him. It wasn't actually on the market place at all and when he finally found it the building looked exactly what he expected to find.

He had hoped that once he found them and offered his paperwork, they'd know what to do with it and tell him. They didn't and couldn't! Padre was insistent. He was definitely meant to be reporting-in to someone, somewhere, locally. When they asked him who had told him that Padre had to admit, "my mother, actually!" Surprisingly enough, that seemed to translate rather well.

What was made plain, during the process, was that no one seemed to be expecting Padre anywhere! A telephone call would, hopefully, go some way to remedying that.

In the meantime, the mission house was quite pleasant. A bit run-down admittedly, but sturdy enough. The housekeeper-cum-manservant, Pops, seemed to be a permanent resident. He simply came with the house. It could do with a lick of paint, a bit of colour. Padre found himself rather admiring the way everything was so much more colourful over here.

The mission house didn't appear to be well known for its Sunday Services so much as rapidly gaining a reputation as a soup kitchen.

Padre had always admired the alchemy of chicken soup: a few vegetables and a jug of stock, transformed into something magnificently delicious. "All in the seasoning and simmering," he recalled with a quiet smile to himself.

The exchange rate for the fizzy pop was very agreeable and Pops had done wonders eking out the chickens. Although Padre suspected he had some supplementary dealings going on. Neither man said anything about that. After all, Padre could quote a few instances within his own family, where such situations arose. It happened even in the best houses!

Porter's delivery of the radio to the mission house had been a very pleasant surprise and the Engineer had been true to his word, whenever he could 'swing by from the railway station to the mission house'.

Until then, somehow, with the occasional welcome 'contributions' from the likes of John, they'd manage.

Another unexpected donation had come from one of the local policemen, explaining his gesture as being 'for an office-key' and there had been the generosity from one of the cafés too, sending over a couple of chickens with a new coffee pot, with a message about a 'mantlepiece'? Padre still hadn't got to the bottom of that one.

And there had been others, some with notes, some simply left on the doorstep. Nothing untoward, usually just groceries, some a little more obscure. But, all things considered, Padre felt they might just about be able to keep the chicken soup kitchen 'ticking over nicely'.

Padre was well aware Porter was a man of 'many talents', many of which were best not mentioned in the mission house, but that didn't mean a weekly bath and a fresh change of clothes wouldn't go amiss. Padre was the first to admit he could benefit from Porter's bargaining-skills and that would make it simpler for Porter to get between camp and town, too, if he was 'just on an errand for Padre'.

Padre hadn't given much thought to having visitors staying over. Whenever his mother had visitors, they just visited and then left. But this was not his mother's house. Pops had his own room. He didn't seem to like going upstairs, except when something had to be taken up that way. Pops much preferred the couch in the front room, which Padre rarely used, except when he needed the desk for writing. He read in the kitchen, or out in the yard, with some of the locals over coffee.

The bathroom was basic and essential, as were the bedrooms. No wardrobes, just a blanket box and a book-case. There may once have been more furniture, but Padre rather preferred the simplicity of the space that was there now.

Padre had everything he needed to provide proper services, should the need arise. It hadn't yet, but just for the sake of good-form Padre thought he ought. He never spoke of such subjects during supper, that wasn't why they came, and he knew that.

Sometimes he would listen, sometimes he would simply sit with them. They'd enjoy their chicken soup and he'd read one of his books. They seemed to like seeing him sitting quietly reading. No sermons, no singing. His mother would not have approved! But then his mother wasn't here; and Padre was very happy.

He was quite sure Head Office would send someone up,

eventually, to check in on him. He would keep the mission house active with good works and kind gestures, they wouldn't be able to find any fault in that.

It did feel rather wonderfully active, Padre thought as he walked from room to room. Yes, it was dusty on the inside and shabby on the outside, but the floors were swept regularly, and the windows were cleaned when they needed to be.

There were books to read and tea to drink, sometimes coffee, and always enough ingredients for a pot of chicken soup to be simmering before supper time. Pops was happy preparing the chicken, whilst Padre preferred taking charge of the vegetables and seasoning.

Padre could already hear the noise from the main streets ebbing away. The chatter of the gathering evening, stirring the sounds, sweeping away the day. He'd sit with Pops in the kitchen yard, listening to the radio, reading one of his books and wait until his evening visitors came with bowls and spoons.

They would sit and talk and eat together, until the soup was gone, and the bread-basket was empty. Every day had a reassuring simplicity to it, with just the most wonderfully invigorating dash of the unexpected!

The bicycle was now in the yard, sent over from camp, the note had said. The Engineer must have mentioned it. Padre felt that bit more ready for whatever the next morning might bring. "I can do a spot of visiting myself tomorrow. How delightful!"

CHAPTER 5

RADIOS AND RACKETS!

PADRE

"Simply brilliant to have three! The red one for the market, the blue one for supper-services and the yellow for feeding the chickens!"

Padre had initially thought Porter had got the alarm clocks by way of a bit of bartering, perhaps. Not all at once of course, that would have been silly! "So useful."

It was just until Padre's allowances started to come through regularly. Until then, it had to be a bit of muddling-through for them both, which Porter had proven very adept at. Padre would have been happy to have made him verger, if it had helped. After all, a verger on a bicycle never needed explaining!

Pops helped with the chickens and he favoured the yellow alarm clock! He would have liked a radio of his own too, but when it came he was prepared to share it with the chickens!

The Engineer brought the blue alarm clock, not Porter. It had come from an office desk at the railway station. He'd come by whenever he could and was always considerate, although he never did explain how the blue alarm clock had got into that crate of fizzy pop.

Padre kept the red alarm clock for the market days. That was the one he kept by his bedside. Nice and cheerful, a sort of a little celebration, to start each morning!

The markets were very colourful. Far more exuberant than back in Blighty! More like those summer bazaars, Padre recalled, less bunting perhaps, but with a joyful racket of haggling! As soon as the first sellers set out their wares, the shouting and calling started ringing through the streets, even before the coffee-vendors had time to get brewing.

"Ah, the smells on market day. Such a revelation!" Padre always enjoyed walking through them. Most days there seemed to be some form of market-trading going on. Some vendors would use old blankets on the ground for the dust and umbrellas over their heads for the sun, those that had them. Those that didn't stood and didn't seem bothered by the sun. Invariably there seemed more sellers than there was space. There were those that just wandered about with trays or baskets in the hands, colourful and loud.

Market days meant perhaps a new book and invariably a few more ingredients for his chicken soup. Padre was soon getting the hang of the haggling. It was all very respectful. You had to observe the proper-form of such proceedings.

Padre had started by asking if Porter could fetch him a few things from the market. He didn't think to ask how he managed it, whilst Pops just tended to disappear and come back with random items.

It took a few weeks and, by then, it seemed most of the market knew who Padre was. They certainly recognised 'Pop-home'. Padre had spent pleasant hours about his local village markets back home and had enjoyed the more bohemian markets of his college days, but this was not a market like either of those.

Padre was still hopeful of hearing from Head Office before his own money ran out. He wasn't entirely sure how it worked, but Pops and Porter were proving invaluable in the meantime!

Then he'd had a message through the clerk at camp. The office didn't have his records but *had* taken note of the Padre's Letters of Introduction and it seemed to be 'all sorted' from there, as far as he could tell.

It appeared the necessary records were somewhere between office desk in-trays and filing-cabinets! But they had his Letters of Introduction and a regular allowance eventually began to arrive at the mission house for Padre.

"Very helpful," Padre observed gratefully, but there was still no indication of what Head Office actually expected from him! Apparently, they were simply satisfied he had got that far and someone was in residence!

The blue alarm clock was always kept on the kitchen table. The kitchen door opened into the back yard, that led on to one of the myriad of narrow side-alleys that came away from the market. The blue alarm clock was set to go off when the chicken soup was simmering nicely, reminding his visitors that Padre was ready to commence supper-services.

The first time it had happened was before he'd had the blue alarm clock. Padre hadn't even been thinking about visitors, he was simply hungry and someone had given him a chicken. It was very basic that first time but had got better as he'd got bolder in the market.

He hadn't given much thought as to how he would deliver his services from the mission house. But the soup was ready and the woman with her children had come to see if there was any going spare. Well, if chicken soup was what was needed, then Padre would do his best to oblige. And when they heard that blue alarm clock on the kitchen table, then they knew the 'pop-home' chicken soup was ready for serving.

Padre and Pops were soon needing more soup bowls. The first few had brought their own, but there were never enough. That had been the same market day that Padre had found the book stall. Such a delight, he'd always enjoyed reading and the chatting was rather pleasant too. Chatting involved far more listening than talking and he was rather good at that.

Padre had a good ear and was soon picking up some of the local words and phrases. He never tried to talk too much and was always ready to listen to what needed to be said.

His radio was a joy for Padre and his visitors didn't seem disturbed by it. He never had the music on so loud it could be heard beyond the kitchen. It was just like their market day noise had sounded those first few weeks to him, perhaps? Until he understood what it all meant a little better.

He never asked the Lads, when they came by, to explain anything about what they did, and they never asked Padre about what he'd heard. That was understood. They'd bring him books occasionally, sometimes even a newspaper. It felt very strange reading about home on the other side of the world, when he was feeling more at home where he was! Strange, reassuringly strange, maybe. The way it ought to be.

The market book stall was almost always there, not always in the same place, but if Padre was going into market, he always looked for it. Lovely old reading books, dusty and faded, rather like the way he felt some days! But the flamboyance of the market never failed to lift him up again. It made Padre feel more enthusiastic, more confident to talk with his hands!

He'd always enjoyed reading books, but he liked to listen more, especially when someone needed to talk. It was one of the reasons why he'd thought being a vicar would suit him: he didn't want to be a country parson. He'd wanted a little more colour than that and he'd certainly got that now!

The language had become part of the noise of his days and, gradually, Padre discovered he was listening in on conversations he wasn't meant to be able to understand. He didn't think about what he'd overheard until much later, long after the market had finished and after he'd finished supper, when he'd had some time with the radio. It helped him think.

Reflecting on what he'd witnessed, Padre thought it a strange location to have a chat. He'd noticed that straight away. It was a strange way of chatting too, not in the usual animated manner. They'd been talking to each other with a corner wall between them. Padre hadn't wanted to pry, but it simply didn't look 'right' to him. There was something about it that made him think "I really ought to mention that to someone."

Not Pops, nor Porter. Padre didn't want to get Porter into trouble, he was far too capable of doing that for himself. Padre needed to ask someone's advice about what he'd witnessed. He didn't think they'd noticed him; it was as if they didn't want anyone to realise they were having the conversation!

Maybe the young woman hadn't noticed Padre standing there, trying to decide which book to buy from the stall? Maybe she had thought he hadn't noticed, or couldn't understand, but Padre did and had! She had been quite near to him and he'd heard her voice clearly, although he couldn't be so sure what the man was saying on the other side of the corner. His voice was very low, muffled, but Padre was certain he'd spoken using words that didn't belong in the market place.

And there was something else. Padre hadn't realised it initially, not until much later that day. The two people talking through the corner hadn't 'spoken' with their hands at all and the woman's face had been expressionless. But Padre recalled their voices, singularly so, they had sounded menacing.

Padre had quickly appreciated there were many languages threading through the transactions of town and its markets, but this had been a hushed harsh anger and out of place. He'd recognise her voice again.

They were plotting something, and he didn't like the sound of it.

PORTER

He'd not expected to be quite so easily happy. It had surprised the heck out of him the first time he realised what it was! What had shocked him even more was that it had been going on for far longer than he'd first thought!

127

It started somewhere on the ship, coming over. He could have probably got away with putting it down to being injured, loss of blood and all that, probably got a knock to the head about then, too. But he was definitely happier than he'd been before. Since the ship and the train and the truck and, for that matter, once he'd stopped hiding, it had got easier.

He'd been happy to help. Not because he wanted anything in particular, except maybe just to be useful!

He'd had some small jobs en-route before settling into the new situation but after that, between the cook house at camp and Padre in town, Porter was rather happy. Not just pleased with himself but actually, honestly, happy!

He'd managed to slip into his day, between kitchen-duties, good works and errands he had all the connections he'd need for a while. It had taken him longer than usual to find his feet, but he'd found he rather liked the way they did things over here. Relaxed wasn't the word for it, there was more tolerance, so long as you didn't rock the boat.

There was a refreshing honesty about the way they did their 'trading' and 'dealing' in town. Everywhere seemed to be a back-alley, and every table had something getting kicked-back or going on underhand, as far as Porter had been able to tell!

Porter had been quick to make himself useful. At first, he'd thought by making himself useful he would blend in! Keeping his head down and finding what needed to be done and getting on with it, he knew how to do that, but he hadn't expected the kindness.

Then there had been the times when he'd just had to be honest! That hadn't come naturally to him. He'd been dreading that moment, those questions, but then they'd come, and nothing. No one marched him off. No one told him they'd send him home. He'd been helping them, so they helped him. It was an extraordinary concept to Porter and took some getting used to!

Porter could turn on the charm and be a character when it suited him. The funny thing was, over here everyone was a character. He just slipped in, got to know his way around and made himself useful.

No one had much, most didn't have enough, and Porter found he had more than most. That took some getting used to, too!

JOHN

He'd only come into town for a book. He'd been reading the same one for the third time.

He'd also been asked about bicycles. Daks had mentioned it a couple of times and between the pair of them they'd been able to rustle up a few spare parts, but after John had taken a look at a couple of the bicycles Daks had been talking about, it was obvious it wasn't just spares they needed.

They could do with bending out the buckles for starters and John could do that in the garage, then a bit of oiling and tightening to the chain wouldn't go amiss, and Daks' friends could do that for themselves, now he'd shown Daks how and what to use.

John had already figured that showing Daks the 'how' was half the solution. The other half was encouraging the locals to feel able to bring their broken bicycles to him for repairing. That would be part of that 'hearts and minds' scheme he'd been hearing the officer going on about. The trickiest part of the whole arrangement turned out to be finding spare bicycle pumps.

It was just as well John needed to go into town to find the book stall again, maybe he could find a stall of bicycle parts too. Otherwise, Daks' friends were going to be using them on bare-rims again which, come to think of it, might explain the original buckling!

John was happy to see what he could do to help, but he'd have to run it by Sarg first. And Sarg would have to check with the officer in charge of that sort of thing. If John had known which officer that was, he would have asked the guy himself. Instead, he left it to Sarg and waited for a reply.

Daks wasn't quite so patient. All John could do was tell him, "I'll see what I can do!" That seemed to mean, "Yes, I can definitely do that," to Daks' way of thinking!

Daks' people were part of the hill-people tribes. After two days of waiting, John got an answer back from Sarg. It was an 'OK', but only if they got their repairs done at the garage. That way they could see who they were dealing with. That wasn't as helpful as John had hoped, but at least it was something he could work with.

Daks was satisfied with that, apparently, as the next morning he came back to the garage with a crate of chickens in payment. John was trying to explain the deal was already done, there wasn't any payment due, to which Daks very eloquently expressed how his people wouldn't be satisfied with that arrangement!

So, John took the crate of chickens he'd been given into town, still hoping to find himself a book and wondering how the chickens could be bartered for bike parts. If not, he knew Padre would appreciate them.

Somehow, when he explained what he was doing taking a crate of chickens with him on the truck to get some bicycle spares, the Lads at the gate didn't bat an eyelid.

"Sort of speaks volumes, don't it?" one of the other Lads grinned, as they jumped aboard the waiting truck, hitching a ride as John drove. So long as all the Lads were accounted for at the gate, going out and coming back, then John was allowed to use the truck. Chickens and all!

The Lads in the back were a riot! John could hear them laughing and joking between them and calling to the locals as they passed, making some observations about what they saw, that John was glad Sarg couldn't hear.

The road between camp and town in the back of the truck was a bit of a 'free-speaking' area. They were all aware of the white, grey and black areas. The back of the truck sounded a lot more colourful than any of those.

John didn't say much. He hadn't given the passenger seat to any of the Lads and none of them had asked him why. They were glad just to get a lift into town. John was happy to have a bit of space to think about everything. He still hadn't figured out where he was going to get the bike spares from, but was determined he would, somehow. He couldn't let Daks' people down.

The chickens would be useful. John had learnt early-on how a crate of live chickens seemed to be the going rate for all sorts of trades. It was just going to be a matter of what he might be able to trade them for.

John had put an order through official channels for all the bicycle parts already. That had been the simple way of doing it, but that might take weeks and he'd got the distinct impression Daks' people didn't do that sort of 'official channels' waiting-time very well.

There would always be more than one alternative route. John knew that. He'd checked with Sarg first, just to be on the safe side. Sarg hadn't said 'yes', but he hadn't said 'no' either, which was as good as a nod in the right direction.

Driving always helped him think. He needed to focus on the road, but he was starting to get to know them, too. John knew if he couldn't trade the chickens, he'd give them to Padre, that felt like the right thing to do. Padre had done well during his time onboard ship and his visits to camp. The Lads all liked Padre, a more practical example of his type than many of them had encountered before. He was doing his best to do good works in town and John had heard all about Padre taking care of the injured Porter onboard ship. That was the sort of Padre John could work with.

He reached the edge of town, stopping to let the Lads get down, then drove the truck in as far as he could to the market place.

"Driver!" came the shout. One of the locals had recognised him. It had been a while since John had taken that tanker through, but it seemed a couple of the stall holders were worried he was going to be attempting a repeat performance.

"Just parking it here," he yelled down from the cab. They were getting a bit agitated, so he climbed down and calmed them. If he parked the truck there, it wasn't in their way.

They quietened after that. John picked up the crate of chickens and his backpack and started walking. He knew where Padre lived and decided it might be wiser taking the main street way, up to the front door, 'proper'-like.

The chickens didn't like the walking and were getting restless. John got a couple of offers en-route for trading them, but he resisted those. He just had to mention "for Padre" and they seemed to understand and stopped hassling him. It was a longer walk than John remembered. Hadn't he been carrying chickens that time too?

John didn't have any hands left so kicked at Padre's front door. Pops opened it and yelled back behind him for Padre. "John-John-dump-truck." John grinned at that. It sounded like Daks had been this way before him.

Padre greeted him and directed Pops to take the chickens, reminding his housekeeper, "It's 'Driver', not 'John-John-dump-truck'!"

Pops seemed to accept this new form of address. When he came back from the kitchen with the tea-tray, he very particularly offered John the tea cup with a courteous, "driver dump-truck."

John chuckled, "Near enough!" and accepted the tea cup.

Padre was laughing as he explained he'd almost got stuck with the title 'Padre-more-tea-vicar'. "He's very keen on titles, you see. It's traditional around here. The more names you have, the more respect you have, and Pops seems to think I am a very respectable person."

"Well, that's always good to know about our local Padre!"

Padre was happy to receive the gift of the crate of chickens. He was also delighted to have John's company. An opportunity to catch up with what had been happening over at the airfield and camp. Nothing specific about orders and activities, just about what some of the Lads were getting up to.

"Now, what's brought you into town?" Padre eventually got round to asking.

"Glad you asked me that one. Books and bicycles, any suggestions?" John didn't bother mentioning he'd fleetingly considered the chicken-bartering method himself, deciding Padre would have better use for them.

"You've got the book stall in the market, but the bicycles? They're at a premium, everyone wants a bicycle!" Padre wasn't sure he could help, until a notion occurred to him.

"Unless … do you need the whole bicycle?" he ventured.

"Good question!" John agreed. "Actually, just the tyres, tubes and pumps really."

"Ah! Yes, it would be, wouldn't it? Those are always the first bits to wear out!" Padre understood perfectly.

"Not the market then?" John checked.

"Not likely!" Padre confirmed. "But I might have an idea where you could get a few bits from, but it's rather a distance and off the beaten track. Off from the old station road? Do you know where the bridge used to be over the river? It's about there."

John didn't know it, but it sounded like Padre did.

"Oh, I had reason to go on a visiting errand that way. They have a large family and one of their grandparents was rather poorly. We have a first-aid tin now, you know? So, I do quite a bit of visiting with a book and a tin in my bag, and a packet of biscuits, whenever I can."

"Sounds like a good plan," John approved. Then he offered, "How about your bag and my truck?"

"You need me along with you?" Padre checked, just to be clear, and Pops wanted in on the invitation too. Neither Padre nor John were exactly fluent in the local languages. "We're going to need him."

That didn't seem to be a problem. Pops knew what was needed. Padre packed his bag and John checked his own backpack. They were soon walking back to the truck on the outskirts of the market.

"No going through, this time," Padre reminded him, just to be clear.

John smiled, "Fair enough. The long way round."

Between the three men and with a variety of directional expressions, they managed to get the truck out from the market side of town onto a road that seemed to follow and then separate entirely, away from the main station road.

They could see the bridge after a few miles, which was reassuring, but it felt further. And Padre hadn't been kidding when he'd described the route as a 'bit off the beaten track'!

John had got used to the building materials employed by the roadside villages. The bridge-house was a little more substantial.

"We're here!" Padre announced. Pops had been sitting in the back of the truck and enjoying the ride from his elevated position.

When the truck stopped, Pops jumped down and picked up the Padre's bag. He would have taken John's backpack too. "Driver?" he offered.

John smiled, patted his backpack, explaining, "Driver."

As they approached the building it seemed more an official residence, rather than the family home Padre had described. Nor had John appreciated quite how large a family were living there.

"Oh yes, four generations at least!" Padre confirmed happily, as he walked forward, waving and greeting his friends.

John stayed back a pace, waiting until formal introductions could be made. Pops had already joined Padre, to help with some of the chatter.

The chatter seemed to be getting more excited and faster. John gave up trying to translate but used his eyes instead. He could recognise there were at least two young patients waiting for Padre's attention, they'd managed to get a few scraps and cuts. Padre had just the thing for that, opening his tin for iodine and clean bandages.

John could already see he would be needing more supplies from camp and made a mental note to mention that to Sarg when he got back. Sarg wouldn't want Padre to be short on essentials. Much better to lead with something like that than to tell Sarg he'd been driving around the countryside. John wouldn't have liked to guess as to what colour area he'd been taking the camp truck through. Yes, not a good idea to offer Sarg that detail!

John was duly introduced, once the youngsters were all fit to play again. The elders were all seated, and the packet of biscuits produced, which seemed to be the cue for the tea to be served. The tea was aromatic and delicate, but it was the tea-cups that got John's attention.

"Regulation railway station crockery, Padre?"

"Oh yes, didn't I mention that. This is the railway's Lost Luggage Office!"

It was the location of the office, as Padre had already pointed out, so far off the beaten tracks and not really on the station road at all, that had John baffled.

Padre kept the explanation simple, because it was. "It was on the station road, the *old* station road! Before they had to move the bridge. The first one got washed away. Once they'd moved the bridge to a more stable location, the road just moved that way too. It happens regularly around these parts. The Engineers and builders used bicycles to get about between the old and new sites to begin with, but by the time they'd finished, the trucks could get through and they didn't need the bicycles any more. So left them behind with the lost luggage *and* the Lost Luggage Office. It happens more often than you'd think!"

"The rebuilt bridge I can understand," John confirmed, "but losing the entire Lost Luggage Office, Padre? Didn't anyone at the railway station notice it was missing?"

"Of course not!" the Padre happily explained, with some of

135

his friends nodding along. They understood enough English to appreciate the events being referred to. "The bridge was far more important that the lost luggage!"

"Oh!" John grinned, enjoying the ridiculous. "Of course, it was!"

They drank their tea and enjoyed the day, talking of railways and bridges and rivers and rains.

"So, what seems to be the problem here, then?" John had become aware of what looked like a shed, or at least what had once been a shed, but wasn't leaning-to so much as leaning away from the main house.

Pops stepped in. He knew the answer to this question. John had been pointing to the original office. "No more room!" Pops informed John, judging by the response of their hosts, the family seemed to agreed.

"No more room for what?" John asked.

Pops checked with the family. It seemed to take a while for them to all agree on that answer. Finally, Pops was ready to explain everything. "Not luggage!"

"Not luggage?" John queried.

Padre realised what Pops meant. "The family are happy to keep the suitcases and contents, but they're river-people. They don't do road-travel. They haven't any use for bicycles and crates make their boats unstable."

"The family keep the suitcases? The lost luggage suitcases?" John checked, slowly, deciding it might be wiser to break this down into more manageable chunks.

Padre checked from Pops to a couple of the more vocal elders. "Quite right. They can pack suitcases into their boats and take them down river, for trading, very useful for trading, suitcases are."

John could understand that bit. "But not bicycles? And not crates?" John checked.

Padre shook his head. "No, they don't like bicycles, too bouncy! And the crates are awkward. They've only got the small boats now, not the bigger one."

Padre checked with the elders again, "Big boat not working?"

The elders shook their heads mournfully, and Pops piped up, just to be clear. "Quite right, no-go."

John was starting to do some figuring out. "Did you know about the bicycles before now, Padre?"

"I never thought to ask, I was only visiting. I didn't want to seem too inquisitive."

"But it's OK for me to be, Padre? Just checking." John's smile remained steady, save for a small twitch in the corner.

"Oh yes, of course it is, you're the Driver!"

"Quite right, Driver!" Pops reminded John.

"Let me get this straight. If I can take the bicycles and the more awkward crates out from their family house, they'll have more room? And if I can get their big boat working, they can do more trading on the river? Is that right, Padre?"

"Quite right!" Padre told him.

"Quite right, Driver!" Pops seconded John's summary of the situation.

"Right. Then we'd better get started, hadn't we?"

John got to his feet and lifted his backpack, then went to the cab of the truck and took out his toolbag. "Let's have a look at what you've got." Striding forward to where the lean-to sprawled, John could already see the house itself was cramped. The lean-to would likely fall down as soon as he'd emptied it. He only hoped it didn't fall down during the process!

The unclaimed contents requiring clearance overflowed from the lean-to into half the main rooms of the ground floor, depriving the large family of much needed living space. Emptying the bikes and crates was a process requiring John's ingenuity and tact.

The elders were on-hand for advice, whilst the younger more able members of the family were soon organised. John had got them lined up in a chain. Two of the sons of the house went into the shed and handed the items out. John and Pops accepted them and started handing them down the line, one at a time, whilst Padre stayed by the truck to direct the loading.

The bicycles took a while to get to. Although the sons brought out the items, it was the daughters who checked they were acceptable for being released in the exchange.

A couple of times they disagreed, loudly.

John kept out of that, waiting until the language had calmed and the daughters had duly redirected said items back to the family rooms. Normal service could be resumed.

They definitely didn't want the bicycles.

John could see immediately some were bent and buckled, most didn't have tyres, but a few did. Enough for John's purposes, and with a truck there was no need to waste anything.

The crates, once they were reached, were another matter though. The smaller lighter ones went immediately into the hoard for trading by the family, along with any stray suitcases. There were about half a dozen crates that were too heavy for river-trading. These took both sons, with John and Pops, to wrestle into the truck.

"Do we know what's in these ones, Padre?" John queried, but quietly. Just by the way Padre was standing, he'd sensed this might not be the time to enquire. There were no military markings on the boxes, John had checked that first.

Whilst John helped Padre re-arrange the loading in the back of the truck, Pops walked back with the sons to make sure they hadn't missed anything.

"Why didn't they just open the crates and unload the contents? Weren't they curious?" asked John.

Padre smiled at the ancient wisdom he was about to impart. "Why would they do that, they've got plenty for their trading and too much to keep in their home. Why would they want to know about what they didn't need?"

With the truck loaded, John walked back with Padre and the youngsters who'd been helping them. They were joined by the elders and the sons at the riverside.

"That's the one that's causing the problem," Padre pointed out.

It wasn't significantly bigger than the other boats in the family's fleet, the main difference being it was big enough to have a motor.

Pops reminded John, "Driver."

"Yes, Driver," John agreed, patting his toolbag. "Right!"

It took a couple of hours, although he knew better than to check his watch. When an engine needed fixing John never checked his watch. The two sons seemed to know what he was doing, agreeing enthusiastically with each piece of kit he checked. Between the three of them and John's toolbag, they got the engine fixed.

"Go on, take it out. Give it a go," John invited the pair of them, standing back away from the engine, wiping his hands clean and resolutely repacking his toolbag on dry land.

Padre had joined the elders sat in the chairs brought down to the riverside to better follow the proceedings. As the engine started there was enthusiastic applause from the spectators.

John was feeling equally relieved, but slightly light-headed, likely from the fumes and the heat, as well as the bending and lack of food. He sat down on the riverbank and took a few deep breaths, rather pleased with himself.

"Tea?" Padre enquired politely.

"Thanks. Do you think that'll be enough, Padre?" John asked Absent-mindedly accepting the cup. He'd been expecting that, but hadn't realised a remarkable picnic of fragrant hot foods and freshly baked flat breads were being brought out to them.

Padre smiled at John's expression.

"Enough meal or enough trading!?"

John had been uncertain, but the way Padre had asked, evidently the trading wasn't done.

"Crikey Padre! What now?"

John had checked his watch and was about to object that fixing the engine ought to be enough in trade for the bicycles, then saw over Padre's shoulder another crate being brought out, a very heavy crate, by the way the men were carrying it.

Padre followed John's gaze. No. The trading definitely wasn't done.

"Oh!?" John caught sight of the markings on the crate. This time it was quite clear what it contained. "Books!" he beamed and saw Padre likewise delighted.

John drained the cup and rubbed his hands together with glee. He was ready. "What do they want for them?"

First, the matter of settling the previous arrangements needed to be concluded before any fresh dealing could be done. Pops was called back over for this, but Padre took the lead, at least to begin with. Referring to John as 'Driver' as this seemed to extend from deliveries to engineering, basically being able to handle anything that could move, or needed to *be* moved!

John didn't interrupt. It sounded like it was going quite smooth enough without him and the meal was delicious.

The bicycles were bartered for fixing the boat engine. That seemed to be a direct-exchange. There also seemed to be some confusion as regards Padre's medical services and the packets of biscuits he'd been able to bring with him each visit. That seemed to be an acceptable contribution towards the crates.

"The crates. *All* the crates?" Padre checked.

"This one, with *all* the crates?" looking to John, who winked and nodded.

"For all the crates. Books-and-all!" Padre enquired, patting the lid of the crate that had just been brought out.

One of the sons asked one of the elders, who asked a couple of the others. They didn't want the crate of books, they didn't want any of the crates, the room was needed for something else.

"Ah, now we're getting somewhere," John murmured across to Padre. This sounded hopeful. His next question was obvious.

"What do they want on the floor of that room?"

"Quite right." Padre muttered back, before looking to the elders now. "Quite right?" he asked and waited.

"A bed." That was what they wanted. "A bed for the books-and-all?"

John took Padre to one side. "You know I'm never going to get away with that. How about you?"

Padre considered this. He did have a spare bed at the mission house, but that was the only spare bed and Pops was already sleeping on the sofa in the front room. There was another sofa in the kitchen yard. "Do you think they'd accept a sofa, it's a nice long one. It might do nicely as a sofa-bed?"

The two men were talking in hushed tones, but they hadn't turned their heads, that would have been rude, they'd just lowered their voices.

"Sofa-bed?" Pops blurted at full volume to the gathered family members, continuing their meal. One of the sons stepped forward, hand held out to shake theirs.

"Sofa-bed for books-and-all."

John wasn't convinced. "We can't just bring it straight back. It'll be a few days before I can come by with the truck again. Are they willing to wait that long?"

"Oh, don't worry, 'waiting that long' doesn't mean anything to them. Most of them will be away for days, if not weeks now whilst the rest of them will be rearranging the furniture to fill the space we've just made. You've got their main source of income back up and running and they've got a lot of trading to catch up on. Plenty of markets to visit. They'll be busy for weeks."

"Busy?" Padre checked to one of the young local.

"Ready-ready," the son shook Padre's hand vigorously again. Then reached to shake John's.

John had already got his backpack halfway onto his shoulder, shrugging it secure, before reaching for his toolbag, deciding that would translate to him being satisfied with what he'd done. With his free hand he reached across and shook the hand of the river-trader.

"Sofa-bed next time?" he clarified.

"Next time. Busy," the son agreed, and shook his hand again.

"Right-ho." From the smiles from Padre and Pops, John would have to be content with that and they started back to the truck.

John wasn't entirely sure, with the way they were loaded, if he was going to make such good time getting along those 'off the beaten track' roads back to town.

"We need to get back before market finishes," he suggested. That approximation of time seemed to register with everyone.

The last of the crates was loaded and Padre said his goodbyes, as John sat in the cab waiting. Pops was already in the back, calling to the family of the Lost Luggage Office, some of whom seemed to already be loading the repaired boat in readiness for their next trading expedition.

John churned the ground as he turned about, yelling up to Pops to keep a lookout for anything coming. The way they were moving and with what they had in back, wasn't conducive to sudden-breaking!

Padre added his thoughts, "And don't forget the bends!"

John wasn't sure if that was meant for him or Pops, but they all kept their eyes on the road ahead, leaning into each bend and leaning the other way as they came out from them. The bikes were wedged in between the crates, mostly, rattling reassuringly. The only problem was that Pops wasn't so well wedged!

"Hold on back there," John shouted, before looking across to Padre, with one hand holding tight to the toolbag in his lap, the other on the door. "Good idea, Padre. You hold on too. Nearly there."

They could see the edge of town by then. John called it. It was a straight road. A proper full-width clear-floor road, nothing in the way, and John hammered it, grinning as he glanced across to Padre.

"We didn't check the brakes properly, did we?"

Padre hurriedly warned Pops in the back.

"Coming in!" John called out and slammed on the brakes.

The truck hurtled, then screeched, the wheels locked, scuffing up a dust storm from the road. The truck came to a halt with about two foot to spare before the entrance to town. The people coming out from the markets had long since taken the hint and scattered.

Some of the Lads John had brought in with him that morning were waiting, more heard the truck and came running, ready for the lift back to camp.

"Where've you been?"

John thumbed towards Padre. "Mission business!"

A bruised but unbroken Pops peeled himself off from where he'd been clinging to the top of one of the crates, whilst wedging a couple of bicycles against the side of the truck with his hip.

"Driver!?" he informed them. The Lads gave Pops a cheer and helped him down.

"Right Lads, crates to the mission house. Padre you'd better help Pops. I'll be waiting for you."

Taking the toolbag away from Padre, John reached over and opened the passenger door for him. Padre thanked him a little shakily.

"Mission business?" he enquired.

"More or less, Padre! You sort out those crates for me and save me a few books, I'll be back next market day and we can get that sofa-bed of yours sorted, ready for the river-traders." John laughed, before adding, "Send the Lads back as quick as you can, can't be late back or Sarg'll start asking questions."

Padre looked over John's shoulder to the back of the truck where the tangle of bicycles and bike parts were still clattering about. "Sarg will *start* asking questions! You think!?"

John waved Padre and Pops on their way back and waited for the Lads to get back to him, turning the truck round in readiness.

Whilst he waited, John took the opportunity to climb in the back and have a proper look at some of the bicycles. Some were in pretty decent nick, some were only fit for spare-parts and some looked like they'd already been stripped for such! But any bit of a bike was better than none.

The Lads didn't hang about at the mission house. They did what they'd been told to: get Padre home and drop off the crates with him. After that they were ready to get back to camp. They'd had enough of town.

John couldn't remember bringing that many Lads in with him earlier. "Where did you lot come from?"

There wasn't time for arguing, but he wasn't going to be able to carry all of them in the truck, not with the bicycles back there, and he couldn't leave them behind in town.

"Right Lads. Pick a bike and start peddling!"

"You're not gonna leave us behind, are ya?"

"No, I'm keeping you lot well in my sights! You're in front, I'm right behind you in the truck," John told them.

It was slow progress going back. There were only about half the bikes that had peddles and both wheels with tyres, but that was enough. Not all the Lads could ride bikes anyway, and some weren't willing to get out of the truck since climbing in, and a couple of those who'd said they could, proved they weren't in any fit condition to do so!

One came off almost immediately. John hadn't even got a chance to pick up steam when that happened. The Lad's mates picked him up and propped him in his saddle, whilst they rode either side, one hand on their handlebars and one hand each holding him upright between them.

"It's going to be a long road back into camp," John muttered, but he was smiling. At least this way he'd be sure they all got back, more or less in one piece.

The second Lad who came off got a bit over-enthusiastic with the pace. He'd begun to recognise where they were, only a mile or so from the gate, and decided there was a race to be had.

It was just the pair of them racing ahead, being cheered on by the rest. John couldn't keep his eyes on them as well as keep the truck slow enough not to lose the Lads struggling behind. Next thing he knew there was a fight going on in the middle of the road ahead.

Neither of the racing bikes got to the gate. One Lad had kicked the other Lad off his bike. There was a right old fuss slap-bang in front of the Sarg at the gate.

"You've got to be kidding me!"

John pulled the truck up to a stop. Flung open his cab door and stormed over to the two culprits for the chaos, grabbing their collars and separating them.

"I DON'T CARE!" he roared in their faces, before either had a chance to offer a word of explanation. John's face was thunder, and he was still holding on to their collars. He stomped towards the gate. "HERE YA'ARE SARG. THEY'RE ALL YOURS!"

He thrust both men forward with such force they almost bounced off Sarg's chest, before they could steady the momentum. John didn't even look where they landed, he spun round and stormed back, still bellowing, "You lot! Pick up the bikes and GET 'EM OVER

TO MY GARAGE."

John kept walking. His expression hadn't changed and he didn't look back until he got to the cab of the truck. It only took a few seconds, but as he climbed back in his tempered had calmed.

He could hear Sarg hollerin' now, "Go on then! You heard him? Fetch the rest of those bikes."

John waited in the truck, whilst the Lads did what they'd been told. When they were clear he drove the truck to the gate but Sarg simply waved him through with a barely concealed wry grin.

"Best get over to that garage of yours, looks like you've got your work cut out for you."

"Thanks Sarg."

It only took John a few minutes to drive over to the garage, sit down and then stand back up again as Sarg approached.

"Got everything you need?"

"Yes, Sarg."

"Not bad for a crate of chickens, then?"

"No, Sarg."

"Look forward to getting your report."

"Yes, Sarg."

There was no sign of Daks, but he managed to find out within the hour about the bikes arriving and came over to help John.

"Think we've got enough here?" John wondered, as Daks looked wide-eyed at the outrageous haul. It was going to take them a few days to work out how many whole bikes they had and what could be stripped for spares.

As for the rest of the 'Mission business', John needed a shower and supper before he was ready to make sense of that!

Daks wasn't good at waiting.

Sarg wasn't either.

The report was all very well, up to a point. Chickens, truck, Lads, market, Padre, medical-visit. That much John could get away with. But the Lost Luggage Office? Now, that was going to take some explaining and John wasn't sure he could!

"Come on Sarg, you know what 'Mission business' is like!? Delicate stuff. Can't be going around upsetting 'Mission business'. 'Hearts and minds' and all that."

John did mention the crates, but only in passing, as in 'passing' from the river-traders to Padre. Which was true.

What was in the crates? The only thing John knew, because he'd checked, was there wasn't anything that ought not to be there!

Sarg would have to accept that. He'd already had enough stories coming in from some of the Lads and wasn't sure he wanted to know any more than that!

John had almost forgotten about those books. It wasn't until he took the truck back into town and discovered Padre had already unpacked the crates that he remembered. Between them Padre and Pops had moved the sofa out from the kitchen yard, back into the mission house, just so it didn't get any more dusty.

John had been correct in what he'd reported to Sarg, there was nothing untoward in the crates. There was the crate of books, another crate of crockery, two crates of bed-clothes and a crate of household bric-a-brac.

"Not another radio then?" John teased Padre, guessing he'd been rather hopeful there might be. Padre wasn't too disappointed though.

"The crockery will come in useful for the services, some lovely soup bowls in there."

They'd gone through the books together. There was a wide choice and John picked four for himself. His reading tastes were not quite the same as Padre's so it was all very amicable.

"I'll keep them at the mission house, and you can change them whenever you come by," Padre suggested.

They didn't need the linens, the mission house had plenty. There was no indication as to where the new batch had been destined for. "How about you use them for your 'Mission business' then, a donation? I mean no one bothered looking for them, so they didn't really need them?" John reasoned, continuing, "That's what they do don't they? When they've got anything they don't want, they donate it to 'Mission business'?"

Padre wasn't sure that was quite the correct theory but couldn't deny they needed the soup bowls! And most of the other crockery, somewhere. They could probably do with a few extra sheets, but not those fine-and-fancy ones.

"We could take them to market?" Padre tentatively suggested.

John shook his head. "Not me, Padre. I've had my fill of chicken-trading! But I'll do your driving for you when you need me. Anytime!"

"You'll bring your toolbag? And you won't forget those extra medical supplies?" Padre checked.

"Always got my toolbag with me and your extra supplies are in-the-works and on their way," John assured him.

He left Padre with the crates, linens and chickens, whilst he held on to his books and walked back to the truck, wondering how those river-traders were getting on. He'd take the sofa-bed over next time Padre was heading in that direction, but there wasn't much point going until they knew the river-traders were due back.

It was Porter and one of the local officials who eventually got the business with the household linens sorted.

"No money. Always a bit messy when it comes to money, all that paperwork! Never been a fan of paperwork!" Porter explained to Padre later. "A crate of one thing for a crate of something else, seems to be the going rate around here."

Padre had to admit that did sound so much more agreeable. "Just a straight swap, then?" he asked Porter.

Porter didn't exactly say a 'straight swap'. "More an agreement, Padre. Gentleman's handshake-sort of an agreement, Padre. Proper-like."

Padre was pleased to hear it was all 'proper-like'. He also knew better than to enquire too deeply into the details of the 'agreement'.

"How are you going to get this lot back up to your hill-people?" John asked Daks later. He'd been wondering about that ever since he'd realised the size of their haul back at the garage. Daks had never given him any reason to doubt it was possible, John was just wondering on the actual 'how' of it.

This was where the contact with Padre came back round, to help John and Daks, by way of the river-traders and their big boat. It might cost the ferry charge, but John and Padre could work that one out.

Daks didn't mind helping with transporting the bicycles, but he wasn't going on the boat and he wasn't going to get involved in the ferry-charges. As far as he was concerned, that was all part of the deal his people had made with Driver.

Padre had his extra medical supplies from camp by then and there would be a regular supply, now they'd got it all authorised and recognised as 'Mission business'!

"We could have just left the bikes here and brought you back with us," he teased Daks at the riverside. John knew that wouldn't have worked, but it would have made things simple.

But the locals did 'simple' differently. There were 'channels' and 'rituals' of getting things done, that needed to be observed and respected. John understood that. It wasn't about money and deadlines. It wasn't about orders. There was a direction. There was a reason for everything. It just took a while to make the connections, sometimes.

"All part of being a Driver, hey, Padre? Somewhere between chickens and bicycles, books and ferry boats?" John wondered with a smile.

"So much more colourful, don't you think?" Padre asked him, as they made their way back to the truck.

"D'you know what?" John didn't take his eyes off the road ahead, but felt his foot relax the pressure a little on the pedal as he steered the truck back into town. "You're right, Padre. Much more fun this way."

CHAPTER 6

COVERS, CLOCKS AND CORNERS!

PORTER

The officer had called Porter over 'to have a word'. Apparently, the café owner with the mantlepiece clock had been talking! According to the local it seemed that one of the Lads from camp could fix clocks just by tapping on the front of them!

The officer had made enquiries and the man in question appeared to be Porter. Technically Porter wasn't 'one of the Lads from camp', but the officer didn't seem interested in that detail, only in Porter's clock repair skills. Porter could explain his regular trips into town simply enough, 'for Padre'. The officer accepted 'that would cover it.'

Cookie, however, didn't like the idea of his kitchen-hand working for a town café owner. It had taken Porter days to explain that there wasn't any cooking, only clock-mending and eating! Cookie had got used to Porter running around for him, keeping the stores and tables sorted. He seldom had to leave his kitchen at all, just the way he liked it!

The Lads had got used to Porter too, and he'd rather liked the way that felt. They'd got used to him being about the place and he'd got used to the way camp worked.

Town was a little different, although being seen to 'work' for Padre made it simpler, usually. He was able to get about and on with some business for himself when the opportunity arose. Although Porter didn't mention any of that to the officer now. As far as he was concerned this was a camp porter who worked for Padre in town and could fix clocks.

"Just the man I'm looking for!" the officer explained. "There's a small matter of needing to repair the town clock." And he made it clear this wasn't a request. "Can you climb?" the officer suddenly thought to ask. He'd forgotten to mention the clock was up on the market place tower.

"Climb?" Porter checked. "Depends how far and what with?"

A good question, but the officer couldn't help him with that. He was able to scribble a pass for him.

Very tidy. That would go nicely with the others Porter had managed to collect.

"You should be able to get what you need with this."

The paperwork didn't say much, but Porter correctly assumed that any checks would simply recognise the header and the signature at the bottom. The only thing Porter thought he ought to take with him was a couple of the ladders, and there were plenty around camp.

John was fireman-driver, he'd know where the ladders were.

"Even better if I go with you," John suggested helpfully. "Not market day, you can't use that excuse again," he reminded Porter sternly.

"Padre is trying to get some more medical supplies over to the river-traders. I think he's trying to arrange an expedition. So, you can't tell them you've got mission business that way, either!"

John had got wise to Porter. It wasn't like he was trying to trip him up. They both had their own reasons and neither asked too many questions. He was just checking they weren't heading into any more trouble than absolutely necessary!

"What do you need the ladders for?" John began to ask, before Daks interrupted the query, with a full explanation.

Apparently, the town clock had been donated by one of the crews going through. No one seemed to know why they'd done it. Maybe it was meant to be a symbol of progress. The only problem was that particular crew never came back again, and no one else knew what to do when the clock stopped working.

"Is it the *only* clock in the town?" John queried.

"The only town clock," Porter corrected him.

"They've got their own ladders in town, why do you need to take ours?"

Porter had already thought that far.

"If I need to take the ladders, then I need to take the truck for the ladders. And that suits me fine, an empty market place means I won't have to worry about dropping anything on anyone walking under the ladders, and I can get the truck right up to the clock tower. It is a clock tower, isn't it?" Porter checked.

John checked with Daks, before replying.

"No. It's a Calling Tower. You know one of those the local holy man uses to call his followers to prayer. Kind of like our church bell tower, I guess, but without the ringing!"

John knew Daks wasn't religious like that. They weren't going to offend him.

"We'd better take him along with us. Just for appearances," Porter suggested.

"You and I might be able to follow the locals around here, they've learnt to talk a bit slower, but in town you should see the way they speed up!"

Daks was happy with that plan.

Sarg already knew what the pair were up to. At least with John driving, it didn't look quite so suspicious. They'd almost got outside the gate when one of the young officers came over waving another bit of paper at them.

"You've forgotten this. You'll be needing this!"

John sighed and caught the look of exasperation on Sarg's face.

"What now, Sarg?"

Sarg had to shrug at that. "You'd better wait, it might be important."

They waited for the officer. Sarg accepted the letter, while the officer explained. It wasn't orders, but some bright spark had arranged for a film show for the Lads. They'd got the location and the equipment, just not the cans of film. That had somehow managed to get left at the railway station.

John muttered a rueful, "Hope it ain't lost," but only loud enough for Daks to hear.

"You're heading that way, aren't you?" Sarg confirmed with John, on the officer's behalf.

"Looks like it Sarg," John agreed, accepting the note.

"Any timeline, Sir? We're meant to be mending the town clock first. If that's still on?"

"Oh, very definitely yes!" the officer agreed earnestly.

"A clock and a film? Wow, who knew?" John muttered, this time in Sarg's direction, both men watching the officer heading back to his office, obviously relieved to have that cleared off his desk!

Porter piped up at that point. "If we're heading to the station, can we scoop up Padre, Sarg? And those medical supplies he's been waiting for?"

"There you go! That's what I like to hear. Initiative!" Sarg approved.

"Oh, Porter's not short on initiative, Sarg!" John assured him, finally feeling able to get on with their errands before they got any more convoluted.

"Hang on back there!" John yelled, then stamped down on the pedal, scuffing up the road dust, hearing Sarg spluttering at the cloud thrown back in his general direction.

Daks immediately fell against the ladders in the back and started up a fierce tirade of loud-jabbering at the pair in the cab for the next mile or so, whilst he was flung about.

"Don't worry he's just enjoying the scenery."

Getting from camp to the station meant going by the main roads and the main roads were busier than ever, and slower. With it not being a market day in town, everyone was trying to get everywhere else, and their between-village business done, as well as the actual getting-to-station travelling.

"If Padre is caught up with all this lot, we'll probably get to the railway station before him," John wondered to his passengers. "Any idea how he was meant to be getting there?"

Porter hadn't thought to ask.

"Abso-ruddy-typical!" John muttered, trying to get through a little more of the traffic of bicycles, carts, barrows, animals and villagers.

It was slow going, but they didn't have a deadline. At least they weren't meant to be meeting the train. Only collecting what had come in on it.

The journey of twenty miles between camp and station had slowed to walking pace. Daks was the one to solve the hold up. Climbing over onto the roof of the cab, he sat down there and started shouting.

Neither John nor Porter wanted to know what he was shouting, but it seemed to work! Most of the traffic began moving to the verges ahead of John's truck.

The station road wasn't designed for two-way traffic, but no one seemed to be particularly bothered which side of the road they were travelling on, so long as they were moving. There was the road and that was it! No matter where you were trying to get to, or how you were doing it, there was one road to get there and back. Porter liked that, nice and simple.

It was four hours before they got to the railway station. Padre was there already, with his supplies and completely exhausted! He was sure he hadn't requested that much, but it was all here! Now he didn't know what to do with it!

John grinned as they came to Padre's aid. "You see, we knew you'd be needing us this morning!"

"Oh, thank goodness. I don't know what happened," Padre flustered. "I've been writing to Head Office for weeks to try and get the medical supplies and I wasn't sure whether any of my letters were reaching them. Then one of the engineers said he'd take a message for me, and it appears they all got through together!"

Judging by the size of those heavy boxes, that's exactly what it looked like.

"Must think you're running a hospital up here, Padre?" Porter wondered.

"Come on," John took charge. It was obvious someone needed to. Daks and Porter helped Padre load the truck with the supplies, whilst John went over to the station office to see if he could locate the films destined for camp.

It hadn't seemed a complicated errand to John, but the station clerk had to go through the rigmarole of 'due-process', which involved checking three different timetables before remembering where he'd put the items in question and then adding two more stamps to the officer's note, before he was satisfied with that.

The ink-pad was worn to threads, with not a trace of ink remaining. The only way the stamps made any impression on the paper, was for the clerk to lick them before slamming then down.

John was no longer surprised by how much got left behind in lost luggage. If no one was actually waiting at the station to snatch it directly off the train, then it got stuck in the 'waiting' office.

"I need that back," he reminded the clerk, who was just about to file the 'paperwork', opening the top drawer of his rust-riddled, battered cabinet, poised to plonk it on top of the pile of existing paperwork, 'waiting' there.

"Back?" the clerk queried, defiantly checking the note, whilst inching towards that cabinet drawer.

John had his hand out. "Now!" Deciding the clerk needed a reminder, he stepped forward a pace to the clerk's side of the desk.

The clerk suddenly looked horrified that anyone would come into his office and expect to get anything back. They didn't do things like that! John stood his ground and the clerk seemed to shrivel a little as John's glare deepened. Handing the note back to John, the fellow reluctantly shut the filing cabinet drawer again, taking a moment for one last admiring glance at his collection.

"Not today!" John took the note, and folding it, put it back into his pocket.

"Not today?" the clerk queried.

"Quite right!" John agreed and slammed the door behind him. It felt ridiculously satisfying to have managed to obtain both objectives.

"Got everything?" Porter asked cheerfully.

"Only just!" John admitted, the last remnants of tension leaving his voice. "Crikey, those clerks don't like letting go of anything, do they?"

"Really! I didn't think so?" Padre was all amazement.

"When I came to collect my supplies, they had everything ready. I didn't even need to show them my letter."

"Ah but Padre, you've got better cover than any of us," John reminded him. "Your dog-collar! Any office clerk sees that and knows that's a go-anywhere, do-anything pass. They can't argue with that. There's no stamps or signatures that's going to beat that!"

"Goodness, how did I get such a fearsome reputation!?" Padre was quite impressed with himself from that description. He knew John was referring directly to the dog-collar, but Padre had never thought of himself as being a man able to influence anyone else. As Padre, at least around here, he seemed to be able to get things done. It was a new sensation and a rather exhilarating one!

They returned to town without much trouble. The morning rush seemed to have eased, everyone that needed to get somewhere else, seemed to have got there!

First stop was the mission house, only then did John think to ask Padre about the chicken situation.

"Oh! We're doing rather well at the moment."

It sounded like it. They could hear Pops out back playing the radio to his chickens, whilst they unloaded the medical supplies into the front room.

"Oh yes, please fix that clock," Padre pleaded when he heard of Porter's errand.

"Every time I walk past it, I have to check my own watch, it's quite annoying, you know. And you've no idea how many arguments it sparks!"

Porter would have been happy to inform Padre he'd been in the middle of one such argument, but there wasn't time. He didn't know what he was going to find up there and was feeling more grateful for John volunteering, by the minute.

Porter had his tools and just hoped he could get the clock working. Everyone else seemed to think he could!

"We're in between the callings, so now would be a good time!" John reminded the pair of them to hurry up.

Daks thought that was funny, "Hurry up clock?"

Padre was finding John's garage-mate, Daks, a very agreeable fellow, "That's the ticket. Hurry up clock!"

Porter knew the Calling Tower in the market square. "Good location!" he admired, and John agreed. Both men found themselves thinking of another use for the tower, other than clocks and callings. But this was a 'white area' town, with only a fringe of 'grey' in some areas, so they should be safe enough.

It did feel a bit exposed though, Porter hadn't considered that.

"Glad you're here!" Porter muttered as they put the ladders in position. Daks and Padre seemed to be doing a bit of their own scouting. It was amazing how many people had time to exchange pleasantries when it wasn't a market day!

The fire ladders could reach as far as the clock, but John was still impressed by Porter's steeplejack skills.

"Didn't know you had it in ya!" he said, as he waited for Porter to get into position.

"One of my covers," Porter admitted.

Porter had been wise to request the camp fire-ladders, as the ones being offered by the locals seemed to be in a far less reliable state.

With Daks and Padre on the ground, anyone coming up with any questions could be kept out of the way. John preferred to stay at the door of the tower, keeping a wary eye on both the ladders and Porter's progress.

Porter had climbed to the clock and got started, but the wind was picking up and there were more locals starting to take an interest.

"I'm going to need some of those ropes," Porter suddenly yelled down.

John had been watching the watchers, but now jumped into action, grabbing the ropes from the back of the truck and without a word ran up the stairs of the tower. There were a couple of startled locals who thought he shouldn't be doing that.

Catching up with one of the older ones who'd been shouting, John brought the Elder up with him. "Look, see. All I'm doing is making it safe. Safe?" John could gauge the nature of the Elder's concerns, even if he didn't entirely understand them. "I'm not touching anything.

Just ropes to make safe? OK? Hurry up clock safe?" John checked, trying to work out the local words for the translation.

He seemed to have done enough to satisfy the man, who nodded sagely, then helped him tie the ropes. John hadn't realised how tense the momentarily stand-off had been, until he felt his grip relax.

Porter was leaning precariously out from the wall of the tower on the ladder, waiting for the rope. "Clock safe?"

John threw the tail-end of the rope to Porter's grasp. "Check!" he called back.

John looked to the Elder who'd accompanied him up the stairs. "Check?"

The local man seemed to want to stay and enjoy the view, but John shooed him down in front of him, before resuming his position outside the door to the tower stairs.

Anyone approaching after that, John gave them the same information as he had their neighbour. "Hurry up clock safe!" and the Elder took over the explanations from there.

Porter had tugged on the ropes and decided they'd take his weight. The ropes around his waist might take his weight if he fell, but Porter was still putting his hope on the ladder proving enough. He was also hoping his knowledge in watches would prove adequate to the task in front of him.

He'd assumed the tower clock would be just like the café mantlepiece piece, only bigger. It wasn't nearly as old, but it had just been put in place and left. Porter was hoping a general clean would prove the solution and had tucked the tools into his pockets, all within reach. He leant back and let the rope take the strain at his waist, his top half unsupported, his feet and knees braced into the ladder frame, leaning up against the tower wall.

Porter was aware of the gathering crowd beneath him. He'd also noticed John resuming his post at the tower door. John had since been joined by a couple of local men, who seemed to be guarding him!

To fix the clock Porter really needed to get behind it, to get behind it he needed to take it off the wall. He didn't have enough hands to do that. The best he could do was bring his knees up to the bottom edge of the clock and tilt it forward into his chest.

It was awkward, but not as awkward as it might be if he tried to take the whole thing down to the ground. The crowd was curious, and Porter didn't like being so much on-show. Instinctively he tried to move himself closer to the wall.

The clock was almost working, he could feel from the way his tools had stopped finding looseness in the mechanism. He could hear the way the gears were sounding. "Purring like a kitten," he muttered to himself, resecuring the clock, then tapping the face, as he always did when he'd finished a job.

Wiping it clean with his handkerchief, Porter brushed away the dust that had crept in around the rim, finding his hand continuing to sweep a few inches further across the wall surrounding it. Flecks of dried mud fell away from where his hand had found a ripple in the brickwork.

"Wires!?" He was high enough and forward enough that none of the locals seemed to notice what Porter's movements had uncovered. "Definitely too exposed up here," he muttered.

"Almost done, Padre!" he shouted down, indicating to John that he could do with a hand the other end of the rope. He could see John start to open the door to the tower entrance, but the locals seemed intent on following him.

Porter waited. He couldn't do much else. Hoping John somehow sensed the problem. John was looking to Padre to explain to his shadow.

"Clock safe, hurry up all done," Padre indicated to the men, then to one of the older men, standing by the Elder.

"He's their Imam. The one that does the calling. He needs to give you the OK for going up the tower." As Padre explained, he pointed up. The Imam understood.

John and Padre both stood in the doorway. They were out-numbered but kept calm. Daks kept his distance. Porter stayed up the ladder and waited and watched, and wished he hadn't been so keen to do this job. It was becoming more uncomfortable by the minute!

"All done now?" John checked with the Imam.

Padre tried to say something about too many steps and not enough rope. John wasn't quite sure he got all the words right, but the Imam seemed to comprehend.

When the Elder stepped away from the door, his neighbours did likewise. Padre stayed beside the Imam. Somehow that seemed appropriate, whilst John opened the door again and started up the stairs.

He could feel their eyes on his back. He didn't want to be here anymore than Porter but remembered Sarg going on at him about 'hearts-and-minds'. As far as John could tell all that was happening right now was his heart having to cope with way too many steps, and Porter was going out of his mind with being left dangling!

Those thoughts had got John taking two steps at a time. When he was eventually able to lean out the window, he wasn't hiding the relief in his voice.

"Hey Porter, I'm here. You OK there?"

Porter looked at John, but the look of concern on his face had nothing to do with the ladder or the clock anymore.

"John," his voice a hoarse whisper. "What d'ya think of this?"

Porter had both his hands in front of his body, so no one except John could hear or see what he was gesturing to. Keeping his elbows tucked in, he pointed from wrist to finger only.

"There. Wires. What's that all about?"

John raised his own voice to compensate. "Undo your rope, Porter. The ladder'll take your weight. You can get down now."

Porter followed the direction and within the movement of

returning the rope from his waist over to fellow, John got a better angle on the problem Porter had found.

"Looks like tannoy wire or some-such to me, hang on I'll follow it this way."

Porter's laughter was real. "Can you maybe not use words like 'hang on' to me, right now?"

John gave him the thumbs up, and Porter called down to Padre. "You got the ladder down there?"

As Porter began climbing down, making plenty of fuss as he did so, John quietly disappeared back into the tower. Quickly gathering up the rope and untying it from the column where he'd secured it, he soon managed to locate the destination of the wires, they were only crudely concealed. Whoever had put them there hadn't expected anyone else to be coming that way.

That done, John yelled down the stairway, to those he knew were listening at the door, "All OK here, coming down."

Making a lot of noise coming down, John waited for one of the Imam's neighbours to open the door for him. He was right, they'd been waiting for him. "All OK?" John checked.

Padre looked to Porter who gave a thumbs up, then to the Elder. "All OK?" Thumbs up were given.

By the time John got to Padre and Porter, there seemed to be another problem. "What are they arguing about now? Not the time, surely?"

"No," Porter decided. "I think they're trying to decide how many chickens the job's worth!"

Padre looked up to the clock, then back to his own wrist watch, then to the Iman who was watching him. "Quite right?"

The Imam checked his own, before pointedly observing Padre's dog-collar, and nodding sagely. "Quite right."

"What now?" Porter muttered, eyeing up the distance between

them and the truck. "How do we duck out of this one?"

"I don't think we can."

Porter followed John's eyes as he spoke to the man approaching them with an ornate tray carrying coffee cups.

"Ah yes, the formalities," Padre smiled graciously, recognising the gesture.

"The formalities," John understood, briskly nudging Porter to follow his lead. "Hearts and minds remember."

John had seen Porter taking a breath to ask him about the wiring he'd found. The nudge became a sharp prod. Enough to stop the query.

"Got it, not the time," Porter coughed at the impact.

"Coffee a bit strong for you?" John checked, with a smirk.

Porter glared but regained his composure. "Head for heights, remember? Not for coffee!"

"Ah yes, the formalities," John agreed, lifting his cup to the clock, then to the Imam, and then to Padre, before drinking its contents.

Porter followed, never so pleased to catch sight of Daks coming over to them through the crowd. He was holding two chickens high.

"Looks like it's been a good business day for you?" John observed.

Daks cackled, "Very good."

Pops had also made his way through to them by then. Padre's housekeeper could also confirm there was room enough for a couple more chickens in the yard.

Porter didn't mention the wiring again but walked back to the truck in silence behind John. Both men could guess what the other was thinking, but this wasn't the time nor place to discuss it.

It was only when they were back in the truck, with ladders, ropes and Daks onboard and with the engine running and the cans of film held on Porter's lap.

"Well, what was it? Have we got time?"

John smoothly changed gear and got them moving out of the town first, before responding.

"Plenty. Not that sort of wiring. Looks like a sort of tannoy system. Crafty one that Imam."

"They shouldn't be there," Porter suggested.

John agreed. "No, they shouldn't be there, but I need to find out *why* they're there before doing anything about it."

He wasn't so much talking to Porter, as thinking out loud. John still needed to take the truck round to the address the officer had given him to start getting setting up for the Lad's film show.

"Never a dull moment," Porter smirked. He'd meant that to sound sarcastic, but it hadn't. More interested than anything else. "Film show, hey?"

John had done his thinking by then. "Not you, Porter. You're just holding those for me. Back to the mission house for you. I need to know where I can find you."

JOHN

They'd only wanted to watch a movie. A 'Yippee'! Who the heck thought that was a good idea?

John hadn't had much of a choice, a comedy would have caused a riot, a romance wasn't a possibility, a drama would have been lost on the men and a war-ee wouldn't have been helpful. So, a 'Yippee' it was. A few blokes riding around on horses, shouting and shooting at each other. Who could be offended at that? It was ridiculous, but just the right-side of ridiculous for the Lads to enjoy it.

They'd come back into town with Sarg to watch a movie. The officer had organised the loan of the compound for the evening, from one of the plantation owners. It was the grey-side of a 'white' area, but large enough to get them all in and able to keep an eye out!

John had been able to drop off the films earlier and they'd got it set up. Somehow, he was running the 'show', but how he'd got talked into that, he still couldn't quite figure!

It had happened somewhere between collecting the films from the railway station, finding where the address was to deliver them and before returning to camp to pick up everyone else. The officer seemed to have simply assumed and Sarg hadn't got anyone else in mind!

There were plenty of house chairs to bring out into the courtyard and a few benches at the back. John suspected most of the Lads would prefer sitting on the floor or leaning against the wall. He'd got the screen and lighting organised. The house was large, proper white plaster and paint on the walls, none of the local mud and crumbling bricks. The outer walls all seemed sturdy enough. John had checked them out as soon as he'd got down from the truck. He wasn't on security this time ... but old habits.

Porter hadn't been expecting to be included in this part, but John appreciated the extra pair of hands, and he was good with the lights.

"Should have known you'd know how to handle yourself in the shadows," John teased him. Porter took the compliment but was ready to get back to the mission house before Sarg and the Lads arrived. "Wise move," John agreed.

Daks knew how to move about in the shadows too. John knew that and listened for him now. He couldn't hear him moving, but he could feel the air return to the space where he'd been.

Whilst the film got started and with everyone getting settled, John found himself calming. His hands and ears were working on muscle memory, his eyes had adjusted to the focus beyond the light, to the shapes of movement in the darkness.

The flicker of the reel spinning in front of him, steadily became part of that muscle memory, it didn't register anymore. What was registering was the way the air felt, behind him.

John was standing nearer to the outer wall that bordered the courtyard. The Lads were all seated further in, facing the largest wall of plantation town house, watching the show.

He'd heard something very slightly behind him. Where there shouldn't have been anything. They'd posted guards. John had heard Sarg bellowing at a couple of the Lads earlier. There should have been at least two, if not three behind him by then.

He'd heard them walking the perimeter, but until then hadn't realised he'd been counting their paces. They'd stopped walking since then. He'd smelt one of them light up a cigarette. His thoughts had gone 'idiot.' If they'd just waited another five minutes, he'd have been changing the reel and they could have had a light up back there, no problem.

"Idiots!" John heard himself repeat out loud this time.

Daks was instantly at his shoulder. Without turning round to the Dayak. John talked naturally, without moving a muscle from his position.

"Check perimeter will ya?"

Daks ducked down and disappeared.

John kept his eyes front for a moment. Not a twitch from the Lads to indicate they'd registered the incident. John just hoped he'd miscounted those steps, hoping that Daks would bob right back up again, give him a thumbs up and they could get on with the 'Yippee'.

No chance!

Even before Daks got back to his shoulder, John was tensing up and had one hand on his rifle. His head hadn't moved the entire time, his shoulders had remained perfectly still, but John was no longer watching the screen. His attention was focused behind him. His ears were listening for footsteps, for the sound of a hand on the wall, or a foot further back than where he'd gauged the patrol had been pacing, straining to feel if he could find the air moving where it hadn't been before.

He was still waiting for Daks when the thud came. That was it.

That was all John needed to know. His hand went up turning the movie off in a fraction of a second, before yelling, "INTERMISSION!" at the top of his voice.

Daks was scuffling with one of them. John could hear the scrape of knuckles and metal against the other side of the wall. It wasn't Daks doing the shouting. John hadn't expected to hear him, that wasn't the way he fought.

John had no idea where the Lads from the patrol had got to. Then heard all three of them running after another of the CT rebels. Most of the Lads who'd been on the ground were already on their feet, those who had been seated had been a heartbeat slower, knocking the chairs in all directions. All they'd heard was John yelling 'Intermission!' Then the grenade came flying over the wall.

It was nowhere near where John had first heard Daks dealing with one of them. It must have been the one the patrol had been chasing. That thud? You don't usually get to hear that thud.

Sarg went forward to kick the grenade out of the way, but a couple of the Lads got in the way as they scattered and scrambled to help! The grenade went thud, then clatter, as it rolled across the ground between the chairs, a dud?

No, Sarg wasn't that lucky. The pin was still in it! Sarg picked it up and ran to the wall, yelling at his men. He couldn't leave the grenade there and couldn't throw it so close to town. The movie might be halfway through, but the show had just got started!

Sarg had the grenade held high and the Lads followed Sarg, John amongst them. The compound only had a single entrance. It was meant to be safer, but with a full-on charge in progress, it was a bit of a bottle-neck!

Some of the men at the back had already lost their patience and were chucking chairs over the wall. John saw Sarg turning to reprimand them. He hurriedly shrugged and offered.

"They don't like their 'Yippee' interrupted, Sarg." There was no time for more.

Sarg had his truck and John had the other. Some of the Lads had time to get in, the rest ran ahead, it wasn't helpful. The headlights startled and silhouetted them. Their eyes hadn't adjusted, and their boots were trampling any tracks.

"Which way?" John called out. Daks was opening the passenger side door, without answering, pointing off to the left. John gave Daks a quick, "Alright?'

Daks was scuffed up and there were a few scratches across his right arm. His right hand was down, close against his chest. He'd used his left hand to get the door, but he said nothing. It was a stupid question. The Dayak sat down and put his left hand back over the gashes to his right arm.

"How's the other guy?" John asked a better question.

Daks beamed, "Worse!"

"How many?" John checked.

"Only two now," Daks cackled.

The Lads were all out from the compound by then. It's boundary wall opened onto a long, curved path, framed between the high wall of the property on the one side and a half height wall on the other, almost holding back the jungle.

The house lights were beaming out, but there wasn't much to see, except the two bodies of the 'dealt with' rebels, that no one seemed particularly interested in. They weren't going anywhere. However, the other two were.

They were way out of range of the main market area by then, but well within chase-range of the less-reputable 'grey' corners of the town.

The Lads had long since got ahead of Sarg. Sarg was driving his truck, the grenade still with him, wedged safe down the side of his seat. It wasn't going anywhere unless he wanted it to and, right now, he needed both hands on the steering wheel.

It was only when Sarg decided to get out and do his share of charging-about, that the Lads in the back of the truck suggested they took the grenade off him for safe-keeping!

"Don't want you lobbing at the locals, Sarg!"

Some of the sprinters amongst them had started hammering on the townspeople's doors, before the officers could stop them. That wasn't going to do any good.

The Lads were furious, kicking at the nearest doors. A couple had already been opened for them, but they weren't going to get anywhere with that tactic. The officers managed to reason with them before anyone made it worse, although the officer screaming at the Lads didn't help anyone's sleep. The rebels wouldn't have needed to have got that far, much easier for them to disappear into the darkness and the jungle.

By the time Sarg had managed to get the Lads back into the trucks, the officers had decided it was too late to do anything else. The officers' car was back at the compound, so they had to walk back. Sarg offered them a lift, but they declined. Far better for Sarg to get the Lads loaded up, before any more of them got a chance to run amok!

John waited for those Lads assigned to his truck. He wasn't happy about it and nor were they. Given half a chance, and following Daks, they'd probably have been able to get a couple more answers before the morning!

Daks was itching to get out and start the hunt, but John had a suggestion. "Best get you patched up, or they'll smell you coming." It was good advice, and they both knew it.

Back at camp, the story was told enough times over that by morning there were tigers and elephants somewhere between film show and front doors!

Daks hadn't said a word and John hadn't slept much. The only way they were going to find out who'd been responsible for ruining the 'Yippee', was to get the locals wanting to tell them. This was all part of that 'hearts and minds' stuff. John had never doubted it had its part to play, but so did Daks' attitude to the situation!

There were plenty of medical personnel available on camp, but John knew that wouldn't suit Daks.

"Lucky it was you, not me!" John told the Dayak next morning, when he took another look at the wound across the top of his friend's arm.

Daks gave him that slow angry look. John knew what it meant. "No, you twit. I didn't mean if it had been me I wouldn't have stopped fighting! You only stopped because you'd got your man. I only meant if it had been me who'd got hurt, we'd have to get it treated on camp. With you we've got good reason to go back into town and see what Padre knows about last night!"

Daks expression steadily shifted, he understood. Pointing to his injury, "Cover?"

John nodded. "Got it!" The anger had quickened into a cackle by the time John was explaining to Sarg, he'd be needing the truck again.

"Really!?" Sarg asked. "You sure that's a good idea with him in that state!?"

"Padre, Sarg. Town medic. You know they don't like our doctors patching them up."

Sarg waved them through, but not without reminding John he still had to fetch back what had been left behind at that compound.

Daks knew John wasn't bothered whether he wanted to see Padre for his injuries, or not. They just needed to get them back into town before everyone started talking and changing their stories.

John didn't want to ask anyone directly. He'd worked out a while back that wasn't the way they liked to do things around here. It wasn't as if he could just walk up to the nearest café owner and ask him if he'd noticed anything suspicious yesterday evening! He and Daks would need to sit down in a café and wait until someone felt like talking. They didn't ask for information, they waited. The talkers would find them, that's how it worked!

Whilst they drank their coffee and waited, they watched and listened. John had learnt there were café owners who liked to talk, and there were café owners who liked to listen. He needed to find the talkative ones, that would give him the chance to listen.

Most of them knew John somehow, either from his stunt with the Australian tanker or with the chickens. Maybe they'd seen John by the book stall or driving Padre, or just seen him with Porter fixing the town clock. Right now, John simply needed to be noticed! If they knew who he was and tried anything unfriendly there would be enough curious eyes watching to warn John. That was the plan for the cafés but before then they needed to get over to the mission house.

Padre had already received a full report from Pops at first-light that morning. He'd been expecting a visit from John at the very least, ever since. The chatter was all about town, already way beyond any exaggeration the Lads could have come up with.

Padre was pleased to see them looking so healthy. From the way one of the descriptions had come into him, "the sky was dark with arrows, there was a screaming banshee and you had to tear the doors off the houses to protect yourselves."

Padre didn't believe it for a moment but, just to clarify, John repeated the actual details. "It was four men, one grenade, and an interrupted 'Yippee'. Daks got one, our patrol got another and two got away. We're looking for them, or someone that knows something about them."

John didn't expect Padre to know anything. No more than he expected anyone in town to tell him they knew where the two culprits actually were. All John wanted was someone who knew something.

"Oh, there's plenty of that," Padre was pleased to confirm.

That was all John needed to know. He didn't like asking Padre for information directly, it made him feel uneasy.

"How about a bit of a medical patch-up for Daks here?" Padre was delighted to offer aid.

Daks wasn't so happy about it, but when John explained it was 'all for show' Daks proved to be quite a consummate actor. Padre did the patching-up out in the kitchen yard, so that anyone who wanted to could listen in and anyone who came to watch, could be seen. Only with that part of theatre completed, were the pair ready for the second act over at the café.

They would have happily invited Padre and Pops along but didn't want them involved. Meeting Porter at the café was fortunate, though. They could talk about the town clocks and legitimately avoid referring to the later incident. Acting as if it never happened seemed to work; Porter was talking enough for all three of them.

John was impressed. Porter had learnt the local lingo better than he had. With Porter chattering on about clocks John was better able to listen to what the elderly local approaching them seemed to want to say on the matter.

He had come over to say thank you and then to complain. The Elder seemed to feel more comfortable directing this to Porter, as John was in uniform. Daks remained silent. The bandage made him look quite harmless. If they thought that, then more fool them!

John was gradually starting to recognise what this respectable senior was saying. One of his neighbours was being lazy. That didn't sound like it ought to be quite so objectionable. There were always more details to these sorts of stories.

Ah yes, now it was starting to make sense. The neighbour to this talkative Elder just so happened to be the Prayer Caller. John remembered those wires going up the side of the clock tower, he'd thought they looked like tannoy wires!

The Imam's neighbours would prefer it if he actually got out of bed in the mornings to call the faithful to their early prayers. No wonder they were complaining. John was listening and waiting for Porter to make the same connection he had. Sure enough, a few minutes later Porter started hissing, under the cover of his cup, "Wires!"

John picked up his own cup and nodded as he moved in to take a sip. John wasn't religious, but even he could see how the tannoy system sounded disrespectful.

Porter was agreeing to something. John had let his thoughts wander for a second. Idiot! What had Porter agreed to now? Daks was grinning and nodding too. John felt like he wanted to knock both their heads together!

They'd only just managed to get out of one scrape, why were they agreeing to jump right back into another? What had they just agreed to and why were they both now looking at him!?

Whilst the local was talking, John needed to work out why he'd chosen to give them this information! Porter was asking more questions, not too many, he didn't seem to be able to get a word in edgeways to the local's complaint.

The story was becoming more complicated, but John recognised that tended to be one of those local customs. "Never tell one story when you can put half a dozen more into it." John reckoned it must be something to do with the culture, they don't like to make it obvious they were complaining! He wasn't sure if it was a quirk of the language, but Daks didn't bother telling stories of any sort!

Daks didn't say much, but when he spoke, he said what he meant and nothing more. So maybe it was more to do with the town locals? They didn't want to broadcast their private business to any visitors. If that was the intention, this Elder was talking to the wrong man!

Porter explained soon after the Elder had taken his leave. He'd sat down, drunk three cups of coffee and said his piece. He didn't wait for a response. When he'd finished speaking, he got up and left.

"Well!" Porter looked to John, grinning, "What do you make of that!?"

"Idiot!" would have been John's first response, though he didn't say it. He wasn't even sure who he was calling an idiot, the Elder confiding in Porter, or Porter agreeing to get involved, or John himself!? "Idiot!"

Porter couldn't even tell John and Daks the local's name. He hadn't introduced himself, which seemed to be another of those cultural quirks.

"So, who was he and what did he want?" John got right in there with the questions, "and why did he tell you all of that?"

"Ah!" Porter smiled. "He recognised me!"

John gave him that 'Really!?' look they all knew.

"He recognised you too," Porter explained blithely. "From the clock tower. He seemed to think you'd know what to do."

Daks was chuckling up to full cackle already. John wasn't! And Porter wasn't finished.

"He thinks you can speak to the Prayer Caller without being disrespectful, or impolite, or too subtle. Basically, he wants you to tell the Imam to get his backside out of bed, stop dragging his heels, pick his feet up, and get the job done proper-like!"

"Oh, is that all? And what does he want you for?" John asked.

"Ah well, I repair clocks, don't I?" Porter smiled, seeming to think this explained everything. It didn't.

"The Elder thinks I might be the delicate-soul amongst the three of us."

John looked suitably doubtful.

"All this without implicating himself, I'm assuming?"

Porter gave the thumbs up. "You've got the picture."

"So, what's in it, for us?" John looked at Porter. No way was Porter going to agree to doing anything this stupid without there being something in it for him. As for Daks, these weren't his people. Daks didn't say much about the townsfolk but the way he held his chin when he considered them spoke volumes.

"It's all about respect, you see," Porter began. "You know, that 'hearts and minds' lecture they gave back at camp."

"You weren't there," John checked.

"Ah, but I was listening!" Porter informed him.

John wasn't surprised.

"So, the job is to get the Prayer Caller back to work then? That it? Without anyone knowing how it happened, or who's involved?" John checked, just to be clear.

Porter considered that summary. "Not quite. Bit more than that. We've got to make it look like no one knew what the Imam was doing to begin with. He can't be blamed for any of this, either!"

"OK, so let me get this straight. This is going to be a deniable accident, that never happened?" John checked, with a sceptical tilt to his head, finishing his coffee.

Checking over to Daks. "Quite right dump-truck!"

John asked for fresh coffee.

It was good coffee, but it needed to be drunk quick and hot. That's the thought that went through his brain now. That's the way they'd need to do this 'job'. Quick and hot! Don't give anyone time to think too much about it. That was the only way this was going to work.

Draining the cup, John returned it to the table. "Got it. Let's move."

Daks got to his feet without a word.

Porter was stumbling. "Just like that?"

John didn't look back at him but made to leave the café. Porter seemed to be needing a little more than that.

"Why? You did all the talking, not me!" John reminded him.

"Oh! Come on, that's not fair!" Porter blurted.

John swivelled round to face him. "You want fair, Mate? Cripes! You're in the wrong place for that one!"

"OK. OK." Porter put his hands up. "Fair's asking a bit much.

How about making sense, then? How about that?"

John's thunderous brow cleared somewhat. "We need to go see Padre. I need to run it past him first." They walked in silence after that, as John thought the rest of his plan through. At least what there was of it so far.

"We'll need to get the truck out of the way. Don't want it stuck when we need it quick."

Porter didn't like the sound of that, one bit!

"I've got that we're starting with Padre, seeing as how we're going to do something to the Prayer Caller, seems only right. I'll give you that, John. And I've got that we'll be needing the truck when we're done, maybe in a hurry. Sounds about right. But … just a bit foggy on the bit in the middle there, John?" John wasn't in a talking mood so Porter being Porter kept on talking. "I get we've been asked if we can do something about …" Porter couldn't wait until they'd reached the mission house.

John spun round at that.

"*We* weren't asked," he reminded him savagely, stabbing at Porter's chest with his finger.

"*You* were saying 'yes' before that Elder actually got to the asking bit!"

"Did I?" Porter was genuinely amazed. He never volunteered for anything.

"And what about you Daks?" John demanded, as they arrived at Padre's front door.

"Didn't say a word, but you weren't saying 'no' neither."

Daks didn't say a word now.

Both men knew from the way the Elder had been talking, the way he'd told the story. That sort of man with that sort of story, if you don't say 'no' clear enough, then it's taken as a 'yes'!

"So that's why he was talking so fast? So, we didn't get a chance to get a 'no' in there?" Porter finally cottoned on.

"Really!? You've just figured that out!? As I recall you were doing all the talking with him. If any of us could have got a 'no' in there, it should have been you!" John was prodding Porter again.

There was no point arguing about it now. Porter just shrugged. He'd volunteered and even he didn't know why. So how could he explain it?

Daks didn't seem to mind, whatever his reasons were. And John knew a Dayak never did anything without a reason, he wasn't saying anything. So it was only John who thought the whole idea was an idiotic one!?

At least talking it through with Padre meant he wouldn't be the only one saying it. It was an idiotic plan! But if Padre gave them the nod, then John could see they might be able to get away with it. It was idiotic, but he'd had worse ideas!

"So, we're trying to get the Prayer Caller to get out of bed in time for early prayers. Is that it?" Padre needed to be clear what they were telling him.

Porter wasn't. He only knew John had a plan. Daks seemed to know more than he was saying, but then Daks always knew more than he was saying!

John was the only one being clear on anything. "We've got to get it done quickly, before next morning's prayers. And done so no one can blame anyone else, including us."

John started at the start of the plan. Padre could appreciate that much. Nothing idiotic so far!

"We've got to attack from two points. Firstly, getting the Imam awake and secondly, stopping him from being able to use the speaker."

"Then it's a four-man team you'll be needing?" Padre queried, just to be sure, because he could only see three men in front of him.

"I think we can manage it with three Padre, but we'll be needing a few bits of kit from you. So, I guess you'll be the silent fourth?

No harm done. Actually, come to think of it, hopefully a bit of good because everyone will have respect for the Imam and no one to blame for the damage. They'll put it down to natural causes."

"Natural causes?" Padre queried.

"Oh yes, Padre," John's eyes crinkled in laughter, "on account of the chicken did it!" Ignoring the look of gormless confusion on Porters' face John continued. "We'll need one of your chickens, maybe just a loan, but if not, I'll make sure you get another. And we'll be needing one of your alarm clocks, too. I suggest not the one Pops keeps for the chickens and probably not the one the kitchen, either. They might be recognised by one of your regulars. You've got another one, haven't you?"

"Yes, the red one by my bed," Padre confirmed, before blurting, "I do so like a cheerful alarm clock by my bed in the morning. Will I get it back?" Padre queried, rather afraid he'd already guessed the answer.

"Sorry Padre. That one won't be coming back. Can we consider it a donation? I'll do my best to find you a cheerful replacement, might not be red though. Little hard to come by round these parts! Can we manage Porter?"

Porter checked he'd heard properly. "A cheerful red alarm clock? No Padre, shouldn't be too much of a problem."

John waited for Padre to fetch the alarm clock from his bedside and Pops to decide which chicken would do the trick. Padre came back first. They all waited for the chicken.

Pops came in with the bird under his arm.

"Ah excellent choice Pops, thank you."

Padre explained to his partners-in-crime the reason for Pops' choice. "That's the one that always goes for his slippers when he goes out to the yard. Gets Pops hopping mad every time. It hides behind the crate until it can hear the heels of Pops slippers flapping, then makes a beeline for the toes and starts pecking."

"Perfick!" John took the offered bird. "Thanks Pops."

"Don't put him down on the ground. If you hold him, he'll just sit there nice and calm. He's only gets aggressive when you put him on the ground," Padre cautioned.

John thanked him for that detail. "Good to know."

Padre guessed he wasn't going to be told any more of the plan. So, he could deny knowledge of it, without qualms.

"Quite right!" John told him, as they took their leave. The alarm clock was tucked in John's pocket, the chicken was stuffed under Porter's jacket, held as if he was too warm to wear it. Daks walked ahead of them both.

They needed a distraction, an alibi for being where they were. It wasn't too far from the truth. 'Close enough' so the officers wouldn't question it when they got back to camp. As far as John decided it, it wasn't so much an alibi, as 'just following orders'.

"Clear up the mess in the compound, remember?"

"Oh Blimey, forgot about that!" Porter laughed, recalling something he'd heard about an 'interrupted filmshow'.

"Couldn't we have left the chicken and the alarm clock til later, with Padre, and gone back for them after the clear up?"

"Don't be an idiot, if we visit Padre after dark, that would be suspicious!" John growled across. They needed to load the truck with the mess the Lads had scattered in the scuffle after the 'Yippee'. They'd also need to tidy up the furniture sent sprawling. It wouldn't take long, but long enough for it to get conveniently dark.

It wouldn't be difficult for them to create a noisy enough alibi, if anyone asked, effectively pinpointing their location as being at the plantation owner's compound, and nowhere near the market place in the middle of town.

"Not you Porter, you stay with the chicken!" John directed. "He needs to feel comfortable with you. We don't want him in a flap, drawing attention to us when we do start moving."

"Oh! OK John." Porter was starting to get an inkling as to his part in the plan and sat quietly in the cab, checking his repair tools, nice and sharp, nice and quiet.

Porter's toolbag might not be as heavy-duty as John's, but then Porter didn't 'tinker' with truck engines! He listened to Daks and John loading the camp benches into the back of the truck, scraping the chairs and sweeping away the breakages, with a loud running commentary for anyone listening.

By the time the truck was fully loaded and the compound presentable, as per Sarg's orders, it was getting dark, and Porter had got quite attached to the chicken.

"Got everything you need?" John checked.

Porter knew what he was referring to. "Toolbag? Always."

John smiled, "Thought so. Knew I could rely on you."

Porter liked the sound of that compliment.

"We need to leave the truck outside town," John was figuring.

"As far as anyone is concerned; we came into town to tidy up the compound and that's it. They'll already know we visited Padre, but that was just us being polite, they' d expect us to do that."

Daks remarked. "Coffee-polite?"

John remembered the talkative local. "Ah yes, but he'll never admit he mentioned anything to us. As far as he's concerned, he just complimented Porter on his clock-repairs."

"Neatly done!" Porter admired. By then it was fully dark and the truck was where they needed it.

John checked his pocket. Yep, the alarm clock was still there. Daks was lower in front of him, scuttling under windows, avoiding doorways.

They began moving through town. Porter wasn't quite as low nor as quick as either of them, on account of the chicken he was carrying. Porter didn't like the idea of being exposed. John knew that and took him to the door of the clock tower first.

"Get in, get up, and leave the chicken at the speaker. Have you got something to make it look like the speaker wires have become frayed, rather than cut?" John checked.

Now it was Porter's turn. "Idiot!?"

John grinned; he deserved that one. "OK, stay inside the door. We'll come and fetch you."

John left him there and rejoined Daks, who seemed to know where he was going.

There didn't appear to be anyone out this late. It might even be early. John hadn't bothered to check his watch. He knew Sarg wouldn't be happy, but he could also imagine Sarg wouldn't bother the officers until they'd finished their breakfast and were back at their desks.

If John could get the truck back before then, no harm done. And if they didn't, then it would be the least of their problems!

Daks indicated the house. John couldn't tell it from any of the others they'd scuttled past, dodging the occasional lights from windows and ducking down lower every time they heard so much as a murmur.

John's eyes had adjusted and his ears were picking out the various snores and yawns and more-distance scuffles of the town's night-life.

"Here!" Daks whispered, indicating up to a window.

John had no idea where they were.

Keeping Daks low, John took one quick look up, through the window into the room. He could make out a table and a bed, nothing much in between them and the window.

"No obstacles, straight up, in, out, OK?" he checked.

Daks nodded and gave John a moment to alter the setting on the clock, before taking it from him and skipping from the ground into the Imam's bedroom.

John listened but couldn't swear he even heard Daks feet touch the bedroom floor. It could only have taken a couple of seconds. John watched for any movement outside, whilst his ears listening for movement within. Nothing. Next second Daks almost leapt out the window, landing to neatly crouch down beside John.

"Done?"

"Done!"

"Right."

Both men nodded and immediately began to scuttle back to where they'd left Porter.

Porter had spent his time well. Getting past the door to the stairs of the tower wasn't the problem. Doing it quietly, came instinctively. Doing it whilst holding a chicken quietly under his arm was a little more challenging! It took Porter longer than he would have liked, but he'd worked in more awkward conditions. Maybe not quite so ridiculous, but definitely more awkward!

Porter was up the stairs to where the speaker had been secreted in seconds. He leaned out and looked across the square. He couldn't see anything for a few moments, then saw two shadows moving, low and silent.

The pair didn't hug the sides of the buildings but came directly out from one shadow into the next. Porter heard himself sigh with relief. With John at the door Porter knew he was safe.

The chicken came out from his jacket with a bit of a flutter, but quiet-enough. Porter didn't have slippers, so no toes for the bird to peck at. But she seemed happy enough when Porter started tapping at the wiring under the speaker. They needed the damage to look 'natural', whilst the mud covering-up the wires on the tower wall would remain relatively undisturbed.

"Just there, little chicky. You keep pecking there."

Porter scrapped at the cover of the wiring, working one of his file edges into it that effectively disabled the entire system. He kept tapping at the wire, 'encouraging' the bird to continue its own contribution to the effort. "That's it little chicky, you keep doing that til morning."

Job done and chicken content, Porter started back down the stairs. Daks heard him coming and indicated to John, who opened the door silently, beckoning Porter out.

"Now lock it." When it came to locks, they were always more difficult to relock. "Don't stand up," John hissed, as Porter had instinctively lifted himself from the crouch to look into the lock he was working on.

"Sorry, forgot meself!"

"No, don't do that, we need you!" John softened the hiss. He and Daks were looking out, only Porter was looking at what he was doing. They didn't need to know.

"Finished." Porter tapped John on the shoulder.

All they had to do now was get back to the truck before anyone in town saw them. And back to camp before Sarg got a chance to say anything to anyone. Sarg was going to yell at them no matter what. They'd been following orders of 'clear up that mess', the rest was covered by the 'hearts and minds' lecture. At least that's what John was going to be reporting back.

"You'd better not say anything", he suggested to Porter on the drive back.

Porter assured him he had no intention of doing so. He was preoccupied with how he was going to find another red alarm clock for Padre.

"Better not forget we owe Pops another chicken, too," John reminded Porter cheerfully, as they approached the gate. "Oh Cripes, I had!"

PADRE

He missed his little red alarm clock. He'd never relied on the alarm, but liked to see it there every morning, that little bit of cheerfulness.

It was market day. Padre briefly wondered if he'd be seeing Porter today before remembering what they'd been doing the night before. Unlikely. A couple of days away from town, the market, and the vicinity of the clock tower, might be a wise precaution for Porter and John.

Padre could already hear the market getting started down in the square. He could remember the markets back home; they'd taken an hour or so before anyone was ready for business. Not here! "As if by clockwork!" Padre murmured to himself.

Padding down the stairs in his slippers, Padre saw the satchel waiting for him on the post at the bottom. "Ah yes!" He clapped his hands. How wonderful! He'd almost forgotten about the delivery of medical supplies. By the looks of it several deliveries!

Padre still couldn't decide which boxes had come by way of his pleas to Head Office, which from the enquiries by the Engineer privately on behalf of the mission house and which had come through official channels from the camp clerk, putting in the correct paperwork for Padre!

He was just glad *any* of it had arrived and had no doubt it would all be called upon, eventually. In the meantime, Padre was enjoying the pleasant sensation of feeling a little better prepared.

He suspected the satchel had arrived with one of the boxes from the military channels. As a visiting Padre to camp, it had been a quite legitimate request. "So kind of them." He wasn't really needed at camp, but the Lads seemed to appreciate his visits and little chats.

Packing the satchel was a joy in itself. Padre wasn't fully medically trained, but he'd a good idea about what might prove useful on his rounds. He'd been offered plenty of good advice from his old Nanny on the subject. He could remember her words: "It's all about the cleaning and the patching-up, if you get that right you're heading in the right direction."

There had been a few broken bones along the way of those days, so he knew approximately how to splint-and-set. Padre packed the bottles of cough syrup and iodine, in amongst the bandages and dressings, smiling to himself, 'yes, Nanny would approve!'

Anything more serious and Padre would very sensibly seek advice from the camp doctors. For now, the next thing to do was check there was room in the satchel perhaps for a couple of books from the market stall.

He was smiling at the prospect by the time he came into the mission house kitchen to bid good morning to Pops. "A new satchel and a book stall day!"

Padre greeted Pops breezily, but Pops wasn't happy.

Padre had forgotten about the chicken! It wasn't that Pops missed that particular chicken, it was a bad-tempered chicken, but Pops didn't like wasting his chickens!

Padre began to try to explain it had been put to a good cause, but Pops soon waved him down, he'd heard all about what had happened at the first Call to Prayer of the day. More to the point, Pops seemed to feel the need to warn Padre about what he'd heard.

It wasn't really any of Padre's business, to Padre's way of thinking, and it seemed to have sorted itself out, just the way the locals like it to, without bothering anyone else.

Pops was starting to talk too fast again, something about the clock tower, Padre heard that much.

"Oh good. I'm so glad it's working well." He slapped his housekeeper on the shoulder and informed Pops he was going for his morning stroll. "Can't go wasting satchel-space when there's a book stall beckoning, now can I?"

Pops didn't have an answer for that.

Padre always enjoyed the slow stroll around his 'parish' on market day. He'd discovered it far more effective than trying to rush anywhere. It was a strange sort of 'parish'. Padre didn't think they had such things over here and the mission house wasn't really on a mission. As far as he could tell Head Office just needed to know someone was in residence!

As he was walking and thinking, Padre found himself wondering what Head Office actually expected of him. It was a good question. No one had really told him yet. They'd sent him the supplies he'd asked for and they'd provided him with a regular allowance, but they hadn't given him any ideas! At least they knew he was there now, that was surely an improvement! Maybe they simply expected Padre to do his best in the circumstances? Padre considered the notion further and decided, if that was the case, then he well content with that.

"Right."

The more he considered it, the more the similarities become apparent to back home, once Padre translated the flamboyant customs! A few enquiries as to their health. No front garden gates or invitations to take tea, but there were cafés and always someone happy to tell him more.

Making his way through the trays and stalls of the marketeers, Padre was happy to find one or two able to let him know how the river-traders had been getting on.

Padre noticed some of the plantation workers had come in. He always made it obvious who he was, for their benefit, just in case they needed to find him!

If they wanted to complain without causing any problems with the locals or their bosses, then Padre was the person they needed. He liked that. Padre felt if he knew where the problems were, then he knew where he might be able to help.

As far as Padre was concerned, being able to listen to complaints was just as useful a skill as knowing how to make a good bowl of chicken soup.

The chicken soup services were continuing at the mission house and having 'received' the crate of redirected kitchen crockery meant they no longer needed to keep asking for the bowls to be returned.

They did come back, eventually, but it was the fresh supply of soup spoons that was particularly welcome.

The books too! Padre smiled to himself, as he recalled that 'donation' of an entire crate of books. He hadn't really had time to look through them all yet. Which would explain why he hadn't given it a thought until he found himself already heading automatically over to the book stall corner of the market. "Old habits!! he murmured happily to himself.

They expected him over at the book stall, it was part of his parish and he liked to be seen to visit his parishioners. Padre greeted the stall-holder as an old friend, and they exchanged a few pleasantries. There wasn't really anything they could say about the weather, but Padre was pleased to admire the enthusiasm of the market this morning. "Plenty of noise?" he enquired.

The stall-holder was glad to agree. "Plenty time for talking," it sounded like the stall-holder had said, but he'd spoken to Padre at the same time as he turned his head, mid-haggle with another customer, so the Padre couldn't be sure.

Padre politely kept on browsing until the man came back to him, satisfied with the outcome of the previous bargain.

"Plenty of time?" Padre checked, looking over to the clock tower. The book seller seemed very happy Padre had noticed.

"Much better."

They agreed before Padre continued his errands.

With Pops being so excitable first thing, Padre hadn't really had a chance for a second cup of tea, but there were plenty of cafés around the market. Some had proper shops with tables and chairs, others just came by with trays through the throng and the chatter.

Padre sat down at a table at one of the quieter cafés. He could watch the whole market travel past him from there. The first time he'd done that it had made him giddy, as he struggled to follow who was selling and who was buying. It had taken him a few more market days before realising that wasn't the way these market places worked.

There were two or three cafés the Padre had become rather attached to. He didn't like to always go to the same one, a little variation was pleasant and offered different perspectives. He couldn't be too random though, 'regular enough to be reliable,' that sounded about right.

He sat out the front, at a table that had two other chairs. "Yes, this'll do nicely!" Padre declared when the owner brought him his coffee. If anyone needed him, he was here.

The owner seemed just as pleased to see Padre, offering the observation on how well the 'new' clock was keeping such good time.

"So I hear. It's wonderful," Padre agreed amiably.

"Much better!" the owner agreed.

Padre thought how nice it was that the locals appreciated Porter's efforts to get the clock working again, tapping his own wrist watch and checking it.

"Yes, very good time." He looked to the café owner, who appeared to be expecting something more.

"Proper time?" Padre checked.

The owner nodded vigorously at that suggestion. "Oh yes, very proper. Much better!"

That seemed to satisfy his enquiry and the owner left Padre to his coffee in peace.

Padre was starting to wonder if the café owner's references had more to do with John's recent 'ridiculous plan', rather than Porter's clock repair services, but he kept that to himself.

Most of the locals recognised Padre's dog-collar by then. They didn't have much of an opinion on his book choices, but they did seem to have an appreciation for anyone who could make good chicken soup. Some of the locals, it seemed, had also begun to hear of Padre's 'medical training' from the river-traders. Padre hadn't needed to do much. He could manage iodine for scrapes and syrup for sore throats. He bandaged firmly and held frail hands gently.

The river-traders took the news out with their trading boats to the villages along the riverbanks. The river-village people tended to work for the large houses and their vast plantations. They didn't work the hillsides with the rice terraces. The river-village people were plantation workers in the main, only coming into town occasionally.

A few had come in to market that morning and seen Padre, hesitating until they watched how easily the café owner spoke with him. Padre had evidently been described to them by the river-traders, but it was his new satchel that caught their eye. They recognised the red cross first, the dog-collar second.

They weren't local, so it needed to be done without making it too obvious. Padre wasn't the stranger here, they were. They steadily worked their way over to his table. Padre had seen them approaching and could also recognise their apprehension.

He calmly read his book and sipped his coffee, waiting until they were ready. When he looked up, the plantation workers were looking directly at him. That was his cue. He got to his feet and invited them to sit.

Immediately both the plantation workers explained they didn't have time for that.

He offered them coffee. They didn't want that either.

It was his move. It usually took three. Padre had learnt the way of such introductions, the etiquette.

"How may I help you?" he asked, without flourish, without demand. Padre's hands were open, his book laid resting on the table, as he sat down and waited for their response.

They didn't sound as if they were complaining. They didn't sound as if they were offering a story. Padre listened, but his expression must have been telling, as one of the elders at the next table felt it prudent to offer some assistance in the matter

"They say need you visit village," the elder explained.

Padre thanked them sincerely. He always liked to receive visiting invitations. So much better than barging in where he wasn't welcome!

Padre needed a little more help from the elder as he wasn't yet able to follow this particular dialect.

He didn't want to be rude, but he wouldn't be able to get over that way yet. Not with just his bicycle. And the other dilemma was that he had no idea where their village was.

The elder requested a few more directions from the plantation workers. "No hurry." He turned to Padre.

"Oh good, then please tell them I shall be delighted to visit them, when I can get over that way," before adding, "maybe I can get some help with one of the smaller boats from the river-traders?"

"With bag?" the elder enquired, pointing to Padre's satchel.

Padre understood perfectly. "Oh most definitely, I shall come with bag. Very good."

Padre liked this pace of getting things done, the 'no hurry' pace of everything. Just as when he had no idea where he was going. It was quite simple. Padre had learnt you never asked directions, you found out who else was going that way and made yourself useful.

With the plantation workers satisfied they'd completed their message, they took their leave and disappeared back into the market. But with the introductions now made, the elder came to sit with Padre. He too complimented Padre on the town clock. Padre was starting to wonder if they thought he had anything to do with it, but was still glad the elder sounded happy with the clock.

"Proper time."

"Quite right," Padre agreed, as they both had another cup of coffee together. Padre had put his book down as soon as the plantation workers had approached him. With the elder seated beside him, a further courtesy was called for. Padre put his book back into his satchel and returned it to the side of his chair.

"Quite right!" The elder agreed, acknowledging the gesture.

Padre was glad it met with his approval.

The elder's attention was suddenly distracted. There seemed to be a general movement through the market towards the pair of them.

"Quite right!" the elder indicated to Padre, pointing to the Imam approaching, with a limp.

"Oh dear!" Padre was all concern. "Poor fellow." He stood up to offer his seat to the Imam.

The Imam straightened, observing Padre's gesture. He'd also caught the elder's expression, which was revealing. He groaned loudly as he sat down, resting his outstretched foot away from anything that might touch it.

Padre made all due fuss with the Imam but was sure he heard the elder murmur a 'quite right' under his breath again. He ignored it, considering that the wisest response. The Imam wasn't saying much either. Certainly not before another cup of coffee. The owner was at his elbow before Padre could ask.

"Nasty stub!" Padre offered, as he began rummaging through his satchel. "I have just the thing for that." Without waiting for the Imam to say anything else, Padre pulled the third chair into position to provide a rest for the sore foot. "That's better, isn't it?"

The elder smiled knowingly but said nothing, preferring to drink his coffee and enjoy the theatre.

The Imam had leaned forward to take his slipper off. The foot was a bloody mess.

"Oh dear. Yes, indeed. A very nasty stub! Too many sharp corners?" Padre offered ingeniously.

"Too many sharp corners," the Imam muttered inscrutably, putting his slipper down on the floor and permitting Padre to request a bowl of water. The café owner had been standing by, anticipating the request.

Padre brought another chair for himself from an unoccupied table, positioning it beside the foot-rest chair. He could see the faces of all three men from there. The Imam, the elder, and the café owner.

It was definitely theatre now!

The elder was fascinated by the soaking and the dabbing of the cotton wool, leaning forward in his chair to better observe the meticulous process, almost exactly replicating the posture of the Imam. The café owner was leaning in by then, too, and Padre was starting to feel a little uncomfortable.

"Shall I bandage that for you?" he asked, pulling the roll out from his satchel to show the men what he was referring to. "I really ought to put a little iodine on it. It'll sting, but it ought to be done properly."

Only now did the Imam look to his elder. "Properly?"

The elder nodded firmly. The café owner was equally adamant. The Imam looked hesitant but braced himself for the sting.

Padre was a gentle as he could be, carefully dabbing at the damage until he was satisfied. Then with a clean dressing and the bandage, he smothered the bruised and bloodied hen-pecked toes with a swathe of clean white cotton lengths, until the Imam could bear to tolerate putting weight on it again.

Padre gave him his shoulder, to stand and test the 'mend'.

He seemed satisfied.

The elder was not. Not yet. He looked to the Imam. "Properly," he prompted.

"Ah yes!" the Imam nodded, able to remain standing unaided. He finished his cup of coffee, then put it down and thanked Padre, before calling to one of his students.

The young man seemed to have been waiting out of sight of the café table. He stepped forward, ready to take over supporting the Imam back to his office. He produced a chicken for 'Pop-home' in payment of Padre's medical services.

"Oh, how lovely," Padre gushed. "Much appreciated. Thank you."

The elder approved of Padre's manner. Padre had learnt the

politeness of their ways.

By now, even Padre had realised the elder knew *exactly* how the Imam had received those injuries. From his grin the café owner knew too and likely most of his customers as well as the locals on their market day business. All Padre had needed to do was just as he had done. Shown the 'proper' respect and been the one to say 'thank you'. Somehow, in the eyes of the elder and every other man there, that put an end to the entire business. Properly.

And the payment of the chicken? That was the Imam telling them all he knew he'd been an idiot!

Padre took the chicken home for Pops to prepare for supper. He had his 'with-bag' visiting invitation to plan, he seemed to have gained approval from the Elder in the process and the coffee had been excellent. The books looked interesting too. Padre was content to just sit somewhere cool and quiet and do a little reading for a while, waiting for the chicken soup to simmer until supper time.

He was still wondering about the plantation workers and what they might need him for. The elder had told him they required a village-visit, but hadn't been able to explain the problem. That usually meant something medical a little more complicated than cuts and scrapes. Padre was just wondering if perhaps he needed to pack more than his satchel for that?

Not yet, no hurry. He'd wait until he could check when there was word from the river-traders and that they could take him that way.

Perhaps he'd mention it at camp, on his next visit over there? It was nice to get out on his bicycle every once in a while. He could let the clerk know he'd got the delivery of supplies they'd so kindly arranged for him. And he could check how John and Porter were doing, too. Padre didn't want to think they might have got into any trouble. After all, the matter was closed. The clock was working and the Imam had a sore foot, so it was all sorted … and there was chicken soup for supper!

So long as he kept serving chicken soup every evening, his 'flock' came to visit him in the kitchen yard. They came with bowls and stories, and Padre would sit on the little stool beside the pot and ladle the soup into their bowls, for as long as the soup lasted.

Some would thank him and walk away, some would sit closer by and return for more; some had begun to sit beside Padre, bringing their own stools and cushions and he'd read to them from his book, or they would tell him their own stories.

Chapter 7

INTELLIGENCE!?

John

I t had been a few months but the questions weren't getting any smarter. One of the Lads had already queried 'and who's daft idea was it to go *this* way?' John had reminded them they'd been told the reason for the patrol: the same reason given for *most* of their patrols.

"The powers-that-be have received intelligence of suspicious activity in the area. They need us to check out just *how* 'intelligent'!"

Daks had his own way of expressing what he thought of this particular route! It was a river bed, the rains were coming and he was hill-people. Daks was at the back of the patrol with John, and they were both in muttering-mood.

Daks was only coming along to make sure the river-traders had remembered to deliver the bicycles to his people.

"Why do they need them up there?" one of the other Lads had asked Daks. The Lad doing the asking hadn't quite got his head round the way things were done on patrol in these parts.

Daks would have liked to have been a bit more direct in his explanation. His people were hill-people, they also happened to be head-hunters. They were friendly, but even so, John wasn't sure of the wisdom of questioning their errands. He was all for banter, but that might have been a step too far!

Daks had remained silent for the next hour, although John was sure he could hear him fiddling with one of the knives in his belt, as some of the less experienced Lads up front continued to grumble.

"You alright?" he queried, when he heard Daks 'tock'. John had learnt this was the local dialect for a 'tut-tut'.

Daks looked to John.

"Idiot!"

"Right. Now we've got that agreed, d'you mind explaining to *me* why we sent those bicycles up to your hill-village, rather than wait until some of your friends could collect them next time they came down in to town?"

It was the same question, just a little better phrased. Both men knew that, but Daks was calmer and had stopped fiddling with his knives. John felt a little bolder.

"You'd better speak up Daks, you know they're all listening."

According to Daks the hill-people needed the bicycles first, to bring their trade down from the mountain, to the markets

The Lads decided now that Daks had started talking to them again, they had more questions. John thought it unwise, but waited.

"If the river-traders can get the bicycles over to your friends then why can't your friends use the same boats to take their trading to market?"

Daks 'tock'ed again, John was grinning. He kept the pace steady. They needed to keep moving, safer that way.

"Hill-people are not river-people, we use bicycles not boats," Daks reminded them. "Bicycles on mountain paths. Hill-people don't travel on river." He made it simple.

That seemed to satisfy their curiosity and the patrol continued in silence for another couple of hours.

Someone up front started grumbling.

John gave Daks a nod and they moved up to lead.

The inexperience of some of the Lads was getting louder. In the jungle getting there quicker wasn't the point of the exercise. That would be 'getting there in one piece'!

As the pace had slowed, they were getting a little easier in their travelling arrangements and that seemed to be the cue for restless tongues. Daks was keeping silent and John hadn't been asked any questions for a while.

The other Lads seemed content to grumble amongst themselves: Distance? Direction? Description? "Weren't we given those back at base, before we started this 'ere patrol?" "What was that officer talking about anyway?" "Why didn't they write it down for us?"

John could answer that last one. "Because no one wrote it down for him."

"He's got the reports, ain't he?" one of them asked. "He's the intelligent one, that officer?"

John corrected that delusion in short-order. "No, he's the one who *writes* the reports! As for the 'intelligence'? That's what we're here for!"

Sure enough.

"So, where the heck are we?" a fresh grumble came up the line.

John could sense a rhythm now and called back smoothly. "That would be that 'Intelligence' we were talking about."

Daks suddenly clamped down to his haunches and signalled silence.

John followed without question.

Someone behind started to ask "wha …?" when his fellows dragged him down to their level and slapped a hand over the idiot's mouth.

Daks started crawling forward.

The forest seemed impenetrable. No telling which direction they were going. They'd been pushing branches and stepping over leaf-litter and dead wood for what had seemed like miles already. Now Daks was getting them to go directly through it!?

He had his reasons, and John wasn't asking, just reminding the Lads behind him to stay low.

The greenery was clearing slightly. It smelt different.

There must have been some traffic up ahead. The dust smelt of engine-oil and wheels. John tapped Daks and signalled he'd recognised it too. Daks answered the signal with the gesture that meant they were too late. He stood up.

John waited for the rest to catch up. "All clear Lads. Looks like we missed 'em."

"At least we know which way they're using now," one of the bright sparks offered.

"And that's about as 'intelligent' as it's going to get!" John agreed with Daks gesture, as they started looking for something to eat.

The 'clearing' in the jungle was no more than wheel ruts that had passed through in the last twenty-four hours. The vehicle had shoved, scraped and trampled the vegetation. It was 'clear' enough for Daks.

"How can you tell it's them not us?" someone asked, whilst John made a brew and Daks got the meat prepared. No one asked the Dayak what it was, they'd learnt that much already. The Lads had got rations, but whatever Daks was cooking it smelt better than their tins.

The Dayak liked the Lads' biscuits though and their cigarettes. A good sign, if Daks was allowing them to smoke, then they were definitely clear of anything that might be tracking them.

"That's part of the 'intelligence' too, always two-sides to it," John reminded them.

The Lads were relaxing and ready to ask more stupid questions. "Which side are we on, then?"

John snorted. "We're on the side that doesn't have enough intelligence. Apparently!"

Daks 'tock'ed in exasperation again.

There was still the unanswered question of how could they tell whose vehicle had made that path they'd just found? It seemed to overlay older tracks. Across every inch of the jungle were older paths. It was simply a matter of how ancient, and who was using which most recently! That was the crux of what Lads were wondering now.

"How can you tell it's them and not us?"

John laughed, almost managing to crack his laughter into the same cackle as Daks.

"They're not our boot-prints, and there's no bicycles tracks."

With that they agreed enough 'intelligence' for now.

They'd been following the path now for a day or so. Generally, it seemed on a heading away from town, towards one of the rivers John knew about. It would be stupid at this point to attempt to reckon which one. Too many rivers and paths, and the mountains swept up in every direction beyond the jungle canopy.

They next camped just off the path, three paces into the jungle. John knew one of the Lads was going to get lost during the night as soon as he moved away to relieve himself. Everyone would need to watch, but at least they'd be able to sleep this time.

The tea was stewed but drinkable and they emptied the tins and made a mash with the biscuits and jam. The rest of the rations were given to Daks to use as bait.

The meat was good, a bit stringy, but it was too dark to see what they were eating, and they were too hungry to ask. They'd have to put the fire out in a minute, so whatever it was, it was good enough.

Rope and empty cans were tied around the borders of the camp area, as an early warning. They weren't expecting visitors, but they weren't expecting a restful night's sleep either!

The next morning the cold tea was drunk. The less experienced Lads were already running out of cigarettes. John knew better and suggested they give what they had left to Daks. "May be some trading to be done up ahead," he explained. They cleared the area and checked their equipment and numbers. All accounted for, everything ready. Pack and load up. This time no one was grumbling. This time everyone realised where the intelligence was coming from.

Daks led.

They'd found what they were looking for. Now they were following it. The only problem with following a path in this area was you knew that, sooner or later, you weren't going to be the only ones using it. The 'intelligent' part was to decide which were the currently favoured paths and why.

Distance wasn't a matter of miles in the jungle, no matter what the maps and the officer back at camp said. Wrong numbers! When you were on patrol it was a matter of days and supplies. And on what you found before they ran out!

The directions could have been given some prompting with the compass, but it only helped so far as they could find a path to follow in that general direction. The best they could do was be aware of 'markers' and just keep turning towards or away from them.

They'd got an approximate pick up in two days, give or take a day or so! They'd got the path and were following it. If they weren't there when the truck had to leave, they'd miss it. The truck would report back to camp and the officer would make his report.

John's patrol were following the 'intelligence' ... not the officer!

The description of the route they were taking? Someone was going to have to explain where the path was on the map, for the officer's report, once they got back to camp. No one was offering to know that much yet.

"No wonder they don't try and map this place," one of the

Lads had started grumbling again, but he was learning. "Trying to describe the route depends on who you ask, and which season you're travelling through."

Daks thumped John's shoulder, thumbing back. The intelligence was brightening up!

They got to the river on the third day, sometime in the afternoon. The path was there but joined up with a more established track. More tracks, plenty more, and they weren't theirs!

No cigarettes now, no fire, no tea. No one was thinking about what day it was. No one was thinking as far ahead as when the truck would be waiting to get them back to camp.

The patrol was thinking boots and eyes. The weight of their packs didn't register anymore. They'd tucked their hats into their belts, with a knife and water-bottle within reach.

The tracks were definitely following the river, criss-crossing it from time to time, wading across it. The Lads were starting to get a sense of direction.

Daks might not be of the river-people tribes, but that didn't mean he didn't know some of the river villages. The river villages had bicycles too, the bicycles were used to get from their village to the main trucking-route to their plantation-working.

"Trucks don't come this way from the plantation. But if anyone needed to get to the plantation without using the working routes, this would be a good way?" John was asking the question, as well as answering it.

Daks appreciated the efficiency. "Good-bad way," he agreed.

They'd need to get a safe distance from the track and the river. It would be dark soon and there was no such thing as being safe enough in the jungle in the dark.

There were too many tracks to follow any further. That was as far as the 'intelligence' went.

The best thing the patrol could do now was keep moving until they met up with one of the working routes heading out from the plantation, through to one of the trading villages beside the town road. That would take them, sometime tomorrow, to where the truck could pick them up.

No one argued, everyone kept walking, following John and Daks.

"Any chance of a cigarette?" one of the Lads behind queried.

"If you've got 'em, smoke 'em," John agreed, waiting for the inevitable, adjusting the coil of rope he carried across his chest and shoulder, signalling to Daks there was a deal brewing his way.

"Daks, can we have some of the cigarettes back?"

Daks winked across to John. "What you got to trade for them?"

PADRE

These weren't the trading boats of his friends from the Lost Luggage Office. These were fishing boats, longer and broader in the beam, shallower, for working the nets and holding the catch, but no more than that.

It was fascinating to watch how they steered and produced the power by a single oar. Padre also noticed that although the trading boats and fishing boats appeared to be near-neighbours, they had very different manners. Thankfully the dialect was similar enough for his ears to follow.

They found him odd but allowed Padre to treat the injuries one of their number had received from a fighting fish that had taken objection to the nets. Not the anticipated patient, but Padre had come 'with bag', so was prepared for the red cross to be recognised.

Padre wasn't a boat doctor, but it seemed to impress them that he'd come onto their fishing boats and treated them on the water, rather than insisting they come on to the shore to be treated.

The fishing boats traded no further than the edge of the water. Anything further in land than the dock and it was down to the river-village people. And with the help of the fishing boat that was where Padre was heading, on his with-bag visit to the river-village. The nearest hospital was three days walk away. Padre-with-bag was the next best thing!

He'd got the message they needed a doctor at one of the river villages, but wasn't sure which one, and had been waiting for the next fishing boat heading over that way. Padre was ever-hopeful.

That had been a few days ago, but Padre didn't want to let them down. He knew the message had come from plantation workers, but most of the river villages sent some of their people to work on the plantations. It could be any one of a half dozen villages along the river, and the plantations were vast. Padre would just have to go by fishing boat, from one to the next until he found it.

He'd left Pops in charge of the chickens and the mission house and had packed everything he could think might be needed in either the satchel or the backpack Porter had 'found' for him.

Padre had even thought to leave a message for Porter for next time he came by the mission house. It was simple enough, just to let the camp know where he was heading and why.

Padre had managed to get over to camp before taking his trip but had been too busy to mention his intentions then. He'd only seen the Engineer briefly. Busy man, coming by from the railway station before going on over to the far side of the plantation. Something to do with building works.

Padre was always welcome at camp. The Lads found it helpful to have someone who didn't know 'anything', to talk with and he was given a remarkable degree of freedom to say what he thought. The dog-collar and the stories of the soup kitchen seemed well received too. As were the books that had come 'his way' through the crate-dealing with those lost luggage fellows. There were a few which Padre decided more 'suited' to camp conditions than the mission house book shelves.

During that visit he'd also been asked to offer a little guidance to a couple of the officers regarding their attitude towards local customs. Padre had also heard something of the matter in question from one of the café elders he'd got to know.

Padre decided the two officers concerned would respect his direct approach in the matter. Some plain-speaking, to ensure no possibility for confusion.

The incident had only been a minor misunderstanding, but the Elder wanted it nipped in the bud. Next time it would be viewed with far less tolerance for their ignorance.

Padre got the officers sat down with the door shut. "Now gentleman, do you want to tell me what you were thinking, when you did that?" Neither of them could defend their rudeness and both men were left in no doubt as to Padre's opinion of their behaviour. With that being said, he suggested neither returned to town until the matter had a chance to blow over.

Sarg heard about it from the clerk who hadn't dared open the door until Padre was finished, but had listened. "Nothing official, nothing on the record. Neatly done. No injuries, only a couple of noses out of joint!" said the clerk when he retold the story to the Lads, who thought it 'abso-ruddy-lutely overdue'!

After the talking to, Padre had just enough time to visit the medical tent to deliver a couple of reference books he'd found, a little dated perhaps, but he couldn't see them go to waste.

The camp had plenty of fully qualified medical staff, two medical tents, and another less obvious, designated as surgical-theatre tent. They seemed to be manned by constantly quarrelling teams of English and Australian, with some South African members contributing their efforts too.

They only quarrelled amongst themselves and never when it came to actually getting on with the work. They'd always been friendly enough towards Padre. It helped to have someone in town with at least a basic first-aid knowledge and Padre was glad for any advice they could offer him.

He spent the remainder of the day with them, discussing the various benefits of classroom learning and practical hands-on training. By the time he was ready to head back, his satchel supplies had been supplemented considerably.

He ought to have mentioned his intentions then, but the doctors were more intrigued to learn how Padre had become so well-appraised of the local customs so quickly. His message to Porter, about letting the camp know about the fishing boat, would have to suffice.

The occupants of the fishing boat had been glad to take him aboard. Padre had done his best to tend to the wound. His backpack and satchel were ready, now all he could do was wait for wherever the fishermen next docked.

They'd been able to explain they couldn't help him once he stepped off the boat, but they agreed to wait for him to return from the village, for as long as they were fishing that way. When the fishing was done, they'd move on, with or without Padre.

Not all the locals were ready to trust someone from the camp. It might be the way they walked, or smelt, even before they started to talk! But Padre's chicken soup remedy had persuaded many that maybe he had a touch of good-medicine in his ways!

John wasn't surprised to hear about what Padre was planning. The message was vague, but sufficient for him to hazard a guess at his intentions. John could imagine Padre would have thought no more of the risks of 'visiting the sick', than of offering a bowl of chicken soup to his neighbours! John would have been quite happy to have got angry at Padre's fearless attitude, except he admired it too much.

As Padre sat quietly out of the way on the fishing boat, he wondered about what he was heading into, absent-mindedly patting the side of his satchel, murmuring, "let's see what we can do, shall we?"

It wasn't the first village, but it was a very good practice-run for Padre at dealing with both the dialects and quite a few minor ailments. As for handling the language barrier, it was quite fortunate one of the men on the dock waiting for the fishing boat did most of the yelling.

The fishermen soon explained Padre's errand. The dockman was doubtful, but was eventually persuaded to call back to his friends. From then on, there seemed to be some degree of trading at the dock, the dock being neither land nor water. The fishermen and the villagers were both happy to attend to business, whilst Padre sat on a stool that had been brought out to him.

The villagers seemed well able to take care of their own injuries and ailments but for a couple of infants there was cough syrup offered, taken by their mothers first, as a precaution. Then there was an elder who needed some muscle-ointment applied. Padre very respectfully showed him how to do so, demonstrating on himself first. Then with a magnificent bow presented the tube to the elder, who accepted the gesture with no less formality.

Stepping back onto the fishing boat, Padre sat down and gave a low sigh and a whistle of relief, amazement and amusement at his own audacity, and his admiration for the ways of the locals. He'd a lot to learn.

"Best doctoring is don't think you know better."

The fisherman agreed, whilst they packed away their trade. Padre thanked them again and settled himself.

The next village proved to be the origin of the message and Padre was going to be busy for more than a few hours, perhaps days. He hadn't thought that far ahead and was rather glad he hadn't! The fishing boat wasn't going to wait for him this time. Perhaps he could borrow one of the village bicycles to get to the truck road heading back to town, but they didn't seem to have many. Most village residents simply walked the paths until they reached the road and then kept on walking, until one of the working-trucks picked them up.

Padre could do likewise, they suggested helpfully. Anyone who stood and waited long enough was bound to have a truck stop for them. There might even be one with a spare bicycle on it.

He couldn't help but smile, as he stood there ready to be guided to his patient, when he thought of what he'd managed to do so far with hardly more than a bowl of chicken soup and a trusty satchel. It was quite simple: kindness and consideration and patience. Politeness, too, that was important, and the listening.

Chicken soup! Who knew? But like his mother's cook had always told him: 'it's the simmering and the seasoning that does the mending.'

"The simmering and the seasoning, hey?" Padre wondered quietly to himself. The 'simmering' would be the listening. The 'seasoning' would be the help he hoped to offer. Giving his satchel another reassuring pat, informing it, "and you're the chicken soup this time."

PORTER

He'd got the message from Padre. Porter had been getting restless recently and wouldn't have minded going with Padre on his visiting. Pops didn't seem unduly concerned, but it had already been two days since the fishing boat had left.

Porter had got chatting with a couple of the elders in Padre's favourite café to see if they knew anything about where he'd gone. Porter learnt about the fishing boat and the river villages. He'd always assumed a fishing village was a fishing village! It had taken another chat with the elder to be corrected. The fishing boats were their own village, the river villages did the trading, not the fishing. That had been when Porter made the connection with the plantation workers coming to town looking for Padre's 'mending-bag'.

Porter knew there were regular work trucks heading out from town, for the plantations. What he hadn't appreciated was the way some of the trucks were used between the plantation and the railway station as buses by the locals, for travelling and dropping off between villages and market.

It wasn't like the old buses he'd been used to back home. They seemed clumsy by comparison. This was a much easier arrangement. If it went past and slowed down, you got on. If it didn't, then you didn't! No one needed to know where you were going. It didn't matter where you wanted to go, you got off when it stopped. If you didn't then that was your problem.

You could take whatever you could carry onto the back of the truck, to bus it wherever you needed, so long as there was room, and so long as none of the passengers already in the truck objected and threw you off. Of course, there was always the possibility they'd throw you off the truck-bus and keep your trading-goods, but hey, Porter didn't have anything worth trading right now!

So, a hop onto one of the truck-buses to try his luck along the way to the next stop seemed at least a step in the right direction to finding where Padre had got to.

Getting into the truck was the easy bit, staying in it once it got started was a whole different matter. Porter was off his feet and on his rear-end before he'd managed to grab for the sides. If he hadn't got to his knees, he was at threat of being trampled by one the goats that had got on earlier. He was safe on his knees, holding on to the side of the truck. It took him another minute or two from there to gain his 'truck-legs' and stand with any degree of confidence.

It wasn't so much that the truck lurched from one pothole to the next, but the road was rutted, acting like tramlines for the truck wheels, until it crossed one of the other local paths and then the ruts took a turn and the truck driver had to make an effort to steer the truck clear of the diversion.

The goats weren't so bad. Porter found himself happier with the goats than the chickens. At least with the goats he could nudge them away, without being too obvious. The chickens just pecked at his ankles until Porter moved out of their way!

Admittedly most of the chickens were safely contained in a crate, only a couple had got loose. Porter made the mistake of trying to help put them back, only to be told those two chickens didn't belong in the crate. What had given him that idiotic notion!? Who would have been stupid enough to try and bring a whole crate of chickens onto the bus? The crate belonged to the truck driver!

The goats were only meant to be going halfway to the next village. Porter was fascinated. So, what happened in between one village and the next? He'd just assumed it was all jungle.

"Nothing is all jungle!" he was told, by the same man who'd informed him of the ownership of the chickens.

"Nothing is not-market," seemed to be equally true.

That was information Porter could work with. That was intelligence! Roadside traders, truck-back trading? Oh yes, Porter knew how to do that.

Most of the current occupants in the back of the truck seemed to be going further. That gave Porter at least a couple of hours to get the lie-of-the-land, at least as far as the back of the truck was concerned.

They were coming up to another pick-up drop-off point by the looks of it. Porter could already see a couple of locals waiting by the roadside. They didn't appear to be carrying anything, which meant they were likely plantation workers. Porter wondered if they might have heard of Padre anywhere in the vicinity.

He was so engrossed in his enquiries, Porter almost stumbled again when the truck caught the next rut. He hadn't asked anything about the trading conditions, or what the market was like on the roadside. All he'd asked about so far was whose were the chickens and if anyone had seen Padre.

"What about when no-market no-jungle, the villages?" Porter asked the only man who seemed to have noticed he was asking questions.

"What about the villages?" the man asked him back.

Good question. What exactly was Porter trying to ask?

"Padre?" he explained, clumsily, not sure how much information to offer. "Padre?" he repeated, gesturing to his collar and drawing a cross on an imaginary bag.

"Visiting? Mending-medicine?" He could hear himself starting to sound a little desperate by then.

The look on the local's face was slightly bemused, apparently waiting for the jabbering idiot to make more of an idiot of himself before they stopped again. Always nice to have a little amusement on the journey in to work.

Porter had learnt something useful about laughter a long time ago. If you can get someone to laugh at you, they no longer see you as a threat. Unfortunately, the man couldn't help with Padre's whereabouts, but seemed to know a lot about goats!

Porter was starting to wonder if it mightn't have been quicker by boat, then shrugged the thought aside. He still didn't know which village to head for. At least going by truck, someone from one of the villages would surely know something, eventually. He just needed to keep on asking.

Porter's thoughts had been wandering even before he'd got the message from Padre. He'd been thinking about going home.

Porter wasn't trying to run away, he just wanted to be able to get home. But to do that he needed some real money, not just living expenses and free meals. Porter had even considered doing a payroll job on the plantation office. He didn't like the idea. It didn't feel right. None of his old-ways felt right anymore.

That was Padre's influence, and now Porter was on his way to rescue Padre. It simply felt right. Porter couldn't explain it any other way. He simply needed to do the 'right' thing now.

He'd done enough dodgy jobs in his time, but, truth-be-told, Porter had discovered he rather liked the way it felt walking into a café with the owner welcoming him with a cup of coffee and congratulating him for the work he'd done. It had felt strange the first time, now it just felt right, and Porter liked the way that felt!

Standing in the back of that plantation truck, trying to find Padre, Porter realised there was only one way he was going to get home and it had to be the right way.

Porter had been kept busy, mostly between errands from camp to some watch- and clock-repairs in town. He'd even been able to get a regular deal set up between the river-traders and one of the station porters. After a week or so of that arrangement, Porter realised they thought he was the same as them, something between a trader and a porter.

As far as Porter could tell, that's what most everyone was around these parts, in some way: porter and trader. The plantation workers, the book-sellers, even the chicken-keepers. The funny thing was, and this was abso-ruddy-hilarious, Porter found he liked the way it worked!

It had started with that sack-barrow and Cookie's store room. Crikey! How long ago was that? Weeks? Months? Years even? It might as well be, to Porter's reckoning!

He'd found himself rather enjoying the sensation of being able to sit somewhere in the open and relax. Not constantly looking out for someone looking for him! His ears had become accustomed to the sounds of their language. He'd been able to read most of the facial expressions from day one, the words took only a little longer.

Porter had always had good hearing. He knew how to keep quiet, without seeming to. He recalled an incident now. It had happened just a day or so ago when someone had been saying something they obviously didn't want to be heard beyond their own café table and Porter's ears had started tingling. 'Something wrong here' his ears had told him. He'd quickly recognised the words for 'plantation' and the whisperers didn't sound like they were grumbling about work-load. The mention of 'payment' sounded off too. If he'd heard it right, and Porter trusted his tingling ears, they were intending to hit the plantation, but not for the money. Then what was their reason? A target?

The café owner had interrupted Porter's ear-wigging momentarily with some more coffee. Porter took the hint and spoke loudly, thanking the owner with clumsy words and a terrible accent.

He caught the surprised expression of the owner and feigned a headache in mitigation for his rudeness. The owner laughed at him for drinking with the Australians. That should do it. The owner left him to his coffee and Porter tried to find out more.

The occupants at the next table had almost forgotten about Porter being there, until the café owner had come by. They were obviously in a hurry and that made Porter even more nervous. The last bit of conversation he'd caught before they left was enough to make him think he'd made a mistake! It wasn't 'plantation' they were talking about, it was 'plantation owner', something about his car, his personal car.

The truck hit another rut and the sudden lurch yanked Porter back to his senses. The plantation owner's car wasn't his business. Right now, his business was finding Padre!

Somewhere between the mission house and the plantation there were rivers and villages and roads and jungle and, somewhere there, Padre was doing his good works-visiting. Porter didn't have a clue on the 'where' except for the message about 'visiting a river-village'.

Whatever those café table plotters were whispering about, it would happen on the road, somewhere between the owner's town house and his plantation. That wasn't Porter's business. But that particular detail meant this was not a safe road to be on right now … and Padre was on it, somewhere!

CHAPTER 8

BOTHER AND BUS STOPS

JOHN

He'd only just got back to camp the day before. They'd managed to find the truck. It had only been waiting a half day.

Sarg got their 'intelligence' report first, whilst the officer got what he asked for: distance, direction and description only.

"Two days out, one path, more than one truck, recent and regular use. The tracks suggest the trucks are following the river, but not using the main local routes. Criss-crossing at intervals, where seasonal flood water could easily obscure their record."

It didn't sound particularly helpful, but with the general sense of distance and direction it was more than the officer had before their patrol. So he could add that to his maps!

Sarg was just glad they'd been able to find anything. After the reporting-in was all done, the Lads needed a shower and a change of clothes. That took most of them at least an hour.

The truck back to camp had given them time to loosen their limbs and shake the jungle out from the heads, mostly. They'd needed to get the talking over and done with, then hit the showers. Kit to one side. Just stand there and let the water wash off what was left on them, peeling off the layers of the past few days.

After that, fresh clothes. Then they were looking for the mess tent, a cold drink, then hot tea. It had to be that way round. None of them could explain why, but it had to be that way. Then the cigarettes. Whilst they could stay awake, until they couldn't. Then they could crash out on their bunks.

When they woke, they were ready to return to the mess tent again. John was glad to see Cookie. He'd heard someone talking about Padre coming into camp with some medical books. He was thinking about going into town to the book stall and checking in on Padre.

John was halfway through a massive breakfast when he noticed Cookie loitering by the door. That was telling.

"Come on, what's up?"

John knew Cookie wasn't a man to loiter without good reason. Normally he skulked, did a bit of slapdash sullen ladling and offered a running-grumble when he came round clearing the tables, invariably closely followed by some annoyed clattering at the sink in the back room.

John hadn't noticed it yesterday, but now he was awake.

"What's wrong? Porter? What's he got himself into now?"

Cookie laughed. Yes, they both knew Porter. He could take care of himself. Even so, it wasn't like Cookie to loiter.

John waited till he had another mug of tea, then walked outside with Cookie. "Come on, let's have it, what's wrong?"

For once, it seemed Porter wasn't the problem, the message Cookie had got with yesterday's delivery of market vegetables was: "Padre's gone fishin!"

"Don't be daft, Padre don't fish." John was about to call Cookie 'stupid'. His hesitation was well-timed. Cookie hadn't finished.

"Fishin-errand. Visiting river-village. Market-message for mending-bag."

Ah, that made more sense. Now John could understand what Padre was doing … and he wasn't happy about it! John knew about the various village peoples. They were friendly, mostly. The initial message sounded like Porter had accompanied Padre on the fishing boat.

Cookie couldn't be clear on that though. From what he'd heard they hadn't actually gone together, a day apart maybe, maybe two, maybe in the same direction!

"Right." John's jaw tightened, as he chewed over that detail.

Cookie gave him cigarettes for Porter. Neither man was going to admit to being worried. There was no point. Cookie couldn't leave and John could.

"Does Sarg know this? Any of it?"

Cookie indicated he hadn't told Sarg. John hadn't expected him to, but that didn't answer the question! Considering the timelapse since anyone had seen Padre, John needed to be straight with Sarg.

"Any chance of me taking one of the trucks into town, Sarg? Need to check up on Padre."

Sarg was interested, he liked the way Padre handled the young officers and the way he talked with the Lads, too. Sarg would've been happier if Padre had stayed on camp and John's tone wasn't making him feel any easier!

But Sarg couldn't tell him much more than he already knew. Padre had gone with his first-aid satchel and a backpack, visiting one of the river villages by fishing boat. The truck wasn't going to be able to reach most of the river villages, but the road would take John a fair way there.

"Come on Sarg, you know I need more than that. You tell me to go 'fetch' Padre and I can get a whole lot further than if I'm just 'looking for him.'"

Sarg knew what John was asking. It wasn't difficult, a couple of bits of paper to get through town and onto the road quicker.

John got himself ready, whilst Sarg cleared it through official channels. Less than an hour later they were both back at the gate.

John could use the truck or the paperwork to deal with any queries he might encounter, and if the paperwork didn't work, John had other options at his disposal. That wasn't on the paperwork, but Sarg could see John was ready. By then neither man was in the mood for stupid questions!

No one blamed Padre for getting himself lost.

The last thing Sarg said to John was simply, "OK?" John nodded, responding with a, "Thanks Sarg," and with that the mission was fully briefed and approved!

First stop would be Pops at the mission house.

Pops couldn't tell John much that he didn't already know, except John would likely find Porter already on the tail of Padre's visiting. John couldn't decide if that was a good thing or not! How Pops knew that much wasn't clear either. Something to do with one of the plantation trucks heading out of town earlier. John knew his truck could make better time. He could also guess Porter had no clearer idea which village Padre was visiting than he did.

"Idiot."

John didn't say much after that and didn't stay long with Pops, but before he left he made sure one thing was understood.

"I'll be bringing Padre back."

Going down to the boat moorings proved helpful. Although Padre's boat had not returned yet, there were sightings of Padre in at least a couple of the river villages coming in with the 'catches and trades' by then. That gave John an approximate timeline and location. He could work it out from there.

The plantation road was still his best bet.

Setting out from town the first few miles were good wide road with plenty of traffic. It wouldn't stay that easy, but at least John could see what was coming, making up some time between himself, Porter and Padre. A couple of bicycle traders proved useful, too. He used Cookie's cigarettes for the information. John learnt Padre was well and making himself useful.

John was looking forward to learning how Padre had managed to persuade the fishermen to take him up to the river villages. At least most of the river villages had bicycles. He was starting to feel a little more hopeful.

"Should have brought Daks with me!"

It would have been useful having a navigator beside him, as the town road met up with the plantation road after a couple of hours and the conditions got rougher by the yard!

John was stopping at each cross-ruts, where the village paths came to meet the plantation road, checking in with any locals there.

This would be the only route open to Padre now, a bicycle from the village back up onto the town road, if he was lucky. Or a walk up with the plantation workers to the cross-ruts and wait for the next truck.

And that was where John found him. A few more hours down the road looking a little tired but remarkably cheerful, considering. Padre had somehow managed to get himself a little stool and was sitting there with his bags at his feet.

"Afternoon Padre. You miss the bus? No bicycle today?"

Padre heard those words that seemed to come to his thoughts from a world away. Looking up he saw the grinning John, leaning causally out from his cab window with his hand over to help Padre to his feet.

"Come on Padre, let's get you home. You've got Pops worried. And you know he never makes chicken soup as good as you. As for the poor café owners, they're in a right old flap! They've got your favourite biscuits waiting and you're not there!"

"Ah John!" Padre sighed. He knew he'd been an idiot.

John drove in silence for another mile or so as Padre began

telling him about his visit.

"No one is saying you shouldn't go visiting, Padre. Only to be expected. Just next time you get the call, could you maybe wait until one of us can give you a lift?"

John sighed with relief, right alongside Padre.

"I mean, really!? You could have come to camp. We'd have taken you all the way there and back. You know that, don't you?"

Padre did. He'd just got swept up in the opportunity of the fishermen heading in the right direction.

"You even got Sarg asking question about you!"

"Oh dear! Oh, poor fellow!"

Padre looked so concerned, John had to laugh.

"You were really just going to sit there and wait for the next bus to come by?" Then something else struck John. "Did you even know which way you were heading?"

Padre had to admit he might have got a bit turned around. He'd walked from the village with some of the workers, but they'd had bicycles for the road. If he'd got the next truck heading up to the plantation, at least he'd have been able to get a lift back from there. It sounded vague and far more dangerous than John suspected Padre realised.

There was no room to turn the truck round where they were, so John was going to have to take them nearer to the plantation where the road started widening. They hadn't quite got that far when Padre suddenly noticed Porter peddling towards them.

"Good Lord!" Padre exclaimed. John slammed on the brakes and Porter's bicycle tripped over a rut before swerving off to the side of the road.

"How the heck did you manage to get that far ahead of us?" John called down from the cab.

Porter looked up and beamed. "Got the bus, didn't I?"

"And the bicycle?" John queried.

"Ah well, it was like this. I missed Padre, so I was expecting him at one of the stops on the way over this way, but he wasn't, so I started back."

John realised that didn't actually answer the question of where the bicycle had come from.

"You took the truck-bus all the way from town to the plantation, just to find Padre?"

John wasn't convinced and waited for the rest.

Porter took a breath and admitted. "Not entirely, actually …"

That was enough for John. "At the plantation?"

"Bit of bother brewing, maybe." Porter was getting to the point.

John sensed it too. "Bother brewing, hey? How much of a 'bit'?"

"Rather a lot, I think."

"OK." John needed to be clear. "Am I trying to stop it? Or start it!?"

"I think we can stop it. I think I've managed to get ahead of them and bring you back a bit of help."

John hadn't expected *that* development.

"What sort of help?" John couldn't help but sound dubious and was already checking over Porter's shoulder for anyone coming.

"Intelligence," Porter offered, in case there was any confusion, before continuing. "Plantation owner is due back from town business. Now you know."

John was listening.

"That puts us ahead, by my reckoning," Porter offered.

"It does, does it?" John asked steadily. "And that's your business, why?"

"It *wasn't* my business!" Porter agreed. "But seeing as how they were talking so loud in the café, that I couldn't help but get in the way of it, what else could I do? You'd have done the same thing, wouldn't you?" he pleaded across to Padre.

"Right." John had made a decision. "Give me the rest." He didn't want Padre involved but had the uncomfortable feeling it was too late for that!

Porter told them more about what he'd heard back at the café and what he'd learnt about the plantation owner's driving habits! Porter also had intelligence on the likely path the wrong-uns would be taking to avoid the locals. He checked his watch, tapping it, before presenting his wrist up for John's inspection. "See, told ya. We haven't got much time."

John nodded to Porter before turning to Padre. "I think that drive home is going to have to wait. Bit of a detour first."

Whilst they had time, John asked Porter for some more details about the boat bringing the ambush party to the jungle path. They were intending to get onto the plantation road from there, before the plantation owner's car came past, and lay in wait.

"We ought to get you away from this, Padre."

Padre smiled and patted John's shoulder, shaking his head slowly, as all three men took a clearer look at their situation. "I don't think so."

"You sure they're not going to hit the house?" John checked back to Porter, but he was adamant it was the plantation owner and his car they were going for. "Makes sense, too many men at the plantation," John reasoned after a moment's more thought. "If they can stop the car on the road around here…?"

There was something about the way Porter had described the plan of the ambush, giving John cause to look at him sideways, "From one who knows?" he wondered.

Porter looked to Padre, then to John. He'd obviously been doing some thinking of his own. "Not anymore. I just want to get home. The right way."

"Good enough." John took him at his word.

Checking his watch, he said, "I need you both to help me delay them. Padre, have you got enough puff to get that bicycle back to your village friends? Tell them a truck's gone into the ditch. We'll need all of them to get it out, and do your best to get them to hurry-it-up, will you?"

"Right-ho!" Padre took the bicycle without a moment's hesitation.

John had the distinct impression Padre was more game for this bit of bother, than Porter had anticipated!

"Porter, you're the runner. Back to the plantation house. I'll tell you what to say. Then you can tell them I've sent you, OK?" John paused for a split second, before checking, "The right way. OK?"

"Good enough," Porter agreed, waiting for John to scribble the note, before turning on his heels.

"Get them to send up an escort car. Armed, but not obvious. They'll know what to do," John told him.

Before Padre started peddling, and just because he was curious, he asked, "What's *your part* of the plan, John?"

"Me? Oh, I'm going to drive the truck into the ditch!"

John chuckled softly at the stunned expression on the other two men's faces.

"Then I'm going to wait." Padre and Porter were waiting too … for John to go into a little more detail on the plan.

It was simple enough. "With any luck your friends from the village will show up, Padre, and make such a noise recovering the truck it'll take the wind out of those 'unfriendlies' Porter overheard, at least for tonight."

Their bewildered expressions were starting to lighten into comprehension, as John continued. "With the message I'm sending with Porter back to the plantation they'll get to the owner's car in plenty of time and divert it off the main road. And they'll be ready up at the house by the time the owner gets there, just in case those 'unfriendlies' try re-thinking their plans."

Now both Padre and Porter were nodding steadily.

"No one will question Porter on how he got the intelligence, or what he was doing this way, because I've sent him. No one will question you, Padre, because all you've done is told the truth. There *is* a truck in the ditch!"

"The only problem I'll have after that," John recognised with a shrug, "is hoping your lot can help me get the ruddy truck back out the ditch again! Then we'll need to get it back to camp … somehow. And I'm relying on the both of you to back me up with Sarg! 'Cos otherwise, I'm going to have an awful lot of explaining to do!'"

Porter's legs and John's note worked up at the plantation. They mobilised the house, half at the ready around the perimeter of the grounds, half out in the rest of the fleet of cars to bring the owner back in safely.

Whilst Padre's cycle legs were perhaps not quite as fast as Porter's, and the bicycle wheels tended to skip alarmingly over the ruts, but he soon found the route back to the village. Padre's return there was unexpected, but the message he brought prompted immediate action … with all the enthusiasm and commotion John had hoped for!

The villagers quickly declared it 'safer' to carry the Padre's bicycle back with them, whilst the cleric trotted merrily behind, feeling absolutely confident everything would be 'quite right' soon.

No one actually saw the 'wrong-uns' that evening, although they'd been heard sure enough. The trackers from the river-village would surely find evidence of their scuppered plan in the abandoned boat, come morning.

In the meantime, the villagers proved to be highly skilled with their ropes, and Sarg's truck got duly hauled out of the ditch … with plenty of heaving and hollering!

John's idea was to make the 'accident' and subsequent recovery so obvious as to not rouse any suspicions amongst the 'wrong-uns' that their plan had been rumbled. He was hoping they'd just feel thwarted and skulk off somewhere to stay low awhile.

If the 'wrong-uns' tried a plan-B up at the house, they'd find the owner at the ready behind some formidable defences with the perimeter being double-patrolled and with very visible armed guards at strategic locations.

"Pretty damn impressive convoy. Like one of those royal cavalcades!" Porter described with a satisfied grin, as he joined John back in the truck.

The truck was looking a little worse-for-wear, but John seemed optimistic they'd be able to limp it back into camp. "I'll sort it out at the garage. Daks will probably be waiting for me by now."

"Sarg'll likely be waiting for you, too!" Porter reminded him.

"Yeah, maybe. But he'll be pleased to see you two," John reminded Padre and Porter, as they sat together in the cab on the way back listening to the noises from the road and the truck and trying not to listen to the thoughts going through their heads.

"What do you think they'll do?" Padre was the first to ask.

"If they think they've just lost the opportunity, I'm hoping they'll relax back into the shadows for a while," John tried to sound confident. "If they think it was simply down to poor-timing and that otherwise their plan was sound they'll keep talking about it, I'm hoping. That way we'll be able to listen out for them, won't we?" he asked Porter, pointedly.

It took them longer on the return journey back to camp than John's earlier outward brisk pace, with a fully fit truck. There wasn't a lot of talking in the interim.

It was pitch dark and past midnight by the time they saw the lights of the camp ahead of them. John pulled up and waited for the inevitable.

The Lads at the gate had woken Sarg who came charging at

the truck. He'd started shouting and was already halfway through a second stretch of expletives before he realised John wasn't on his own in the cab.

Then it got serious.

Sarg opened the door for Padre, who climbed down.

The Lads recognised who the passenger was and called for the officer, by which time it seemed like most of the camp had woken up. Cookie was already screeching. Something about losing his sack-barrow! Daks was cackling so loud they could hear him from the garage to the gate.

One of the medical staff had the presence of mind to bring Padre a cup of tea. Padre accepted it and immediately began looking for somewhere to sit. This prompted a further fluster from one of the young officers who came dashing out with a torch in one hand and bringing his own chair in the other.

"Sorry Padre, we weren't ready for you."

Padre recognised the officer and thanked him, perfectly politely. Then proceeded to sit down, back straight, head up, hands in lap, calmly resting the strap from his satchel on the back of the chair.

"Oh, how kind of you! I don't suppose you have some biscuits, do you? Rather peckish, you know?"

Porter didn't want a cup of tea. He was way past that! But he did have the presence of mind to take charge of Cookie. "Come on, let's see where you put that sack-barrow? You know you keep losing it in the store room. I have a system, you know, and the system is start by not losing the sack-barrow!"

Cookie's screeching had subsided by the time Porter had steered him back towards the kitchen where there might be something to drink a good deal stronger than a cup of Padre's tea.

Padre, in the meantime, had been presented with the officer's personal biscuit tin. He looked up at the officer and smiled, murmuring a grateful, "Much better," to the young man. Then with a clearer voice, admiring the illustration on the top of the tin, he remarked, "Oh how charming! Reminds me of home."

The officer got the clerk to bring out another chair from the office for himself and sat together with Padre, enjoying their tea and biscuits and talking about the various county fairs they'd attended in their youth. In the middle of the night, sipping tea by the gate of the camp in the middle of the jungle, neither man batted an eyelid. It was perfectly civilised, as far as the officer and Padre were concerned.

They weren't going to discuss the matter of the truck until Sarg had calmed down and was ready to listen to John's side of the story and Sarg didn't seem quite ready to listen yet! He'd got John cornered between the side of the truck and the gate.

"What on earth have you been doing with this truck?"

John knew better than to try and answer that one!

The officer didn't know what all the bother was about. As far as he was concerned, Sarg had sent John out to 'fetch Padre' … and that's exactly what John had done! The state of the truck was irrelevant. Especially as it would undoubtedly be John taking the truck back to the garage to work on … just as soon as Sarg had finished shouting at him!

Sarg was still shouting when the clerk came back out from the office again.

"Telephone call."

The officer hopped off his chair. "Now? At this time of night?"

Padre took his cup of tea to hold it whilst the officer got up to take the call.

The clerk had to stand in his way.

"No Sir, not for you, Sir. He's asking for John."

Sarg spluttered to a halt and glared at John. John grinned, taking a guess at who it might be.

"Think you'd better take that one for me, Sarg. They'll likely be able to explain better than me."

Padre took the hint, no one else seemed to be ready to.

"Sargeant, I *strongly* suggest you take that call. If, that is, you want a comprehensive report on the events on this evening."

Sarg stormed in and grabbed at the telephone. There was silence for a fraction of a moment. Then a "WHAAAT!?" before a hasty, "Beg pardon, Sir, but what did you say?" A pause, then a slightly unsteady, "HE DID WHAT?" Then an even more hesitant, "*AND THE PADRE!?*"

There was a lot of muffled spluttering and a bit of a coughing fit of expletives, then a remarkably loud silence!

John hadn't moved. He hadn't stopped grinning either. Looking over to Padre he asked, "Got another cuppa going over there, Padre? I'm gaspin."

The clerk took the hint and went to fetch another cup of tea.

By the time Sarg emerged, the sequence of events that had brought John back with Padre and Porter, with the truck in the state it was, seemed to have been thoroughly explained. Certainly, to the officer's satisfaction. Sarg, however, looked like he could do with a few more answers, but decided not yet.

"You alright?" the officer came back to John and Padre.

Padre had already been able to assure the bright young man he was "Comfortable thank you." The officer was directing the question to John this time.

"Nothing we couldn't sort out, Sir," John assured him.

Sarg had got one of the Lads to take the truck over to the garage, with the officer's approval, ignoring John for the time being.

"Sorry, Padre. Looks like you're staying here tonight."

The officer had already got the bleary-eyed clerk to get something organised.

Sarg returned his attention to John.

"Get yourself cleaned up, something to eat and some sleep, you're up early tomorrow. Market day remember. They'll be needing you and whilst you're at it, make sure Porter's fit, too."

"OK, Sarg."

John turned and started walking. Nothing more to be said. He was too tired to think of anything else to say anyway. Clean. Eat. Sleep. Yep, John thought, as he trudged over to the showers. That sounded good to him. As for the early start. Well, it didn't sound like he'd get a chance to start on the ditch-dunked truck for another day. It would be stinking by then. He was laughing by the time he'd reached the showers, thinking of what Daks would make of it!

He caught up with Porter over at the mess tent, Cookie had let him get on with prepping his own food in the kitchen.

"Crikey, he must be trusting you something special. He doesn't let any of the *other* Lads get in there."

Being referred to by John like that, as one of 'the Lads', made Porter feel even more clear about getting home the 'right way'. He was the first to admit he hadn't exactly got out there the 'right way', but he'd done his best, barring a few hiccups, since then!

They sat down at one of the tables together. There wasn't more than three hours before day, but at least the coffee was strong and hot. John didn't ask what Porter had slugged into it. It tasted sweet and smooth and potent and that was all he needed to know. The food was damned welcome too.

"Where've you been hiding that bacon?"

"I wasn't hiding it, just packed a few supplies in front of it. There wasn't enough for everyone anyway and I only used six rashers between us!"

Porter had taken a loaf and split in lengthways and layered on the well-griddled rashers with some brown sauce.

"Got that from the Australians, doesn't taste the same as ours, but it's edible!"

"Edible sounds good enough to me," agreed John and took his half of the doorstep sandwich in both hands.

Neither man had realised how ravenous they were until they started eating.

"I hope they're feeding Padre? Do you think we ought to have invited him over?"

John finished chewing before answering. "Can't!"

"Why not?" Porter asked as he drained the mug and the last of the liquor that had settled down the bottom, eyeing up a second pot.

"None left!" John laughed. "But I bet there's more coffee where that one came from?"

Porter managed halfway down the refill, then stayed at the table resting his head down into his arms and fell asleep.

John left him there. He just about managed to get back to his bunk, kicking off his boots, dropping his pack on the floor and fell onto the bed. He'd shut his eyes before his head found it.

Then someone was shaking him awake, yelling at him. John almost grabbed the collar of the idiot and yelled right back at him, about it being dark and he'd only just got to bed. Only it wasn't dark. John's eyes were blinking in the sunlight, and he could already feel the heat of the day.

It was four hours later, and it might have been Sarg yelling at him again, except he wasn't! John just had a thumping headache. What the heck had Porter put in that damned coffee!?

"Hey Sarg, can you turn that volume down just a tad," John pleaded.

Sarg took a step back and waited for John to roll off the bed.

"You've got half an hour. Get yourself ready and at the gate."

John staggered to his feet, none too steadily. "Ready for what, Sarg?"

Sarg waited, there was the hint of a smirk on his face. "Go on then," he indicated for John to 'grab yer gear'. "It was *your* idea!"

John still hadn't a clue what Sarg was going on about but picked up his pack. "What was my idea, Sarg? Yesterday? I thought we'd all got back. Someone was drinking tea and saying 'well done' weren't they?"

Sarg left and John was still trying to work out what that 'idea' had been, when Porter came stumbling past. "Good coffee last night!?" Porter wasn't sure if John was asking or telling. "What was that all about, with Sarg?"

John shoved Porter ahead of him. "For Gawd sake have a shower. I don't know where you've been, but you stink!" He chucked the soap and towel over.

John went through his kit. He knew the essentials and was starting to remember *why* they weren't finished yet.

"Where did the rope come from?" John asked, as they both washed and started thinking about fresh clothes. Porter still didn't have an official locker, but there were a couple of spare lockers over at the garage. The only problem with going over to the garage meant they would be running the gauntlet of Daks' wrath, for leaving him with the ditch-stinking wretched truck! John would have been happy to explain why he wasn't working beside Daks in the garage today but couldn't remember that part of yesterday's plan. Solution: ask Daks to come with them! They could work it out on the way over to the gate. Sorted!

Daks was happy with that. Even happier with the mug of coffee Porter offered him. John declined.

"I think I'll stick with the tea, I've a feeling I'll need a clear head for what's coming."

Padre was waiting for them. Looking as fresh as a daisy.

"Clean living?" Porter teased him.

"Avoiding your coffee," was John's shrewd suggestion.

The officer had got them a lift in one of the Australian cars into town. "Less obvious," he explained cryptically.

John was still desperately trying to get a hint of what they all seemed to think he'd got planned. He still hadn't got the foggiest!

The Australians would drop them off just outside town. No one seemed to be talking about how they were going to get back to camp. John was wondering about that, but more worried about the bit-before that. And Sarg knew all about it!?

The Australian car was nice, plenty of room. John was just pleased he wasn't expected to do any talking about the 'plan' on the way in, and by the time they'd got to the edge of town his headache was easing.

"First stop the mission house. I must let Pops know we're all back and in one piece."

"You do your reporting Padre, I'll find the plantation blokes," Porter agreed, helpfully. "They told me which café, so I'm guessing they should be there by now and once I know they're in position we can get started."

"Ahhh! That's it!" Finally, John remembered.

Porter and the plantation car 'heist': they'd managed to stop the ambush, that was why the truck was in the state it was, but they hadn't caught up with those responsible, but Porter had heard them plotting at the café on market day. Now John had it.

"We're rounding up the culprits, then?" John checked he'd got the 'plan' straight with Padre, who was already returning from checking in with Pops. Everything seemed tickety-boo at the mission house, apparently the chicken soup went down well.

The café was 'at the ready' too, according to Porter, coming back with a thumbs up. "All we have to do is give them the signal if we recognise anyone," Porter confidently informed his fellows.

"How the heck are we meant to do that? You're the only one who saw any of them in the café," John asked the obvious.

Padre stepped in. "Porter saw a couple of them, but I'm sure I overheard a bit of corner-talking before they got bold enough to discuss it in the café. I'd recognise the female's voice again and you said we only needed to find one of them, John? Well, if we can get three of them then the plantation blokes will soon find out who else was involved."

It took as long as the walk from the front door of the mission house back into the market place for Porter to decide his 'bit'. If he thought he recognised any of the culprits, he'd ask them the time. If they hadn't got a watch, then he'd offer to sell them one, that wouldn't raise any suspicions.

John and Daks would be on the lookout. So too, would the plantation blokes. "That should be enough, don't you think?" Porter checked.

"I hope so," John mumbled and sent Daks as back up for Porter. John would follow Padre, which was less obvious as both men were known locally for visiting the book stall. They were both regulars to that area of the market and John wasn't convinced how well the plantation blokes could see from where they were sitting in the café.

Padre was still certain he'd be able to recognise the female voice he'd overheard by the book stall corner, and was convinced she would be there again to find out what had gone wrong.

"If you hear her voice, just try and recommend a book to me. That'll be all I need to know to signal over to the plantation blokes. That way you're not getting stuck in the middle of this, Padre. It's ok for me and Porter to get a bit sticky, but not you."

They noticed the plantation blokes had already split up and were now seated at cafés in different quadrants of the market place.

John walked alongside Padre, who clutched a little tighter to his satchel. "Just stick with me Padre and no one will know you had anything to do with it."

Porter's men were found first. They'd reacted to the abandonment of their original plan, just as John had thought they might, finding the same local café, they sat themselves down and started arguing loudly about who amongst their team was to blame. One was sure it had been an inside job, the other seemed convinced they just picked the wrong day.

Porter was able to amble over and look as if he was half hungover, a fair approximation of what John had felt a couple of hours earlier. He ordered a coffee from the café owner who knew him well, and started joking about the 'last night's brew.'

This all helped set up the clumsy seating arrangement, as Porter shambled into position, before seating himself heavily, almost falling off the chair. Then, lumbering into a lean across to the plotters, he asked them if they had the right time, tapping his watch, as if he wasn't sure it was telling him right, and holding his head as if the ticking of it was a set of hammers.

They laughed at him and teased Porter, in the same vein as the café owner. They couldn't help with the time but sympathised about the hangover. Porter made an offer to sell them his own watch, assuring them it was a bit slow, but otherwise reliable.

They declined and Porter thanked them for their sympathy, declaring the coffee helped but he'd need to walk off the rest of the thunder between his ears, staggering out of the café as a pair of plantation blokes strode in.

Whilst John silently browsed, Padre was more than happy for the book seller to recommend a few of the 'new' titles to him. The corner behind the book stall was quite regularly occupied, but John wasn't sure how much Padre could overhear with the book seller doing so much 'recommending', until Padre suddenly thanked the seller and turned to John.

"Oh yes, that sounds excellent. You ought to try this book."

With Padre and the seller occupied with deliberations on the price of that particular item, John was able to give a discrete signal to the plantation blokes in the café to one side of the corner.

John stayed put, whilst the scuffle happened, his body shielding the two men at the stall from the brief flare-up. Then calmly guiding Padre's trembling elbow, he helped to lift his book bag back up onto his shoulder.

"Come on, let's see how Pops is doing at the mission house."

"Did we get everything done?" Padre enquired, in a whisper that quivered a little at the end as Porter joined them at the next turn.

John didn't pause at the question. Nor turn to acknowledge Porter's presence. His eyes remained forward, as both men now continued to steer Padre clear of the fracas at a steady pace.

John answered out the side of his mouth. "Oh, I think we did well, Padre. Excellent book choice by the way!"

Pops was waiting for them at the front door. He'd had visitors, too.

"Delivery?" Padre queried, "I wasn't expecting anything?"

Pops couldn't tell him what the delivery was. He would need to show him. Guiding both men grandly through to the kitchen, he gestured to where a new stove of gleaming white enamel with polished metalwork stood.

"Chicken soup," Pops announced.

"Good Lord!" Padre exclaimed.

"Where did that come from?" Porter wondered.

John could guess. They all could. "Seems like that plantation owner found just the thing to say 'thank you', Padre. Perfick ain't it?"

"Oh, it's wonderful. My very own stove!" Padre stepped closer to inspect it, genuinely touched and humbled that anyone would recognise how vital his chicken soup services were.

"You sit down, I'll make us a cuppa," Porter offered to the emotional Padre.

Pops hadn't finished. "Oh no! No! More for you!" He was dragging Porter outside to the kitchen yard. "For you, from plantation."

There in the yard was a brand new motorbike.

"For me?" Porter couldn't believe his eyes. Looking back to Pops he asked, "Really, for me? Really?"

John gave him the thumbs up. "Looks like it!"

"What about you, John?" Padre queried, reluctantly stepping away from his beloved stove as the tea was poured into the waiting cups. "The plantation owner really owes his neck to you."

"Well, he did call the camp last night, didn't he, and put Sarg in the picture. That pretty much saved my neck! So, I guess we're quits on that front. Don't need anything more than that."

Padre and Pops had a lot to be getting on with, restocking the first-aid satchel, sorting through the rest of that crate of books and getting the chicken soup ready for evening services.

Porter wanted to get out on his new motorbike.

"Need to get the feel of it. You don't mind? You can get back to camp, can't you?"

John nodded. He hadn't decided quite how he was going to get back to camp yet, but actually wasn't intending to go directly back that way. He had an errand of his own first.

He walked back into the market place. The plantation blokes seemed to have disappeared, the cafés were going about their business as usual, so too the stall holders and tray-traders.

There were calls from some of the locals to let John know they were glad to see Padre had got back safe from his recent visiting. The last time they'd seen him he'd been setting out on one of the fishing boats.

A couple of the river-village people had returned to market with their own trading to do. They also seemed more than happy to tell anyone who wanted to listen how helpful the town Padre had been with his mending-bag!

John was glad to see them. He was hoping when they were ready he could travel back with them on the truck-bus. He'd got a notion about building them a slightly more substantial bus stop.

The two river-village traders had come on bicycles. John waited with them until their trading was done. By then one of the plantation trucks appeared to be heading out. John mistook it for the regular working truck-bus.

"We can load your bikes in the back and have enough daylight to start on that shelter," he suggested.

But the traders seemed surprised to see the truck. Far too new for a plantation work truck! John stepped forward and pushed both traders behind him, slowing his approach to the truck, a hand on his side-arm. He knocked on the cab door. No response. He couldn't see anyone in the cab from there, but they might have ducked down.

This time he thumped on the truck door, yelling up to the cab, "Anyone asleep in there?"

John's voice sounded sharp. There was menace is his movement, as he turned his body to grab the handle of the cab door, avoiding a direct line of fire from whoever was hiding in there.

The two traders stayed back with their bicycles, behind John.

Suddenly a little head popped up at the window of the cab.

"Daks!? How the ruddy-heck did you get there?"

Daks was cackling and jabbering furiously. And whatever he was saying seemed to include the two villagers, who gleefully joined in.

"Where did you get to in the market?" John started to ask, as Daks clambered down. "One of the Australian trucks?" he checked. "Plantation truck?" His second guess seemed more likely, but Daks was quite clear with a 'no' to that, too.

"OK, I give up! Where d'you get the truck from? Who was crazy enough to give you the keys?"

Daks positively relished the opportunity to confound John, even better if he was asking stupid questions! John went silent. His hands were relaxed, although his head still had a lingering throb to it. Maybe that explained why he felt like a dolt!?

Daks was standing in front of him with the keys to the truck in his hand. Beaming from ear to ear.

Finally, John erupted into a "WHAT??"

Daks handed John the keys. "Idiot! Plantation, 'thank you.'"

John's smile matched Daks at that. Both men were beaming as they climbed up into the cab and beckoned the village-traders to fetch their bicycles into the back. "Let's get over to your stop and see what we can do."

During the next few days, John and more of the Lads from camp, used the new truck regularly, helping in the construction of a more substantial bus-shelter at the roadside, from town to the plantation. The river-villagers were accomplished builders and the truck proved invaluable bringing in heavier supplies.

The bus-shelter looked little more than a glorified hut, but it made a heck of a difference. If anyone came to wait they'd have somewhere to sit and even trade whilst they waited. Any truck using the plantation road would have no excuse for missing the stop anymore.

"Nicely done!" one of the Lads observed, when they were packing up ready to return to camp. John was already waiting for them to load up the last of the tools, looking along the plantation road, considering it for a while ... the past few days and weeks. "Yeah. Turned out alright didn't it."

CHAPTER 9

FERRIES AND FORAGING

JOHN

John spent the next two weeks trying to prove to Sarg the 'old' truck wasn't 'ruddy-well-wrecked'.

Daks was happy as they had to keep taking both trucks out on the road to test how the old one was working, taking the new truck with them in case the old one broke down and needed a tow.

"You wouldn't want us stuck out there again now, would you, Sarg? You saw what happened last time!" John was happy. Two weeks on camp in the garage meant two weeks with no walking.

Porter came by less often since he'd forsaken his sack-barrow for the new motorbike and his trading had started taking him places.

John was steering clear of town, just to let the dust settle, but the Lads brought him regular reports on how well Padre was doing.

One day the office clerk had come over to the garage. That got some of the Lads talking: never a good sign if you've got an office clerk looking for you. He was asking when John was next due over to the mission house. A couple of items had come in for Padre from home, months late, according to the date stamps.

The clerk was in luck.

"Right-ho. I was just thinking this old truck was about due a proper rough-rut off-road test-drive anyway," John informed him.

"Good Grief! I can't even say that, never mind repeat it," the clerk complained.

John chuckled, as he wiped his hands on a rag. "Just tell 'em I'm heading into town and will see Padre gets the parcels. Keep it simple."

John knew he'd have to go over to the office himself to collect them, but was smiling as he tidied his tools away, imaging the clerk attempting to repeat that tongue-twister of a tease.

Taking the truck on a test-drive and delivering Padre's parcels wasn't going to be the problem. It was the second half of the message waiting for John at the office that caught him off guard.

"Whilst you're out that way, pick up the Engineer from the railway station, will you?"

"What happened to his car?" John queried. No one seemed to know. Only that he'd be on the next train coming in.

John wasn't satisfied.

"Why didn't he come back with the Australians, weren't they all working on the same bridge?"

John could imagine the Engineer preferred to see the whole job through to the polishing-off; whilst the Australians tended to get their gear in position, go full-steam ahead, get what they were there to do done, then move on! The fine-tuning they left for those with a little more patience, like the Engineer. That combination actually worked quite well.

The British needed the heavy-machinery and heavy-footed attitude of the Australians to get everything in place, then a few of their own engineers to fine-tune and smooth-down the local hackles ruffled by the Australian's reckless progress!

There were some Canadians and South Africans out that way somewhere, too. But John hadn't been able to keep up with them in recent weeks, only seeing them when one of their flights came in.

"Do we know where the Engineer has been?"

John was trying to figure out how long he'd been on the train and what state he'd be in? The best the office could give him was 'one of the new bridges, over to the west. Not really our region of interest - ports, ferries, cargo ships and islands - Navy business.'

No wonder John had lost track of the fellow he thought, as he and the clerk gazed over to the map of the country.

It was all very well for the Australians, with their quarry lorries and thundering trucks, to sweep out great swathes of road-ways; but when it came to crossing the water-ways they were going to need bridges, they were going to need the British engineers.

That still didn't explain what had happened to the Engineer's car. The office clerk didn't have any paperwork on that. John put a tow-rope in the back of the truck, 'just to be on the safe side'.

At the station the Engineer was glad to see John, who he knew would understand his predicament! It seemed his car had got into some trouble a way back.

"I asked if they were sending you."

John was pleased to hear that. Two weeks between bunk, coffee and axle grease was enough to make him feel slightly clogged up.

"A problem then?" John had already guessed the answer from the greeting.

"I thought you might be ready for a change of scenery," the Engineer offered to navigate.

John was in no hurry to return to base. Padre's parcels had waited two months already, a few more hours weren't going to make any difference.

They drove past town and camp, far from John's regular driving routes. They were way-over-west and onto the ferry road. The old truck handled the road well, just the sort of rough-rut road-test John had been hoping for.

When they eventually arrived, John could see for himself the ferry over to Penang Island was in worse condition than the roads!

"They're hoping to build a bridge here," the Engineer explained his problem. "It's a hell of a project."

John pulled off the road and up to slightly higher ground, where they had a better view of the problem.

"*Your* problem?" John checked. The Engineer nodded.

Together they observed the organised chaos that was the local ferry service.

"What's so important on Penang Island?" John checked.

The Engineer explained that was the port for most of the larger ships coming over from India and Burma. "It's all about the Trading Routes."

John wasn't interested in trade-routes and even less interested in the political scheme-of-things, but if the Engineer had a problem, then John was interested in that.

They stayed up on their perch, studying the ferry workings, whilst the Engineer told John more about himself. He was well educated, well-travelled, and had quite a lot of opinions, but they tended to be more socio-economic than political, as far as John could tell.

"We want to leave this lot in a better position this time. We don't just want to get them out of a sticky situation with the Communist Terrorists wrecking everything, we want to give them a chance to pick themselves up and run with the resources they've got," the Engineer was explaining quite fervently.

"Bigger markets, better transport, that's where my interests lie. If we can get them started for the locals, then they'll be stronger and healthier and won't need help from anyone in the future."

That sounded like a damned good plan, and John said so, before letting the Engineer continue with his ideas.

"Roads and bridges. That's what this is all about. We need to get them right first. Then anyone can get anything anywhere! From the middle of the country out to the ports and onto ships. If they can do that, then they can get to world markets and demand fairer prices for their goods."

John felt almost sad he didn't feel as passionate about the situation and said so.

"Maybe not, but you know how to protect your friends," the Engineer offered a timely reminder. "You fight for the life of the man who's fighting beside you." It was a quote they both recognised.

The ferry boats were ancient, in poor condition and struggling to cope with the number of passengers demanding to use them, never mind the freight that was relying on them. There were only two ferry boats in service between the mainland to the island.

The cargo ships were coming in to the main port on the other side of Penang Island. "Some of them unload part of the cargo there, the rest goes on down to larger ports on the way to Singapore," the Engineer explained. "All I'm interested in are roads and bridges. I'm not trying to make sense of what they're moving. That's the merchants' business."

As they moved down to the waterfront the ferry boats looked in even worse condition from that angle.

"You've got a bottle-neck, haven't you?" John could see the problem.

"We need more ferry boats?" The Engineer queried.

John grinned. "No, you were right. They need a bridge!"

"We need roads to build the bridge though," the Engineer began to explain. John could see that connection too: merchants and markets, trade and politics. John found himself preferring the garage and the jungle!

"I'm very glad to hear that. Men like us need men like *you*, because you're going to be doing the driving for us. And whilst we're working, you're going to be the ones watching our backs."

The two men walked through the masses of traders and travellers arriving to taking the crossing from the mainland to the port of Penang Island. From the looks of some of the traders, they weren't too friendly towards the likes of John. It made the Engineer feel slightly awkward but didn't bother John. "If I'm making them nervous then I know who to watch; makes it easier for me."

The ferry had worked well for generations. The bigger ships had used the port on Penang Island for as long as that, but the traders had become greedy, demanding bigger ships and better profits. The ferries had tried to cope with the trucks, but making room for trucks meant less room for travellers and smaller traders. That meant there was some unpleasantries simmering.

"Not healthy!" both men agreed. Already some rowdy hot spots were developing.

"Do we go in and break those up?" John was already moving forward.

The Engineer held him back. "Not yet. No authority. They'll just think we're trying to take control."

John stepped back beside the Engineer. He was right. John calmed his hands. "OK then, what's the plan?"

"We've got communications in place and a fairly reliable logistics route, the railways are good, but the roads need upgrading from the stations to the port. The Australians are working on the roads."

"They might be bringing their heavies, but we're providing the man-power mostly," John reminded him.

"You've got another advantage over the rest of us coming in," the Engineer told him. "You know the jungle and the locals. We're needing them on our side if we're going to help them."

"Ah! You're talking hearts and minds again, aren't you?"

The Engineer nodded. "Except in this case it's ferry boats and bridges."

"You can get the REME in?" John suggested.

"We can, but they bring it, secure it and move on. We need a bridge that's going to stand the test of time, that means a long build. And you know the weather and traffic conditions around these parts, constantly changing."

Both men knew the Engineer wasn't talking about the 'weather', but whether the locals would tolerate such lengthy disruptions. The Engineer was right: "Hearts and minds, hey?"

"You're the Engineer. Your job, bridge-building," John reminded him.

"And you're the mechanic, you could fix a boat engine as well as truck-engine, couldn't you?" The Engineer asked him pointedly.

"Could I?" John queried, without a twitch of a smile on his face, then a slow breath as he realised the answer. "Probably. But I'd need to get a closer look at them."

John was trying to figure out how that sounded suspiciously like he'd already volunteered. Big mistake! That's what the Engineer had been waiting for.

"The sooner the better, then. Glad you agree! I'll come back to camp with you and have a word with your officer. He'll be able to sort out the paperwork."

"Sort out *what* for me?" John felt like he'd just missed a step.

"There are two larger ferry boats stuck over on Penang Island. We can't put them into service, they're too unreliable. What we need is a mecky on them, someone we can trust over there, whilst we get started for the bridge works on this side."

"How's that me watching your back? From all the way over there?" John queried.

The Engineer laughed, "Don't worry we won't leave you stranded. I'll be coming over every day or so. A bridge needs to be able to work from both sides, you know! And we've got local police. But if we had a couple of your Lads getting familiar with local arrangements, it sure as heck won't do any harm, would it?"

"No, it wouldn't," John agreed. "But you want us ear-wigging and watching? In between trying to fix those ferry boat engines?" John checked, still not convinced what he'd just agreed to.

Returning to the truck, they both had plenty to think about and didn't speak again until just before reaching the camp gate.

"Damn! Forgot Padre's parcels."

The Engineer realised John needed a bit more time to think. "Let's get the post to the Padre," he agreed and the truck sped past the gate and on to the town road.

John could feel the difference in the roads between the ferry road and the town road. The railway station road was better still. He was starting to appreciate the Engineer's problem. They *did* need to build that bridge, no question. But to bring the equipment to where it was needed, they'd have to use the roads and the roads weren't ready for those sorts of loads yet.

Some of it could come by rail, but the railways only came so far, then it was back to the roads again with mountains and jungles in the way of everything, whichever way they tried. The Engineer had his work cut out for him! By comparison, a couple of ferry boat engines didn't sound so complicated.

Padre was surprised to see them. "For me?" Holding the parcels, he turned them over in his hands reading the labels, not quite sure what to make of them.

"From home?" The Engineer enquired.

Padre confirmed, so it seemed. "But I wasn't expecting anything from home."

That needed a little more explaining, to satisfy John and the Engineer's curiosity. Padre pinked up. "I got packed off over here as the 'best' they could think to do with me! After that, it was up to me to make the most of the opportunities I found here."

"Well, you've done that and-then-some," John congratulated him.

The Engineer had heard of Padre's efforts too. "You've got quite a reputation."

"I have?" Padre wasn't sure he wanted to know what for.

"Oh yes, your chicken soup services and that mending-bag of yours." The Engineer was more than happy to clarify, "you've been mentioned in a couple of the doctor's reports going up, you know? We've even had some of the men all the way down in Singapore talking about sending you extra supplies to help."

"You talk straight Padre, you don't lecture, and you listen, makes a world of difference that does!" John reminded the cleric.

"We'll leave you to your post-from-home, Padre," the Engineer was discretely gesturing to John. "We'll be by again in a few days, just some things to finalise at camp before we're off again."

"You're off again, too?" Padre checked.

John sighed, with a 'tut' of shrug towards the Engineer. "Not far, just over to Penang ferry, boat works by the sounds of it. Navy's got its hands full with cargo ships and smugglers."

"Are you taking Daks with you?"

"Daks is hill-people, Padre. You know what they think of boats! But you're right, I could do with him as mechanic's-mate." John brightened at that prospect. Persuading Daks to tag-along made good sense.

Padre shook John's hand. "I worry about you, you know?"

John had to laugh at the 'clucking' tone Padre was using.

"Don't worry, I'll be back to borrow more books in no time."

Padre watched both men climb into the cab of the truck and waved them on their way. John waited until they were out of town, before he spoke again, turning to the Engineer. "Come on then, let's have the details, what are we looking at? You'll need someone with a little more than mechanic-training."

It wasn't a question. And the Engineer sensed John's questions had also shifted focus. He needed plain-speaking and he duly obliged.

"We might have a sabotage problem."

"Do you mean you're maybe going to have a problem with sabotage?" John checked. "Or the sabotage you've already got, might become a problem?"

"We've got a problem John, definitely. And you're the best solution I can come up with."

"Well, hey, thanks for that vote of confidence!" John laughed as he drove them back. He could have taken exception at the way the Engineer worded the invitation, but he didn't. He was rather relishing the prospect. Maybe two weeks in the garage was enough, John was starting to recognise that itch.

"Truck's running smooth for you, Sarg," John reported back at the gate.

"About time," Sarg growled. John stopped to let the Engineer get down, who immediately walked over to Sarg.

"Can I have a word?" Both men turned away from John as he drove the truck back to the garage where Daks was waiting.

"Well?"

"Drove good," John reported.

"Wrong well!" Daks informed him sternly.

John could see that his garage-mate's hearing was as finely tuned as ever. He'd heard the Engineer come in with him and the Dayaks would know all about where the construction sites were.

"You going?" Daks got to the point.

"Want to come? Didn't think you got on with river-people."

"Don't! Ferry isn't river-people!" Daks educated John.

"Going to be useful, then?" John checked, just to be clear.

Daks ever-inscrutable picked up the pack he'd already prepared. "Useful," he confirmed.

John was guessing he'd get a yell from Sarg in the next few hours. The Engineer wasn't the sort of fella to hang around once he'd got the nod.

John hauled out his own 'working' toolbag from the footwell of the truck, then added a few more items from the garage racks.

Daks waited.

"Too obvious?"

Daks nodded to a couple of pieces and John returned them.

By then Sarg was looking for them. "Ready?"

"How long we out for, Sarg?"

"Could be a week or so, up to a couple of months, maybe."

"That's a long 'maybe', Sarg." John gauged the weight of his bags.

Sarg muttered a, "Best I could do," before clearing his throat. "Your Engineer wasn't especially helpful in that department," which sounded suspiciously like the Engineer had been helpful in other 'departments'. Sarg liked to be in-the-know-of-things! John knew that and waited for the rest. "You're going in as ferry engine mechanic, for starters."

John nodded with a grin. "Yeah, that's as far as I got too."

Daks was eyeing up the vehicles in the garage behind them.

"Didn't want to take one of the trucks away from you, Sarg," John took the hint and began to query, but Sarg pointed over to where the Engineer was ready for them. "All sorted!"

The Engineer was astride his packed motorbike, waiting for John to take the second leaning beside it.

"Right." John could work with that. "Daks, hop-on!"

Sarg saw them out the gate.

"Alright, let's have the rest of it." Now John had Daks with him, he was ready to hear what the Engineer thought wiser not to mention within earshot of camp. They pulled the motorbikes over to the side of the road.

"We could have gone back mob-handed with the Army Lads, but that wouldn't have solved the problem. The sabotage isn't the CTs. At least I don't think so, but I can't be sure. Just got a feeling about who's involved. They're not angry. They're more scared than we are. That's not CT, is it?"

The Engineer wasn't asking John. He was asking Daks.

"No."

"I thought you might be able to help me get a chance to change their minds about us. Don't want to bully 'em or make 'em think we know better. Just trying to help them help themselves."

John considered this, before getting back on the motorbike. "You mean you're doing a bit of missionary work, hey?"

"Don't do missionary work." Daks was clear on that.

John had to agree, they didn't!

The Engineer was happy to assure them, he wasn't asking them to do that. "I can manage the missionary bit, along with the bridge planning. I just need a bit of protection and maybe a couple of pairs of more experienced eyes checking what's happening where I can't!"

"Can do that," Daks told him.

John nodded. Yeah, they could do that!

"I'm sure that ferry boat engine didn't blow itself up, but I didn't want to start shouting about it." The Engineer sounded like he'd got it figured and John and Daks were listening.

"If I simply bring a couple of mechanics in to fix it, then maybe the locals will be a little more reasonable. If they're not, then I know you'll have them in your sights, long before I know where they are."

"Can do," John agreed, checking with Daks.

"Deal."

There were no more stops on the way over to the trading town that met the Penang ferry where the Engineer's office was. John and

Daks would be over on Penang Island, the other end of the ferry operation.

"Hope you've brought everything you need?"

They pushed the motorbikes through the town, packs on backs, toolbags on the seats beside them. It was the best way to get the feel of the place, walk straight through it. Easier to hide in the mayhem!

The mainland ferry town was like a market town, a merchant warehouse and a cargo packing yard, all rolled into one. Pretty much what John was expecting, and Daks didn't hide what he thought of the place!

"My office is here, but I thought if you're on the other side with the ferry engine then we'd be able to get a better idea?"

"Depends what sort of 'idea' you want? Because if you think I think this is dangerous, then I can tell you now. It is! I think your idea of building a bridge is a good one." John could feel Daks stiffen his pace in objection to that statement. He hadn't finished, "but you're trying to do too much too soon."

The Engineer stopped in his tracks. "Why didn't you tell me that before?"

"Because I didn't say I disagreed with what you're doing! I've already told you, I think it's a good idea. I just think you need to do the missionary foundation work before you start building bridges!"

As soon as John had said those words out loud he laughed at them. "Yeah, I know, ridiculous!"

Daks wasn't laughing, but he was agreeing. "Idiot!"

"Here's my office, come on in and we can talk about this, before we get any further." The Engineer didn't sound like he was disagreeing with either John's or Daks' assessment of the situation.

"I Hope you've got plenty of coffee?" John asked.

"Oh yeah! Way ahead of ya!" the Engineer assured him.

They talked about the bridge plans, but only briefly. John was right, it was going to be a while before that got any further than the 'paper calculations'.

"We thought if we could get all four ferry boats working and put two to cargo and vehicles, with the other two for locals and livestock, that might be a good start?" the Engineer explained his idea.

"Bicycles?" Daks reminded him.

John seconded that. "Bicycles?"

"Oh! I hadn't thought of that," the Engineer realised.

"Then I think you'd better think of that! You need to put the bicycles in front of the cargo and trucks, or you're not going to get anywhere."

They were on to the second pot of coffee by then.

"OK, how about this for a start?" the Engineer was sounding more confident. "I get the authorities to agree the bicycles stay with the locals and livestock, but you need to get those ferry engines fixed for me. At the same time, I need to know if there's any more fireworks coming over from Penang Island? There's the port office on the island, if you need to contact my office in a hurry."

"You're making yourself a target you know?" John asked him, just to be clear. "They always shoot the missionary first."

Daks nodded, "We do!"

"Then I'm glad you're on our side," the Engineer laughed, downing his coffee, "I know my plan isn't ideal, but someone needs to *do* something to help this start moving. The longer it stays all bottled-up and broken-down, it'll only get worse."

"Sounds like a plan." John agreed and shook the Engineer's hand.

Before they parted that evening, the Engineer had one more question for John, about his training back at Changi. It wasn't that he needed to know, he already did. He needed John to know he knew. "Sniper qualified?"

"If you're asking whether I can shoot straight and hit what I'm aiming at? Then yes."

That satisfied both men.

Over on Penang Island, John and Daks had got rooms right next to where the ferry boats were docked. They were rotten rooms, but fitted the cover well. "Rough and ready, hey Daks?" John checked as they unpacked and settled down.

"Ready," Daks agreed.

They got started on the first of the ferry boat engines next morning. This would be the easiest one to get working. It really just needed a bit of cleaning up, probably wouldn't take them more than a day.

The other ferry boat engine was going to need re-building. They could order those parts and keep the other one working whilst they waited.

John was figuring it out as they got themselves familiar with the set up. The two regular working ferry boats were struggling to carrying everything between the island and the mainland. There were the larger ships dropping off directly at Penang Port, on the ocean side of the island and deeper waters.

The smaller ships were able to come into dockside at the mainland and the ferry boats were trying to avoid hitting them, whilst bringing everything else the larger ships weren't bothered about. Neither of the working ferry boats could cope with demand.

Getting the third ferry boat up, meant at least they could put the walking traffic, whether on two feet or four, and the bicycles on that one. It would take the strain. The crossing would take longer but at least they wouldn't be constantly threatened by a lorry slipping or piece of cargo crushing them.

By the end of the first day, John and Daks took their 'repaired' ferry boat over to report in to the Engineer's office with a list of parts they needed to re-build the fourth engine.

"Cripes, there's a lot here. Could take a while?"

"That's your problem," John reminded him.

The Engineer wondered what they were going to be getting up to whilst they were waiting for the delivery of parts.

"Ah, we've got a plan."

"Already?" he wasn't sure whether he should be impressed or nervous.

"You brought me in as ferry boat meck." John reminded him.

The Engineer looked to Daks, "Both of you?"

Daks shook his head. "No water. Bicycles."

John explained. "He's following the bicycles. Wouldn't do for a hill-man to start working on the water."

"Right." By then the Engineer was impressed, nervous, *and* bewildered. "Sounds like a plan?" he cautiously suggested.

"Except for that part about you telling us we could use the telephone in the port office. Too much Navy. Not gonna happen!" John sounded clear on that point.

The Engineer decided it was wisest not to ask why. Instead, he asked what John was planning whilst they waited for the parts.

"Not yet," he was told by Daks.

"Yeah, way too soon to bring you in. Too obvious." John exchanged glances with Daks, before continuing. "Give us a week. I'll be back to see you then. Deal?"

"Done." The Engineer wasn't quite sure what he was shaking on. He'd asked for John to join him, but it wasn't feeling that way! "You'll tell me about the plan, then?"

"We'll let you know some of it then. Never a good idea to know everything."

"You're telling me it might be wiser for me not to know, aren't you?" the Engineer was starting to get the idea.

That didn't seem to need an answer. Daks had done talking and John had said as much as he wanted to. Already the Engineer could see the way John had changed in just the few hours and miles since leaving the camp gate.

"You get those parts on order. I'll check in with you this time next week. You'll be here." John wasn't asking.

"Right-ho, John." The Engineer would do his part.

They'd got the third ferry boat working, but John and Daks decided it could do with more work for the next few days.

It was all about the 'time and motion' element of their plan. Daks was on the ground, travelling across the island from the ferry dockside through the streets of the port town over to where the large cargo ships did their business ocean-side. They had the rooms but didn't stay there, again, too obvious. John was the ferry boat mechanic, staying onboard made better sense, both for himself and for the benefit of anyone taking any notice of what he was doing. Daks would be doing the trading and the listening, with or without the bicycles.

'Time and motion'. Between the pair of them, gradually, they began to recognise the timings of those around them. Their comings and goings, movements, just as Daks and John were establishing their routines.

John would see to it that the third ferry boat would 'work' when he needed it to and 'breakdown' when convenient, for as long as they needed it. The work suited them both, fitting into their respective roles. Neither of them looked out of place, with where they were nor what they were doing. They traded, argued, worked and ate.

Watching those around them, and letting anyone interested see them, John and Daks appeared to be exactly what they seemed to be and behaved as anyone would expect them to!

Nothing to hide, best cover John could think of. Becoming part of the everyday and ignored. Only then, could they really start watching those who were not!

On the third day, John tried to do a ferry run across the water just with a couple of bikes. The ferry boat broke down on the other side of the water. John swore at the engine and anyone else who tried to board it, showing them that he was trying to fix it as fast as he could. He managed to get a couple of the locals to help, just enough so it could limp back over to the island. It was late by then and the locals were agreeable to a 'coffee break' at the nearest café. John argued with the café owner but paid his share.

When he left the café, it was getting dark. He slept on the ferry boat, no one expected him to do anything else. In the morning he finished 'working' on the engine repair. There were more locals gathered, waiting for the return to the mainland.

His two customers of the day before had been talking. They didn't consider him a very good mechanic, but if he could get the third ferry boat running, then they'd keep using it and his prices were reasonable.

John made sure none of them were in any doubt, the engine was dodgy. The two that he'd kept waiting could attest to that! They might all end up swimming back. They accepted the risk, and he got them over.

On the fifth day, Daks came by to let John know how he was on the trading.

"Doing well?" John queried.

"Noisy!" Daks informed him, indicating success. They were working together, but as far as anyone else was concerned they were no more than passing acquaintances.

That would be the rhythm of it for the next few days and weeks, however long it took for them to decide if the Engineer had good reason to feel uneasy.

John had a few regular customers looking out for him now. They knew he'd got an unreliable boat, but if he could get it going and they didn't bother him when he was tired, he'd take them across. No questions and cheaper than the more reliable ferry boats.

John and Daks watched those who looked as if they didn't want to be noticed. Those were the ones who moved out of the way when someone got in their way. It was the wrong way round! No one came to a ferry town to be polite! Movement.

John noticed those that didn't argue and seemed to be rushing, a little bit too restless. A bit too anxious to seem to be doing something all the time, without going anywhere. No one came to a ferry town without good reason! Timing.

At the end of the first week John went back over to the Engineer. He'd brought a crate of pop over with him. "For Padre."

The Engineer didn't try to find out what John and Daks had been doing. He knew John would explain when he was ready.

"Could have done with Porter. Any idea where he might be?" John asked.

The Engineer couldn't help with that, he hadn't been back to camp since they'd left.

"Take that to Padre and check up on him, will you? And don't spend all week in your office waiting for something to happen. Your timings off. You're looking awkward."

That was it. That was John's report and 'fresh instructions.'

The Engineer was sure John had mentioned there would be more of the plan by now. Had there been? Before John reached the office door, he managed to get one question in. "Next week, then?"

"If I've got anything to tell you," John agreed and shut the door behind him.

The Engineer looked over to his office door. "Then I guess I'll have to be satisfied with that, won't I!?"

Daks was 'on' with the trading and getting a reputation! It was only to be expected when one of the hill-people spends too long on an island! But the bicycles were a good idea. Daks was doing well with them. Every few days or so he'd find something to argue about with the ferry mechanic. Nothing to obvious, but John and Daks knew what they were doing.

John was managing to get enough to eat from the dockside stalls. He seemed to be able to keep the ferry boat working, despite always hitting something or having to take something off it to 're-start' the engine.

The locals had gotten used to seeing him where he was. They'd got used to his habits, his temper and his lack of hygiene. They also got used to the way he handled his tools!

It had taken until the second week before the ferry boat began to run 'regular'. After that John only needed to break it again a couple of times a week, for 'on-going repairs'.

By the third week it had got a reputation as being 'the bicycle ferry', so Daks' trading could move nearer, away from the main market areas, to the waterside. There were perhaps a few less-reputable dealings getting done, but that was only to be expected. If they weren't, it would have been noticed!

That's what John and Daks had been trying to achieve. For them to become no more than expected, whilst keeping an eye out for anything or anyone that wasn't!

John didn't want too many passengers too often. They'd tried it a few times that fourth week. One of the fish traders had been chucking his bucket in to the water to keep his catch alive and John had got the ferry boat to suddenly lurch, and the full bucket had yanked the trader over into the water. He could swim, but John had to stop the ferry boat to pick him up. John gave him time to climb back into the boat, before giving the fish trader a piece of his mind and throwing his catch overboard.

After that most of the locals got the hint. They only used John's ferry for their bicycles and smaller trades, like the port-crates brought to the waterside by barrow, then left on the 'bicycle ferry' for someone the other side to collect.

By this time, from their respective 'angles', both Daks and John had a couple of individuals they were interested in.

What they needed next was Porter. That needed another visit over to the Engineer's office and another crate of pop for Padre.

"Crikey! John, you alright?" the Engineer blurted, hardly recognising him.

John muttered, "Convincing ain't it?"

The Engineer shook his head. "I thought you said a week, it's been a month? I wasn't sure what to do?"

"You don't do anything, except what you've always done," John reminded him steadily.

There was no news on the whereabouts of Porter.

"Can't wait for him." John seemed to decide on the spot. "I'll have to do it myself, are you ready?"

"Ready for what?" The Engineer asked.

John ignored the question, asking, "Do you lock your office?"

That got the Engineer a bit fidgety. "Ummm. Yes."

John finished his coffee. "Don't! If they want to get into your office, it'll be better for us, less of a disturbance and harder for them to explain."

"You're expecting someone to try something then?" the Engineer needed to know he'd understood.

"We've got eyes and ears on a few 'likelies' and they're getting restless, so probably soon," John confirmed. "You want the locals to support your efforts? We're just going to make sure no one gets the chance to chuck a spanner in your works, right?"

"Just a spanner?" the Engineer checked. He could guess John was trying to reassure him.

"They're not coming in heavy, just troublesome. We can handle that!"

From the state of John, the Engineer could well believe that.

John had been hoping they'd get the final parts for the fourth ferry boat engine re-build. They'd only managed about two-thirds so far and they were running out of time.

When it happened, the 'Rice cargo incident' wasn't as subtle as John might have come up with, but it worked just as effectively!

A small cargo ship had been moored up on the mainland, ready to unload, waiting long enough for some of the deckhands to get land-happy and careless with alcohol and cigarettes.

John had been waiting for something like this.

He'd come across with a couple of local drunks onboard just for good measure. They were rowdy enough to make up for him being quiet as he watched what was starting to happen.

They all smelt the smoke.

By the time they got close enough to see it was coming from the cargo hold and not from the engines or the decks, the dockside was already shouting mayhem.

John shoved the two drunks ahead of him and ran to the Engineer's office, demanding "FIRE EXTINGUISHERS!"

The Engineer stumbled to his feet and managed to point, as John grabbed at it, and then for the Engineer himself.

"Come on, this is the diversion. Get help," John yelled. The Engineer hesitated. "GET THEM TO FOLLOW YOU. Fetch every fire extinguisher up to me. I'll be at the cargo hold, ready."

That was it, that was the Plan?

"You didn't!?" the Engineer managed to splutter.

"Didn't need to. FIRE EXTINGUISHERS. NOW!" John had the one extinguisher, and the Engineer quickly managed to round up some of the hysterical locals to help him get more. They got the message and followed the Engineer.

He was running and kicking in doors. No one was arguing. Not with a mob behind him.

The Engineer kicked, grabbed and handed the fire extinguisher to the next man, who took it to John on the deck above where the fire was burning its way through the rice cargo.

John got the more capable deckhands to catch the fire extinguishers as they were flung up from the dockside.

The Engineer knew most of the government offices and nearest business residences most likely to have extinguishers. He'd exhausted all those within a ten-minute radius of his sprint. After that he was gasping and winded but kept shouting at those still behind him. "Find the rest! Anything with authorised noticeboards in front of them, or brass plaques."

They were following the Engineer. They were following the man trying to save their rice cargo, the man willing to break into official buildings to do his utmost to stop the fire from spreading to their own shops and property. This was a man who knew what needed to be done and how to do it … and he was helping them.

That might not have been John's plan, but it was working!

"Didn't even need Porter for the doors, neither!" John muttered to himself, as he kept on hammering each extinguisher open as it got lobbed over to him. By now he'd got two of the ship's crew up beside him, catching, hammering and chucking the extinguishers into the cargo hold of smouldering rice.

John slipped back behind them, then down onto the dockside, before slipping away. By then the Engineer and his followers had a chain going from dockside to cargo hold. Kick, grab, shout, haul, fire extinguisher after extinguisher, until the fire was out.

John smiled approvingly at the effort: "respect and trust," he muttered to himself. The Engineer had the right instincts and those locals would be more inclined to listen to him now, "that'll help his bridge along nicely."

The cargo was lost, but the ship was intact.

The ferry boat remained at the dockside, but John wasn't on it that night.

There were a lot of drunken sailors that night in the dockside cafés and bars. Amongst the locals and traders who'd come to find out what had happened, there were three or four hill-people, who'd been bringing in their own rice harvests for loading. They were miserable and getting even more drunk. The fourth of those hill-people had a couple of bicycles with him.

Daks reeled out to where he'd left the bikes, over to a sleeping fisherman just a few yards further along. Daks kicked his foot and John looked up.

"Ready." They walked away with the bicycles.

They'd take up the position they'd seen earlier, high and clear of town, ready for the morning in a few hours. If they could slip through like that, then those two local troublemakers could too. They were young and stupid and this was too good to miss.

"The Engineer managed to save the cargo ship. Should be a good start for his 'missionary works' don't you think?" John reflected.

Daks muttered something about it not being the way he would have dealt with a missionary, but looked over to John, and shrugged. "Good enough!"

"Now all we have to do is see who starts what!"

The deckhands started cleaning up the mess the next morning, between cargo hold and dockside, with thick heads and stinking buckets, none of them were particularly steady.

Daks took his bicycle back down to the ferry mooring, apparently waiting for the ferryman mechanic to return. John watched him, whilst Daks watched those around him, waiting until he saw someone make a move towards the Engineer's office.

John saw Daks suddenly lean the bike down onto the ferry deck.

Check.

John's gaze followed that direction. "Gotcha," he muttered, signal received. He saw the young pair of 'likelies'.

The Engineer emerged out of his office with a couple of the local elders and an official from one of the offices ransacked for fire extinguishers the evening before. They were arguing, John noticed.

That was a good sign. They weren't looking beyond their hands and the paperwork!

One of the troublesome youngsters looked like he had something in his hand, the other was looking around to decide which way to run as soon as they'd thrown it.

John waited, one step for them, one breath for him.

Feeling the reassuring coolness of the rifle against his cheek, he shot the bucket at their feet. It instantly threw up its contents, spraying the stinking slop of smouldering rice into their faces.

They never got the chance to throw whatever it was in their hand. The one nearest the exploding bucket jumped into the water, the other fled down a side-street.

John didn't wait to see who hauled the sodden troublemaker out of there. Just long enough to appreciate some of the outraged local businessmen giving chase, whilst the elders were making ready to give the sodden wretch a screeching earache for disturbing deliberations with *their* bridge-engineer.

John needed to get back to his ferryboat and start working.

Daks was waiting for him, sitting on one of the crates.

John took the toolbag he was carrying and put it down by the bicycle.

"Missing that truck yet?"

They'd need to settle a few outstanding details over on the island, but that shouldn't take more than a few days, maybe a week.

The Engineer never saw when John and Daks finished work on that fourth ferry boat. They must have got those last few parts from somewhere else. He found it moored up at the mainland dockside a few days later. He didn't even know if they'd managed to get back to camp. He still had both motorbikes. When he asked the port office to send someone to check if the ferryboat mechanic was still at his rooms, according to the locals, the ferryman mechanic had never been there.

The Engineer sent in his report over to camp, then waited a couple of days before telephoning.

"Oh yes, John and Daks are here," the camp clerk was able to confirm.

"Where?" The Engineer asked.

The clerk presumed they'd be where they always were these days. "In the garage. Do you need them for anything?"

The Engineer had sent in his report. He'd done his part and John and Daks had definitely done theirs, helping him with his 'missionary work'. Those that needed to know, knew. Those that didn't, didn't!

It had been a couple of weeks since the rice cargo incident and John and Daks had got into town on one of the camp trucks. Daks had a 'few errands' which meant John wasn't expecting to see him for a few days.

Padre was glad to see John. He had news of Porter. That was good to know, John could do with Porter in the second truck.

"Thank goodness!" Padre couldn't help the relief in his voice.

John waited for an explanation.

It seemed Porter had got himself into a bit of bother with one of the village-traders. "A misunderstanding, nothing more," Padre was quick to assure John. But a timely 'hauling out' was called for. Fortunately, it had happened out of town, so officially it hadn't happened!

"Right." John was pleased to see Padre looking well, and as for Porter!? "I'll sort it."

John took Porter back with him. Cookie was pleased enough to see him and Porter decided it might be wise if he left the motorbike with him, for safe-keeping.

"Truck might be a wiser choice for a while?" John offered him the job.

Porter was still a little uncertain about using some of the roads around town, but as John explained, they weren't heading that way. "Got a bit of a haulage job to do."

They didn't want to involve Padre. From the way it had come in, it didn't sound like a 'medic' was going to be needed.

"Ropes and canvas." A helicopter had gone down in one of the lowland rice terraces.

"Oh, thank goodness for that! I thought you meant we were going to have to get up one of those hillsides!" Porter stopped sounding so relieved, as he realised what he'd just said. "Sorry John. Any chance of any survivors?"

John didn't have any more details than that.

Porter waited, until he had to ask. "What's the plan when we get there? Two trucks? One pilot?"

"We've got to find it first. And in this area, it's always useful to have a spare truck," John reminded him.

They were halfway up, when they reached the road-block. Some of the hill-people had come down to meet them. Daks was with them. John relaxed.

"Cavalry has arrived."

Porter took a moment to realise John was referring to Daks, not the other way round.

The hill-people piled into the back of John's truck. Porter had the rope and canvas in the back of his. The toolbags were stowed in the cabs. They were taking the long way up, because of the trucks. It would take the rest of that day to get to the crash-site.

Daks explained to John what he'd managed to negotiate. The job was to haul the helicopter out from the rice-field. The locals would help with that. John and Porter could use their toolbags to take out any engine parts or instrument pieces they wanted to take away with them. Whatever John and Porter didn't take away would become the property of the hill-people, in repayment for the damage done by the idiotic pilot.

John couldn't agree with that, he didn't have the authority. But as he didn't have the authority to disagree with it either, he didn't say anything, and got on with what he could!

"Get the body out first," John told Porter, who was already getting the ropes and canvas out the back.

The locals had begun arguing amongst themselves about what they could do with the remains of the helicopter. It was mangled, but once it was out from their field they'd put it to 'work' in one of the village-trades on the market roads.

Porter wondered if he ought to say something.

John didn't think there was anything to say.

"It was his own fault. He'd been flying over the wrong area, doing the wrong thing. He was being stupid, now he's dead. He clipped something and went down quick. No chance."

They got the body out and wrapped it into the canvas, then put it in the back of John's truck.

Porter hadn't said a word whilst they worked. John told him what to do. Daks kept the locals out of their way, whilst the farmers tried to find all the scrap that had got loosened on impact.

The longest part of the job was retrieving the instruments from the remains of the helicopter. They worked methodically. It was a remarkably quiet day.

One day up, one day back, and Daks came back with them.

They left the trucks near the garage, for those that needed to attend to the body of the pilot at a respectable distance. Only when they were finished would John return to the trucks and unload everything else.

John was sitting with Daks eating when Cookie came over to tell them Porter had gone back out on his motorbike.

John wasn't surprised. "Probably gone to spend some time with Padre. First time he's had to do that sort of thing, makes a man think.

Having someone like Padre to talk with will help him."

PADRE

Those packages from home had been his birthday cards, with a piece of fruit cake and a set of Sunday-best embroidered handkerchiefs. Padre had forgotten all about his own birthday! He'd slipped into the local calendar of harvests and markets, services and visits.

He kept picking up the cards and reading the words, looking at the pictures on the front, and thinking of home.

Padre used one of the embroidered handkerchiefs to wrap the fruit cake in. Then unwrapped it and sniffed it. It smelt of home, of the family cook's baking, of Sundays, of every day he'd spent at home. He couldn't remember the last time he'd thought of it like that, as being home.

Porter's return had been a relief.

Padre had got a couple of helpers coming in regularly from the plantation, but Porter and Pops were better at organising services when Padre was called out to take his mending-bag on a visit.

Padre had learnt the news of the rice cargo fire, as well as the damage done by the recent helicopter crash. It had meant some of the hill-villages were struggling with supplies. The rice cargo was not only their food source, but also a significant means of trade, too.

Next time John came into town, to the book stall, Padre called him over to sit with him in the café. They needed to talk.

Padre wasn't sure how much of the rice cargo incident John was aware of, or involved in, and wasn't sure he wanted to know. They'd saved the ship for the captain and his crew, but the cargo had been lost. That meant the farmers and the traders would be struggling.

John waited for Padre to ask the question. "Can we get a re-supply convoy sent up, to help them?"

John was still getting his bearings back into camp-chatter mode, after the past couple of months. "What are you asking me for Padre?"

"I need to know if you think it's possible," Padre explained.

John sat back in his chair, enjoying his coffee. "You'd better get a list of what you think is needed then."

Padre hadn't expected John to just sit down calmly with his coffee and accept his request like that. "Don't you need to get anything ready yourself?"

John grinned and glanced down at his pack beside the chair, patted his hip, then looked at the book on the table beside his coffee cup. "Ready."

"You put in all the official requests and reporting, Padre. I'll take care of the driving, and I'd better take Porter with me, and Daks, if he wants to come."

Padre agreed. "Yes, you'd better take Porter with you. He's got a few unpleasant individuals asking some awkward questions."

John muttered a rueful. "that didn't take him long," but knew there was work to be done. Making the necessary requests would need to be done in person. "Come on then."

"What now?" Padre followed John's example and stepped away from the café table.

"Over-land convoy," John explained. "It'll take some favours, and the sooner you start, the sooner we can begin to bring it in."

The Army could help, but they'd need to get it through the proper channels and the Main Depot was down in Kuala Lumpur. It was going to be a heck of a hike and some of the area in between was rather colourful!

Padre had made a comprehensive list of what he thought was called for. He wasn't disregarding the warnings, but this was important! It wasn't simply about the need for 'a bit of extra food', and he'd spent over an hour explaining that concept to the officer. Everything on his list was absolutely essential.

Later, when the officer went over to consult with the camp's medical team, they couldn't fault Padre's understanding of the situation. The next few months would be difficult for some of the locals. If it was 'hearts and minds' they were aiming for, then Padre's idea was a solid step in the right direction.

That got things moving!

Food, first aid, and some practical equipment for the farmers, traders and workers, a few comforts for home and for business, and for the bargaining in between. Padre had thought of everything. The rest he was leaving up to John!

Three trucks would be allocated to the task. John would go down and fetch the other two direct from the Kuala Lumpur Depot.

The telephone calls had already been made and John had his paperwork. The getting there and back was up to him. Porter didn't argue either, he could take his motorbike with him in the back of John's truck.

John had only one requirement of Porter. If he wanted to do any 'sightseeing' then he'd have just the one day in KL, once they got down to the Depot gates. John expected Porter to be back at those same Depot gates before the convoy was ready to drive out and start back. If Porter wasn't there, then John would leave without him.

PORTER

He was still trying to figure out how he was going to get home the 'right way.' Unfortunately, the figuring out had taken him down a few wrong turns in recent weeks. His new motorbike had proven useful for getting about, and for getting away, but some of those 'wrong turns' seemed to be catching up with Porter.

He'd been wondering why John had asked him to tag-along on the drive. There was only the one truck and John was never going to let him drive, unless it was one of the trucks coming back. It had taken until the second day of the journey down to KL before John mentioned it had been Padre's idea.

Porter took it as a compliment and blurted idiotically, "If we get into problems on the way, I'll blend in better than some of your guys!?"

"You're not getting into anything!" John told him firmly. "If we have any problems, I'll be the one getting us out of them. The only thing you're good at blending into is bad habits!"

Porter could guess Padre might have mentioned a few of his recent 'wrong turns' to John. John knew he couldn't stop Porter having a look around KL for a few hours and he wasn't going to begrudge him that. "All I need from you is to keep your ears open, your mouth shut and your nose clean!" John concluded.

Porter grinned a little sheepishly. He couldn't help but think that sounded just like something his mother would have said to him.

"Sorry John."

When they got down to KL, John dropped Porter off with his motorbike just short of the Depot gates.

"Back here in six hours, got it?" John checked, already shaking his head as he watched Porter disappear into the city traffic.

It hadn't taken Porter six hours. He'd lost the motorbike even before the second hour was up, down to a misunderstanding with a couple of traders and a pack of cards. From there on in, it only got worse.

Porter had gotten used to the ways in the market town, with Padre within reach, and being able to work his way out of a bit of bother, with John and the Lads back at camp.

There were too many temptations and not enough tolerances in this place. Porter was soon out of his depth.

Problem was, Porter didn't know his way around this place. The right ways or the wrong ways, they all looked the same! And during the course of the next few hours, he'd hit a couple of brick walls, and he looked like it!

Porter needed to get somewhere else, anywhere else, and

climbed on the next bus going past. He found a seat at the back, out of the way of any more trouble, just for a while to lick his wounds and think about what his next move might be.

Sooner or later, he'd see a sign telling him which way to get to the Depot. That was as far as he'd figured it.

Porter could guess he looked just about as wretched as he felt. He slumped into the seat feeling sorry for himself and out of ideas of what to try next to get home. Home, that's all he wanted now, no more deals, no more bright ideas, just home. If he could just get as far as the Depot, that would be a step in the right direction. His thoughts kept coming back to the 'right way', whilst his gaze wandered across to the other passengers.

The bus had a marine on duty standing up front by the driver. Porter stared at him in disbelief. His first thought caught him off guard. 'Your mother would be so proud of you.' Porter thought of his own mother now, what would she think of him!?

He sat up straighter in his seat, combed his fingers through his hair and rubbed the top of his boots on the back of his trousers. Looking down at his hands, Porter rubbed them on the tops of his trousers, and felt his knees. He remembered she always checked his knees and elbows when he came back home after school, to see what he'd got up to. He was smiling at the memory. Bringing his hands up to his face, Porter felt the bruises from his most recent altercation. No, he didn't want her to see him like this.

He could see her face so clearly and hear her voice. He remembered how she had always tried with him. Every morning, before school, she done her best to make him presentable. She would have everything ready for him, clean and pressed, darned and mended. He'd come down and she'd make him wash his face and hands again, before getting dressed.

Every morning before he left she'd make him stand there for her to take a look at him from head to toe. His mother would sit there at the kitchen table, with her cup of tea. He remembered her face, her smile. "Smart as a band-box", she'd always tell him. He remembered the way her smile shone in her eyes then. It didn't matter what happened for the rest of the day, that was the bit he always remembered.

Porter never quite knew what she had meant. Not until now.

He had never forgotten that look in her eyes before she had shooed him off to school. He hadn't thought about it for years, but he still remembered it. Looking at that marine standing there, pressed and polished, clipped and courteous, intimidating but helpful, Porter understood.

Porter had been staring out of the bus window for a while after that, his eyes damp and red. He wasn't really watching the streets, but then a lady walked past wearing a pretty sun hat.

"A fancy hat," Porter muttered to himself. His mother had always wanted to have a really fancy hat, just for church. A fancy hat with ribbons and flowers on it, why did that make him homesick?

Did they have hat shops around here? Porter started noticing where the bus was going. It seemed to be travelling through a very different part of the town now, a better part.

They were passing town houses. Porter found himself staring at the roofs first, his gaze coming down to the balconies, porches, columns and steps. He stared at the large smooth windows, all lined up, scrubbed clean and painted white, with shutters; and lawns and railings in front of some of them, or white painted stones as they came to meet the pavements before the road. The railings flowed on to the railway station. It looked faintly familiar, like a railway station Porter had known a long time ago.

He almost got off the bus then. It was the little flower borders planted in front of the railway station that stopped him, it reminded him of that 'fancy hat' for his mother. That stopped him.

The thought of being able to get home the 'right way' reminded Porter he was meant to meeting John at the Depot gates. They'd passed the magnificent railway station by then, no more smart white polished pillars. The verandas had gone and the clipped lawns delicately sprawling in the sunshine had faded away.

The pavement had also disappeared. There were now beggars and peddlers, market traders and rough-dealers, some being moved on by some of the marine's fellows, by the looks of them.

Porter readied himself. They must be getting near the Depot. He got to stand, and the marine turned to notice him. Suddenly Porter wanted to apologise for the state he was in. He wanted to apologise for everything, to this complete stranger, who'd reminded him to remember his own mother!

"You with the trucks loading up?" the marine enquired.

What on earth had given the fellow that idea!?

"Yes, Sir." Porter lifted his chin, and grinned, grateful to be able to answer. Close enough to notice the marine was wearing white gloves, spotless, chin smooth-shaven square-set and boots brilliant black. Porter was close enough to smell the soap and polish, it made him hesitate, feeling the need to say something more.

The marine smiled slightly and stood aside, waving Porter off from the bus. Porter managed only a, "Thank you, Sir." And he had never meant those words of gratitude more sincerely in his life before.

That marine would never know what he had done for Porter, but Porter would never forget it.

Porter got to the Depot gates. He'd promised John he would. Probably the first promise he'd kept so well for a long time. He didn't try and sneak past the guards. He didn't need to sneak. He told John he'd be there, and he was. Porter could see through the gates and wondered what the hold up was. John would tell him when he was ready.

Porter could see all three trucks were backed up in the yard. There must have been a dozen of the Lads working on the loading, and more in the warehouse bringing fresh batches out to them.

John saw a figure waving at him from the gates. "He's with us," he informed the guard.

"Right you are."

Porter was in.

"Come on. We've got some foraging to do!" John invited him into the Aladdin's cave of trading goods.

Porter was staring wide-eyed, but his thinking was clear. "What does Padre need?"

"From the looks of this list, just about everything! We've got the emergency rations all loaded, blankets, tents and the like, and the first-aid kits, talking of which ..." John took a longer look at Porter. "What have you been doing?"

"Um. I got into a bit of bother, maybe," Porter admitted.

"Lost your motorbike too?" John asked, without a hint of surprise in his voice, and not waiting for Porter to answer that one. "Glad you made it back."

No more questions now.

One of the Lads handed John a first-aid kit.

"Sit down. Let's see if I can clean you up before anyone else notices." John caught Porter's shoulder and perched him on the edge of the nearest crate.

Both men were silent for the next minute or so, as the loading continued around them, steadily filling up Padre's three missionary trucks.

Porter broke the silence first. "How about some nice biscuit tins?" he suddenly blurted brightly.

"What?" John was the one spluttering, fumbling with the swab he'd brought up to clean a few more of Porter's scratches. "Biscuit tins!?"

"Yes, you know those *nice* biscuit tins, with pretty pictures on the lids. Padre would like that, wouldn't he? Maybe we could get one for Cookie too, or I will? I can't pay for it, but I'll get it for him, just to sort of say sorry. I think I need to, don't you?"

That was too much for John to take in one breath.

"Biscuit tins?" Porter tried again, as John took a step back to see whether he'd been able to remedy enough of the damage to Porter's face, before checking he'd heard right.

"Biscuit tins?" John queried hesitantly.

"Yes, the ones with the pretty lids … I thought …" Porter started again.

John stopped him. "No, I got that bit. For Padre, and Cookie? I hope you're not going to start suggesting Sarg gets one too?"

Porter started again. "I just thought it would be a nice thing to do, for Padre and Cookie, they'd like that, wouldn't they?"

John stopped him there, putting up his hands. "OK!"

"OK? Really??" Porter stared at him, grinning from ear to ear, even with his face still aching and tender.

"Go on then. I'll cover it for you." John was already shooing him off the crate. "You're right. Padre would appreciate it, and you definitely owe Cookie an apology, at least!" John agreed, before adding, heedless of whether Porter heard him, "It's a good start."

Porter dashed off and John had another look at Padre's list. He had his own list too. The loaders from the Depot already knew how far they could go.

"Space on the paperwork, room in the trucks," that was the rule-of-thumb, so long as they could smudge the signature!

He and Porter would take the first truck. There'd be another pair of drivers in each of the other two.

A couple of 'passengers' had got themselves included in on the inventory. They hadn't been John's choice, but he'd seen their papers, and if they wanted to 'cover the story' for the newspaper, that wouldn't do Padre's missionary work any harm. Might even get him noticed back at his Head Office. "Padre's long overdue a mention," John observed.

John kept an eye on Porter's errand. He was still looking for those biscuit tins. After another ten minutes John called him back over. "How about we send those two tag-along reporters out to get your biscuit tins for us?"

Porter suddenly realised John was telling him to send those two official-looking chappies where to go and what to do. He hesitated.

"Might as well make them useful whilst they're waiting for the off." John gave him a nudge. "Go with 'em, show 'em what you want, and you can tell 'em more about what Padre is doing whilst you at it. For their article."

Before Porter 'organised' the two reporters, John had one more suggestion. "Whilst they're doing that, you might make sure they know where Padre's home-patch is. So they can send a copy or two back home for him?" John never doubted Porter would know the address and Porter never thought to ask how he guessed.

"You've got half an hour. Think you can manage that?"

Porter nodded and dashed off, eagerly dragging the pair with him. "You want a story? Then we'd better get started!"

They got back within the allotted half hour, but not before John had time to pack in a few extras. Nothing that the warehouse would miss. "A bit of foraging for good works," John smiled as he tugged down the cover on the back of the last loaded truck.

The Depot gates were opened and they started out, leaving KL behind them. Everyone was loaded in. The trucks were full and moving slow. John had the lead truck, with Porter beside him. They weren't carrying any passengers. Porter had his biscuit tins and John had his toolbags.

For the first day it was chaos on the roads. During the course of the second day the traffic disappeared. By the third day the road had disappeared with only a dirt track, scrubbing jungle, between a few scattered straggly villages and trading posts with drains and bridges in between. They made good time then.

In the days that followed they slowed through the villages and over the bridges. The rest of the route was taken at a steady pace, and they kept moving.

The drivers kept it tight together, four hours each, then swap. That included John and Porter. Four hours each, then swap.

They stopped when the jerry cans had to come out. If anyone needed to get comfortable that was when they did.

Mud and dust, bugs and flies!

Water bottles were refilled when needed and they slept when they were too tired to stay awake anymore.

Four hours each, then swap. Until they got back up to town.

The news of their progress had been telephoned ahead. The convoy would be 'properly' received in town with all due ceremony. The camp would be sending the Lads over for the unloading and the officers were already there to be formally introduced to the elders receiving the convoy.

John could have told them he knew where to bring the trucks into the town square, but he guessed the officers needed to at least look as if they were in charge of something! He'd done his part. This was just the 'formal bit'.

The officers were doing all the talking and the two newspapermen were getting excited whilst they got set up with the camera and their notepads. John could see Padre amongst them, and Porter was in the middle there somewhere too.

It was all going 'pantomime' and John got out of the way. He found one of the cafés at the corner of the market place and got himself settled to enjoy the show. This was going to take a while.

Sarg had brought some of the Lads over for the unloading ceremony and Padre had been summoned forward and was being formally introduced to everyone, for the benefit of the cameras.

The 'tag-alongs' got their photos and their article. Front page in some of the newspapers back home.

The two photos that seemed most popular was the one of the Padre and Porter holding a pretty-lidded biscuit tin in front of a couple of Army trucks, just beside the town's clock tower. The second was the one with Sarg and the Lads unloading the bicycles and the first-aid boxes.

John lifted his cup of coffee. "Nicely done, Padre." Then drank it down and got up from the table, walking away from all the ceremony and formalities. They'd unloaded his truck long since. He'd done his bit. He'd meet Sarg and the Lads back at camp.

CHAPTER 10

NOT SO SOFT LANDINGS!

JOHN

It had been a few weeks since the 'biscuit tin convoy', the dust had settled and John was getting comfortable with his garage duties again, a nice steady rhythm. There were new blokes coming through the camp. A variety of different languages could be heard, but they could all speak some form of English, enough to get about the place. Some of them were loud, you could hear them coming a mile off. Not wise. Then there were those that managed to make you feel uneasy just watching the way they sat at the table. Best avoided.

There were a lot of youngsters arriving, over-eager, heavy-set and tall. They'd stand out like sore-thumbs, that wasn't going to be helpful.

"We need more little-uns, like Porter," John observed with a wry smile. They hadn't seen him about the place recently.

John was hoping that meant he'd been able to do some of those missionary errands for Padre. For the moment John couldn't imagine what they might be, but anything to keep Porter out of mischief would be better than letting him loose on the roads with another motorbike!

They'd been talking about the state of the roads that morning, with another of the cars coming back into the garage. John gave up asking for an explanation as to how it happened!

Amongst the new arrivals seemed to be a fresh batch of road-building engineers. They seemed to have a plan, a *new* plan. John had heard a few of those already.

"Damn! We've been called out to another crash. You coming?" John grabbed his toolbag.

He'd had enough of the garage for a few hours. Daks would have happily stayed, but John didn't give him the choice. "Come on. If we take the paths we can avoid all the works!"

There was no such thing as a 'back road', only the roads, which these days were regularly clogged with military vehicles, construction traffic and plantation trucks, or the local village-to-market paths. The paths were the ones used by anyone with more sense than to get caught in the clog.

If they were taking the paths, Daks knew John would be needing him. It was the only option. If the call out had been somewhere on the roads, they would have been found already. If it was on any of the market-routes then the locals would have taken care of it and the car would have shown up in one of the villages by now.

That only left the option that an idiot had tried to avoid both the clog and the locals! So, he'd taken his vehicle down a way blind? He'd be lucky if he only needed a mechanic!

"Not one of ours. Construction-jobbie by the sounds of it, one of the new lot. Must've taken a wrong-turn." The Lad at the gate took a stab at 'stating the bleedin' obvious.'

All John had been given was a vague address in a general direction of 'over that way'. Daks was navigator and they'd only got the rest of the day. After that, after dark, no one was going to be able to find anyone. They'd just have to wait for the patrol to reach what was left.

Both John and Daks were aware the directions would be taking them down some rough routes. Anyone else attempting those would be taking a ridiculous risk. John didn't bother asking why, Daks had the best explanation. "Idiot!"

"I hope those road builders are good navigators!" John was steering, but it wasn't so much a matter of which turn, as where's the route gone? The 'path' was barely more than scratches in the earth.

John was following someone else's wheels, after a couple of hours. They'd have got further walking the route.

Daks was checking his reckoning. It was a futile errand. There was no way they were going to find where the vehicle or the driver had got to. Not enough to follow.

The best they could do was get as far as a couple of the nearest villages and do some asking. John was recognised in both as 'Driver', that always made it easier.

The first wasn't particularly helpful, although they did say they'd check their tracks next morning. John wasn't sure if he liked the sound of that, but at least if they found anything left they'd know to get a message over to camp.

Daks was welcomed rather more enthusiastically in the second. Apparently, he'd forgotten he had a few relatives that way.

"That's nice for you," John grinned, as a couple of the females started making suggestions to Daks.

The Dayak grinned broadly and indicated he might be staying a while. John chuckled, "Sensible fellow," matching grin for grin.

"Don't worry, I can find my own way back. I'll see you again when you're ready." John climbed into the truck and watched Daks walk back into the village, losing sight of him amongst the huts.

Getting the engine started again, John looked back one last time. "Sensible fellow."

John knew the heading and the ruts steered his wheels, the tracks scuffed astray a few times, but soon enough the paths were starting to resemble one of the regular roads. The light was already fading, and it might be the longer way, but he felt a damned-sight safer.

John's thoughts wandered back to Daks' grin and that slight shrug that went with it, and the way his footsteps lifted when he was on home ground. John found himself wondering just how long it had been since he'd walked on home ground. "Cripes! I wish it were that easy for me."

Approaching the gate, the Lad on duty was ready for him. Sarg wanted a word. "Gimme a break! I've only just got back!"

Sarg wasn't there yet, and John calmed. "Any idea why?"

The Lad could help him there. "Seems like they've got a couple of spaces on the truck taking some of the new'uns out for a qualifying jump. You due one?"

John guessed he must be, he wasn't keeping count out here. "At least it'll give you a change of scenery from the innards of a truck and garage tool boxes," the Lad offered cheerfully.

Sarg seemed to think so too.

"Be ready for the truck in the morning." He spun round and strode off. Sarg didn't expect to see John until then.

"I'd better get this truck back then, hadn't I?" John slapped the door shut again. The Lad wished him 'good luck' under his breath.

John had no way of knowing when he'd be seeing Daks again. No telling how long the jump would take, no one was telling him anything much. That was another not-good sign!

Eat, sleep, and be ready for the truck in the morning. John had learnt not to eat before a jump. Tea the night before. Coffee in the morning. He took the mug of tea over to the table in the mess tent. It was quiet there, plenty of noise about, but quiet just there.

He read his book in peace until he'd had enough. Lifting the mug of tea to the shadows, he smiled, "Good luck to ya, Daks."

Jumping out of a perfectly good aeroplane? No, John didn't have a problem with that. He'd done it enough times now. He'd also done far more stupid things since! He couldn't really describe them as 'fears' anymore. They were more like a terrible sense of 'acceptance'.

The coffee had helped the next morning.

Plenty more Lads were waiting for the truck along with John, but he might have been the most experienced amongst them. That gave him something to think about!

They waited at the gate in silence until the truck drew up. The driver recognised John and offered the passenger seat to him, directing the rest of them to climb in the back. "You'd better stay up here, or they'll be badgering you the whole journey. That ain't going to help no one."

John didn't argue.

The jeering and laughter subsided after a few miles. They were starting to think about it.

John didn't.

He thought about the coffee again, once he was on the plane going up. That was the whole point, you kept that taste in your mouth. Think of the axle grease, swallow it down, then feel it kick from behind your ears, grate either side of your nose and crawl down the back of your throat. You think about the coffee and nothing else. There was no point thinking about anything after the coffee!

You were going to jump. That was it. You got loaded up, and sat down, and if you could still taste the coffee, you were going to be OK.

A few of the Lads weren't, but the rest waited in silence. Waiting their turn. Waiting for the yell. The yell takes over from the coffee, as you stand ready and start moving forward.

Someone said something about it being 'like riding a bicycle'. John couldn't taste the coffee anymore, but the bicycle reference helped!

He remembered racing his bike along some of those lovely little green lanes back home. Early mornings, crisp air, he knew every route that way. All those old stone walls, boundary markers for some long-dissolved estates, the walls keeping pace with the lanes. The stones worn and weathered, seeming to grow out from the dark soft soil itself. A tolerance between them, a respect as they braced themselves against the ages. Whilst the trees towered over them both. Branches weakened by age, draping themselves on the length of the walls, as if seeking support from them. Spring twigs vigorous enough to nudge a few of the crumbling top-slabs aside. The loftier branches, stronger, reaching over the top of the lane, yearning to embrace their brothers on the other side. Long-gates and narrow lanes, where every corner seemed to wander towards you, with no intention of giving you a hint of which way it might turn, or what lay beyond.

The man in front of John stepped forward.

He felt the weight behind him. Hands to his chest, his turn to step forward, feeling the weight of his boot as he lifted it.

Jump!

Let your breath go when you jump. Don't bother looking up. There's nothing you can do about that now.

Enjoy the view. John was still thinking about his bicycle. He'd learnt that, join the step-out with the step-down with something else entirely, and it doesn't feel so far.

Breathe and brace and grab. His body jolted back, to the 'now' of the jump. Coming down steady, a few seconds to breathe and look about.

Back at training it had been different. The confidence of knowing that wherever you were jumping, there was likely to be a nice soft patch of field somewhere. The farmer might not be too pleased about it, but he'd still give you a lift back to where you should have landed with Sarg ready to ask you stupid questions!

He'd done his regular jumps then, and a few more since, a couple of times over here, but not this way.

"Third time," John reminded himself. Jumping down into dense jungle where the canopy was going to be coming up hard to hit him, before he could get his boots on the ground.

No, John didn't have a problem with that.

His kit bag was down on the strap and way ahead of him.

The canopy would break the fall. Cut the strap to the bag and let that drop. Then use the remains of the strap to get himself down to ground-level. That was the theory.

It was always reassuring to feel yourself going through the manual on the way down, like there was anything you could do about it! John knew his kit well enough to trust it. He knew the jungle well enough too and didn't trust it an inch!

They'd been heading for jungle last time he looked. Most of them still were. Who put that barn in the middle of the jungle!?

WALLOP!

The roof of the barn broke his fall. The chute collapsed. From there the slap against the side broke a couple of ribs, and the drop to the ground broke his leg. His head didn't feel too good, somewhere between the roof and the ground, either!

It had taken the other Lads a few minutes to find John. There was a medic amongst them. "You hurt?"

John would have thumped him, if he'd been able to get up. He hadn't had time yet to realise how badly he'd been hurt. He would.

"What kept you?" John mumbled, not sure if that had been out loud, or in his head.

"We didn't expect you to be all the way over here!" someone was shouting.

John had muttered something about, neither had he! Why were they shouting at him?

Someone was saying as how he'd given the barn a good kicking. Which confused John because he was sure it had been his head not his feet that had found that ruddy barn roof first. He muttered something along the lines of "had it coming!"

John wasn't unconscious but wasn't far from it. It wasn't

unpleasant, the phases of drifting in between the pain. He wasn't sure he was following all the sound and movement that seemed to be swirling in front of his eyes. There seemed to be a load of shouting and boots about the place, and he was sure he'd told them to 'stop moving', why weren't they listening to him. But John hadn't said that, someone was telling him.

John felt crumpled up, but when he tried to straighten up his chest wasn't having any of it. The earth smelt metallic, but that was his own blood in his mouth, on the ground. He preferred the axle grease coffee. Too many boots down here, he couldn't see who was doing what.

Someone was holding his head between their hands bringing it back down to the ground telling him to 'stay there.' John wasn't thinking of going anywhere. He just wanted to get a bit more comfortable.

Someone was shouting about legs. John could remember looking down to check his were both there. They were. They didn't hurt, until he thought about them, then they did! It was starting to get difficult to decide which bit of him hurt most.

"Should've gone by bike!" If he'd just come off his bike, he wouldn't be in this mess. "Where's my bike?"

It wouldn't have been the first time he'd come off on one of those corners, skidding off the loose gravel, or a smudge of mud left behind one of the tractor wheels. Or one of those ruddy pot-holes, devils they were for catching you, just as you swung wide to really get the best line. Yeah, he'd just come off his bike, that was all. Just a bit of a wobble, that was all.

"Don't worry it's only broken a bit," the medic was telling him, his hands already checking where the breaks were.

That was when John started feeling the pain again.

"Oi!" he yelled up at the medic, snapping back and making a grab for one of the hands. John thought he'd been quick, but his hand was moving slowly, everything was moving slowly ... suddenly ...

He'd only lost consciousness for a few seconds, but it felt like everyone had changed around since then. The guy that was holding his head was cupping the side of it in the palm of one hand and restraining John's wrist with the other, stopping him from making any more sudden movement. "That's not going to help!"

John was duly reprimanded.

"Stay down there. You're OK, we've got you."

"That ruddy barn roof got me first!" John mumbled, the sudden anger crumbling into a chuckling curse.

"It did that alright!" the medic cheerfully agreed with him.

The medic seemed to lean over the top of John, to say something to another guy. "There's at least two breaks down here, could be a nasty third one lurking. Can't quite be sure of the state of it, though."

John groaned. "That third one ain't lurking. It's up 'ere."

"That's just your broken ribs," the medic patiently reminded him. John was still gauging how he was going to throttle the medic … but he could feel himself slipping again … suddenly …

Concussion.

"We've got to get him down from here, somehow." That was the guy by his head.

John was sure he was already down as far as he was able to go. He could taste the dirt in his mouth, spitting it out, trying to bring his hand up to wipe it away, but someone else was quicker, a flash a white fabric across his line of sight. They were cleaning the side of his face for him.

"Thanks!" John murmured, then remembered something he'd heard. "Down where?"

There were more boots approaching, and some bare feet this time, John thought he recognised, "Daks?"

No, it wasn't Daks, but it looked like one of his friends.

They were talking over the top of him again. John tried to raise his voice; he couldn't seem to raise his body for the time being. It was the best he could do. "Down from where? I thought I was down?" John asked someone, anyone listening.

"You're down from the barn roof, but we're up the side of a hill," someone helpfully explained, very near to John's head. It wasn't the medic this time. The new guy was at least being a little more helpful.

"Oh!" John sighed, that seemed to explain everything.

Someone else was still working down by his feet, maybe on his knee? He could feel them, but now his legs felt far away from his chest. His head was starting to feel that way too.

The medic was by his right shoulder, prodding at it. "This'll help. It shouldn't be hurting so much soon. Then we can move you."

"Wrong. It hurts like hell." John tried to get up onto his elbows, to get an idea of what state his legs were in. His head felt heavy, his neck felt weak, his arms weren't moving the way he wanted them to. "What?" Slowly … suddenly …

"John? John?" Someone was shouting at him again.

At least they'd stopped talking about bicycles. And who'd put that ruddy pothole in the way?

"Still here," he grimaced, as he regained consciousness.

The medic was talking to him again. "We're going to try and start moving you now."

"Good luck!" John offered, then groaned as the lift started. They'd strapped both his legs together to splints. His right arm was strapped close up across his chest already. When did they do that? He felt like one of those Egyptian mummies. How the heck was he going to be able to cycle like that?

Ah, now he saw the bicycles! Some of Daks' friends, and the Lads packs, had been loaded on them. The Lads had made a stretcher of sorts between their jackets and branches.

"You OK there?" someone was asking up by his head. John was looking down to his feet. Why were they asking about his head, they'd bandaged his legs. Idiots!

He could see there were at least two bicycles leading the way, ahead of what he could see of the stretcher the Lads were carrying him in. He couldn't see much further than that. "Hill ambulance?" John asked.

"Yep! Works a treat, don't it?"

Someone gave him a sip of water. It took the taste of the mud and metal out of his mouth. The water stripped his tongue from where it had got stuck to the roof of his mouth. He half spat and half swallowed.

"Slow down," someone was telling him.

His head was starting to throb. When he felt pressure back on his lip and liquid across his teeth, he swallowed again.

John slumped back onto the stretcher. Whatever the medic had given him, it was starting to work.

He didn't remember much after that, except thinking something about it being easier than walking. He could remember thinking he must say thanks to Daks' friends for coming over. How did they know? He hadn't. Why hadn't they warned him? What was that bicycle doing up there anyway? Slowly … suddenly...

John lost consciousness again as the 'ambulance' got him the rest of the way down the hill.

"Easier than walking," a different medic told him as he came round again.

They weren't in the jungle anymore. John knew that much. They were in somewhere, not a room though. It didn't feel like it had walls.

The medic leant over John to finish cleaning the dried blood from the side of his head. "Took a bit of a knock there," he observed, reaching for some fresh dressing and bandages.

"Everywhere." John tried to laugh, but his chest hurt. The weak laugh became a groan of pain. "Where?" John repeated, not sure if his first attempt had made any sound.

It was difficult to make himself heard above the noise. It was windier and colder. Did he come off his bicycle by a busy roadway? It sounded like it, but he hadn't come off his bicycle. Why did everyone keep telling him he'd come off a bicycle?

"On the way to hospital now, mate. Best place for ya!"

John wasn't going to argue. The helicopter must have taken a while to get where they'd been. John had wanted to ask how long, instead he went for what he really needed to know. "Anyone else?" The bandages must be helping, his head was clearing, he was thinking straighter. He needed to know. "Anyone else get hurt?"

"No, just you. You were lucky!" the perverse medic informed him. John felt his hands clench, another idiot he'd like to throttle.

"Lucky!?"

"At least they found you," the chirpy medic offered.

"What?"

"The locals, they found you. Almost as soon as the Lads got to you. Must have seen you come down."

John felt stupid. He didn't know how to answer that.

"Seemed to know *you*?" the medic asked him.

John could answer that one. "Friends."

"See. Told ya, lucky! They said if it had been anyone else, they'd have taken much longer getting you out!"

John grinned. That sounded like the first thing to make sense to him all morning. He thought he recognised those feet, and the bicycles!

He just needed to get a bit more comfortable. John tried to move his head and ask for some water, but he was starting to get out of breath. It felt like he was only able to breath out, when he tried to draw in any air it wasn't there. There wasn't enough room for it to get in.

Maybe the helicopter was taking all the air? Maybe if he just turned his head a little that would help? John tried to move his head, but his shoulder wanted to move too. That was the arm that was strapped to his chest. Everything tried to move, and everything hurt!

"Don't do that," the medic told him sharply.

"Can't do that," John murmured, "bicycles!" and fell back unconscious again …

The helicopter lifted to climb, then lunged forward over to the landing site, checking out the surrounding area, before turning to come back in, down to the hospital ground.

The air started getting heavier. John could feel his chest. Someone was sitting on it! The same someone who was smothering him!

It was the medic kneeling beside him, trying to put an oxygen mask over his face. John was struggling with him, trying to claw it off. "I'm just trying to give you a bit of air."

John was gasping, it tasted different from what he remembered. When was the last time he breathed air. Not mud and blood and dust and rust, just air!?

John was jerked fully awake, then. His body felt like it was being dragged over cobbles, bicycle wheels? No. It sounded like trolley wheels but felt like a sack-barrow! Hospital trolley! It didn't matter. He was moving again, away from that idiotic medic who kept on asking him about bicycles.

He hadn't come off a bicycle, he'd jumped into the side of a barn roof. John knew that much. Then some of his friends had come on bicycles, that was it! That was where all those bicycles had come from. He'd already explained this, why were they asking him the same questions?

There was a lot of white going on in front of his eyes. Where had all that white come from? John hadn't seen white like that since he couldn't remember when. He wasn't used to pale looking people. Slightly scary!

They smelt weird. He didn't like the taste in his mouth. Only a hospital smelt like this, and they weren't listening to him. They were talking over him. Jabbing at him again. Then someone was counting … back to bicycle wheels and pot-holes …

When John woke next, everything had stopped moving but it was all still very white, very still, very clean, and everything felt. stiff and sore. John smelt clean, like the bed clothes. He felt like the bed clothes. No. He felt worse. They felt smooth and he could move them, slightly. They weren't crushing him anymore, but they were tucked in too tight!

Everything felt ludicrously white. Nothing could be that white! And how'd he get so clean? He'd never smelt this clean.

John felt he'd slept well. He couldn't remember eating anything, but he didn't feel hungry. Thirsty though. He felt very thirsty and very clean! John was blinking in the light, bright clean windows!

He must have slept well; he didn't feel tired. Not like when they'd emerged from the jungle, like it was reluctant to give them up. It clung to them if they let it. The jungle would claim them. He'd seen it happen to a couple of the Lads that had come back, and never did. You saw it in their eyes first, and in their silence, even whilst they were speaking you heard the distance in their voice. The way they walked changed.

This didn't feel like that.

This didn't feel like anything.

John wanted to know what he could feel.

He felt clean and thirsty. He knew that much! And his head felt thick and heavy, but his body felt light and weak.

His legs? What about his legs? He knew about his head and his chest. He wanted to see his legs. He was asking the questions, but his legs weren't answering him. What had they done to his legs? They were there last time he looked. John could lift his head now, and see his hands, that was a good start.

As he smiled, he felt the sides of his mouth feel sore. His mouth still tasted dry, but he could speak. His breath felt stronger, too. Crikey! His hands were clean, even his nails were scrubbed! His hands felt strange, soft?

How long had he been lying in this bed?

He remembered those Lads that didn't come all the way out from the jungle, the way their hands moved. He lifted his left hand in front of his face, turning it at the wrist. "Still works." He wiggled his fingers, clenching and releasing them.

He remembered the look in their eyes, those Lads, that didn't come all the way out from the jungle. Their hands moved differently, they held tightly, and let go too quickly.

John clenched his fist again, and felt the strength throb up his arm. It hadn't been the jungle that had got him. "Just a ruddy barn," he muttered, reminding himself.

His voice sounded clearer. He was grinning idiotically now, still gazing at his own hand, as if he was amazed to find it there at the end of his wrist.

"Oy! It was your leg, mate!" the Lad in the next bed called over.

John turned his head suddenly to see who'd spoken. Too suddenly. Wow! That one hurt. Everything hurt. John was glad. If it was hurting, then it was still there. Good to know! "My leg?" John checked.

The resident in the next bed, yelled. "Yeah, your leg. Gawd you were in a mess! They've been working on you for days!"

It felt like those bicycles had ridden over his chest. John's hand went down to his chest. It was strapped solid tight. It still hurt, but it didn't feel so tender. He tapped at the bandages with his knuckle. Hard. Solid as a rock. How was he meant to breathe through rock? It was too tight! He couldn't get a whole breath in.

John wanted to be able to breathe, and suddenly he couldn't. Why would they do that to him? He needed to get the bandages off, they were crushing him, suffocating him. What was the point in being so clean, if they stopped you breathing?

John must have started to call out, scratching at the bandages on his chest, but the urgent movement in his arms was making his head hurt again. As soon as he raised his voice, it wasn't words that came out, but a long slow groan. He needed to shout but couldn't get enough breath into his lungs. He was gasping.

Someone else had shouted for him. He'd heard them. Must have been that bloke in the next bed. A nurse came up to the side of John's bed. "You're OK, just a bit sore. We've got you cleaned and patched up. You just need to stop moving for a while." Her voice came through the haze of panic and pain, like a dagger into a feather pillow.

She was holding a cup of water to his lips, and John drank. The water helped, it seemed to take the breath deeper into him with every sip. John wanted to gulp it down, but the nurse wasn't tipping it enough for that. "There you go, just slow down now."

He waited for her to stop. She took his hand and turned the wrist over again, taking his pulse.

John grinned. "Still alive then?"

"Oh yes!" she smiled. Then put his hand back down on top of the bedcovers and walked away.

John knew he was in hospital, nowhere else could smell like this. Though how the heck he got from riding his bicycle into hospital he couldn't say. That must have been one heck of a ruddy pothole!

The first week was absolute rest. John couldn't move. Nothing! But he had both his legs and by the end of that week all his toes were moving, although one of his knees felt like it had been put in backwards.

"Are you sure that's right?" he asked one of the nurses, poor thing she must have been one of the new ones. He'd soon recognised the difference: that blithe glide in the more experienced and the startled deer glance of the new ones!

They did tell him what they'd done but he hadn't been listening. He was trying to get someone to fetch him some proper coffee, everything tasted horrible, nothing tasted of anything, and they kept washing him! What was the benefit of that? He'd not been anywhere or done anything to need another wash. All this cleaning was starting to make him itch.

It wasn't an itch. He'd got an infection.

John was meant to have been able to sit in his chair that weekend. They'd been telling him for three days, if he didn't move for the week, he could sit in that chair by the weekend. Now they were telling him he couldn't, because of an infection.

"I'm not having it!" he informed the senior nurse, crossly.

She smiled blithely, "You've already got it and we're trying to stop it. Now shut up and take this. Then I'll roll you over and give you an injection."

"You'll what!?" he spluttered.

She calmly repeated the description of the procedure and called one of her colleagues over to help her, pulling the screens around his bed.

"I can roll meself over," John informed them, starting to prove his point and failing. "Cripes! I can't!"

They'd taken off the tightest of the bandages around his chest, but the strapping was still sufficient to keep him immobile.

Relaxing now, accepting the inevitable, John waited for the nurses to get into position to commence the manoeuvre. "OK, I'll let you do that. If you let me sit in my chair tomorrow?" he bargained a little desperately.

All three of them knew he wasn't going to be able to stop them doing exactly what they needed to. "We'll see tomorrow," was the best he was going to get from the senior of the pair.

"At least can I have a couple more pillows, Nurse? You can let me have those at least, different view from the ceiling, how about a window, maybe?"

They could allow him that.

Bringing the pillows over, each put one of their arms underneath his shoulder, hooking him between them, choregraphed to perfection. "Lift!" And up he was. John's head spun slightly at the sudden elevation. The air tasted thinner up there.

"Oh yes, much better thank you," he grinned and winked over to the fella in the next bed, who was still flat on his back.

"Any chance of a decent cuppa?"

The senior nurse stared him down, wagging her finger at him. "Pillows and penicillin. Three days. Then we'll see about you sitting in that chair."

She shooed her junior to get all the Lads a cup of tea. "It's tea time anyway," she observed, looking down at the watch pinned to her chest.

John got his cuppa, but it didn't taste a patch on Cookie's brew back at camp. He didn't care. He could see his toes. They were clean too. The tea tasted clean. That was the problem with it, he decided.

The view from the window was a revelation, it was all green out there. Not jungle green. It was green grass, and there were cows on it. Just like home!

He wasn't home, John knew that. The blokes in the other beds were always talking about not-being-home. He hadn't said much, but they were talkative enough.

John was just glad to be able to sit up and breath all the way in, all the way out. Every breath. He could feel the bruising on the side of his head, but nothing broken up there. His hair had grown. How long had it been, no more than a week, surely?

There were twenty beds on the ward, but not all of them were occupied. A couple had screens still around them, so he couldn't tell who was in those. The rest of the Lads seemed to be mostly mobile, except for himself and one other. The other bloke, poor Lad, wasn't going to be walking anywhere for a while. John, on the other hand, found himself glaring at the clock, counting the hours to get out of that bed.

"How about a book?" he asked later, when one of the nurses came round. She'd see what she could do. Probably one of the porters could help him.

"Porter? He's here? Good chap, useful to know, reliable." Only it wasn't the 'Porter' John knew. The poor man was only trying to be helpful, but John was struggling to read. Restless legs.

"Don't worry, that'll wear off," the nurse informed him as she signalled to her colleague to join her.

"You haven't been looking after yourself very well. We think you've got some vitamin deficiencies," the one nurse informed him, as the other was already bringing the screens around before deftly removing John's precious pillows and turning him over onto his side again, for yet another injection.

"How many more of these am I meant to have? Can't we just get them all over and done with in one go?"

"The doctor needs to see you again before then, and no, you can't get them all 'done-with'. You'll do as you're told and take them as prescribed, or you won't get out of bed for another week."

"Well, that told me! Didn't it?" John chuckled, winked at the younger of the nurses, and relaxed.

He was sore and itched, his knee ached and there were bruises where he didn't know it was possible to bruise, but apart from that, it could have been worse!

"Quite right," the young nurse approved. "Now stop complaining and drink this."

"Yes nurse." John tugged at the unruly mass of curls flopping down over his forehead.

She giggled, "and I'll get one of the porters to come round and help with that too."

John combed through his hair with his fingers, then brought his hand down around his chin feeling the greasy stubble. "Cripes! When did that happen?"

The nurse straightened the bed clothes and repositioned his pillows, handing John back the book he'd been attempting to get interested in all morning.

John decided he was well capable of shaving himself. The porter brought everything he needed. It wasn't his best work, but at least he didn't feel quite so scruffy. As for his hair, that would have to wait until he could get into that chair and start wheeling himself round a bit.

He got into the chair for the first time a couple of days later. The sense of relief was ridiculous. The relief of being able to sit was momentary, as it required him to use his arms to lift himself into it, and his one 'good' leg to take the weight. Trying to put weight on the other was agony. The plaster went from above mid-thigh to just before his toes. His foot was fine, but they'd needed to immobilise any movement of the leg above and below the knee.

"Everything is in the right place you just need it to mend," the nurse reminded him. John winced as he balanced that plastered leg forward on the rest-extension to the wheelchair. It worked well, so long as he didn't misjudge the turning.

His arms were weaker than he remembered. "You're going to need to exercise them," the porter suggested as he wheeled John out into the sunshine. John had figured that out for himself and was already starting to decide how he could do that. Lobbing books at some of the porters would be a good start!

The air was bright up here on the hospital hill. The sun wasn't as fierce as it had been down on the paths through the jungle. Hot enough up here, but more than anything it felt bright, rebounding off the clipped grass lawns.

There were regular meals and they were palatable at least, though nothing of any substance. But having seen the state of the some of the other occupants in his ward, John wasn't going to complain. Now he was out of bed he intended to stay that way.

He was missing that bunk at the back of the garage. He was missing his toolbag, the feel of tools in his hands, the smell of them. He was missing the sounds of camp and the voices of the Lads.

It was going to take a few more weeks before his leg would mend to where they could take the plaster off. The bed was too hard and too soft, the lights were too bright, and the walls didn't move. But oh, those nurses, those pale-gliding soft-spoken creatures, who had cool hands and called you by your name!

John reckoned he'd probably be stuck in the wheelchair for two weeks tops. He got to one of the tables outside, pulling himself until his legs were under, his elbows on the table. That felt better.

Giving his head a shake he leant across to reach for the paper and pens. His chest felt less awkward, the bandages had taken over from the strapping, but he still felt sore and was reminded of the position of the breaks every time he reached forward. It didn't stop him anymore though.

Whatever they were giving him was helping with the restlessness, in his legs at least. His hands and head needed more than that. They needed a little bit of mischief to keep them happy.

"Two weeks, hey?" John slapped the side of his wheelchair. "Oh, I think we can do something with that!"

He called over a couple more of the wheelie-Lads. None of them had actually got round the entire complex of corridors and wards yet. The hospital building was by far the largest in the grounds, but there were three other smaller buildings. Presumably one was the Nurse's Home, one was the Doctor's Residence, and the third must be the Administration building. That was John's guess anyway.

"OK, ready for a recce?" John queried. The other two Lads were up for it. He hadn't realised the lawns were actually at the back of the hospital area. Around the front was far busier, with much more 'possibility' about it. The trucks and ambulances were coming up the hill through a single guarded gate.

They weren't going to be allowed anywhere near the gate. As soon as their wheelchairs got close, the guards shooed them away.

There were a couple of trucks parked to the one side of the guarded gate, with spaces allocated for the ambulances to be parked between their 'dropping-off' and 'picking-up' errands.

The other side of the guarded gate seemed to be a supply drop-off point. The porters were allowed to get that close, but only with checkable paperwork. The rest of that area that side out front of the hospital was the helipad, clearly marked out and clipped down to the precision of a cricket pitch.

There was no helicopter in residence for the time being. "How often do they come in?" John asked his cohorts.

"Too often, but they never stay longer than absolutely necessary, so don't get any ideas in that direction."

It was just a thought, but none of them could fly a helicopter, so that was a non-starter. The trucks might work. John's legs weren't feeling quite so restless, but his arms were aching.

"You're doing it wrong, lean into the push, you get more power out of it that way," one of the other two wheelers instructed. John tried but leaning that far forward and trying to push down from his shoulders felt like it was clenching his chest.

The grass was starting to get slippery. His arms were starting to tremble. "You need to get some strength back into them, and your grip's wrong."

John had forgotten what it sounded like to be told he was doing it wrong. He didn't like it! But he listened. Between them, that afternoon, they got to grips with how to handle obstacles and different terrain. It might not have been conventional, but it worked for them.

300

They had to stop a couple of times. The first when John's wheelchair got stuck on the grass. His fellows rallied round, one either side, taking up their positions, grabbing his arm rests with one hand each and wheeling their own chairs back to release their fellow from the clod. That worked, but it was enough for all three of them to need a breather. There was squash on the table.

"Any chance of some tea?" they yelled over to the nearest porter, who was struggling to take a cumbersome delivery round the back. "Can't yet, when I've finished this."

The three wheelers were intrigued. "What's that?"

John made a guess. "Tents?"

The porter had yet to answer.

"What for?" ... "Incoming?" ... "How many?" ... "What's happened?"

The porter waited for them to quieten. "No fresh incoming. At least, not as far as they've told me. The Nurse's Home's getting new showers. They haven't got enough facilities apparently and the builders can't move in until the nurses move out. Temporarily. Just for a couple of weeks."

"The nurses are moving into the tents?" John queried on behalf of his fellow wheelers.

"No, just the nurse's showers," the porter corrected him.

"Even better!" John smirked.

The porter ticked the three of them off as best he could whilst holding on to the laden trolley. "If any of you so much as get within peeking-distance of these tents ... they'll ... I'll be for the..." The porter was at a loss for words to adequately describe what horrors lay in store for any poor fool who attempted such.

The wheelers backed away. "OK. No one goes near the nurse's shower tents. Got it!"

"They're putting them up behind the Nurse's Home building,

so you lot won't get any ideas." The porter didn't seem convinced by that theory, but he'd given them fair warning, that was the best he could do.

An interesting development. Something to be discussed over tea, as they recovered. Their heads were clear, but their bodies weren't behaving as they used to, just a little more 'adjusting'.

They waited for the porter to come back their way. "Can we borrow your trolley?"

The porter didn't think he ought, asking a wary, "What for?"

"'Cos we're not ready to swipe your bicycle yet!"

The porter left the trolley and went to find his bicycle. He'd finished for the day anyway.

For a couple of days they used the trolley to help with getting used to how to move their bodies, in and out of the wheelchairs. It loosened the chest and strengthened the back and arms. They'd all spent too long lying down. Even if they could only stand by holding and hauling, it was a start. At least for the first day 'out', just to feel the weight of their own bodies. They could 'work' with that.

The trolley got put to one side where the porter could find it again, and by the time they got back to the ward they were ready for it. Heads weary and bodies aching, but no longer restless. They had plans and they slept well that night.

They stayed away from the shower tents although the workmen coming to do the plumbing for the Nurse's Home were a constant source of amusement. John had even seriously considered taking a few pieces left recklessly within reach. The damned plaster on his leg was making it ruddy inconvenient.

"Come on Doc, even if you just take half of it off, it'll be enough," he bargained next time the doctor came round. The nurses had already told John 'absolutely not yet' but it was worth a go if the Doc said yes. "Just a half a leg, it's only me knee, ain't it?"

The doctor began to argue, a lot of long-winded medical-jargon.

John didn't want to listen to that. He politely waited for the doctor to finish his explanation, then resumed his argument.

"So that's a yes then?"

That wasn't what the doctor had been saying, but he could see the determination in John's face.

"I think I'd better. I've heard you've been threatening to use one of the workman's woodsaws to wriggle yourself loose."

John was wondering who'd blabbed, but it didn't matter. If Doc believed it, then mission accomplished!

"I think we can change that," the doctor decided and duly beckoned a nurse, who indicated to the porter to bring the screens around.

John gritted his teeth and let them get to work. He was glad of the screens. Within the hour he had the plaster off. There was his leg, exposed and intact in front of him, for the few minutes it took for the nurse to clean it. Her touch felt strange on his skin. Sort of lop-sided. Not numb, but without the same level of sensation he recognised in his other leg. John was sitting in his wheelchair, resting one hand on the thigh of his 'good' leg and gripping the arm rest on the other side. The clench of John's jaw had started to work its way down to his chest.

"John, get your breath back, or you're going to start feeling uncomfortable," the nurse suggested gently.

"Start? Crikey nurse, where've you been for the past half hour!" John winced again, as she removed more of the various dressings that had been under the plaster. His leg looked rather patriotic. Pale white soft flesh, angry red scars and blue blotches.

"Don't worry those will fade."

"Think I need to start working on my tan," John tried to sound light-hearted, but that first sight of his leg had been a bit of shock. He'd been focused on his knee. That had been the only bit he'd been worried about, but by the looks of it, his whole leg had been damaged to some extent.

"Gawd! I did make a mess of it didn't I?" his voice rang out louder than he realised.

"Told you so!" called the Lad in the next bed over, from the other side of the screen.

John laughed. "You did that!"

He didn't need to look at the worst of the damage for much longer, as the nurse had turned and obscured the view. She was still cleaning it, she needed to give it a bit of a scrub in a couple of places, by the way it felt. John couldn't be sure he could tell between the scrubbing and the tugging, even the sensation of liquid across its surface felt distorted. The sooner she stopped doing whatever it was she was doing, the better.

When she moved again, John could see the nurse had re-bandaged the area with plenty of padding, but to no more than four inches above and below the knee this time. He couldn't move the knee itself, but at least he could see and touch the rest of his leg.

"I can stand with that?" he queried, as she took a step away from him, clearing the trolley away from his reach.

"Take it slowly and hold on to something." She wasn't going to try and stop him.

That was all John needed to know. She hadn't cleared the screens away either, so if he was going to make a mess of this first attempt, it wasn't going to be obvious.

Grabbing both arm rests, pushing himself up and leaning slightly forward, John could feel the weight going through both legs. More or less. Mostly down the good side, the dodgy side he tried to lean away from.

He wasn't going to try and step. He just needed to get his balance. He moved one grip to the end of the bed, wobbling precariously, close to toppling.

"No!" he stopped the nurse from stepping forward to steady him. "I can do this. I just need to get the feet in the right place." Why had he said it like that, 'the feet'? Like they weren't his own? They were, he could see that, only one felt a little 'off' from the other.

He had one hand holding onto the corner of the bed frame, the other free, the wheelchair behind him. He knew where it was. "Just gotta stand on me own two feet, that's all," he told himself and the nurse. He'd got the balance about right, about seventy-thirty. If he turned just slightly enough, he didn't start feeling that crunch into his knee so badly. John could manage that.

Straightening up steadily, he felt his spine lengthen and his hips felt more certain, though they were aching too. But he was grinning now. Easing off the tension in his chest, relaxing his shoulders and lifting the hand that had been holding on.

"OK, that's enough," the nurse commanded.

John didn't argue. He'd proven he was right, that was enough.

"Standing only and only for a minute or two. You'll be needing the wheelchair for at least a couple more weeks and I don't want to hear any more talk of bandage-tampering," she commanded.

"Deal!" He would have shaken on that, but she had brought the wheelchair forward and his hands were occupied twisting his body back into the seat.

He was blowing hard from the effort and slumped with exhaustion.

"You OK?" the nurse asked, before moving the screens away.

John nodded, "Thanks nurse, I can work with that."

Before the end of the day after that the wheelers from John's ward had made contact with the rest of the wheelers in other wards. There was a very brief foray into relay-racing down the corridor. It had sounded alright in theory, and they had look-outs posted either end and the corridor could take it, but the wheelchairs couldn't turn soon enough when the alarm was raised when someone was coming!

There'd been a bit of a crush at one end, two of the chairs had got locked blocking the escape route entirely. There was a lot of jeering and yelling, a few scuffs, but no (more) bones broken, and although someone said they needed a crowbar, it only took one of the nurses to take charge and clear it all, just before Matron came sailing through.

Matron didn't even blink, but the Lads knew she'd be having words later. "Better take this outside," they decided before they'd been split up.

Meeting up in the grounds the following morning, a couple of the Lads weren't ready for anything quite so robust yet, but the rest of the wheelers started with some practice runs; 'circuits and bumps' took on a new meaning. The circuits were simple, as there was a concrete path laid down around the main building, presumably for the trolleys when they came off the trucks or helicopters. There was no one about, so it seemed a good time to give it a run.

A couple of them, including John, got a bit over-confident third time round and started nudging each other at the bends. John went over, and it was on his 'bad' side too. The pain came up to meet him and slingshot his senses back to the memory of the jump. He was clear on the pain he'd felt then, this felt worse.

His knee felt as if it had just been smashed by a sledge-hammer, his hands were down, cradling it. John hadn't even realised he'd actually gone down on his shoulder and head, too.

They'd managed to get his wheelchair righted and him back into it before the workmen got there. "You alright!?" one of them asked. John stared blankly at him, still clutching his knee. He daren't let go, or it might explode again!

His shoulder had started to throb, and his head was spinning slightly, but if they'd just let him sit there … and no one dared touch his knee. "Lend me a spanner will you, and a couple of bolts? I'm gonna get this fixed!" John blurted in furious impatience.

He raised his hand to thump his knee, all the rage of the past weeks in that fist, about to come slamming down onto the precarious joint. Two of the workmen grabbed hastily at his arms, restraining him. John yelled at them and they let him until he didn't have any more breath left in his lungs and his chest was starting to tighten again.

The nurses had got to John by then. "ENOUGH OF THAT!" the senior scolded him.

John went silent, she was right. That was enough. It was gone, done, passed. He'd spent his rage and his knee was still intact. John was mending. He was just being an idiot. His hands were no longer clenched, they rested, as she talked over his shoulder down to him, pushing him back to the ward.

"You're doing well, now stop trying to mess it up!"

"Sorry nurse." He knew she was right. He could hear some of the Lads resuming their racing, good for them. He'd join them again in a day or two, but maybe not tomorrow!

The screens came back around his bed for the rest of that day, as they checked his knee *and* shoulder, this time.

"You'll need that cleaning again," the nurse observed and went to fetch the trolley. She'd a few more choice words on his behaviour when she returned.

John listened and didn't argue when she beckoned her colleague to help him back into bed. They both worked on him after that. He took his medicine and felt his body sink back down into the mattress beneath him. His knee felt secure, his shoulder sore and his head heavy.

It was later the following afternoon before John got as far as getting his wheelchair outside again. They were glad to see him, they'd been practicing and he was ready for them!

Yesterday he'd been an idiot. Today he knew his limits and wasn't going to make the same mistake. He'd worked out how to move and how not to. The wheelchair was only temporary, a 'couple of weeks' that doctor had told him. Give or take a tumble or two, that's what it was going to be.

"Come on then Lads, let's make this a bit more interesting, let's get some obstacles there."

It was a good idea, there were no straight races in this place, and there were going to be enough obstacles ahead, they might as well start getting used to them! It wasn't about avoiding the obstacles. They needed to work out how they could get around them and get on with what they wanted to do.

They hadn't seen the trolley porter for a couple of days. By the time he showed up again he was impressed with the layout of their course. They'd already moved it away from the paths, so they weren't in the way of the hospital workers. They'd borrowed a few items from the workmen, who hadn't noticed them missing yet.

That was the way of it for the next week or so.

By the time John was ready for the sticks he'd got his bearings about the place, the schedules of the locals and the routes that the irregulars tended to prefer!

The doctor had told him they needed him to start using the steps as well as the sticks. Walking didn't feel too difficult. Stiff and slow, but not difficult. He'd been doing it for decades. How difficult could it be?

Apparently, more than he'd appreciated!

The standing and shuffling from bed to table and chair was one thing. Walking from one end of the ward to the other was a different matter! Exhausting and disorganised. How could his legs have got so ill-disciplined in so short a time!?

"Shorten your stride and stop trying to swagger so much. Roll your hips." The Lads were only trying to help. Although at one point John picked up one of the sticks and threatened to wallop the twit who suggested he wasn't picking his feet up enough!

A flat floor was one thing and by the end of the day he'd got it right. The steps were another thing entirely. He knew how to climb stairs, what he hadn't realised was his knee didn't like the idea of bending going down. How do you get down stairs without bending your knee!?

He was swearing a lot in those first few days, but John was down to the one stick by the end of the week. He'd got better with the pain too.

There was a football match going on the grass. He didn't try to join in, maybe a bit too soon for that, but a walk was going to help. Both legs and one stick, yeah, John could manage that.

The knee was mending, it wasn't crunching anymore, but it was stiff and only bent begrudgingly. This place gave you a lot of time for thinking and John didn't feel so easy with that! He needed to walk, that had always helped with his thinking before.

The workmen were making a mess of the Nurse's Home bathrooms. They'd been struggling for weeks to get the plumbing right and it was still leaking. They didn't seem to mind John about the site. More than once he'd been able to tell them what they were doing wrong. At least it stopped him thinking about the 'everything else' he didn't want to.

That week they'd got hold of the record player the doctors had been using in their lounge. The lounge door wasn't locked, and the Lads were bored and the one who still needed the wheelchair caused the diversion. The one who didn't, got ready to do the 'swipe', whilst John got into the room and did the 'lifting'. Neatly done! They weren't taking it far, just relocating it to one of the side rooms for the Lads to enjoy.

Every time the doctors realised it was missing, the porters were sent scouting for it. They'd find it and report back and by the time the doctors came to fetch it, it had been 'relocated'.

This went on for another week.

John had only been involved in the first couple of days, after that there were more than enough Lads to keep it going for as long as it amused them. Eventually the doctors got the message and organised another record player.

John didn't need the stick any more by then. He was walking and stepping and striding, maybe not fit for running anywhere yet, but he was ready to leave hospital. The doctor wasn't convinced though.

He'd read John's notes and history.

"I can't send you back, not as 'fit for duty'. You can't drive."

"Oh, can't I?" John asked him squarely. He knew he couldn't run, but he didn't need to run to drive a truck, or a car for that matter. "Give me a chance and I'll show you I can drive anything you give me," he argued.

"You might be able to, but I'm not sure your knee can," the doctor countered.

John couldn't be sure of it could either. But he was about to be given the opportunity to find out!

They heard some of the porters beginning to scurry and the junior nurses had quickened their pace too.

"We've got a load of emergencies coming in!" one of the Lads shouted.

It was serious. The Lads could tell by which rooms were being made available and that the nurses were ignoring their teases. The Lads were ready to 'scramble'. How could they help?

They'd noticed some of the porters putting up one of the tents 'further back'. That was never a good sign. The Lads started moving their own beds.

"More room this way," they called over, showing the porters where, returning the chairs they'd borrowed to back under the table in the middle of the ward. Some of the Lads had been using them beside their beds to get moving, to ease-off the restlessness. No one was going to have time to be restless that afternoon!

The first helicopter came in.

The medical team were ready for them, and the trolleys were on standby. The Lads stayed back and watched from the windows.

The helicopter was packed.

One of the men hadn't survived the journey. No one said anything, as they watched him being taken directly to the tent. The pilot didn't hang about. From the gestures the onboard medic was making they needed to hurry back for more.

"What the hell happened? Where are they coming from?"

No one was going to have time to tell them anything for a while.

The Lads who could help, made themselves useful. The doctors 'indicated', Matron 'commanded', the nurses 'directed', and the porters 'yelled', whilst the Lads kept up with whoever was telling them what, and got on with that! John included.

There were trucks coming up the hill too. They were only the regulars with supplies, but they were already getting in the way. John and a couple more of the Lads got themselves over to the trucks as soon as they came in through the gate.

"Move those out the way," John shouted. The drivers were too stunned to ignore his direction and did as they were told.

"We've got supplies!" one of them started to explain.

"I know that. And we've got emergencies! Don't just sit there, the porters are busy, get shifting on those supplies."

As far as John could see with the number of emergencies coming in, whatever medical supplies were being delivered the sooner they were unloaded the better.

"We'll bring the trolleys, you stop wasting time and start moving. The Lads will help, we know where everything goes."

"There's another couple of trucks coming up behind us," the second driver warned them. "Where you gonna put 'em?"

There wasn't enough room for another truck that side of the gates, and the helicopter was going to need the space on the other side for landing and unloading.

"Oh hell!" John could already see the next truck approaching the gates. He couldn't get over to it quick enough to stop it. He couldn't unload the trucks already parked quick enough to get them moving out of the way. And they could all hear the helicopter returning.

"Oh hell!"

"GET OUT!" John roared at the driver nearest to him.

John stepped up, grabbed the handle of the cab door and pulled himself in. His knee objected. John ignored it. Muscle memory kicked in, quicker than the pain of the knee.

Waving his arm to clear everyone out of the way in front of 'his' truck, John drove forward onto the grass, running over a couple of chairs in the process, making enough room behind him for the next delivery truck. Leaning over from the cab, John gestured to the new driver who'd evidently heard his earlier order and was already climbing down from his cab. Just to be clear, John thumbed him over to the rest of the Lads. "Get on with it, then!"

The helicopter came down with the next batch of incoming and the medical team rushed forward again. The Lads stayed back with the delivery drivers, just as John had told them, out of the way and making themselves useful.

No one was arguing.

They could see the nurses and porters with the trolleys. No more being taken to the tent further back this time, at least not immediately.

They weren't done yet.

John heard it.

There was a second helicopter coming in.

"DAMN," John swore to himself. "Where the heck are we going to put that one?"

They were all looking up and over to the second helicopter. It was impossible. There was no way they were going to get three trucks *and* two helicopters in that space.

Something had to give, someone had to move.

John was still in the cab of his truck. The pilot was still in the first helicopter. They'd only just got the last passenger off and his medic was still giving his report to the doctors gathered around. There was nowhere for the first helicopter to go up, and the second helicopter needed to come down.

"TOW!" John yelled at the top of his voice, slamming his foot down hard on the accelerator, repeating the instruction, "TOW!" Skidding the truck into a sharp right turn, tearing up the grass he careered towards the front of the landed helicopter. "TOW!" he yelled over to the pilot.

His cab door swinging wide open, John got the nearest truck driver to grab hold, first to wave frantically to clear the way ahead, between the truck and the landed helicopter, then to clamber into the back and 'be ready with the rope'.

John could see the staff and injured were clear, and he'd got the attention of the pilot, showing him what he was intending to do. The pilot gave a thumbs up.

"THAT'S A GO." John was still at full bellow, signalling to the man in the back.

"COME ON YOU LOT." The Lads within range got themselves behind the truck and grabbed the rope flung from the back in their general direction, hooking up the connection between the front of the helicopter to the back of the truck. John had another man hanging on his cab door by then. "GET 'EM CLEAR," he yelled, loud enough for the Lads to hear for themselves.

"Clear this end!" John looked back at the cockpit of the helicopter; the pilot was ready. "Right." John steadied himself, reached over and yanked the 'spare' truckdriver, clinging to the door, back into the seat beside him.

John brought the truck to pull-speed smoothly. Until he felt the rope took the slack. Then the helicopter began to roll.

"OK?" John checked.

The 'spare' driver looked out his side. "Looking good."

John kept his truck hauling. They could hear the second helicopter starting to come down.

"You might want to pick up the pace a bit," the 'spare' driver suggested. John was already ahead of him. He got to within about a half yard of the next brick wall, before he stopped. By then the medical team were running past him to start unloading the third batch of incoming patients.

Some of the doctors and nurses were already busy working on the men who had been brought in earlier. The available nurses were being helped by porters, whilst the porter's duties had been seamlessly delegated to more of the Lads, who were doing their best with the trolleys and supplies being called for.

The 'spare' driver leaned over to John. "Nice work. Quick thinking."

John grinned. "Who said anything about thinking!"

The pilot of the first helicopter came over to thank him too. "Didn't think there was enough room for doing that."

"Neither did I!" John admitted, with a grin and a groan, as he collapsed out of the cab, unconscious.

CHAPTER 11

REHAB AND RALLIES

PADRE

The mission house had been inundated with offers of help since the newspaper article had got published and the photos had been reprinted in some periodicals. They seemed to especially like the one with Padre and Porter and that pretty biscuit tin. Padre hadn't expected that sort of a response at all! He'd simply wanted to help the farmers who'd lost their crops in the rice cargo fire.

Head Office had decided they needed to get involved with all the enquiries and responses and sent two assistants for Padre. Very efficient they were. Very capable, and more than able to make Padre feel like he really wasn't needed there anymore!

Padre hadn't intentionally begun looking for a new situation, but his current one seemed to have been taken out of his hands, and the advert he'd found did sound rather urgent. He'd read it a couple of times and it just seemed to say 'we need you.' Padre had thought he would be sad to leave the mission house, but when it came to it, he wasn't.

He would have been quite content to continue his chicken soup services from his kitchen yard, and more than happy to continue his visiting errands with his mending-bag. But Head Office weren't sure that was safe for him, that wasn't the way they expected things to be done, as Padre's new assistants kept reminding him!

As for those letters from home, they'd brought Padre mixed messages and he wasn't quite sure what to make of them. He recognised some of those who wrote to him, old friends he hadn't heard from since college days informing him of their impressive achievements and the advancements they had accomplished. Padre wondered why they'd spent so much paper telling him that.

There were letters from family members who'd never spoken to him before, writing to congratulate him on his 'good works'. He wasn't really sure what to do with those, either.

They made him feel restless. Not homesick, just ready for a change. And with so much 'help' from Head Office, Padre was starting to feel he was getting in the way again, just as those letters from home had reminded him of how he'd felt before.

Time to move on.

Yes, he'd decided. That advert was just the thing. That hospital on the hill sounded quite a change of pace for Padre.

Before he took up their offer of the position, Padre had taken the opportunity to get over to camp again. He hadn't been able to for the past few weeks and was shocked by the changes. The camp was half empty. Padre knew better than to ask for any details. He'd already heard there'd been a 'warming-up' of incidents in some areas.

When one of the doctors had brought him up to date with what had happened to John and where he was, Padre found himself wondering, "So, 'change of pace' for John too?"

Daks hadn't been seen anywhere near the camp since. Whether he knew about John, or whether he was staying away for another reason, no one knew. Padre for one didn't doubt it. Daks knew.

Padre had heard about the incident with the barn roof previously, but hadn't realised it was John who'd been injured, nor so badly, nor where they'd taken him. With the camp doctor adding his own letter of recommendation to the communications heading for the hospital on the hill, Padre felt easier with his decision.

"A change of pace?" The doctor had enjoyed that expression. "Oh, yes! It'll definitely be that for you, Padre. The pace over there is *all* up-hill!"

If he had intended to caution Padre with that assurance, it missed its mark. Padre had come to realise he preferred a bit of an uphill struggle. It was that sense of achievement inside him when he'd managed to help. Whether it was with a bowl of chicken soup and a quiet place to sit down and chat, or with his bicycle and mending-bag.

Padre hadn't understood how literal that 'uphill' expression had been from the camp doctor, until he got there.

It was an ingenuously simple arrangement and worked marvellously well, so long as you knew the time! The roads up to the hospital on the hill were only wide enough for a one-way flow of traffic. One hour up, one hour down, then swap around. "Odds up, evens down." Even Padre could remember that.

There were regular trucks heading that way. Padre waited for the next to get a ride up the hill. He travelled light, hardly much more than the same luggage he'd carried onto the troopship, the same leather bag and the small suitcase with just a few more books and letters in it this time.

The mention of the clock hours had reminded Padre of Porter. He'd heard plenty of stories of Porter since he'd gone off on another one of his business ventures. It always worried Padre when he did that. Porter really wasn't very good at those. He was undeniably a very useful fellow and if he'd only stuck with repairing clocks, he might have been safer. Porter just tended to get distracted by ill-advised 'opportunities'!

There were plenty of clocks between the railway station and the check-point at the bottom of the hill. Padre was already wondering how he might be able to get a message to Porter.

It was the Padre's second day at the hospital Chapel. No one had told him anything yet. He'd found his own way there, and had settled himself in, then waited.

He was still waiting when he heard the commotion over by the gate at the top entrance. They had to check everyone's papers at both gates, and they could only do that if no one got stuck halfway. It sounded like someone had forgotten to check the time before starting out. Padre listened and wondered what Porter would have made of that, he was particularly good at synchronising watches! Maybe he ought to mention that to someone? When someone came to tell him what he was meant to be doing there.

Once they'd got the delivery trucks and the ambulance unstuck, the first of the Lads came by the Chapel to have a chat. Padre made them both a cup of tea. There was a nice little kitchen for that.

The Lads hadn't been expecting to find Padre there at all. "We had a Chaplain but he went off!"

They sat and sipped their tea and talked about where they'd been and what had brought them to the hospital on the hill.

"You're a good listener, Padre. You don't interrupt and you don't remind us what we did wrong."

"Well, thank you," Padre chuckled, looking down at their cups of tea. "You know what this needs? Biscuits, we need some dunkers. Where's the canteen?"

Nothing in the canteen but tables and chairs at this time of day. All the Lads knew where the kitchen was and that it was off-limits to the likes of them. "But if you're after biscuits, Padre, best try the doctor's lounge. That's what I'd recommend. Of course, there's probably some in the nurse's office, but I wouldn't try that way if I was you! Come to think of it you can get into the kitchens, Padre, can't you? I mean you've got a pass to be just about anywhere."

"Well then, that's going to be useful, isn't it?" Padre agreed, getting the Lad to laugh along with him. The Chapel was quite small, but nicely set out. A quiet place to sit and pray or talk about whatever was needed to be talked about.

Padre decided he was there to listen. His quarters behind the Chapel comprised a small kitchen to one side, that doubled as the vestry, and his study-bedroom behind that, just enough for Padre.

He didn't go into the hospital canteen until supper time, still not quite sure who he was meant to be presenting his paperwork to, but it seemed about time someone ought to know!

Padre saw Matron first, and immediately decided that was probably the best person to introduce himself to. Matron made it easy, by speaking first. "Ah! There you are. You're late."

"Yes, Matron. Sorry, just got settled in." Padre decided it didn't need him to add the bit about being there since yesterday.

"You'll have supper with me," she indicated the seat next to her. There were four seats at each table and all were empty. It wasn't so much an invitation as a command.

Padre found that quite reassuring. It was always easier to accept a command. "Thank you, Matron."

She was happy to introduce him to the staff as they arrived for their supper, but made it clear she wouldn't have time to give him a tour of the hospital.

"I'm sure I'll find my way around," Padre ventured boldly.

"I'm sure you can, but there are some areas which are restricted, unless we call for you, Padre." Matron wasn't being rude, and he didn't take offence.

"Of course." That seemed to be agreeable to Matron.

As for the doctors, they were interested in Padre's recent experiences. They'd had the newspapers too! They had also received a letter from one of their colleagues at Padre's 'old camp'. "We can always make use of someone with your skills around here. There are times when some of the Lads get a little 'shy' of the nurses, and you don't look like a doctor, that'll help too."

Padre found that equally reassuring. He was also happy to assure his dining companions that he was looking forward to improving his 'hospital training'. That raised a few smiles. As one of the doctors kindly explained, from what their colleague had mentioned in that letter, Padre was already remarkably well 'qualified by experience'!

Padre took his meals with the staff mornings and evenings, but otherwise, for that first week, kept himself where he could be found, tucked in the Chapel. Just as he suspected after his first visitor word got around and every few hours someone found they were 'just passing-by' the Chapel and thought the Padre might like a 'chat'.

In between the visitors, he read, and when he found he was running low on supplies in his little tea-making kitchen, he waited until the canteen was empty and made enquiries.

"You should have just sent us a note, Padre. Any of the porters will bring you whatever you need."

"Oh, you have plenty of porters?" Padre wondered.

"Never enough porters. That's why we've got wheelchairs and trolleys in so many awkward places!" The canteen lady was very helpful.

Padre had wanted to say something then but realised that hadn't been the right time for making such a suggestion. He waited until his supplies were brought over to the Chapel. It hadn't taken much to persuade the porter to have a cup of tea and tell Padre more about how the hospital worked.

Padre had learnt long ago that although the doctors were the brains of a hospital, it took Matron and her nurses to run it, whilst it was invariably the porters and canteen staff who knew how the place actually worked.

Padre was at a slight disadvantage then. He could write to the mission house directly to request they forward a note on to Porter, but had no idea if they had any clearer 'fix' of Porter's location than he did! "Worth a try," he decided and posted the letter the next day.

Padre drank a lot of tea and did a lot of listening in those first few weeks. Unfortunately, he was also called over to the 'isolation' unit a few times, to attend to a couple of the Lads in the side rooms.

He kept up with regular services too, never fretting about a sermon, but always happy to 'waffle-on' a bit.

The nurses approved of the way he was with the Lads and the doctors were pleasantly surprised. Not what any of them had come to expect from a Padre. A sensible fellow, he understood the men's strengths and the officer's weaknesses!

Padre had found John and was relieved to see him looking better than he'd been led to believe.

"Took a while," John admitted. "You here for good, then?"

Padre winked, "Well if I was here for mischief, I think I've got plenty of competition in that department, haven't I?"As for how long the Padre was staying for. "For as long as needed," was his best guess. They talked about books and men, the camp, the hospital and, eventually, everything in between.

John couldn't help him with the riddle of the disappearing chaplain, "But if you're getting an inkling to go off anywhere for a while, let me know, will you?" They both got on to the matter of Porter fairly smoothly after that. It didn't seem too far-distant from the riddle of 'going-off'. "Any ideas where he's got to? What he's been getting up to?"

Padre was able to let John know he'd sent a letter to the mission house with enquiries, but nothing yet.

"Do the mission house keep track of him?" John asked doubtfully.

"Probably not directly," Padre considered. "But they'll likely know someone who might."

"Do you need him, Padre?" John suddenly thought to ask.

Padre wasn't prepared to say that much but had a feeling Porter might be needing them! That was something they could both agree on. But Padre had sent the letter and there wasn't much else they could do except wait, until someone, hopefully Porter himself, got in touch with them.

They didn't have to wait too long for news. Porter turned up two days later.

"Got your note Padre," he beamed. "Thought I'd look you up and see how you're settling in?" he said, before turning to John, without a flicker of hesitation. "Heard you got a bit banged-up when you kicked that barn roof!"

John's smile was a little more knowing. "So, you needed somewhere to hide out, did you? And the hospital Chapel seemed like a perfick sanctuary! How did you manage to get past the gates?"

"Ah!" Porter waved Padre's letter. "They never read 'em. They look at the address at the top and the name under the signature at the bottom, but they never read 'em!"

"Are you in trouble Porter?" Padre's voice came earnestly, he needed to know. "Is anyone looking for you?"

Porter sat down, finally ready to be honest. He had run out of all other options! "They're not exactly looking for me, so much as maybe it would be better for my health to avoid certain areas for a while. I might have outstayed my welcome, Padre."

John could well believe that but waited for Padre to say something. Porter's confession was to him.

Padre sat quietly for a few more minutes. He was thinking. He remembered something that Porter had said months ago, and wondered if Porter remembered it too.

"Porter, do you still want to get home 'the right way'?"

"It's about time, isn't it, Padre?" Porter was sounding sheepish. "I did give it a try, honest I did! A while back … Maybe I ought to give it another go, hey? 'The right way' this time, though."

"Yes, Porter." Padre's voice was calm and steady, almost-stern but nearer-kind. "I think if we're going to be getting you home, then it's going to need less trying on your part, and more doing."

Porter was listening.

John suddenly slapped Padre on the back. They weren't going to leave him out of this hair-brained scheme! "Then that's what we'll have to do."

Padre looked at John, nonplussed as to how he seemed to already have got a step ahead of them. "*We* will?"

"What? You think we can't figure something out between us?" John demanded recklessly.

Padre could see Porter still seemed a little nervous.

"Are you sure no one knows where you are. How did the mission house get my letter to you?"

"They didn't, I sort of happened to be passing-by and picked it up myself … when they're weren't looking," Porter confessed.

Padre gave Porter that 'you-know-that-was-the-wrong-thing-to-do' look.

"Sorry, Padre."

Porter kept a low profile for the next day or so, but gradually began to show his face. Padre kept him busy with errands, always referring to him as 'Porter'. It had worked before.

John was amazed it was that simple. But no one questioned a new porter about the hospital. After all, they needed every porter they could get!

John was getting around pretty well on the sticks. He got Porter on book duty. That was a great way for getting about the place. If anyone saw him with a pile of books in his hands, they'd just assume he was taking them somewhere else. Porter just had to looked like he was in a hurry, and no one asked him any questions.

That worked for a few more days, until Padre was called to one of the side rooms. He'd need to stay by the bedside. The night-duty nurse would only be a few feet away at her own desk. Neither could leave their posts.

John never did get a straight answer from Porter. "What on earth possessed you to pop up then and offer to make them a brew?"

Porter grinned stupidly. "It seemed like a good idea. You know, a step in the 'right' direction?"

"And was it?" John had only heard about it the morning after.

Porter wasn't able to answer that. In truth even he didn't know why he'd done it!

"It felt strange, but sort of nice. But I don't know why."

John had seen in a heartbeat Porter wasn't up to talking about it yet.

Padre was tired too, but always found whenever he'd come from a bedside vigil, it helped to walk in a garden. "I always find walking in a garden afterwards uplifting, like the sadness is spent," he explained.

John had been with some of the Lads when their time had come, but there had been no bedside vigil for them, most had been in the dust and mud somewhere, quick and bloody painful. No clean sheets, no calm words, no quiet hours.

"How do you know what to say in those hours?"

"If they can talk, you let them. They need to know they've been heard. Sometimes they just need to know someone is beside them," Padre explained, as they continued walking.

"So what was Porter doing there, all night?"

John had been trying to figure that out ever since he'd heard about it. It didn't make any sense.

Padre had heard Porter out in the corridor. Then he'd appeared at the door with a cup of tea. Porter had only said a few words, but the poor Lad had wanted to talk.

"Right place, right time, then, Padre?"

"Seemed to be," Padre agreed. "Sometimes it just happens like that."

Padre had simply sat to one side and let them talk a while. The nurse had checked in, but when she saw what was happening she hadn't said a word, only brought another chair into the room.

Porter had stayed all night with the poor Lad.

John didn't ask when, or what, or even why, only, "Was it peaceful?"

Padre nodded slowly, "Oh yes, and Porter had a lot to do with that. I think he was like a 'voice from home'. In the end that was all the Lad wanted to be able to hear, just 'a voice from home.'"

"In the end, that's all any of us want isn't it, Padre?" John wasn't expecting an answer.

They continued walking for a while after that, both too busy thinking to talk. Padre was still thinking about John's question later, when he overheard one of the doctors in the canteen mentioning the transport problems and the impending arrival of the next scheduled hospital ship. They usually came every couple of months or so.

Padre didn't usually listen in like that. He certainly hadn't intended to, but there was something about the doctor's dilemma that sparked his interest. An inkling of a notion, a possibility, perhaps.

Padre already knew he'd need to speak with John. It was only a rough idea, not really even-nearly a plan yet, but he could guess John would want to know.

In the meantime, the doctor was happy to bring Padre in on the problem.

"We usually manage to organise a hospital train down in plenty of time, but there was that nasty landslide a couple of weeks ago, and they're still trying to clear it. We can't chance that route this time."

Padre could sense there was a question in there. Not in so many words, but definitely there. Was the doctor asking him for an answer?

For some reason something John had mentioned came to Padre's mind, something about not all routes being regular roads, and even the most irregular of paths still managed to get those who-needed-to-know from where they were to where they needed to be! Was that it?

"An ambulance could get through if it had the right driver?" Padre blurted.

"It would have to be one heck of a driver!" The doctor solemnly eyed his colleagues for a second opinion.

"And I wouldn't give him much of a chance of reaching the ship in time," another offered ominously. "The main routes will be clogged with the traffic unable to use the trains."

"What if we could get an ambulance through by an 'alternative' route, not one of the main ones?" Padre wondered. Was that the answer?

The doctor was ready to listen to *any* answer! If Padre could find a driver willing to take the ambulance, they knew which Lads would be ready to try. "They need to be on it." It was as simple as that.

Both the doctor and Padre knew not all the Lads would survive the journey. Some of them probably wouldn't even get as far as the ship. The Lads would know that too, they just wanted to get home.

"The crews are working as fast as they can to clear the landslide." The doctor was still holding the message. He'd been midway through updating his colleagues on the progress, or lack thereof, checking the details again, as he sought Padre's advice.

"The train will probably still manage to get through." The doctor's voice was saying the words, but even Padre could hear he was far from certain. The 'probably' was a bit of a giveaway.

"When's the next sailing after this one due in?" Padre asked.

The doctor checked, just to be sure. "Couple of months away."

He knew the next question.

Padre didn't need to say it.

Some of the Lads wouldn't be able to wait that long.

"What about the roads?" John checked, butting in on the private conversation. He'd noticed Padre and the doctor with their heads together from the canteen doorway. The other doctors had distanced themselves. Never a good sign!

The doctor slowly tucked the message into his pocket, before turning to John. "I'm sorry …."

A doctor starting a sentence with an apology? Another never-good-sign.

"But you know the state of the roads," the doctor was saying to both John and Padre. "At least with the train, we know the route and the schedule."

John muttered something along the lines of "so do the CT!" but kept that to himself, before raising his voice. "What you need is a driver who knows how to handle those roads down that way."

The doctor and Padre exchanged glances. John couldn't see enough to decide their verdict yet. Then the doctor was looking across to his colleagues. No, they didn't seem to have any other ideas either!

"We can't risk the Lads in the ambulance *all* that way," the doctor began to half-heartedly argue, but even he didn't sound convinced by those words.

"Really Doc!?" John countered. "You think they're going to wait for you to ask them?" his voice strident in desperate anger.

Padre stepped in between the squabbling pair. "It's worth a try? Surely?" he said, his hands imploring for calm.

No one else spoke, Padre had asked the question … the one that no doctor ever wanted to answer. No, it wasn't a mistake. Padre knew what he was doing. Suddenly, and abso-ruddy-lutely, Padre knew what he was doing. "If it can be done once at least you'll know. What have you got to lose?"

The doctor knew what he was asking.

"One ambulance, one driver, three of the Lads and me. That's it," Padre reasoned fearlessly on. "If we can get down to meet the hospital ship then all good, regardless of what the train does. If not, then what have we lost? At least you've given the Lads a chance to get home."

Doc looked to John. "You're fit to drive?"

John nodded but didn't speak. He needed the doctor to decide this for his own conscience, now. Padre stepped back too. The tension had eased. He could feel the resignation, and the relief.

Doc knew immediately which three Lads he would pick for the trial-run. Whether they'd want to be part of such a reckless idiotic attempt was another matter.

John was right. Doc needn't have worried.

"How long have we got Padre?" John checked later when they were back at the Chapel and ready to go into the details.

Padre blew hard before answering. "A week, if we're lucky. The hospital will send a message down to let them know we're coming. D'you really think you can get all the way down there, in that time?"

It was time for John to remind Padre of something. "I'm not going to be the one driving. I'm just there to do the navigating."

Padre finally twigged onto John's idea. "Porter!?"

"Porter." John confirmed.

"You'll need a driver who can help with the stretchers too. You said yourself Porter's good with the Lads."

Padre found himself nodding to John's words, even before he realised what he was agreeing to.

"A week there and a week back," John told them when Padre had got Porter safely sat down. "This is the 'right way' home for you."

"We're taking these three Lads to the hospital ship. You're the driver and the porter. You'll help with the stretchers on board ship and stay with them." John waited for that much to register, before continuing. "This time you'll be doing it properly, the 'right way'. We've got the doctor's letter giving you passage home." John handed Porter the letter he'd been given. "This is yours."

Porter was ready to argue, but John was already there.

"I'm not finished here yet, and I'm not the one driving. Not this time. I'm only navigating, and that letter says 'driver/stretcher-bearer'. That's you."

Both men turned to Padre. "You're ok with this?"

It was Padre's turn to check Porter understood what they were asking of him.

"If we can do it, we'll be helping a lot more than just those three Lads in the back of our ambulance. We'll prove it's possible for *all* the other ambulances that will be able to follow the same route. Someone's got to be the first. One week, one route. You just take care of the Lads once they're on board the ship. We'll take care of the ambulance getting back here."

That was it then. That was The Plan.

They had the doctor's letter and the ambulance. They had Padre, and a motorbike too! The Engineer had seen to that. He'd got the address from the mission house and 'thought it might be useful', according to the note.

The three Lads were ready first thing the following morning. Porter checked his watch, John settled himself in the passenger seat and the three Lads in the back gave a holler over to the guard at the gate. Padre revved up his motorbike and they were ready.

"About 500 miles then?" John checked as Porter climbed into the driver's seat beside him, starting the engine.

Padre knew the distance too. How were they ever going to manage it? It took him from the top-of-the-hill gates down to the bottom to realise 'best not look that far ahead.'

Nothing was planned from that point on.

John knew the roads and what to look out for. Porter was a good driver and knew how to keep the Lads calm. They'd leave the praying up to Padre and he was useful to have along, in case anyone else started asking questions.

Porter had driven in silence for about an hour. He'd been thinking. John could hear it. Porter seemed to decide this might be a good time to get something straight.

"If they look, they'll see Padre first. If they bother to ask, we've got enough paperwork between us to bluff our way through it. And if they don't bother to ask, then it's a good thing we brought you along!"

John smiled. Yep. That had been his 'figuring' of the situation too.

JOHN

He'd needed to take a step back into the wheelchair after that truck-and-helicopter incident and wasn't happy about it, but the races had helped.

They'd set up a 'slalom' course for the wheelchairs in the garden, even managing to get a couple of the nurses to 'check it' first. "Got to make sure we're avoiding the parking bays for the trucks and can't go disturbing the landing area for the helicopters," John had argued brazenly. His bones were mending, but something was missing, a steadiness.

Padre's arrival was a blessing.

Porter's arrival had been amazing.

John was genuinely glad to see the pair of them. Even more glad that he'd been able to get out of the chair and up onto the sticks before they saw him! He could move fairly well, from the hips up. His ribs felt like they were knitting nicely, although if he twisted too quickly they pinched him. His knee was sore and stiff, but at least he could bend it now without collapsing.

John knew he was improving when he overheard one of the nurses complaining about him being a nuisance about the place!

"Give me something to do!" John had pleaded with Padre. Navigating the ambulance to the hospital ship was a heck of a 'something!' But John wasn't complaining.

If they needed to get out and stretch their legs, and Porter got it into his head to do a bit of trading, then John could keep an eye on him. When the roads got too rough or uncertain, John could warn

Padre it was time to bring the motorbike into the ambulance for a few miles. It would be a bit of a crush with four and a motorbike in the back, but the Lads weren't going to grumble.

And anyway, the whole thing had been Padre's idea! At least that's what John kept telling him.

PORTER

It had been Padre's idea. It had been Padre's letter that had brought him to the hospital on the hill, and Porter was mighty glad to get it!

Porter had managed to get himself in with a bad crowd, not for the first time. It had all seemed so straight forward. Just a straight business deal. No such thing around these parts! There was always someone else involved along the way, needing a bit of persuading. Then there'd be someone else deciding they'd only look the other way if a minor 'arrangement' could be made.

Porter had learnt from bitter experience, the longer a business deal took, the more involved the 'arrangements' got, the more could go wrong, and usually did.

He'd rather enjoyed the simplicity of just mending clocks. It was the 'just' bit that bothered him. He still couldn't figure out why he'd stopped just doing that. He'd even been quite happy to help Padre, but that word 'quite' was a problem too.

Porter was starting to realise, if he'd been home, then the 'just' and the 'quite' would have been more than enough. But he wasn't home and wasn't likely to get home if he carried on the way he was going.

Then he'd found that letter from Padre. Talk about heaven-sent! It was addressed to him and no one had told him not to come back to the mission house just because Padre wasn't there anymore. They were all so busy and he hadn't wanted to disturb them from their good works. Nothing they would miss, just a few bits of kit he'd left behind, and Padre would vouch for him.

That's what Padre's letter was telling him. Porter was certain of it. He'd learnt a long time ago, when it came to those sorts of letters, you needed to know how to read between the lines! Padre would understand.

Padre needed his help, and a hospital sounded like an ideal place to have as a reference. Porter would be needing one of those. "Like sign-posts to the 'right way' to get home." That was the way Porter thought of it, reading-between-the-lines.

It was Padre's idea. It might not be quite so easy as the luggage compartment on a troop train, but the dash to the docks sounded awfully familiar!

Padre wasn't going to *tell* Porter to do it, that wasn't Padre's way. It was the expression on his face that said, 'we're relying on you.' Porter had heard that loud and clear! He didn't need to read between the lines to find that message. And the strange thing was, he liked the way it sounded, the 'right way'!

And it took only a glance to see John wasn't fit to drive the full distance. Mind you, having John beside him in the ambulance was definitely reassuring.

Padre on the motorbike was like having a pass-key through any town they might have to get through. John would sort out the route in between the towns. And as for after that? Padre had it all sorted. "We get the Lads to the ship. They'll vouch for you as driver/porter and you've got the right paperwork to back you up."

There it was again 'the right way'.

It hadn't occurred to Porter then, but during those first few hours of driving, he began to wonder about something. What about Padre and John? Didn't they want to go home?

Those first few hours were quite direct. Follow the traffic through town, avoiding the general flow still attempting to head to the railway station. There were trains going up, but not down.

Some vehicles already seemed to be back-tracking onto the same road Porter was driving on.

"We need to get ahead of that lot," John suggested.

Porter nodded and put his foot down.

"Don't be too obvious," John muttered, as a couple of the local trucks up ahead started. "Don't try and over-take, just keep up with them until I tell you when to turn."

There were a couple of bridges coming up the other side of the town. They needed to take the first one over, but then turn off before the next one.

"We're going to be taking the hill roads. Less traffic, might be a bit easier to make some progress. Might be a 'bit grey' that way though," John observed, reminding Porter of the colour coding of various areas.

"How much of a 'bit grey' is the hill?" Porter queried, guessing there might be a good reason for there being less traffic choosing that route.

"Fairly dark," admitted John with a grin. "Nervous?"

"I'm not exactly feeling easy right now!" Porter agreed.

"Probably better that way," John approved. "Then if I need to do anything, you'll be ready!?"

"You going to give me a clue as to what the 'anything' might involve, aren't you?" Porter asked, a little hesitantly.

"Probably best you don't know, before you need to," John suggested.

"Yeah, you're right, probably wiser," Porter nodded sagely. Then realised what he'd said and smiled to himself. Him? Wise!?

It was another hour before it became obvious why few of the town traffic had opted to take this hill-road. There wasn't a lot of it! "Local track," John explained. "Don't worry I can still hear Padre behind us. Put your foot down. Might be a good idea to make up some time. It'll be slower-going getting down the other side."

"Why?" Porter wondered, not sure if he wanted to know the answer.

John heard the caution. They'd picked the right driver. "Should be OK. The other side of the hill is far enough from town to allow for more traditional trading, and we've got to allow that might slow us down."

Porter could imagine what John was referring to. He hadn't forgotten about meeting Daks and some of his friends.

The 'up' side of the hill was pretty uneventful, only needing John to get out and walk ahead for a few hundred yards. He was glad for the cane then, where the track got lost in the greenery!

Padre wanted to help. "You'll get your turn Padre. This won't take long, just need to check there's no barns lurking up this way!"

They took a few more turns but no sign of any buildings, barns or otherwise, that Porter could see. No sign of anything but a hillside full of dense jungle.

John seemed reassured and climbed back in beside him. "We're near the top. This is where I need you to make plenty of noise." He caught the quizzical look from Porter, and grinned. "The sooner they realise we have no intention of sneaking up on them, the less likely they're going to get itchy."

John banged on the side of the ambulance and one of the Lads yelled back. "Open the door back there and let Padre know we're clear for a run-down from here. It's going to get a bit dusty, so he might want to use a bit of a boot-leather with the brakes."

"Right-Ho!" came the reply.

"Ready." Porter added his thumbs up.

"If my compass is correct, we'll be going through one of the villages about half way down. They'll know we're coming and they'll be expecting us to stop. Be polite."

Porter could already feel the ambulance tipping forward. "Yep, we're definitely going down." He agreed. The wheels skidded on the dust.

They'd barely gone a couple of hundred yards when John's hand suddenly shot across to slam down in front of Porter's.

"STOP!"

There was a yell back behind them. They could hear the Lads teasing him, as Padre struggled to handle the motorbike.

"What now?" Porter couldn't see anything.

"We've got a welcoming party. Look!" John's voice was sharp and low, enough to give Porter all the warning he needed.

"No sudden movements, got it," Porter muttered and waited for John.

He hadn't pointed but kept his hands in view as he climbed down from the cab, calling round to Padre. "Got your mending-bag with you, haven't you?"

"Always have…"

John shook his head to silence Padre after those words. "Just stand there and look helpful," he instructed, as he took a few paces forward on the path ahead of the ambulance.

There were greetings exchanged that Porter couldn't quite recognise. Something about them that seemed familiar, but perhaps it was the dialect. They seemed very composed. It was unnerving! They didn't make the exaggerated hand gestures he'd got used to seeing in the markets, and their faces were almost expressionless. They were smaller and stood in such a way that Porter couldn't even be sure how many of them there were in front of the ambulance.

As far as he could tell John seemed to have introduced Padre to the locals, who had stepped into view. Porter had also realised John was checking to see who was armed. They all were, except Padre. Porter wasn't sure if he felt easier about that, or not.

Padre was opening his mending-bag and one of the locals was rummaging through it. A couple of tubes seemed to be of particular interest to them. Padre unscrewed the tops of the tubes, showing them the contents, by applying a little of each onto the skin of his own forearm, offering it to them to check for themselves. They seemed to recognise the smell.

This was where Padre needed to lead.

John made a fuss of leaning on his cane for support, allowing Padre to walk down to the village with the seniors.

John turned a little stiffly, managing to give a subtle nod of an 'ok' to Porter, who very cautiously started the engine up again and crept the ambulance forward. His wheels weren't gripping as well as he would have liked.

The rest of the welcoming committee seemed not the slightest concerned that the ambulance might lose its grip at any moment. They filled in the gap between their elders and Padre, and the ambulance, John now walking amongst them.

"What the heck do I do with the motorbike then?" Porter asked thin air.

There was an immediate scuffle in the back of the ambulance, and the motorbike got hauled in by two of the better able Lads in the back. They'd quickly got the gist of the situation, dragging it half in with its back wheels skidding behind. It wasn't the way Porter would have done it, but the Lads seemed to be managing.

Padre seemed to be engaging with the reception committee fairly well. John knew so long as he didn't look too robust, no one was going to be too bothered about his presence.

That was until the ambulance finally found the compacted earth of the village path beneath its wheels. Porter picked up the pace a little then and the locals scattered. Just enough to allow him to enjoy the flourish of a dust cloud as he 'parked', before climbing down.

The motorbike didn't manage such a grand entrance, it fell to one side in the dust. John heard it and decided he'd rescue it before any of the locals got the same idea.

He didn't hurry, that would have blown his cover of a heavy-duty limp but ambled lopsidedly ahead of the local enquiries, leaning down and picking up the motorbike. John paused, giving anyone interested a chance to see he had first-hold on the item.

John didn't try to start it. Instead, once he'd got his balance, he wheeled it forward into the middle of the meeting underway between the elders and the Padre. There seemed to be something about John wheeling the motorbike that reminded one of the locals of something. "Bicycles!"

"Bicycles?" Porter asked, they could have been referring to any number of incidences, none of which he was ready to discuss. "That's not a bicycle, that's just John!"

One of the elders had taken note of the cry about the bicycle. Padre was getting concerned he might be in imminent danger of losing his lovely motorbike.

The interested elder came over to 'just-John', who hadn't moved since the shout had gone up. He stood quite still, rigid almost, ready to move. He'd lose the motorbike if needed.

The Elder wasn't interested in the motorbike. He was looking directly at John. The cane wasn't fooling him! That withered inscrutable expression began moving, into a grin, a massive grin.

John registered the change, shifting his balance and straightening, lifting his weight from the cane and letting go of the motorbike. Someone was going to need to say something.

"What!?" John spoke clearly, with as big a grin as the elder's, who stood hardly more than a yard from him, shoulder height to John, but squaring himself with confidence.

John stood and waited. He wasn't going to be the first to move, not this time. Not with Padre and the Lads within range.

The elder's sudden movement startled John, he flinched for a fraction of a heartbeat, before he caught himself and opened his hands again. The elder was gesturing to his chest.

John heard one of the Lads calling over to him. "It's a pissing match, John. Look!"

John realised what the local was doing. He was gesturing to his own chest at the same time as he was towards John's.

"A pissing match?" he checked over to Padre, who'd evidently picked up on the same gesture.

"He's smarter than you think. That's an ambulance, I've got a mending-bag and you're limping. He wants to compare scars."

"Oh, good grief," John breathed a long sigh, working through his exasperation, relief, and finally amusement.

"You want to see mine?" he asked the gnarled man standing in front of him.

John started unbuttoning his shirt. Porter was standing beside the ambulance, helping the rest of the Lads and almost collapsing in hysterics of laughter.

"Not those ones, John! He wants the ones you got from the barn roof-kicking incident."

John spluttered the query. "You want to see my WHAT!?"

The elder had only started the bragging contest at chest height. He was already twisting his torso to show a longer, more recent, and far uglier scar, jagged and raised, scratching down from a couple of inches above the hip over his right buttock, coming round and forward, and down the middle of the top of his thigh.

"Go on John, you can do better than that one," Porter shouted.

The Lads cheered, and Padre came to John, taking the motorbike safely to one side. "I think you'd better."

"Really, Padre?" John pleaded. Already realising the futility of arguing. More of the village seemed to have gathered for the 'show'. "Oh crikey! What is this, a ruddy exhibition?"

Padre reminded him, calmly, "Yes John, that's *exactly* what this is!"

The elder was getting impatient with John's coyness.

"I really do think you're going to have to."

"OK, Padre. OK!" John sighed, starting to unbuckle his belt. But before taking his trousers off, decided his shirt was coming off too. If they wanted to see what he'd got, they might as well see the lot!

A little awkwardly, John managed to step out of his trousers, chucking them, along with his shirt, over to Padre. "Look after those for me, will you?

"There! Happy now!?"

The scars of John's relatively recent barn roof-kicking were evident, no less jagged and ugly than the village elder's. They had healed since the surgery, but John's skin was a lot paler by comparison. They appeared to be rather more impressive than his challenger.

"Satisfied!?"

John stood there naked, hands on hips, feet braced, defiant now as the locals inspected and compared. He was more angry than embarrassed. His hands had begun to clench again.

Porter strode forward waving his arms at the locals. "Come on, come on, shows over," he shouted, taking the clothes from Padre and flinging them back over to John. "Come on John, cover up. They've seen enough. You're just showing off now!"

Padre had begun another conversation with the same elders he'd been speaking to earlier. Neither John nor Porter knew he could do that.

"What are they saying? They satisfied?"

Padre was nodding and smiling and ignoring John's query.

John waited, there wasn't much else he could do, standing in the jungle clearing, in his birthday suit, in the middle of a local village, with Padre passing the time of day, as polite-as-you-please. "Crikey Padre, any minute now and they'll be offering you tea and cake. What am I meant to be doing?"

"Ah John," Padre turned, as if only just realising he was still waiting. "I think you'll be pleased to know they are full of admiration for your scars."

"Well, I'm glad *they're* happy about them," John growled.

"No, you don't understand," Padre smiled sweetly. "They don't want you to cover them up."

"What!? They want me to stand here naked?"

"Oh no, they're very hospitable. They're inviting us to have supper with them. They just don't want you to put your trousers back on!"

Porter couldn't keep a straight face after that and made himself useful taking the motorbike back to behind the ambulance but John could still hear him laughing.

"They've heard about your parachute jump, the one where you kicked in the roof of that barn? They're very impressed."

"Really!?" John was convinced.

"Oh, they are," Padre assured him, happy to explain. "Apparently, they've never seen one of those parachute jumps come down with such accuracy! They'd been looking for that barn for days and you knocked it out of commission with far greater efficiency than they could ever have managed. They see your scars as 'magnificent' and worthy of admiration." Padre checked if he'd interpreted that correctly with one of the younger men, who seemed to be able to speak a little English. "Magnificent, yes," Padre confirmed.

The same young man handed Padre a piece of cloth, who in turn handed it to John. "They suggest you put this on for the duration of your stay so they can admire your knee!"

"You've got to be joking, Padre. Please tell me you are!?" Padre wasn't.

Porter and the Lads cheered him on.

"Go on, John. We're hungry and we've seen it all before!"

John took the length of cloth and wrapped it first round his waist, more like a sarong, tying it aggressively at his hip, glaring at Porter who immediately objected, at the incorrect manner. "Don't even think about it!" John warned him with a snarl.

He could see the way the locals wore it and wasn't going to try. He was angry and although Padre had sounded sincere, communicating how the locals admired his scars, John didn't need to be seeing them again.

John's face was thunder as he started walking again. It was ridiculous and he knew it. John also knew that Padre was right, which only made it worse!

He'd heard enough stories from Daks about some of the hill-tribes around this way and their customs. John had just been caught off-balance by the elder. That was what annoyed him most. "Satisfied?" he walked over to Padre.

Padre coughed and suggested they sat down where they'd been invited, accepting the cup he'd been offered by the young local on his other side and handing it to John. "At least have a cup of tea, you'll feel better."

"Padre, you're priceless!"

John shrugged at the smirk from the young local, then shifted his weight, so he could sit with his legs straight out in front of him. He was going to struggle to get back to his feet, but at least he wasn't going to fall down this time.

They sat around the campfire in the middle of the village. It seemed to be a bit of celebration supper, as far as John could tell, not the usual way they did things, but then he guessed they didn't usually have an ambulance blustering through the middle of their home-ground.

"Sorry about that, just trying to miss the worst of the traffic," Porter attempted to offer.

"I think they're more interested in where we're trying to get to?" Padre suggested.

The Lads had got themselves comfortable, and were glad of the stop. The ambulance was good for travelling, but if there was a chance of a bit more room for sleeping they were up for that, and the food was good too.

"So, do we tell them, Padre? I knew they were hereabouts, but I'm not picking up as many words as you are."

John waited, but the only thing Padre could tell him was that it seemed this village traded with one of the river-side villages, and they knew Padre from the river-traders.

"Hang on a minute," John felt he'd missed something. "How did they know it was me?" Maybe he was getting tired. Someone had already handed him a blanket.

"Ah, they haven't quite got round to that bit yet," Padre smiled blithely. "Would you like me to ask them?"

"No. Just tell me when it's ok to put my trousers back on," John dragged the blanket over him and snorted something obscure into the flesh of his arm, as he brought it up to rest his head.

CHAPTER 12

MARKERS ... AND MAKING SENSE OF IT ALL

JOHN, PADRE AND PORTER

John didn't wait to be told. As soon as he woke and recognised a new day beginning, he got himself to his feet and dressed. Porter was remarkably chirpy that next morning and, between them and a couple of the locals, they managed to get the three Lads safely stowed back in the ambulance. The locals seemed happy enough to bring them water to refill their supply for the next leg of the journey.

"We're ready. Where's Padre got to?" John had seen him somewhere over the far side of the village. He'd been emerging from one of the huts.

"They've been giving me directions for getting the rest of the way down from here." That sounded useful. John didn't interrupt him. "They're sending their traders down the quick route to wait for us at the bottom where our path catches up with the road on to the next market town."

Porter had been listening but was impatient to get started. "So why aren't we taking the quick route?"

"Because their traders don't need to drive a ruddy ambulance!" John reminded him. "You do. Padre might be able to make it on his motorbike. But we need a 'path' to get them and you down to those docks in time for the ship, in one piece."

Padre got himself ready on the motorbike, this time leading the way, following the path down the hill, heading for the road.

The path was a footpath but well-worn, and with Padre steering their course, and the locals somewhere to the left of them, John felt easy enough. It was a quiet day and downhill all the way!

Porter wasn't too worried. He'd got the Lads back on the road and still had an image of John standing naked on parade in the middle of the jungle village. Priceless!

When the path eventually merged into the road heading on to town, it seemed to be less of a matter of the traffic joining them, than of the jungle gradually releasing them into it.

As they headed towards town the traffic became more noticeable. A couple more hours and it had become almost a constant steady 'flow' of everything, on legs and wheels!

"Where are they? Do you know which way we're meant to be going?"

"South," John reminded him.

John wasn't looking at the traffic so much as the roadsides they were passing for any indication from that way, or from Padre, that their hillside friends had put in an appearance.

It was at least another couple of hours before John saw them and it looked like they had their own bicycles. That was handy, maybe this wasn't going to be quite such a slog. John leaned out and yelled over to Padre, who hadn't seen them. Padre swerved to pull over to the side, to join their 'trackers'.

"I thought they were going into town? To market? To do their trading?" John checked with Padre.

"Oh no!" Padre corrected him. "They can get all their dealing done on the road, well, the roadside at least. They simply take the route that goes round the outside of the town, avoiding everything they don't want to be bothered by."

"There's a road that avoids the town?" John checked.

Padre had to correct him again. "Not a road, a route, that's what they were telling me, and I thought that sounded like a good idea."

It was a good idea.

It took them the remainder of that day to avoid the town and John could well appreciate why so few, except those directly in-the-know, were even aware of the route. It was easier going than the hill path, though not as fast as the market road might have been.

The ambulance was keeping up a healthy pace and the Lads were in good spirits, keeping up the banter between themselves and the locals on their bicycles, and Padre on his motorbike keeping up with any translating and explaining needed in between.

Whilst John wasn't doing much talking, he was the one doing the watching over along the ditches one side of their route and into the jungle on the other. He didn't like this route; it was making him twitchy again.

Every time they got to a village the route didn't actually go through any of them, but rather managed to just skim alongside clearing them.

"Nice arrangement, really." John had to admire it. No one needed to notice anything they didn't feel comfortable knowing about. "Very civilised."

With the last village reached and the light fading, the arrangement seemed to be they'd camp out, just beyond the village limits. "Second day done?" Padre checked, tapping his watch, looking up to the skies.

"Don't know about you, Padre, but this week is feeling an awful lot longer than I thought it would! I've no idea how far we've got," John confessed. "I'm still trying to find one of my markers."

Padre grinned. "Ah! So, that's how you were doing it? I wondered how you were navigating."

"One of the tricks of the trade." John didn't mind telling Padre. "No point trying to remember every road. No telling when you're going to find you need to avoid them! Much better to keep the markers in your sights and just keep heading in that direction."

Padre was nodding when Porter came over. He'd been making himself a bit more comfortable stretching his legs. "Third day tomorrow. Halfway there?" he reminded them.

John wasn't sure on that 'halfway there' part Porter seemed to have reckoned. He was still waiting to see his halfway marker. "We're not going to be able to avoid the next town. Padre you'd better make sure if there's anything you need for the Lads, you get ready to pick it up there. We might not get another chance."

Even Porter could understand that. The 'easy bit' was done.

Two of the three Lads were doing well, but the third one was noticeably quieter than he'd been that morning. John knew what that meant.

Padre checked him. "I could do with getting in to the next town as soon as you can get me there."

John couldn't ask Porter to do anymore driving today. Padre could drive, but he was needed in the back of the ambulance with the third Lad. "OK, if I drive, can you manage with the motorbike in there with you? Porter you'll sleep in the passenger seat."

Porter nodded. No argument from him. He'd be right beside John if he needed him.

John wasn't going to be able to find any more markers tonight. He'd have to simply trust his own healthy sense of direction.

"We know this route takes us into town. The only problem is going to be if there are any more villages or cross-roads."

Porter nodded and murmured, "Fair warning." Understood.

They could hear Padre talking softly in the back of the ambulance. The ambulance was crawling along the route and John's eyes felt like they were straining out of their sockets. He was trying not to grip the wheel too tightly but could already feel the tension in his knuckles. His knee was already starting to gripe at the way he was keeping it positioned.

John was starting to realise he was actually relying on the pain to keep him awake and alert. No point relying on Porter to keep his eyes open, he was already asleep! John smiled; he didn't blame him. "Sensible Lad, get it while you can."

John could probably have got to the next town in a couple of daylight hours if he'd put his foot down. Instead, in the dark, it took him nearer six. Padre came to help him in the last hour or so. They shoved Porter into the back with the Lads and the motorbike, they were all sleeping.

Padre took over and John grabbed a blessed sixty minutes of shut-eye, until he'd got shaken awake as the ambulance found the town roads again, and the pot-holes and haphazard kerb stones! Better than an alarm clock any day!

John would stay with the ambulance. Padre would do his 'doctoring' errands over to the hospital. They didn't have any choice but to send Porter on the rest of the errands. "Re-supply and a bit of a recce. Can you manage that?" John needed to make sure the Lads in the ambulance were safe and he couldn't be in two places at once.

Porter's first foray proved to be successful and without any obvious mishaps, but he was a little too keen on 'another go'. John didn't stop him, but kept a half-eye out for his return, wondering what sort of opportunities Porter might have found en-route.

Padre hadn't returned yet either, but John had expected it might take him a while. Getting to the hospital was only half the task, getting through to the medical offices and supplies would take longer.

A local café owner was able to bring over some fresh coffee and food for the occupants of the ambulance. He didn't seem at all surprised by the arrangement, taking it in his stride, even asking if they wouldn't prefer to wash first before eating.

John apologised. He should have thought of that. The ambulance had towels and soap. The café owner would send over one of his boys with a bucket of clean water.

John paid the café owner and gave the boy a little too. They shared their coffee with him and the extra biscuits they'd got, and the boy was able to help John with changing some of the dressings. Padre ought to be the one helping John with that, but there was no sign of him, or Porter.

John was more concerned about Porter.

Padre was in good hands, he had everything he needed, all correct. Porter didn't. Whilst John was helping the Lads wash and freshen up, the café boy kept an eye out for Padre. John had described him, and he wasn't going to be difficult to spot amongst the town crowds.

Sure enough, Padre was sighted walking with a stride that gave John hope it had been a 'mission accomplished'.

"Saved you some coffee, Padre." John didn't try to hide the relief in his voice.

Padre was equally pleased to see him and all the Lads in good spirits. The café boy grinned, remembering what John had told him. "Jolly good coffee."

Padre took a sip of the cup offered to him and agreed, "Jolly good. Please can we have some more? It's going to be a long day." The boy took the tray and cups that were finished with and dashed back to the café.

It was only a couple of minutes from where the ambulance was parked, but he was gone longer than that this time, returning with the owner who enquired, "Jolly good long-day-coffee?" then bowed to Padre.

Then John twigged. It was the clearly marked medical equipment. "Morning hospital?" he nudged Padre to catch up.

"Come on Padre, he's offering us his back room and washing facilities, they've got to be better for the Lads than the bucket, and maybe we'll have a chance for a proper breakfast too? No knowing when we'll be able to stop next." He glanced over to the café owner, who'd already begun to help one of the more able Lads to climb down from the ambulance.

John and Padre moved the motorbike back up into the ambulance and shut the doors. That was the best they could do. The ambulance was in sight of the café, but with this crowd if they needed to get back to it quickly it might be difficult. John was just hoping they didn't.

John managed one of the Lads, the café owner another and the boy and Padre the third. The third really ought not have been moved, but he wasn't going to be stuck in the back of the ambulance with everyone else enjoying a bit of a change of scenery!

John stayed out the front of the café watching for Porter, whilst Padre and the boy helped the Lads get themselves a little more comfortable.

"Any idea how we're meant to be paying for all this, Padre?" John checked. He hadn't got much with him and suspected Padre hadn't thought about that either.

The hospital 'details' he knew would be taken care of with the letters and notes the doctor had given them at the start of the mission. Padre could already guess where John's thoughts were going on that calculation. "No, we can't use the motorbike yet, this is the last town we need to go through, but we've got three days of travelling through some rather questionable areas, we might need it.

"Fair enough, Padre. We're just going to have to see what state Porter comes back in and hope he hasn't spent all his 'trades.'"

With the fresh medical supplies re-stocked, the third Lad needed taking back to the ambulance. John stayed with him there, but was starting to get impatient with Porter.

Padre would bring the other two Lads back over with him shortly. In the meantime, the boy brought over the fuel cans they'd managed to obtain from the café's own supplies. It should be enough to get them the rest of the way without stopping. The 'not stopping' was their best hope now.

John didn't realise what Padre had done until later. Somehow he'd managed to 'charge' the café costs to the hospital. Padre hadn't broken any rules, it was 'expenses' for them and possibly a lucrative deal for the café.

Porter had definitely been doing some business. He returned with a couple more fuel cans, along with fresh fruit and a pack of cards. Before John could say a word, Porter put his hand up. "Don't ask. I ran into some of those South African engineers! Very helpful and very dangerous. Sorry. Took me a while to wriggle out of where they were heading. Crikey! I thought I could do some fast-talking. Dodgy, seriously dodgy!"

John was laughing as Porter blew hard as he climbed into the driving seat again. "Do we know which way from here? Everything OK back there, Padre?"

"Ready when you are," came the call from the motorbike. "If we're going straight through town, it might be wiser for me to be up front?" Padre offered.

Porter wasn't arguing. He could do with a couple of hours just doing a bit of easy driving through the colourful chaos of the town streets.

John settled himself back in the passenger seat. He might be able to get another hour's sleep. He wasn't going to waste it talking.

Padre was right. It helped having the motorbike in front, ahead of the ambulance, looking like an official escort, something most of the town residents seemed to recognise and allowed for. Not everyone was so obliging, but Porter seemed to know what to shout at those moments!

They were stopped once, but by then John was awake and ready. Stepping down from the cab, he was looking the part of on duty and not to be messed with. They might have been prepared to argue with Padre and Porter, but weren't so keen when they saw John approaching!

Once through town and the outer villages, it was a direct route.

An easier surface but more exposed. They'd be more vulnerable this way if anyone wanted to make trouble for them. No way to disguise their purpose from here on.

"We'll just have to make a run for the docks. We've got three days; we can do it," the third Lad spoke for his cohorts in the back of the ambulance. If he thought they could, then no one was going to argue.

They took it in shifts after that.

One of the Lads managed to get into the passenger seat to help, whilst Padre was driving. John slept for a while before taking over again. Porter kept up with the motorbike.

The motorbike broke down on the fourth day.

"Damn! What the heck have you been doing with it?" John accused Porter of messing about. It had been running smooth and no problem for Padre for all those miles.

"You're the mecky. You can fix it, can't you?" Porter countered, without answering the question.

John took the opportunity to remind Porter of the practicalities of their mission. "No room."

"Haven't you even got an emergency toolbag with you?"

John did, but doubted he'd have what was needed to fix whatever Porter had managed to bugger-up, from the scant few tools he carried in there.

They hadn't much choice but to stop and attempt a repair or abandon it by the side of the road. Both men knew it would have been useful to keep the motorbike with them for emergency trading between here and the docks.

John wasn't going to waste time arguing. "Come on, give me a hand. Padre, you OK with the Lads?"

Padre had already come round and was checking the Lads. The third wasn't looking so good. John didn't need to see for himself, Padre's expression sufficed.

That was the moment John realised the reason for everything! A thunderbolt to his thoughts, blazing a trail through his brain like wildfire … devastating … taking his breath away for a moment, as a heartbeat of awareness slammed across his chest.

The reason why they were all there in the middle of Malaya?

Never mind how they'd got there, or what they'd been told, or done before, none of that mattered. This was the why-of-it-all. It was *all* about 'repairing' and 'not-abandoning' … ANYONE.

That was it, that was everything!

With his next breath John snapped back to what he was doing, to what they were trying to do … got to keep moving, somehow … a dash to the docks … for the Lads.

Porter had no idea why John was glaring at him and the forlorn excuse for a motorbike he was holding!

John couldn't bring his gaze back to Padre and the Lads. There were no words. He needed to focus. He needed to get the job done. Swallow hard, take a breath and get on with it!

"We'll give it a couple of hours. If we have to strap it to the roof, then we'll do that. There'll be a garage or a repair shop of something, sooner or later on this road." John had noticed the state of some of the other vehicles rattling alongside them. It wasn't like the locals to miss an opportunity like that!

It didn't take John more than a half hour to realise the motorbike needed a garage. Porter had wisely stayed silent throughout. The look of John's face was enough to persuade him that might be the most prudent course.

Even as they were struggling to get it loaded up and strapped down onto the roof of the ambulance, they had a couple of vehicles stop and show interest. Not help, just interest. John wasn't willing to sell it yet, not if they could still get it working, and not until they'd got a better idea of what the next day or two had in store for them.

"Only another day or two, we'll be OK for that, d'you think?"

Porter was calling down from the roof. John didn't answer. He was waiting for Padre's response. They'd only been able to put a couple of straps on the job, with Porter's belt added for good measure.

"You're not going to need it, you're driving, and I'm not asking Padre." John got in with that before Porter started protesting.

Padre's opinion of the configuration was never made clear, but John was sure there was a 'we can make it' half-smile coming from that direction, when he sat back in the cab.

"What can you see from up there?" John checked. Porter started looking further. "Should be getting a bit busier with the farms this way by now," John reminded him.

"What am I meant to be looking for?" Porter asked. He'd learnt that 'farms' around here could mean just about anything.

"You should be seeing more cleared areas, brown. Not so much thick jungle greens ... and no hills ahead," John directed helpfully.

Porter took another look. "Yep, got it. More-brown, less-green. Check. No-bumps, no-towns. None that I can see from here."

"Anything else?" Padre called up.

"Anything in particular, Padre?" Porter called down. "Do you think we can make it in two days?"

Porter looked down to Padre, then over to John. "If John does the driving, we'll have a better chance. What do you think?"

That wasn't so much a question, as a plea from Porter. He'd seen the expression in Padre's face, too. John was already trying to sit to one side, trying to ease the pain down the other leg. "More-brown, less-green, hey? That sound about right?"

Padre had already mentioned the references to the 'likely terrain ahead' that he'd picked up in that hospital visit back at the resupply stop. He nodded a confirmation. "Seems like it."

John tallied that with his own reckoning of the location markers he was certain of.

There was also the somewhat less reliable street chatter Porter had brought back with him, of which route those South African engineers had opted for, to take into consideration. "More-brown, less-green," John repeated. "Right-ho, Padre. If that's what we've got, then that's what we'll work with!"

Padre and Porter took shifts with the Lads in the back of the ambulance, in turn cheering them up and calming them down. John kept on driving, stopping when he had to. It was slow, but at least he felt safer on this route, and the surface meant the ambulance wasn't getting jolted so much.

They decided not to attempt another night drive. The Lads stayed in the ambulance. John stumbled out from the driving seat and reached for the ground, before falling asleep. Padre slept round at the back of the ambulance, with an ear ready if he was needed whilst Porter slept where he slumped, in the passenger seat. They were all too sore and too tired to be hungry.

John was fairly sure his markers were telling him there was a village coming up in the morning. He'd started seeing the brown farm land, just as Porter had indicated. Farm land meant farming machines and they'd be needing mechanics to keep them working, that meant repair shops. Hopefully something to get the motorbike working again. There was a lot of hope going on in those weary thoughts that night!

The state of the traffic the next morning definitely indicated a farming village and a large one. That brightened the mood. Porter was eager to get started with sorting something out about the motorbike, and overnight the Lads had somehow managed to calculate between them, "One more day to go!"

Padre was trying to discover how they managed that. This was day five. They'd started with one week, that was seven days to get from the hospital on the hill down to the docks where the ship would be ready to take them home. They had seven days, one ambulance and a driver and Padre on the motorbike.

"Yeah, Padre. But we're awake this morning, so we don't need to count today, do we?" the Lads joked. It didn't need to make sense to anyone else!

"Tomorrow we get to the docks, then it's just a matter of getting onboard and home. So, one more day should do it, hey?"

Padre wasn't going to argue with that.

Porter was driving this time. John needed to keep his eyes open for what they were getting into. He'd already warned Porter, "We're not stopping".

But Porter was ready to argue that. "Oh yes, we are. Got to. Café and repair shop. Can't leave the Lads unwashed and hungry. They'll expect them to be presentable at dockside."

"Damn!" John hadn't thought of that. "Right."

"OK. Then you stay with me. Padre gets the Lads sorted. You and me are on the motorbike and fuel situation. Right?" John got a nod from Porter. He'd have to be satisfied with that.

The traffic was building steadily by then. It was mostly long-distance lorries, but some local labour trucks too and a couple of tractors. That was hopeful.

They found a café easily enough. Padre took the lead then, strolling over and making enquiries, whilst Porter stayed put. John climbed down, reaching back to retrieve his cane, glaring across at Porter, threatening him if he dared mention it.

John checked with Padre, "Everything OK?"

Padre nodded, pleasantly surprised. "They seem to be quite friendly. This might not be the regular route for ambulances, but they're used to seeing a few of the Lads coming through this way. We're definitely heading in the right direction." Then he grinned. "It doesn't sound so far when they start telling you it's the 'next town over' there." Both men knew that could still be a hundred miles away.

"Next town over sounds good to me, Padre." John suddenly grabbed for the back of the nearest chair, groaning in pain.

"Sit down," Padre instantly ordered. "Porter can help me bring the Lads over. I don't think we'd better move the third, but the other two would benefit from a bit of a stretch."

"No, Padre," John gritted his teeth and pushed himself back up to standing. "Sitting ain't going to help this. I need to walk this off."

Padre could see the pain etched on John's face and hear the determination in his voice. No, he wasn't going to argue.

"Can you manage with the Lads, find the café owner? I need to take Porter with me with the motorbike. I've still got to get those cans refilled." John straightened up, groaning at the effort. "Gotta get it done Padre."

Padre didn't answer. This was John convincing himself. He'd heard it before.

"We'll get there, Padre. Like the men said, only the next town over, then we'll be at the docks. One more day, we can do that."

Porter got back on the roof and unstrapped the motorbike. A couple of the locals saw what they were trying to do and recognising it as an ambulance, offered their help.

Porter was about to shoo them away, but Padre stepped forward again and started exchanging pleasantries.

Not for the first time, Padre had impressed the heck out of John and Porter. The two locals soon doubled up as guides to the nearest garage, John walking with them, as Porter pushed the motorbike behind.

Padre and the café owner seemed to be more than capable with the Lads. John could hear one of them laughing already. That quickened his step. Pain or no pain. One of them was calling up cheerfully, "Cor Padre, they serve a lovely cuppa here. Just the ticket hey?"

John's ears adjusted to the sounds again, shifting from hill path to jungle track, to road traffic, to market village, waiting until he caught the garage sounds ringing through. Metal on metal, rust and hammer, that's what he was trying to find scent of. Old grease and fresh oil.

It wasn't a direct path from the café, but John could remember his way back. It was slightly off the main thoroughfare of market traffic. He'd almost forgotten how hectic market days could get.

How long was it since he'd been just going in to town on market day, just outside camp, over to the book stall? Crikey, that felt like a life-time ago! As for the ship that was going to be waiting at the docks to take the Lads and Porter home? Home!? John wasn't sure how many life-times he'd known since then.

He clenched the top of his cane. "We're here, then?" he checked, looking around.

The locals seemed certain, and there was a vague resemblance to something John could recognise as a garage. Turning to Porter he asked, "Ready to give it a go?" Porter nodded. "Right. All we need is fuel for the ambulance. I'm not going to interrupt unless I have to. They need to think you know what you're doing. Can you manage that!?"

Porter smirked an unconvincing wink.

John smiled quietly and waited for the inevitable theatrics, intentionally taking a step back away from the motorbike and Porter. He could see more clearly from there, as they'd opened both doors to inspect the state of the motorbike under 'consideration'. They had a tractor inside they were already working on. That was hopeful.

It took approximately ten minutes for Porter to get into trouble and a couple of seconds for John to reach him and haul him out of the brawl, then an hour for the pair of them to stumble back to the ambulance and this time it was John needing help.

"What the hell have you two been doing?"

Padre hurried forward to catch John as he fell forward from where he'd been leaning heavily into Porter's shoulder.

"You've been stabbed!" Padre exclaimed in alarm.

"I know," John murmured. "Any chance of one of those lovely cuppas I heard someone mention?" His shirt was already soaked through, even with Porter's shirt stuffed inside to mop up the blood.

John was sat down at one of the café tables with one of the Lads. Padre had already got the first-aid bag by then. "Don't blame Porter. It wasn't his fault this time!"

The café owner wasn't too pleased to have a bloody shirtless man seated at one of his tables. It didn't exactly give the best of first-impressions.

"At least most of the market has moved on," Porter was trying to be cheerful. John didn't respond, he'd have plenty to say to him later, but right now he just needed that cuppa.

John took the cup of tea offered and drank it down in one gulp, his hand managing to bring the cup back down to the table, but it felt heavier by then.

"Give him another one," Padre directed the café owner over John's head.

Porter was trying to say something. It sounded like an apology, but John wasn't listening. He could feel Padre and someone else starting to clean up his side. It was a low wound, and he was fairly sure it had missed anything vital.

He'd moved quick enough, almost, to miss the weapon, but had forgotten his knee! John had shifted his weight and twisted, but they'd managed to catch him an inch above his hip.

"It's OK, John," Padre was telling him. "Not too deep, nothing serious."

John grimaced at the pressure of the dressing. Someone was apologising, that might have been Porter again.

John wasn't looking and he wasn't listening, he was going to drink that damned cup of tea and ignore the lot of them.

"Didn't get the fuel. Sorry, Padre."

"Don't worry, John, we've got that sorted." John put the empty cup back down on the table and groaned a few ripe oaths as he leaned back.

"How the hell did you manage that?" he asked, his hands gripping the edge of the table as they started strapping the padding in place.

"Sorry John, got to keep it in place."

"I know, I know. Just get on with it. Sorry, Padre, but ruddy hell! One day to go, and this happens."

"Don't worry, John, we'll get there. We'll all get there."

John caught that look in Padre's eyes. Yep, they were both sharing the same prayer: the 'reason for everything', the 'why-of-it-all' prayer.

"I'm going to put you in the back with the Lads for a few hours, John. I'll drive. I think you might have shaken Porter up a bit, too. So, he can just sit quiet for a while till we're out of here." Padre sounded like he'd got it all sorted.

John wasn't in the mood for the details but did need to know one thing. "How d'you get the fuel?"

"Ah, John. We're not the only ones who like a good story book around here."

John blinked and stared up at Padre, who was already starting to help him back onto his feet to steer him over to the ambulance.

"You didn't give your books away, Padre?" John groaned in pain and anguish. "I can't let you do that?"

"It's all sorted and I'm very glad to be able to contribute to the effort. Although, I think I got off lightly compared to the pair of you!" John wasn't looking convinced. "It did me good, really. I'd been holding on to them for far too long."

John wasn't grumbling anymore. The tea was starting to have the desired effect, and they'd got the ambulance ready for him. John knew something had been added, but hadn't realised until it was too late. "Sneaky Padre," he admired, slurring his mutters.

The two Lads that could sit, sat, the third Lad was already on his stretcher, and John lay flat down in the middle on the floor between them.

"There now, you can keep them company. I'll let you know when we're nearly there." Porter sounded like he was talking to a toddler being put down for a nap.

John tried to growl, but the grunt sounded more like 'good Lad' to Porter's ears.

"Knew you'd understand, John." Porter took one more look at the passengers in the back, before shutting the ambulance doors. "Right-ho, Padre, up to you now!" John heard that and was chewing through a few choice words he'd like to say to Porter, but those too faded as his breathing steadied and the motion of the vehicle began to rock him to sleep.

Next time the ambulance door opened, it was daylight. Full-on daylight. Bright enough for the occupants to blink and protest. "Someone, put that light out!" John growled, pushing himself up on his elbows. "Oh! Morning, Padre. Sorry! Where are we?"

"We're about a half day from the docks as far as I can tell. Can you walk?"

"I can walk, if you can help me stand up from here," John offered. Padre grinned, leaning into the ambulance to pull John to his feet, holding him steady as he regained his equilibrium. "Where did you say?"

He'd instinctively started to stretch his arms and back, only then being sharply reminded of the events of yesterday. "Cripes, Padre, you sure you didn't leave the knife in there?"

Padre was wagging a finger at him. "No, you were very clear on that part. It wasn't a knife. It was a screw-driver! And you kept telling me it was the 'wrong one', anyway! And that it wasn't Porter's fault. You were very insistent about that," Padre reminded him.

John knew what Padre had done, he recognised the after-taste, but there wasn't much point mentioning that now. There was driving to be done.

"Come on, Padre. Last few hours, hey? Then let's see if we can make it count." John had tried to make it sound like he was at full strength, but they both knew he wasn't. Far from it. But Padre had also seen the determination in John's eyes. No, he wasn't going to argue.

"You go in the back and make sure the Lads are ready. I'll make sure Porter's fit for his part." John leaned against the side of the ambulance and made a move towards the driver's door.

"Go gently on him, John. He feels bad enough," Padre whispered. John muttered, "I bet he does!" but nodded back.

Before Porter could start talking, John put his hand up and told him to shut up. "Just give me a moment to get in and started driving. Then we'll talk about it."

They both waited in silence with the engine ticking over until Padre gave them the shout, "All ready, in the back."

John put it into gear and got moving. He drove for the next few miles, feeling his bruised and battered body settle into the new position. He could even see the railway tracks from here. "Not far now. Nearly there." He could feel Porter stirring to start with the explanations.

"Don't want to talk about it," John warned him. "It was a stupid thing to do. All we needed was the fuel, why did you have to go and annoy him!?"

"Sorry John." Sounded the best way for Porter to start. The reasons why he'd been so stupid took the better part of the next hour, though it seemed to boil down to: 'They expect a bit of banter, to sweeten the deal.'

"That didn't feel very sweet!" John flinched as he reached down to feel how tender that patch was under the strapping round his middle. Shifting his weight, the ambulance lurched forward as his knee cramped.

"Damn it. Sorry back there! You all ok?" John shouted to cover over his own yelp of pain.

Padre didn't sound quite the same as he had an hour earlier. "We could do with picking the pace." There was a pause, as he sounded like he was rummaging through the supplies. "I could do with getting to that first-aid station at the docks, John!?"

Understood.

"Right-ho Padre. Picking up the pace NOW!" John warned and slammed his foot down hard.

It was a 'Dash for the Docks'.

"Another Dash for the Docks!?" Porter shook his head in disbelief, before muttering under his breath, "The right way." Another prayer.

John didn't speak again until they were in sight of it, but Porter was doing plenty of shouting from his window at anyone getting too close to the ambulance as they approached the check-point.

Porter did all the talking. Loud and clear and without wasting a word. He had an answer for every question, the paperwork for every check. He had patients to take care of and didn't have time to waste.

Even when the officer wanted to check the back. Porter told him if he wanted to do that, then he'd better lead the way over to the first-aid station because he wasn't going to open the back of the ambulance for anyone, until there was proper medical care ready for *his* Lads.

John caught the startled look from the officer. He'd never been spoken to like that before, not by someone who was so obviously just a hospital porter!

John smiled to himself but remained silent. Porter tapped his watch. "Get the gate to call the office and you get in your car, 'cos I'm not going to wait for you."

The officer blinked first and ordered the gate to call ahead to the doctor on duty that an emergency ambulance was coming through. He handed Porter back his papers and scrambled to get into his car.

The first-aid station wasn't difficult to miss. There were plenty of staff on duty preparing the patients to be transferred onto the waiting hospital ship.

It was well organised, and Porter breathed out at last with the words, "We made it, John. We *all* made it!"

The officer that had escorted their ambulance in, hailed the nearest doctor. Together they opened up the ambulance and greeted Padre, who immediately set about giving them the details of the patients.

Padre was exhausted.

Padre had done everything he could for the third Lad. He was still alive, but only just. He knew where he was and knew what they'd managed to do for him. He also knew he wasn't going to survive the last part of his journey.

"I'm sorry, Lad," Padre told him simply.

The officer stood out of the way, whilst the doctor got busy checking the Lad over. The doctor's face was intent on the study, but his hands slowed their movements, conferring with Padre.

The dying man's hand came up from where it had been resting, to the two learned men talking over his body. Padre took it in his own, patting it gently. "I'm sorry, Lad."

They waited whilst Porter put the officer to use, helping him get the other two Lads out from the ambulance and staying back.

John had managed to climb down and came round to stand by the side of the ambulance, out of the way, but able to hear and see what was happening.

"Don't worry, Padre. I know I'll get home, now. That's all I wanted. That's all I needed to know."

John watched as the doctor moved to one side. Padre stayed at the Lad's side. He didn't need the doctor anymore.

"Come on, doc, let's get out of the way, shall we?" John shut the door to the ambulance. The trolley was there, but no hurry now.

It was only as John started walking, that the doctor realised he was also a casualty.

"How the hell did you all get down here. We got the message from the hospital you were coming, but we didn't believe it. Then we got another mentioning Padre. We didn't believe *that* one either!"

"Not sure I know how we got here, either!" John admitted.

"How did you manage it?" The doctor had got John seated on one of the chairs set outside the first-aid station.

John was scanning the various trolleys and stretchers around him for the two Lads. "Don't worry they're both fine," the doctor was glad to confirm. "They seemed happier keeping the other porter with them. He's good with them, isn't he? Knows how to handle the Lads when it's like that? Could do with a few more like him."

"Look, doc, you can prod and jab me as much as you like in another minute or two, but just let me see them off first." John could see the hospital staff were working methodically with the loading process. In a few more minutes they'd be boarded and on their way.

John made his way through to his Lads. They didn't need to ask about the third fellow. They'd all realised that was going to be the way of it.

"Poor Sod. He's coming with us, though, ain't he?" Porter asked for all their benefits.

"Yes. Padre made sure he knew that."

The nurses had come to fuss over the Lads. Porter released his grip on the trolley. He couldn't go without asking John something, just one thing.

"Why? Why did you give me your paperwork?"

John grinned and almost started to shrug, then remembered the bandages strapping his side. He tapped the side of his head, instead. "Seemed like a good idea at the time," was the best he could come up with.

"It *was* a good idea, wasn't it?" Porter needed to know.

John nodded. "It was the 'right way', Porter, for *all* of us. It was the 'right way.'"

They could see Padre coming towards them. The hospital staff would take care of the third Lad from here on.

They waited for Padre to reach them. "All done?" John checked.

"All done now," Padre confirmed. Then he turned to Porter. He could see John had finished saying his goodbyes. It was his turn. "You did well, Lad."

Porter grinned, trying to remember if anyone had ever actually said that to him before.

Padre took Porter's hand in his own and shook it firmly enough to cover up both their emotions.

Porter managed a, "Thanks, Padre," just as his voice began catching at the sobs in the back of his throat. With a sniff and a cough to clear his throat he finished, "Thanks. For everything. You too, John."

John nodded back but wasn't going to try and say any more. He'd said enough. They all had. They could see the hospital staff beginning to approach, steering everyone nearer to where the crew were helping get them aboard.

Padre moved John out of the way. Porter was hospital staff now.

"We did our best didn't we?" Padre asked as they started walking. Almost as if he was asking himself.

John heard him, and that deserved a response. "We got him home, Padre. We did the best we could."

They walked in silence after that, amongst the clipped tones of the efficient nurses encouraging their patients and the brisk shouts of the officers trying to chivvy along the clattering trollcys and last of the wayward wheelchairs.

"Come on, Padre. Let's see if we can trade in that old ambulance of ours for a couple of nice long train rides back to camp."

Padre smiled, turning to John. "Last time they served some very fine tea, you know?"

"If I remember correctly, Padre, last time I was on that train I ended up sleeping on the luggage rack. Don't think I'm up for that this time."

Padre tutted gently and put a steering arm around John's shoulder as they headed for the gate, leaving the ship, the docks and the ambulance behind them.

"Don't worry, I'm sure I'll be able to find you a nice quiet bunk, John. That's what you need now. A good strong cup of tea and a bit of rest."

"Yeah! Sounds good. Right you are, Padre."

All for Overalls (Summer 1940)

With the news from Dunkirk, a scrawny fourteen-year old errand boy called Gertie is spurred into action. A lanky lad with borrowed specs, smelly feet, awkward elbows and big ears, who liked to keep things simple, plenty in the village had shrugged him off as 'can't make him out.' Then the war had started, things had begun to get desperate, and they couldn't afford to waste anything, not even Gertie!

As the local residents adapt to wartime-ways, the old village and the new RAF hospital have plenty of characters and best-intentions between them, but country wisdom and military efficiency doesn't always rub along smoothly ...

> *"Just because you're out of the way, doesn't*
> *mean you're not in the middle of it!"*

If the Sock Fits! (Autumn/Winter 1940)

The second book in the trilogy moves on to the autumn of 1940 and the harsh reality of harvest time in the countryside as the Battle of Britain rages in the skies overhead and England's Greatest Generation rises to the challenge and, of course, there was Gertie ... as determined and inventive as ever!

Churchill had been right about 'the Few' being the ones to save them through the summer, but it was going to take 'the many' – the Land Army and the locals – pulling together, if they were going to get through the coming winter.

> *"You get them to believe they can fight back,*
> *and they stop feeling beaten."*

Raids, Rallies & Reserves (1941)

Blasted Blitz! Freezing winds and no overcoats ... and now the Americans were coming!

Doug did his best, but his 'lovely lady' still managed to plough up the grazing meadow and send a piece of wing skipping the hedge to knock Riggs from his post. The RAF pilot walked away with nothing more than few scratches and a sandwich, leaving Riggs with two broken legs, a wounded heart and Gertie playing cupid!

Matters came to a head with the news coming through of Pearl Harbour. Mr Tor went missing down a rum bottle and there were a dozen geese to throttle, pluck and deliver. The best Gertie could do was feed the pigs and drag the delirious farmer along for the ride! As for Sarg at the gate wondering about that officer? Gertie could explain everything:

"Oh, don't worry Sarg, he's just there to stop the others falling out!"

Also, soon to be available in the Gertie's Path series:

Not So Safely Forgotten (Spring 1942)

The Biscuit Tin Summer (Summer 1942)

Restless Torches (Autumn-Winter 1942)

The Tunisian Turnaround (Spring 1943)

Not So Safely Forgotten (Spring 1942)

"OK, so they're ALL over-here! Now what are we meant to do with them?"

The Americans had started to arrive by the truckload and Marm was not impressed! She had enough to deal with already: there was a Spring Bazaar to arrange, the village hall was falling down around their ears and the church warden had lost the vestry keys again! It certainly didn't need those Americans to go barging about the place complaining about country corners jumping out at them!

As for the 'it' race? Dr Edwards had 'hazards and hurdles' of his own to deal with! The American approach did tend to resemble a steam roller. Regardless, 'Katy' was ready and at least the Yanks were good sports: "we'll pay for the damages."

As for what the Lads were getting up to in through the library, Matron was soon on the war path. "Better to have it out, than packed away and fermenting!?"

Rusty made sure Jeepers understood who owned the work-bench and Gertie was able to reassure the church warden: **"there's no such thing as a pointless path."**

The Biscuit Tin Summer (Summer 1942)

Allowances would have to be made. "He's American. Ahhh, that would explain it" ... but only so far.

It began with Matron having 'a bit of a morning.' The RAF hospital needed to accommodate the Americans and some delicate handling between trolleys and translations were called for!

There was news from Malta: the convoys were getting clobbered, but at least Churchill and Roosevelt could knock a few heads together! Though not-such-good news coming from Tobruk. Back home, Bracket was a dab-hand with the KP: "whilst-you're-at-it Lads."

No one was prepared to give the whole story of **the Brag and the Dare**, but the 'challenge' stood nonetheless. There was only one thing to do: "gilly-it," at least until the Americans stopped looking. Doubts and decoys in all directions! The forfeit was a cooked breakfast, and the village took the canteen van to-boot.

It took Mrs Toombs to winkle out the confession and the Post Mistress to make the call: twenty minutes, three stripes, one dance and Rusty was leading!

"The paths are always there, heart-paths and life-paths, nature knows how to take care of them ... all you need to do is find your way."

Restless Torches (Autumn/Winter 1942)

Country wisdom: if you want to know how to fix something, don't wait until it breaks!

Malta was holding on and there was news that Monty and Rommel were duking it out in the Western Desert. There were rumours of Operation Torch starting to light up hopes for the North Africa Campaign, too.

Doc Dook wasn't one to miss an opportunity. He didn't waste time either. 'Flapping Jack' was ambitious, 'Maltese Mike' was furious, and Gertie was restless: "We'll see Rommel gets that message from your Malta-mates." There was an ambulance-crew-shaped space on the hospital ship. Mike wanted back 'in' on the fight and Jack wanted 'out' of the office … and "We both knew that work-bench wasn't going to keep you home."

Gertie earned his gills, but bounced back ready for double-duty before dry land and deep trouble.

By the time they got to Algiers they'd acquired a reluctant American truck driver, an intriguing briefcase, two Italian POWs, a German motorbike … and an abiding respect for Aunt Luci's talents. But the **'eye-opener'** was the tall blue stranger called Freddie coming with the fuel … and a suggestion.

"Good grief, Gertie, what have you got us into?"

The Tunisian Turnaround (Spring 1943)

The Yanks were reckless, the French were unpredictable, the Italians were unreliable, and the Germans were relentless.

Jack had his maps and aspirations, Mike had his rifle and the memory of those Maltese airfields and Gertie had his satchel with that battered old biscuit tin, a wide brimmed slouch hat and silver bangles on his wrist. "You're expecting contact en route?" It always interested their tall Taureg 'guide' who asked the *real* questions. "Hell yeah!"

The mountains and the sandstorms weren't going to stop them, and the desert-pirates were neatly dealt with, collecting up a stranded professor along the way of a camel race, before a nifty bit of negotiating gave them safe passage through the skirmish.

They were running on fumes, but **Kessarine** was within their sights, a rough crawl and a screw-driver put paid to the crates on the runway. **Mike's 'message' was delivered!**

After that the heading was Tunis and the **'Longstop.'** They retrieved 'Battered Bess' and Gertie found his ledge. "You've come a long way from those gentle lanes of home, haven't you lad?"

As for that American officer driving them into Tunis? **There was no way he was qualified to deal with a story like *that!***

Three Sides Out, One Way Home (Malaya 1956-58)

The story of three Englishmen during the Malayan Emergency, each with very different priorities. The driver was also a sniper, the porter was also a thief, and the Padre had come open-minded, empty-handed and turned out to be remarkably versatile!

From building an airfield to opening up a mission house, from dump trucks to chicken soup; they'd be working with trackers, traders, head-hunters and river-pirates. For Porter it started with a crowbar and a motorbike; but Driver needed to allow the jungle to take a piece of him if he was going to survive it; whilst the Padre had been hoping for somewhere 'colourful.' Be careful what you wish for! It was going to be a three-alarm clock job and the satchel prompted the negotiations.

Three men: one of them had been sent there, one thought he ought to be there, and one of them really should have known better!

It wasn't until the hillside hospital when the agreement was made: there were plenty of ways of getting home, but for one of them, only one way to do it 'right' and it was going to take ALL three of them going off the rails to get it done.

It was always understood: "No one volunteers, ever, for anything ... but sometimes ... you're asked!"